So Close to Paradise

By Daphne C. Murrell

Mountain Paradise Publishers.
Cover Photograph by Mary Beachy

ISBN-13:
978-0615960616 (Mountain Paradise Publishers)

ISBN-10:
0615960618:

Dedication

This book is dedicated to my mother,
Florine Meredith Simmons Wall.
This was the only book of mine that she and my father read.
Had she had half the encouragement she gave me over the years,
who knows what pages of tales she would have left with us.

A Few Words from the Author

Even though this is my fifth book published, it was the first novel I ever completed. I had started this story when I was in college. Over the years I would pick it up and write a few more chapters, but as I raised children and worked in churches, I never had the time to put it all on paper (and I literally mean "on paper"—with a typewriter—that's how long I had worked on it). After many years of mulling the story around in my mind, I had already created a sequel. Because I had grown tired of drudging through the old manuscript, one day I simply decided to forget the original and write the sequel—that would be this book. As always, the more we do a thing, the better we become, so I would never consider *So Close to Paradise* my best work, however I love the story and feel it's worthy to be put out there. So if you've enjoyed the *Autumn Sunset* series, I hope you find this one another good read!

Chapter One

"One, two, three, four! You ain't got no answer for!" The cheering revved up another notch inside the brown van and so did Meg MacAllister's headache. "Five, six, seven, eight! We eat you up like you was bait!"

She tried to convince herself she was only busy, not overextended. She knew how to say *no*, and regardless of what her mother might think that wasn't the problem. Her dilemma was that everything she did was important, was something she wanted to do, was a commitment she considered vital to her life—and to the lives of others. The pounding in her head made her wonder if it was time to begin sorting through some priorities.

"Nine, ten, eleven, twelve—go crawl back up on yo sad shelf!" Now the girls began rocking the van back and forth so that it started to sway on the road, forcing Meg to grip the wheel tighter. "Thirteen, fourteen, fifteen, sixteen—we's the best but y'all's the sick team!"

That was it. She could handle the noise, but the grammar had to be dealt with.

"Alissa!" she called from the driver's seat. "Change the cheer or zip the lip! I might even fail you for creating such an atrocity."

The lanky sixteen-year-old giggled as she threw her hands into the air and protested, "Miss Mac, we're celebrating! We can't think about English and junk when we're excited like this! Give us a break!" Frizzy red hair stuck out in all directions from beneath the ball cap. "And we ain't Shakespeare either, so don't go complaining about how lame our rhymes are."

"The lameness of your rhyming is the least of what's wrong. Seriously, I should fail you!" The last sentence came out louder than she meant.

The van grew silent as fourteen girls pondered whether Miss Mac would actually fail one of her junior composition students for something outside the classroom. She glanced in the rearview mirror at Alissa and gave a wink. "Good thing I'm your softball coach and you just won the league championship for the first time EVER!"

That's all it took. The girls started cheering again and the headache ratcheted up another degree. The thought of one hundred twenty term papers in the box beside her on the floor wasn't helping. After seven years of teaching high school English, one would think assigning all classes lengthy papers at the end of the year would have changed, but she couldn't bring herself to end the practice. She always hoped, right up to the end, that there would be obvious growth and added finesse.

"One, two, three, four! You ain't got no answer for!"

She shook her head and laughed as she headed to the children's home to deposit the girls. They deserved to cheer. They had won first place in the city softball league for teen girls. She had coached them six years now, and this was the first time the team had managed to keep all fourteen girls the entire season. They were outcasts in every sense of the word. Some were orphans who had lived at the facility all their lives. Some were from troubled families that claimed they needed a break from managing children a few weeks, or months, or even years. Some kids were between foster families—others were kids that foster families just couldn't handle any longer. Each story was unique, but pitifully the same in that each child was basically unwanted by somebody.

As she pulled into the parking lot, they cheered even louder. No, if she were overextended, it simply meant she needed to rethink her schedule and add a few time management techniques—not turn away from those who needed her.

"Don't open that door, Lana!" she yelled as a tall, thin brunette with a long scar down her cheek reached for the handle. "I just want to say that you did great today, and I'm awesomely proud of all of you. Now, if you'll study as hard as you practice, maybe final exams will be just as celebratory! Perhaps Alissa could come up with a few rhymes to help you remember things in some of your more difficult subjects—put her talent to good use."

With that comment, a few laughed, but most moaned. They piled out of the van and started the cheer over again.

"One, two, three, four! You ain't got no answer for!"

Pushing open the door, Meg noticed Carmen still sitting quietly in the passenger's seat. In fact, the typically brooding girl hadn't said anything since they'd left the park. She just stared out the front, her chestnut eyes barely showing from beneath the long, dark bangs.

"Are you okay?"

"I guess so," was the mumbled reply followed by a slight shrug.

"You guess so? Your team just won first place, and you guess you're okay?"

"Yeah, I guess so ... I don't know. It's sort of been a good year, you know ... I mean, not everybody will ever be here like this again ... together. Next year all this will be different."

Meg nodded. "True, but life is always changing—that's just the nature of it. And yes, it's been a really good year, but what if next year is even better?"

"Right. There's always that ... I suppose."

The girl opened the door and left. It would be useless to follow her and try to dig out the explanation of what just happened. She was extremely closed, more so than any of the other girls. Most considered Meg a buddy, a big sister, a teacher, and a coach. To Carmen, she was just another adult. That killed Meg. She loved and cared for these girls, and to be rejected was hard to handle. But they had lived lives so vastly different from the privileged, wealthy life in which she had been raised. She sometimes wondered how any of them could go on at all.

Getting out of the van, she noticed the box of papers sitting on the floor. "Ugh, I know how I'll be spending my weekend."

In the director's office, Meg listened painfully as Mr. Roberts explained the problem.

"He just can't come. He got an offer to do an advertisement that's worth several million dollars. He's not a mean person, Meg—he's getting older every day. One day he won't be playing football on national television every week."

"It's always about money, isn't it?"

"Uh, yes—it is, for some. He's got a future to think about."

"Yeah? Well what about his past?" She was getting angry. "He lived here on and off for five years. He knows what it's like to be a nobody—to be promised big things only to never have them delivered! He could have come for one night!"

"Yes—he knows what it's like, and he could have come. But he's not. So—we go on."

The man's peppered hair was heavy with sweat, and he was winded as he spoke. He had obviously been outside in the warm, Florida, June weather—probably playing basketball with a few of the guys. He was such a tender-hearted man. No one could have more compassion and genuine love for these kids. His disappointment was evident, but he had clearly learned to deal with it long ago. Part of his job was to handle letdowns on a daily basis.

"Well, did you find someone else for the banquet?" she asked.

"Actually, yes—another alumnus from here—not a professional football player though. He's a music and youth minister up in north Florida."

"That ought to go over big," she said snidely before thinking.

"Meg."

"I'm sorry. That was uncalled for. But, how do you tell them? *Sorry, kids. I know you were expecting Max Caldwell, NFL quarterback, but we've got the next best thing: John Doe, a minister?"*

"They say this guy is a good speaker—very motivating, great sense of humor. When I talked to him he was heartbroken too. I think he'd have personally flown up there and broken Caldwell's neck if I'd asked him."

"Yeah, well, I was just hoping this would be different, you know—grand. Every year we have this big banquet. We make them dress up, behave mannerly, use proper etiquette, all to sit and listen to some boring speaker tell them how they need to rise above the odds they've been dealt."

"Boring speaker?"

"Well, you have to admit the last two years have been bombs. The Hinkle family singing their southern gospel, and then Dr. Horatio Smith talking about the amazing open field in botany?"

"They need to be exposed to all kinds of people. Life isn't all glitter and glitz."

"Unfortunately, Mr. Roberts, it is all glitter and glitz for most every other teenager in their world."

"On a more depressing note," he said changing the subject as he handed her a letter. "You might want to take a look at this. I made you a copy."

"On a more depressing note?"

"It's from Carmen's mother. She wants her home for the summer. Apparently she has a new and improved boyfriend and they want to try and be one big, happy family."

"Oh, brother. Does Carmen know about this?"

"Her house mother said she got a letter from her mom last night."

"Great. Chapter ninety-nine of the *Let's Be a Mom When Convenient* story, I guess."

Meg left the office with letter in hand. Opening the door to the outside, the humid heat nearly smothered her—raising the throbbing in her head to a new level. She started the letter as she walked down the sidewalk, and it was just as she thought. Mom was feeling great and really wanted to try and live with Carmen again. If she would just come for the summer and spend some quality time, she knew things could work out for a change.

Focused on the letter, she barely noticed the man passing her on the sidewalk. Looking up briefly, she smiled out a hello then went back to reading. As she neared the van, she heard her name.

"Meg? Meg MacAllister?"

It was the guy she had just passed. He was tall and lean, short blond hair, dark glasses, dressed in a white dress shirt with a tie of space aliens.

"Yes," she replied, not really wanting to talk, but hoping to finish the letter.

"You don't recognize me, do you?" he asked, sporting a charming smile.

"No, sorry—and this isn't a good day for Twenty Questions."

"Still the same after all these years—blunt and honest, straight to the point."

"All these years? You make me sound ancient." Now she was curious. "How do I know you ... or how do you know me?"

"Well," he toyed with her, "I'm a little hurt you don't recognize me, but I'm enjoying the fact that you can't figure out who I am. It's like I'm one-up on you, perhaps for the first time in my life."

The voice was familiar—as if she closed her eyes, everything would become clear. Finally, he removed his glasses and squinted in the sunshine. Those blue eyes. Those beautiful, almost turquoise colored eyes. There was only one person in the world she had ever seen with eyes like that.

"You can't be Phillip."

He just smiled and crossed his arms, not denying or acknowledging.

"Phillip Barton?"

He still only smiled. That smile. There was no mistaking now. It was definitely he. A sudden rush of feelings and memories so overwhelmed her that she bolted to him, grabbed and hugged him nearly in tears.

"I take it you remember me now," he said as she pulled away.

"You stinker! You've changed so much. I would've never known you. Look at your short hair. And what is with the power dressing? A white shirt and a tie? Who did that to you?" She stepped back to get a better look. "What happened to those beautiful blond locks? And," then she hesitated, "no offense, but what about all the muscles? I mean, you're so ... well ..."

"Thin?"

"Well, yes, to be exact."

"All that muscle turned to fat when I got into the real world and stopped working out all the time. I just didn't have the motivation to keep lifting weights. I started in on healthy eating instead. It's a lot easier than sweating a couple of hours every day."

"Wow, I'm just ... so ... well ... taken back. I mean, of all the people I would have expected to run into today, you certainly wouldn't have been on the list. What are you doing here?"

"I'm the unfortunate sap who gets to fill in for Max Caldwell at the banquet."

She giggled. Unfortunate indeed. "I feel so sorry for you," she managed with a suppressed grin.

"Don't give me your pity. I've given myself enough on the drive down here."

"Oh, you'll do fine. You'll probably be more sincere than Caldwell anyway."

"Oh yeah! I'm sure that's exactly what these kids want—sincerity over fame and fortune."

She still couldn't believe he was in Treasure Cove. "What on earth are you doing here on Thursday? The banquet's not until Saturday night."

"Have dinner with me tonight, and I'll tell you all about it."

"Oh, Phillip, not tonight. Of all nights ... of all weekends for you to show up!"

"What's wrong? You've got a date?"

"Yeah, with one hundred twenty term papers! I've got to have them graded by Monday. I have absolutely no time for visiting—period."

"You're the teacher. Finish them by Tuesday."

"I can't do that. I promised them Monday."

"Tell them something came up."

"Sure. Sorry kids, but this tall blond breezed into town this weekend and I couldn't get your papers graded."

He folded his hands together and pleaded, "Just blow them off this one time. I know you—you do everything right, everything you're supposed to do. We haven't seen each other in almost a decade."

She sighed. The papers were weighing heavily on her, yet how often would she get the chance to see him? She could tell them tomorrow there would be a delay, and then she could visit with him as much as possible. But that would mean putting off the inevitable grading process even longer.

"Don't think too long," he cautioned. "You'll reason yourself out of it if you're not careful. I know you. Have dinner with me tonight, and then you can grade yourself to death the rest of the weekend."

"When are you leaving?"

"Monday sometime."

"You'll be here Sunday too?"

"Yep. Now, are you going to have dinner with me or not?"

"Okay! Okay! Dinner tonight. What time?"

"Well, since you have school tomorrow, how about I pick you up around five-thirty?"

"Sounds perfect. What do I wear—I mean, is this dinner or is this just grabbing a bite to eat?"

"Jeans, please. I'm ready to get out of these clothes."

She smiled.

"What?"

"You haven't really changed a bit, have you?"

"You might be surprised."

"I look forward to finding out."

"Do you still live at the beach house?"

"The one and only. Oh, wait. There's a gate now ... with a combination. Let me write it down for you."

"Oooo, Gull Island has high security?"

"Too many of the older people were getting scared about crime. We had a couple of small robberies, nothing serious, but it really bothered them. So, we're well-protected … I guess."

She found a loose receipt on the floor of the van and wrote down the combination.

He stared at it for a moment and then nodded in understanding. "If I'm not there by five forty-five, you'll know I'm stranded at the gate struggling with this thing. Come rescue me."

"Maybe."

"Still so wicked."

"Just one of my many charms."

"Right."

Chapter Two

Driving home, Meg tried to sort through the jumbled emotions and memories. At one point in time she believed she would have married Phillip—then everything fell apart.

They had met the summer after her high school graduation. Her parents owned a beach house in Treasure Cove, Florida. Every summer they made the journey there from Houston, Texas, where her father was the president of a multimillion-dollar oil company, MacAllister Oil. They usually spent two months enjoying the tropics, then boarded the place up and headed back to Houston for the year. Meg hadn't been in three years because she had lifeguarded at the country club. But that summer, she was forced to go. She had committed the unpardonable.

Before her senior year in high school, she had been the ideal daughter, the ideal student, and the ideal leader. She was a staunch perfectionist, and everything she did reflected that. She made top honors always in school. She was president of her class every year, and led most of the organizations. She was an excellent pianist, and had won several awards and contests. Her junior year she was asked to be a guest pianist for a song with the Houston Symphony. Everything in her life had been perfect ... until she met Alan Parsons.

Alan was a philosophy student at the University of Houston. She had met him while studying one evening at the university's library. He captivated her mind with ideas she had never before considered. After several weeks of talking with him at the library, he invited her to a *meeting* on campus. The meeting consisted of a dozen or so groupies that hung on his every word and idea. After a couple of months with him, Meg began to question everything in her life. Was she doing all she did to please herself or others? Was she wasting her intelligence and talent on an establishment that would always demand from her and then throw her away when she was depleted? Was she a *good* girl because that was what was expected of her, or because she enjoyed goodness herself? Shouldn't she have the freedom to express herself from outside the confined barriers where high society and family status had placed her?

By Christmas that year, he had convinced her she was merely a puppet on a string, constantly being pulled by her wealthy parents and narrow-minded authority figures. She resigned every organization, quit music lessons, and then insisted on working Sundays so she would have to miss church. She began to secretly arrange work schedules so she could join Alan and his entourage at a small cabin in the woods on weekends. Eventually, she even delved into drug use and began sleeping with Alan on occasion. She thought she was really free. She felt unleashed from expectation for the first time in her life, and he was her key.

One Saturday afternoon, she had been unable to get her schedule changed. Knowing at least one other lifeguard would be on duty, she left work with no one covering her. She showed up at the cabin unexpected and walked in on a scene she would never forget. Alan was with two other girls, two of her friends, in a very compromising situation. She stood there with the door wide open. She said nothing, her friends said nothing, but he finally broke the silence.

"Meg, why don't you join us? I think you're ready for this now."

She was mortified, humiliated, and disgusted. The reality of what had actually been happening all those months suddenly dawned on her—she had been used. Obviously when Alan had found out she was the daughter of the wealthy MacAllister Oil heir, he had latched on to her and bolstered her ego constantly. She footed the bill for most of their excursions—at her own insistence, of course. She had joined his little group of psycho-babblers, and she had chosen to give herself to him, convinced that she was his life's soul-mate, his one and only, the single completion to all he was missing.

What a fool, she thought to herself as she finished the combination to the gate. *I guess I'll always wonder what might have happened in my life had I not fallen for such a bunch of lies and liars. They were all psychos really. I guess that made me one too.*

She remembered running to her car with Alan frantically following trying to pull on his pants.

"You don't understand, Meg!"

"You're right! I don't understand how I could have been such an idiot all these months!"

"No, no, no," he said out of breath as he caught up with her. "You don't understand what this is all about. You don't understand what I'm all about."

"Sure I do! You're a loony! You're a liar, and you're a fake!"

"See, I knew you wouldn't understand. You weren't ready for this."

"Ready? Ready for what? To find out I'm a joke among those I thought cared most about me? You lied to me! I've sacrificed everything I ever worked for because you fed me a bunch of lies!"

"Look, we need to go inside and sit down and talk this out."

She remembered how he took her hand to lead her back to the cabin, and how, for just a second, she almost melted at his touch. Then she thought of her two friends inside. She jerked her hand away, punched him in the mouth, and then kicked him in the groin.

"That, Mr. Big shot, is the final word you'll ever hear from me."

She got into her car and sped off, hoping to never see him or his friends again. Of course, where would she go now? Home? What a thought! She had no home anymore. Alan had seen to that. She had so rebelled and grown to despise her parents that there was no communication between them whatsoever. What could she do?

Golly gee, Mom and Dad. I know I've been a real bad girl the past year, but I've seen the error of my ways and would like to be welcomed back into the fold. What do you say?

Her parents had been waiting for her when she returned from the cabin. They had received a call from the country-club explaining she had left work irresponsibly. Her parents were stunned. True, she hadn't been the girl they had known all those years before, but they just assumed it was a phase and that it would pass. Her two older brothers had done the same, and they were doing fine. But for Meg to be irresponsible—to put others in danger—that was grounds for discipline, and they were beyond listening or reasoning by the time she walked in.

"Where've you been?" Herbert MacAllister, a man often filled with humor and a smiling twinkle in his eyes, was all business and no nonsense at that moment. This was how he kept MacAllister Oil running at the top.

"You don't want to know," she replied smugly.

"Sit down, and tell us where you've been," he said forcefully.

She glanced at her mother, Meri MacAllister, and saw the evidence of much weeping. She would have to comply at this point—she knew she had no choice. She had obviously been wrong, and there was no apology or penitence that could make up for it. What was worse, they didn't have a clue as to all she had been involved with. If they knew, it would probably be more than they could bear.

"I asked you where you've been," her father repeated.

"And I told you that you didn't want to know."

"Okay, I'll start this whole powwow off then," he continued. "First, you've been fired from the club. They weren't thrilled to know that thirty second graders were swimming with only one lifeguard on duty. The school has threatened to sue. Second, you've apparently been missing many weekends at the job."

"Hey, someone always covered for me then!" she shot back in defense.

"So you could go ... where?"

She paused again. She was so mad at everyone in her life at that moment she decided to just spill it all out. Why hide it? They wanted to know. Why not?

After a thirty minute, detailed description of her life from September to May, her parents were speechless. She expected her mother to start crying again, but that didn't happen. She just stared. Her father finally got up and left the room.

"We'll talk about this later," he said unemotionally, still the businessman, not the father.

That left her alone with her mother—both sitting in silence. Meg hated that, but for some reason she didn't want to be the first one to crack. She had nothing to say, so she just sat. Finally, her mother spoke.

"This isn't what your father and I expected from you."

"Oh, please ..." Meg began, but was quickly cut off.

"Oh please what?!" Meri said loudly. "Oh please forgive you? Oh please don't expect anything from you? Oh please just get over the whole thing? Oh please what, Meg? Exactly what are we to do in response to all of this? Go ahead. You're such an expert on everything now! You tell me—what do we do?"

Meg looked away at the ceiling, then out the window to the plush backyard, finely manicured and perfect. Everything was supposed to be perfect in this family. And Meg had been perfect, until she became stupid.

"I don't know, Mother," she finally managed. "I actually deserve anything you can dish out right now. No punishment would be too severe, I suppose. I know you're hurt. Guess what—so am I. You only have to deal with your daughter's life. I have to deal with *my* life. I've been a bigger fool than I ever thought possible. So, forgive me if you want to—punish me, even kick me out. I've got three weeks until graduation, so that's my only focus right now. Just do what seems best."

What seemed best was for Meg to go to Florida with the rest of the family that summer. She packed light and made the trip in the motor home with her parents and her two younger brothers. She had anticipated it being the worse summer of her life. Instead, it had been the most amazing. She reunited with her best childhood friend from the summers prior. She made new friends who held purpose and meaning in life, one of them being Phillip, an orphan who had been shuffled from orphanages to children's homes all over the country.

Dropping back to reality, she realized she had been sitting in the van on the driveway for some time. The clock read ten after five.

Oh no! Twenty minutes! I'll never make it! I've got to move fast!

Quickly making her way to the bathroom, she started the shower and let the cool water wash over her. It was refreshing after a day of sticky, sweaty, humid air mixed with an afternoon of dust from the ball field. She laughed as she imagined how horrible she probably looked when she had passed Phillip on the sidewalk—her long, brown hair dangling out the back of her cap in a ponytail. Her uniform was covered in dirt from fourteen or so jubilant hugs, as though she herself had actually played the game. She was sure she must have had a nasty scowl from reading the letter from Carmen's mother. At this point she couldn't remember if she had acknowledged him by saying anything, or if she had just nodded her head. No matter. He would be here soon. The clock read five twenty-seven

"No way! I'll never be ready in time!"

She panicked as she tried to brush the tangles from her dripping hair. *Ding-dong.* The doorbell! Now she really panicked. Forgetting her hair was still a wet mess, she quickly threw on a robe and ran down the hallway. It rang again.

"I'm coming! Please don't run away!"

She jerked opened the door and there stood Phillip, beaming as though nine years had never passed and they were still in college. He wore a yellow Polo shirt, starched jeans, and penny loafers with …

"No socks still?" she asked glancing down at his shoes.

"No. No socks. But at least *I* am dressed, and *my* hair is dry and combed."

She suddenly remembered her appearance and blushed, something she seldom did. She was confident in most everything. Embarrassment was not a trait she suffered from often. This time, however, she seemed to find herself stumbling and bumbling all over the place. Finally, she just stopped, closed her eyes, and put her fingers up to her temples.

"What are you doing?" he asked. "Meditating?"

"No," she responded calmly, "I'm focusing. This whole day has been wild and unplanned. If I told you everything from the time the alarm didn't go off to greeting you at the door looking like this, you would leave, thinking I was jinxed from the outset."

Suddenly a shrill bark sounded from the back.

"Spiro?" he asked eagerly.

"Spiro! Oh no! I forgot all about him! He's chained up under the deck! Poor thing—I need to let him in!"

"Tell you what," he offered, "I'll get Spiro and you go do something with that hair. You can wear the robe if you want, but the hair has got to be better than that before we leave."

She *focused* again and turned back down the hallway. "Focus. Focus. Focus," she chanted as she headed for the bathroom.

In some ways, it was like seeing him for the first time all over again. She had gone to a pool party at Janet's house the very first night they rolled in from Texas. She had determined to be miserable the whole summer, but while sleeping on the beach, her best buddy from days gone by, a bubbly redhead they used to call *Roly Poly,* awakened her. With Janet, was Amy, a tall, thin blond who had always been Janet's best friend. The two girls were as opposite as possible, and Meg never understood the bond, but they had always been inseparable. She remembered summers when she and Janet would do the most off-the-wall things just for a laugh, and Amy would always follow along but never participate.

As Meg had tried to focus her eyes in the blaring sun, she recognized Amy immediately and the stern look on her face. She had to concentrate harder to make out Janet, who had gone from a size sixteen to a size six. She was beautiful—but then, she had always been to Meg. It was the boys who had made fun of her weight, especially Meg's brother, Craig. He was five years older than Meg, and three years older than Janet. Janet always had the biggest crush on him, but he was merciless to her, which was always shocking because he was so tender-hearted.

After reacquainting themselves, Janet invited her to a pool party at her house that evening. Meg went, much to the disbelief of her parents. They had expected her to act like a royal jerk the entire summer, never leaving the house for any reason, because that's what she had told them her plans were. But she had forgotten about Janet. Janet was the best. How could she not go to Janet's?

The party had been wonderful, other than the fact that it was a church event. She stomached the Bible study and the guitar singing okay, but really enjoyed meeting Phillip Barton. He was grilling burgers with Amy's fiancé—a guy from Greece named Nikos. Phillip had looked like a god to her at that moment—tall, with shoulder length, shaggy, blond hair dancing in the summer breeze, bright red trunks, no shirt, and all those muscles bulging everywhere. She was introduced by Janet, and then he took up the conversation from there.

"So, you're the famous *Meg MacAllister* I hear about all the time?" he had asked her.

"You know about me? How do you know about me?"

"Well, for starters, Janet has talked non-stop about you since she found out you were coming down this summer. Of course, Janet talks non-stop anyway, but you've been the subject for three weeks."

Meg smiled at the memory.

"Then I know your brother, Craig, real well. He's a great guy."

"Yes, he is," she had agreed. Craig was wonderful, especially since he had gotten off of the drugs and gotten back into church. He had been in New Orleans enrolling in Seminary for the fall. Craig—a minister—that had been a total turnaround.

The sound of Spiro barking brought her back to the present again. Her hair was combed and dry—enough to venture out in public. She quickly grabbed some jeans and thought of wearing a silk blouse but decided against it because of the humidity. What if he wanted to walk on the beach or something afterward? She would be soaked with sweat.

She opted for a yellow sleeveless blouse, pulled on her sandals, and did a little dab of makeup before leaving the room. When she opened the door, Spiro, a small, brindle colored Cairn Terrier leaped into her arms.

"Hello, sweetie," she crooned while ruffling his head with her fingers. "Did you miss me today? I'm so sorry Mommy forgot to get you when I came home, but this big, bad man distracted me from my duties. He even wants me to neglect my students. He's not very nice, is he?"

Spiro barked.

"Hey, pal," Phillip said coming to pet him, "don't you let her fool you. Who's the one who let you out of that little doggie jail down there?"

Spiro barked again and this time wiggled himself down so he could run to Phillip.

"Great! You've turned my own dog against me. He's all I've got left, you know?"

"Now, that is sad. Your life really hasn't boiled down to a dog and a bunch of students, has it?" He raised a skeptical eyebrow.

"Well, if it had, I sure wouldn't admit it to you after a statement like that."

He held his arms up in surrender. "Don't," he said quickly. "Between my sarcasm and your defensiveness, this could be a repeat of a chapter we don't want to remember. Truce, please?"

She smiled. He was the greatest guy in the world, but they could fight like cats and dogs. "Truce? Yes. Most definitely." She held out her hand, and he took it and shook it gently.

"You look great, you know? Were you trying to make us look like twins?" he grinned.

Realizing her shirt was the identical yellow of his, she laughed as she remembered making fun of Craig and Janet when they had started dating because Janet kept buying matching clothes.

"You know, Janet still does that? I'm not lying. When I saw them at Christmas, she had made these cutesy sweatshirts with Christmas bears or trees or something." She grabbed her purse and snapped for Spiro to follow her.

"How are Craig and Janet? I haven't heard from them in a while."

"Let's get going, and I'll fill you in. I'm starved."

She put Spiro on the back deck and then left with Phillip through the front. A beautiful red Dodge Durango sat in the driveway.

"Wow," she cooed, "yours?"

"Half mine, half the bank's."

He had parked beside the big, brown fifteen passenger van.

"Yours?" he asked.

"Yep. I got so tired of having to borrow vehicles to take kids here and there, so I asked Daddy to buy me one—one of the perks of having millionaire parents."

"I suppose so," he nodded with a slight grimace. "But I can't believe you gave up the Porsche for a van—an ugly van too."

"It's not ugly, and who said I gave up the Porsche?"

"You still have it?" His turquoise eyes glowed with delight.

"In the garage."

"Oh man, please let me drive it again sometime this weekend? Please?"

"You can drive it now, if you want. Move your Durango so we can get it out of the garage."

He acted as jumpy as Spiro, skipping to the Durango. He pulled in behind the van, and hopped out, grinning from ear to ear. She opened the garage and revealed the object of his envy—her blue Porsche. It had been a high school graduation gift from her father.

"You really don't mind?" he asked again. "I mean, I was the one who asked you out."

"The more things change, the more they stay the same," she sighed. "We always took my car anyway."

"Don't ever call this just a car, Meg. It's a Porsche—one reincarnation away from being a goddess."

"No speeding."

"Never." He flashed those blue eyes and that smile again, and she knew that where ever they were going would be farther away than either of them had initially planned, and it would need a good back road to get there.

They caught up on everything during the drive to the Crab Shack. Phillip had graduated from Seminary seven years ago and went immediately into ministry. He had done youth and music work at a small church in Georgia to start. It lasted only eight months. The people hated the idea of a single young man working with their teenage girls. He then moved to a church in central Florida. He stayed there two years, but was asked to leave when one of the deacon's college daughters fell madly in love with him and he didn't return the affections. He tried to find a job just working with music, but only the larger churches were looking, and no one wanted a guy with two and a half years experience while others with twenty years under their belts and a family to support needed the job more. He then moved around to two more churches, and finally ended up in north Florida, still doing youth and music, at a *snooty church run by the wealthy in the community*. He had only been there for eleven months, but was desperate for something different.

"I'm ready to get out of the ministry, Meg," he finally confessed as they sipped their tea. She laughed. "That wasn't meant to be funny." There was hurt in his eyes.

"I'm sorry, Phillip, but if anyone was ever meant to be in the ministry, it was you."

"Yeah, I thought that too at one time. I just didn't realize that to serve my crucified Savior meant being crucified myself every couple of years at some little church. They've been merciless. I go in there ready to give it my all, only to have every idea dished by somebody's so and so who doesn't think it's appropriate, or proper, or just simply that it's never been done like that before. I've only been doing this seven years, and I'm already burned out."

She studied his face. For the first time she saw the age in it. Thirty-two wasn't old, but it was older than the twenty-one year old she had met and fallen in love with years before.

"Craig struggled for awhile too, you know?"

"Yeah, I know. We kept in touch for a long time. We prayed for each other, gave each other encouragement, gave each other names of churches that were looking for youth ministers, or in my case, music. Then we sort of lost touch, especially when I moved to this church. I vowed, Meg, to give it my all, to not hold anything back. If it didn't work out, this would be it." He sighed in frustration as he glanced out to the ocean. "So, here I am."

She shook her head. She would never have imagined he could look so defeated. Even when she had broken up with him before he left for seminary, he still had an unwavering hope about life. He would have liked to have had her with him, but if not, it was okay too. God was in control.

"Maybe you could find a church with full time music now?"

"I don't want to. The music part is harder than the youth. The older guard hates the contemporary stuff, and the younger adults hate the southern gospel. The pastor thinks anything with a beat is leading to fornication, and the youth literally look at me and yawn blatantly when I lead anything less than heavy metal. It's not ministry, Meg. It's a big, nasty business of compromise and pleasing. You please the big wigs, and you try your best to make the rest feel loved. I can't do it anymore."

"So what are you going to do?"

"I talked with Stan Allison a few months ago."

"The manager of WJBA here in Treasure Cove?"

Memories flooded through again. During his college years he had worked as a DJ for the Christian radio station. He was well-liked in the area, almost a celebrity, and surprised many that he didn't pursue a career in broadcasting.

"I told Stan about my struggles, and that I was possibly ready to get back into broadcasting. I asked him if he knew anywhere that needed someone. He told me to pray about it, and said he would pray about it, and for me to take my time before jumping back into this. If it was what God wanted, that we would just know."

"And ..."

"And he called me Sunday evening saying he might have found a place

16

for me, and could I come for an interview this Friday."

"Will it be here ... in Treasure Cove ... at WJBA?"

"Yeah, but I'm not sure what the position is. I don't make much now, but a DJ's salary will be quite a cut. Of course, I could take a second job if I had to. We'll see what happens."

Chapter Three

"Ok, who got the crab legs and fried jumbo shrimp combo?" the petite waitress asked as she balanced the tray on one hand. They had talked so long before ordering that their first waitress had left.

"That would be me," Meg said raising her hand to her shoulder like a school girl.

The waitress placed the plate piled with food in front of her. "So, you're the shrimp salad?" the tiny lady asked turning to Phillip.

"That's right, with thousand island on the side."

She set down his bowl of salad and gave another look at Meg's pile of crab legs.

"There's very little meat in them, you know," Meg defended.

"I wouldn't know—I hate seafood." And with that she turned and left.

"Always defending yourself," he noted with a gentle smile.

"It's hard when you're always right and the rest of the world doesn't know it."

The remainder of the evening was wonderful. She told him about her last two years at college and then moved on to describe teaching. She had taught high school literature, language, and composition for seven years and loved it. She talked of how she had worked closely with the children's home since graduating, and how wonderful it was when they asked her to be on the Board of Directors three years ago. She knew the biggest reason was because she had lots of contacts with money. But the fact that she was only twenty-six then, and that they trusted her judgment was an honor—and she had done well for them. She was able to finance a new dormitory that housed only the eleventh and twelfth grade girls. They ran it more like a house than a dorm. The girls learned to cook, clean, do laundry, and were allowed to have dinner parties and guests, as well as be responsible for all their own meals on a rotation basis.

"If they can't live with the responsibility, then they have to go back to a regular dorm."

"How has it worked out?"

"What do you think? This is the first time anybody has trusted or depended on many of these girls for anything. We've had a few who bucked the system just for the sake of bucking the system. You know—the old *you can't make me do anything* routine. We just stick them back in a regular dorm, and it isn't long before they're regretting their hard-headedness."

"I didn't realize you were so involved in the home. Wow, on the Board of Directors—that's pretty impressive."

She talked about coaching softball and tennis, and how she taught Sunday School to the twelfth grade girls at church.

"Don't you get tired of them? I mean all week long at school, then after school with sports, then all the work with the home, then on Sunday too?"

"Nope. What's more, I've become a stable figure in their lives. I'm not some itinerant dorm parent who's there a few months and then gone the next. I'm not a mom or a dad who spends three weeks with them then sends them back because I can't handle the responsibility anymore. I'm not a foster parent who takes them in hoping for some extra cash, only to discover the cash isn't worth the headache of raising problem kids. I'm just Miss Mac, their teacher, their coach, their counselor, and their friend."

"I wish you could have been *my* friend when I was there. Maybe I would have a little more confidence when I moved out."

"Well, I'm your friend now."

He smiled that wonderful smile, and his blue eyes caused a flood of memories again. She was back at the pool at Janet's, meeting him the very first time, listening to him talk about philosophy, and thinking he was the nicest guy she had ever met.

"A penny for your thoughts," he asked.

"Oh, no. It would cost a lot more than a penny to know my thoughts!"

"I am paying for supper, you know. And you did eat a lot of crab legs."

"I need to grade papers, you know. You kept me out a lot longer than I expected."

"Well, I think you needed this as much as I did."

"How's that?"

"You needed some adult companionship for a change. And I just needed some companionship period." He paused for a moment. "It's not really too late, is it? I was so hoping for a walk along the beach with Spiro … and you, of course, if you can ignore the guilt of ungraded papers."

She loved walking the beach, especially with Spiro, but she had many fond memories of walking with Phillip. It had been a nightly ritual in college. They walked, sang, prayed, and dreamed so many things. She had also broken up with him on the same beach. She hadn't thought of that in years. She wondered if he was as over her as she was him. He wasn't married, but neither was she. So what did that say about her? She was overextended—that was all.

Meg had pegged the weather just right. The breeze was gentle, but still warm, and the air was typically sticky. Spiro was too excited to just walk. He ran, hopped, did circles around them, and chased a yellow ball over and over again. He had been neglected more than usual that day. Occasionally he would tease Phillip by bringing the ball to him only to take off with it before he could get it from his mouth.

"I think he remembers you," Meg smiled.

"He was only a little puppy when I left. Surely not."

"He's a smart dog."

"I guess. You know, I've never had a dog in my life. Maybe I should get a dog. What do you think?"

"I don't know. I love Spiro. He's like family to me."

"Ah, I've never had a family either. Maybe I should get a family." He laughed as though it was a good joke.

"Phillip, that's not funny."

"It wasn't funny for many years, but it seems to get funnier the older I get. I mean, I'm thirty-two, never knew a mom or dad, never been married, never had a kid. The first part wasn't my fault, but the second part—well, I suppose I could do something about it, if I really wanted to."

"So, you don't want to get married?"

"Who knows? For the past several years I've had to watch my every move with women. As a minister, you can't just *date* someone for a while and then break up if it's not right. You could lose your job. Shoot! I've lost my job for *not* dating them! There hasn't been a single free and clear opportunity to see a lady since I graduated from seminary. Of course, there hasn't really been anyone I've wanted to invest that kind of time and emotion in either."

"What about seminary? Was there anyone there?"

"Well, that's sort of complicated." She could sense his discomfort as he hesitantly explained. "When I left for seminary, I was sure that when we both finally graduated, we'd end up back together somehow. I just knew we were meant to be. So, I wasn't even looking … you know … *do not look to the left nor to the right.*" He laughed a little at his comment. "Well, seminary was different from college. Nobody was paying for my graduate school. I was on my own. I was in a strange place, working two jobs, studying like crazy because I was taking such a full load. I felt beat up. I kept thinking I'd write you and tell you how wonderful things were, that it was really wise of you to break up because you were too young to get serious with me. I wanted to act like life was just fine without you—thinking maybe you'd be jealous of all that happiness I was having—and change your mind."

"You never wrote."

"How could I? I was miserable. I didn't know if it was losing you, or just the load I was under. I saw other couples there struggling to make ends meet just like me, with even a kid or two, but they were happy because they were together. I decided maybe you were smarter than I ever was. I wasn't the right one for you. When I accepted that, things got a lot better for me."

"What do you mean—you weren't the right one for me? I never said that. I just said I was way too young for where things were headed and that we needed to stop before ..."

"I know ... believe me, I remembered every word you said. But I *wasn't* right for you. You needed a guy who had a little more fire in him, someone who could challenge you. And shoot, I needed a girl who wasn't so bull-headed and controlling."

"Controlling?"

"Yes, controlling. We just couldn't have made it together. I'm glad things happened like they did. You were obviously wiser than your years."

So, there it was. She could take comfort that he didn't mourn too long after the break up and agreed that their personalities would have been more combustible than compatible. And for right now he had no interest in anything other than friendship, which he apparently needed desperately, and she could handle that.

"I'm glad you got things together. I would hate to have thought I was the cause of much misery in your life."

He laughed again. "You were always the cause of misery in my life! Do you realize you argued with me more than you agreed with me? Now, *that* was miserable! I would pick you up, guaranteeing myself to not bring up anything controversial, and doggone it, if I didn't manage to blow it every time!"

"You make me sound like a witch!"

"You were! You were bull-headed, strong-minded ... just fill in the descriptions here with me, if you'd like."

She merely stared as her jaw dropped.

He shook his head. "Don't look so surprised. You were very antagonistic back then."

She kept quiet for a moment—that actually was the truth. She had always felt the need to be forceful for some reason.

Then he gently touched her arm and said, "You're not like that anymore, though. It's amazing, but you've mellowed a lot."

"So, I'm not intense any longer?"

"Well, I wouldn't say that. It's just that you're more mellow now ... with moments of intensity."

That appeared to be kind. It was comforting to know that maturity had managed to creep up on her in spite of herself.

"You're not the same at all," she finally told him.

"Really?"

"No. I mean …" she hesitated. How did she tell him he had gone from being the world's biggest optimist to a depressed, hopeless man ready to surrender his dreams? "Oh, I don't know. I guess you've mellowed too."

He stood quietly. They had stopped walking some time ago and had been gazing over the Gulf into the moonlight for several minutes.

"Man, it's beautiful here. I should've never left. Everything I cared about—or that ever cared about me—was in Treasure Cove."

"That's not true, Phillip. It only feels like that at this moment. Familiar places can do that to people."

"Well, it sure feels like that really strong right now … really strong."

She wanted to put her arm in his and tell him everything was going to be fine. She was disheartened that his life had turned out so different from the dreams he had shared. She hated that his one joy and goal, ministry, had turned out to be the biggest disappointment ever—perhaps even worse than never having parents, or a home … or a wife.

"You want some iced tea?" she asked instead.

"Oh, no, not really. It's late, you know?"

"Yeah, I know. But the offer still stands."

"You have to face a bunch of eager students in the morning, and I have an interview with Stan."

"Well, if I can't twist your arm any more, we probably better head back."

After he left, she felt uneasy. She had never in her life wanted to make the hurt go away for someone so much. It wasn't fair for him. He had such potential, yet so many odds against him from the beginning. He had been shuffled through numerous orphanages, never staying long enough at any to develop friendships, much less his talents. Finally at Treasure Cove he had found some roots.

You probably could have completed his life had you not been so selfish and stupid. She looked at her reflection. Her long, light brown hair, slightly tangled by the wind, framed her tanned face. *So here you are at twenty-nine and haven't seriously seen another man since him. If only you had made wiser decisions when you were younger.*

The real truth about the breakup stayed locked inside her heart. No one knew the whole story.

Had you married him, you would have saved him the single-man stigma, would have given a few pastors and deacons a piece of your mind, then she thought tenderly, *and would have given him a family.*

She changed for bed as the sting of discouragement over what might have been continued to linger. He had been her ideal, but she could never escape the reality of her past. How could anyone have done all she did and then marry a minister? *You reap what you sow, sister—and you're still reaping it.*

As she lay down, she said a prayer for her old friend.

Lord, I don't usually pray for something as simple as this, but please make Phillip happy—please.

Chapter Four

"I'm afraid I won't have your papers graded by Monday," Meg told her sixth period Language Arts class. The response was not quite what she had expected. Every other class had moaned and groaned, with a few cheers thrown in, and always a comment about it being okay if she didn't grade them at all. Instead, this class assured her all was fine as they stared with knowing smiles. A couple of girls giggled, and Jamey Corts, quarterback, just gave her a big thumbs up.

"Well, I'm certainly glad you're all taking this so well."

"No problem, Miss Mac," Alissa grinned. "You just take all the time you need—doing whatever it is you're doing other than grading our papers."

With that the entire class burst out in laughter. A couple of guys did high fives, and Alissa nearly fell out of her seat with hysteria.

"Okay," Meg calmed them down. "I'm obviously missing something here. Could someone please fill me in?"

"Go ahead, Jamey," Alissa called from the back of the class.

"Yes, Jamey, please ... enlighten me."

He got up slowly, sauntering very deliberately toward the front of the class. He cleared his throat several times eliciting a few more giggles, and then began his revealing speech.

"Well, Miss Mac, as you know, we all love you very much."

"Thank-you, Jamey."

"You're welcome." Once again snickers spotted here and there. He held his hand up for silence. "However, no matter how much we love you, we understand that's not enough for a woman of your ... uh ... well ... maturity." Now there was laughter. He again quieted the class. They hushed quickly and looked gravely serious.

"What are you getting at, Jamey? I'm totally lost." She wasn't enjoying being the brunt of a joke, and was especially uncomfortable because she was clueless about it. Beginning to perspire and blush, she fought to keep control.

"Miss Mac, please, let me finish," he said calmly.

"By all means."

"Well, last night, my father—you do know my father don't you?"

"Yes, Jamey. I know your father."

"Well, he had a business dinner last night. It was a bit out of town—one of those out-of-the-way places you go when you don't want to be seen or disturbed. I believe you've heard of it, the Crab Shack. Are you familiar with the Crab Shack, Miss Mac?"

Her cheeks grew warm. "Thank you, Mr. Corts. That will be enough."

"So, is it true then?" Alissa blurted out. "You had a date? With a tall blond?"

"No!" Meg found herself close to yelling. "It wasn't a date. I was having dinner with an old friend."

"A long dinner," Jamey interjected. The class laughed again.

"Yes, Jamey, it was a long dinner. I haven't seen this *friend*," and she stressed the word, "in almost nine years. We knew many people in common and were merely catching up."

"That's fine, Miss Mac," Alissa inserted again, "and we give you our permission and blessing to catch up all weekend and just forget about those old term papers."

That did it. She had lost control of the class. As they enjoyed their moment of having finally pulled one over on the teacher who knew it all, she stared at the clock. Two twenty. She still had forty minutes with these hooligans, and she didn't know exactly how to handle them. One thing she had learned after teaching for seven years, when you lose control you have two choices   either get really mean and hateful and demand order, or let them go for the day. It was Friday. School would be out for the summer in one week. She had nothing of necessity to teach today, just reviewing.

A knock interrupted the clamor, a very loud knock. Apparently the person outside had been trying for some time and was now banging to get their attention.

"Alissa, would you do something constructive today and get the door, please?" Meg asked sternly, letting the class know she did not appreciate the mayhem. The redhead went to the door, peeked out the narrow window then looked back in shock. As she opened it, she motioned the visitor in. It was Phillip.

It seemed at last the class knew better than to respond. They sat still, smiling as their teacher greeted the *tall blond*.

"Hello, Mr. Barton," she said. "Welcome to my extremely loud junior Composition class."

"I wish I had been in a class like this when I was here," he shrugged. "We would have had been given a week's detention for what I heard going on through the door."

"Trust me, they're close to it," she moaned. "Class, this is Mr. Phillip Barton. He graduated from here many, many years ago."

"Not that many," he insisted. At this, the class erupted again.

"Don't encourage them. Is there something I can do for you?"

"Yes, can I talk to you alone for just a moment?"

She motioned him toward the hallway. "I'll be right outside the door," she told the grinning faces. "Please try to behave like you're almost adults."

"I'll take names, Miss Mac!" Alissa yelled out.

"Thank you, Alissa. What would I do without you?"

"Take your time. I have everything under control," she said with a reassuring nod.

As soon as they stepped into the hallway and shut the door, Phillip nearly burst with excitement.

"What is it?" she asked him, still a bit shaken from the whole classroom fiasco.

"I got the job!" he exploded, nearly jumping to the ceiling. He then grabbed Meg and began to spin her around. "I got the job! I got the job!"

"Phillip! Put me down!"

"Sorry," he softened his voice as he let go and whispered, "I got the job, I got the job."

"What is the job? Will you be here in Treasure Cove?"

"Oh yeah. But I'm not telling you any details right now. Have dinner with me again tonight and I'll tell you everything. You won't believe it! I promise—you won't!"

"Phillip, I can't have dinner with you. I've got to grade term papers."

"Okay, I'll bring dinner over. What do you like?"

"You don't understand. I've got to grade papers. I've already lost an entire night because of you."

"Well, I'm not asking for a whole night. You have to eat, don't you?"

She considered it a moment, and her curiosity was getting the better of her. She decided to try and call his bluff first. "I can't—if you can't tell me now, you'll just have to wait until the banquet."

"Okay, if that's how you want it." He turned to go. "See you tomorrow night."

He was actually leaving—calling her bluff. She had to remember, this was Phillip, the silent rebel, the definition of quiet stubbornness.

"All right, all right. What time will you be over?" she conceded.

"Yeeesssss!" he jumped up again. She didn't think it possible for him to be so animated. "Five thirty sharp. And please be dressed this time. That was a little embarrassing last night." As he started walking again, he stopped and turned around quickly. "Do you want pizza or Chinese?"

Still unnerved by all that was happening, she just shrugged her shoulders. "Whatever. You bring it—I'll eat it. I'll furnish the drinks, okay?"

"See ya!"

After he left, she continued staring at the door. Phillip would be back in

Treasure Cove. She would have one of the long, lost gang here with her at last. It was like coming out of a cave after being in there for hours with no light. She would have a friend, someone her own age again, for the first time in seven years. She was unknowingly smiling as she walked back into the classroom.

"Wo, Miss Mac," Alissa yelled out, "he's a fine one!"

"Does he have a brother?" one girl asked.

"Or two brothers?" giggled another.

Meg just shook her head. Any attempt for order at this point would be futile. She decided to sit down and just let them have at it. For the first time in all her years of teaching she had absolutely lost control.

Meg hoped that immersing herself in grading papers would keep her from thinking about Phillip's exciting news. Unfortunately, that wasn't the case. A couple of papers did manage to grab her attention, but generally she found herself drifting back in time to memories of college, friends, and the most wonderful period in her life. After getting reacquainted with Janet, and somewhat with Amy, and then meeting Phillip, along with several others from Gulf Coast Christian College, her plans for that summer had turned around significantly. She had relearned how to have fun. They had played tennis, volleyball, had many beach Bible studies around campfires, gone roller skating (she hadn't done that in years), had picnics, shopped, seen movies, gone to water slides, gone to concerts, did skits in church, and when there was nothing else to do, swam at the beach or Janet's pool. By the middle of the summer, these wonderful people had shown Meg that Christians really could have fun. Alan had so convinced her that their lifestyles were filled with repression and conformism that she began to despise anything to do with religion and church.

Phillip had done the most to change her mind. He was so free-spirited, easy-going, knowledge-filled, and eager to enjoy life that he had caught her off guard many times when she began to argue against the mores' of Christian belief. By the middle of the summer she had grown tired of defending Alan's views. She had thought they were her own, but in truth, she didn't know what she believed. All she knew was that here was a group of people that loved life, cared about others, valued relationships, and didn't need anything questionable to add to their enjoyment. By mid-July, she had made the decision to follow Christ. What forgiveness, what relief, what peace and what purpose had suddenly flooded her life! She was free, contrary to what Alan predicted. He said all who followed religion were in bondage to its rules and all who rejected religion were free.

Spiro, who had been sleeping soundly next to her on the couch, began to stir and growl. She came back to the present and tried to remember what this particular paper was even about. She glanced at the front cover.

"Oh yeah, the space one."

Ding-dong. Spiro jumped up immediately and ran barking toward the front door.

"Pizza delivery!" yelled Phillip from the front.

She opened the door and found him gently smiling, huge pizza box in hand. He was dressed casually in a pair of white shorts and an alien t-shirt.

"That's funnier than you realize, considering pizza hasn't been delivered here in about three years."

"Really? How depressing. Why not?"

"Security."

"Oh yeah, that stupid gate. It took me five minutes to dig up the paper with the combination."

She took the pizza to the kitchen, washed her hands, and began getting ice in the glasses.

"What's with all the alien garb," she asked as he picked up Spiro and snuggled him close.

"Hmmm ... good question. You know I love sci-fi, but there's probably something more subliminal to it."

"Wait, let me guess, you found your parents, and they're aliens!"

He raised an eyebrow. "You're so perceptive—can't hide anything from you, can I?"

"Okay, the real reason ..."

"Maybe I feel like an alien. I'm trying to live out life in places I don't belong. Guess I went overboard, huh?" He stared down at the huge face on his shirt.

"Well, it's like you always said, if you're gonna do it, right or wrong, do it big."

Spiro was now trying to get at the pizza.

"What's the matter boy? She doesn't feed you right?"

"Stop trying to turn my dog against me, and wash your hands. Get your pizza, take a seat, and then spill everything about this new job you've gotten."

He saluted, "Aye-aye, Captain!"

As they sat in the living room, she said a prayer of thanks for the food then started in on the pizza.

Taking a huge bit, she noted, "I haven't had a veggie pizza in years. When I go for Italian, it's always with a group of kids, and all we get is pepperoni or cheese. Don't even mention vegetables of any kind. I'm honored you remembered."

"Remembered what?" he garbled with a mouth full. "It's all I eat. I try to avoid the grease you get with pizza meats. You said I could get anything, so

I got my favorite pizza."

"Okay, then, I'm hurt that you don't remember this is my favorite. I suppose I'll get over it. Now get on with the news, please. I might as well have gone ahead and cooked something with as little as I've accomplished trying to figure out this new job of yours."

"Ah, the grip of anticipation. It's a wonderful thing, ain't it?"

She glared at him. "The sooner you get this over with, the sooner I can get back, or should I say, get started grading papers."

"I'm going to be the station manager."

"You're kidding? Stan's job? You're getting Stan's job? You're going to be in charge of the whole station?"

"Amazing, isn't it? I was shocked too. I went in there expecting to be a part-time DJ or even worse, a sales manager. Then Stan says, *How does station manager sound?*"

"I don't believe it!" Her smile turned into a frown quickly. "How is Ira with all this? Has Stan even mentioned it to him?"

Ira Epstein was the station owner, a very cantankerous fifty-something-year-old man, who had extreme and opinionated views. He and Meg didn't get along at all.

"Ira was there at the interview. He and Stan asked me a zillion questions, scaring the whatever out of me. Ira goes, *So what new ideas do you have for the station?* And I'm dying there. I tell him I just found out five minutes ago that I might be a station manager—I have no ideas yet. He tells me to just brainstorm. Stan smiles and nods at me, like this whole thing is wrapped up. I'm about to wet my pants. I'm sitting there with Ira, probably Satan's distant cousin." Meg bellowed at that statement. "And I have to just blurt out what I'm going to do with his station."

"I can't believe this! All spur of the moment? You had no idea he was considering you for this position?"

"No idea whatsoever! I was a nervous wreck! I'm sweating like crazy. I start rattling off any and everything. *Well, this might be good, we could always do that, here's something I've thought about before.* Ira seemed to eat it up, so I just kept going and going. I'm thinking either I'm scoring big here or digging the deepest grave ever in my life. I finally shut up. I must have rattled on for fifteen minutes."

He stopped, gulped a big swallow of tea and took a bite of pizza.

"And ..." she was dying to hear the rest.

"Ira goes, *Some of that was really good—some of it was crap.* I'm starting to sweat again. Then he says, *But that's what I'm looking for. We need someone with vision here, someone who can dream big. If you ever stand still, you start to die. Would you let my station die, Phillip?* No sir, I said quickly. And then, trying to relieve some of the tension, I said, *And I will never put down pink carpet, either, sir.*"

"You didn't?" she choked. Ira had fired the manager before Stan because he had let the receptionist choose the color of the carpet, and she chose pink.

"Ira and Stan laughed, then Ira looks at me eyeball to eyeball and goes, *Welcome back, Mr. Barton. When can you start?*"

"Phillip, I can't believe it! That's incredible, and you had no idea!" She squinted. "I didn't realize Ira Epstein even had a sense of humor. He hates me, you know?"

"Really? What did you do to him?"

"I happen to have my own opinions and have the misfortune of being able to put my hands on a lot of money if I need it."

He laughed and nodded as he gulped down more tea.

"When the board at the home wanted to consider me, he absolutely put his foot down," she explained. "He even told them that he would remove all his support if they went any farther with the pursuit. I responded by saying I would double whatever his support was, and that they needed someone under forty to sit on that board while they all made decisions that affected the lives of kids five to eighteen."

"You didn't?"

She nodded.

"No wonder he hates you."

"That's not all. When I put forward the idea about the house for the older girls, he ranted about giving these kids too much freedom. He painted a picture of nothing less than beer parties and orgies every night. When he stopped, I looked at him and said, *Are you finished, sir?* He said, *I just hope you are.* I then proceeded to explain how necessary it was for these girls to learn responsibility before they left the home. What happens when they leave and have never had to be responsible for actually living in the real world?"

"You faced down Ira? Twice?"

"He, of course, said he would give no financial support to the idea after it was unanimously voted in, well, except for his vote. I had no problem with that. I raised the money in two weeks."

She couldn't tell if his expression was one of admiration or shock, but whatever it was, she understood. Seldom did anyone stand up to Ira.

"So, Ira's your boss, now?" she commented, finishing off her pizza.

"My only boss," he smiled.

"Doesn't that scare you a little bit?"

"Ira as my boss? Are you kidding? For the first time in seven years I will know exactly what is expected of me. When I make a mistake, I'll be confronted with it immediately. It won't be passed around the office for weeks before I hear about it. No one will complain that my singleness is interfering with my job. When there are attitude problems, I get to be the one who handles them. I don't have to sit around and take abuse until the pastor decides something needs to be done. But most of all," and he groaned with frustration, "I will know all the hoops I have to jump through in order to get it right ... as opposed to working like crazy and finding out I had missed the hoops altogether!"

"My, you're bitter, aren't you?"

His face was flushed as he tossed down his plate, pizza half eaten. "I really am. Meg, I can't get out of there fast enough. I only hope that I can heal from all of this so I can enjoy being in church again period."

"Aren't you going to finish your pizza?" she asked, a bit concerned at how skinny he had become, remembering how filled out he used to be.

"I can't. I'm nauseous. I think I need some fresh air. Do you mind if I walk your beach a while? I'll take Spiro, and you can stay here and grade papers."

She watched him with concern. His whole demeanor had changed when he began talking about church. Suddenly grading papers seemed insignificant.

"Can I go with you, or do you want to be alone?"

"Please go. I've been alone forever, you know? And I've never really cared for it."

They headed out the back porch and down the stairs of the deck to the beach, Spiro jumping around them with excitement.

"Craig's in a good church now," she told him as she tossed the ball for the dog to chase so he could hopefully run off some of the energy. "He says it feels like being in a big family."

"Lucky him," was all he would say.

"He wants to leave, though. He thinks youth ministry is beginning to be too young for him. I just think he never needed to work with youth anyway."

"You think Craig should pastor?"

"No," she laughed a little, "not pastor. But I think he's more suited for adults, somehow."

"Pastoring would kill him."

"You're so cynical about this whole church thing. You've got to stop. Really, there are nice churches out there, and I happen to belong to one, or have you forgotten?"

He sighed and rubbed his temple. "I don't even think I'm going to give them a notice. I think I'm just gonna pack, rent a truck, call the pastor and tell him, I'm outta here."

"No, you're not," she quickly corrected him. "You're going to end this responsibly. You give your notice, and you stay for as long as the constitution says you stay. Besides, you've got to find a place to live."

"Got it already."

"Really? Where?"

"Some place called Treasure Homes. Ira says they're brand new. He's got one that's never been lived in, and it's part of my package."

Meg's mouth was open in shock. "Have you ever seen the Treasure Homes complex?"

"No. Are they bad? Ira said they were nice. I know he owns them. I just assumed he'd put me up somewhere decent."

"They're these incredible two-story condos about three-quarters of a mile down the beach! They're actually on Gull Island. I thought about buying one when they were first built so I could move out of here. Then I realized I didn't want anything to do with Ira Epstein if I didn't have to."

"A condo on the beach? You're kidding?"

She nodded.

"Things are definitely looking up." That familiar twinkle sparked from his blue eyes. "You can hate Ira if you want to, but I'm afraid I'm falling in love with the man."

She giggled at him then shoved him toward the water and ran after Spiro up the beach. He chased her, picked her up, and then walked out into the water with her. Tossing her in, he then took off toward the house, Spiro following on his heels. She struggled to get up in the waves, and then ran after him. She didn't catch up with him until she got to the stairs leading to the deck of her house. Spiro barked at her as she tried to catch her breath.

"You," she took a deep breath, "are going," deep breath, "to be," breath again, "a horrible neighbor." She collapsed into the sand, sticky wet with salt water.

"And you," he was breathy too, "need to grade," breath, "term papers."

She groaned as she inhaled the thick, humid air. Finally catching her breath, she managed to stand up again. She went to the shower under the deck and cleaned off.

He took out his keys and began to toss them casually. "Can I see you tomorrow? I know you've got to grade papers."

"No, you can't," she pouted. "You've dropped me in the water, and you're trying to steal my dog. I don't want anything to do with you right now. Go away."

"Please? I need moral support before I speak at that banquet."

"You should have thought about that earlier. You think I'm the one to give you moral support? You've royally disrupted my life and you're now working for my arch enemy."

"I'll buy lunch. I'm gonna be making good money, you know? Imagine, a great job, and good money too."

"Yeah, but a lousy neighbor."

He came up and hugged her even though she was drenched. "I can live with that, if I have to. Please have lunch with me."

She stepped back and looked up into those incredible blue eyes. She had often wished she could find his parents just to see if there was another person in the world with those same color eyes. They were gleaming now. She was happy for him knowing that this job would help ease his troubles for the moment. But she also regretted that such talent and heart had been damaged in a career he was born to have.

"How have you managed this?" she asked him.

"Managed what?"

"To keep me from doing what I need to be doing. Yes, I'll have lunch with you, but I have to decorate the gym at the children's home for the banquet at three o'clock."

"I won't be eating all the way to three o'clock! Now you? That may be a different story."

"I don't eat that much."

"All those crab legs and then five pieces of pizza ..."

"You counted how much pizza I ate?"

"It was hard not to. You just kept going after it."

She looked down at Spiro who was still ready to play. "Get him, boy!"

That's all he needed. Spiro jumped at the command and began to nip at Phillip's shins as he barked profusely.

Chapter Five

Meg got up early even though she had stayed up until one o'clock grading papers. She left for her morning jog around seven fifteen, finding herself smiling as she passed the place where Phillip had thrown her in the night before. Spiro followed behind her, probably wishing she had the ball, but knowing this was only the morning jog. Back at the house, she didn't bother with showering yet. She immediately went out to the back deck and began to grade papers, planning to stop and shower at eleven o'clock, then be ready to meet Phillip for lunch at eleven forty-five. He was always early, so she needed to make sure there was plenty of time to be ready.

She found herself laughing at several papers, wishing, for the seventh year in a row, that someone were sitting next to her so she could read various paragraphs or sentences out loud.

"Listen to this, Spiro." He lifted his head as though he understood and watched her read to him.

"Alissa wrote, *Then, Darwin, after viewing the brutal surgery, decided to get a real life. Medicine just wasn't his thing. So what's next? The ministry. The next thing he knows, he's in some theological institution still trying to please his dad.* It's a good thing she has another year with me, huh, Spiro? We'll get rid of those contractions, and hopefully do something with that informal style."

She smiled as she thought of the red-headed girl who had come so far. *She does write great stories, though.* She wrote that on the paper too, hoping it would help offset all the red marks.

Trudging through several more papers, she actually got much more done than she had planned.

Ding-dong!

"Just a minute," she yelled as she finished the last paragraph of a paper on Erasmus. She put the grade on the front cover, tossed it into the finished pile and hopped up, following an eager Spiro to the door.

"Ready?" Phillip said as she opened the door. She was stunned. What time was it? "Obviously not," he answered after seeing her appearance.

She looked at the clock over the television where she had peeked in occasionally to check the time from the deck. "It's only ten twenty-five,"

34

she said. "I thought you said eleven forty-five."

"It's eleven thirty-nine," he said as he held out his watch for her to see.

"You must be on a different time zone or something. It's only ten twenty-five."

"You must have some bad clocks. I'm never wrong on time."

He came on in while Meg went to the kitchen to check the clock on the stove. She couldn't be wrong about this. He must be playing a joke on her. She flipped the switch in the kitchen, but no light came on. She did it again, but still no light. She glanced at the stove. There was no display at all. She stood in the dark for a moment, not wanting to face the fact that the electricity had gone off. She pulled her phone out of her pocket. Eleven thirty-nine.

"So, is that what you're wearing?" he asked. "I mean, it's okay if you are. I can make more casual plans if you want."

She came out of the kitchen, embarrassed for the third time in three days.

"No, I'll go change."

"Really, it's okay. We can eat at the park or something."

"No, let me change."

"Well, the truth is, you look great in that little outfit. I mean, those shorts are so ... well ... short."

"I'll go change," she said again, this time going down the hall to her room. "These are not public shorts—they're jogging shorts."

"Whatever you say."

After driving through Fang's Chinese Palace, Phillip drove the Porsche to the park anyway. They found a huge oak tree with limbs supported by metal bars and sat down beneath it to parcel out the rice, meals, egg rolls and soup.

"Here's some duck sauce," he said as he passed her a couple of packages.

She smiled back at him.

"What are you smiling at?"

"You do remember."

"Remember what?"

"Well, last night you made me feel stupid about the pizza, but there's no mistaking today that you remember what I like in Chinese—shrimp with lobster sauce? Egg drop soup? Egg rolls with lots of duck sauce?"

He put his hands up in surrender. "I'm caught."

They arranged their plates, and this time he prayed.

"So, were you lying about the pizza?" she asked.

"What?"

"Were you lying about the pizza? Did you really not remember that I liked veggie pizza, or were you giving me a hard time?"

He smiled, took a sip of his Diet Coke, and leaned back against the tree. "I remember the first time you introduced me to veggie pizza—it was our first real date. We had eaten pizza at all those church things, but this was just you and me. I asked you if you had a particular favorite, and you quickly answered, *Just vegetables, please.* I had never heard of such a pizza in my life. The waitress came and I said, *We want a pizza with only vegetables on it.* She looked at me like I was crazy because I'd been there many times. *No pepperoni? No sausage?* I assured her we just wanted vegetables." He paused, took a bite, and then finished. "It was the best pizza I ever had."

"Are you this antagonistic with everybody, or is it just with me?"

"Just you," he said with a mouthful of fried rice. "I have to stay on my toes with you."

She tried to watch him without him noticing and was glad to see he could have an appetite still. One thing she had always liked about going out with him was that he was a big eater. She was too, and it didn't seem so obvious when he was next to her scarfing down whatever he could find.

"Why?" she asked him.

"Why what?"

"Why do you have to be on your toes with me?"

"Because you're smart."

"And my mental capacity is a threat or something?"

"It's a good thing. See, some people never get it … you know, my humor. So I find myself trying to dilute lots of stuff that I say … never being able to say what's right on the tip of my tongue. With you, it's the opposite. If I'm ever going to pull one over on you, it has to be really good. Take this whole pizza thing, for example. With anyone else, I would have just agreed, *Yeah, I remember you like veggie pizza.* But with you, you get more out of it if you have to mull it over. Tell me, how often did you actually wonder since last night if I did or didn't remember you liked veggie pizza?"

"More than I want to admit," she pouted.

"See. Funny, isn't it?"

"You knew I would stew about that, didn't you?"

"Stew, stew, stew."

"Well, it got to you that I didn't recognize you when you saw me at the home Thursday."

He leaned against the tree again. "Actually, yes. I had shared the best two years of my life with you. You can't know what it did to me when I actually saw you there on the sidewalk. When Stan asked me to come down for the interview, the first thought that came to mind was whether you were still teaching in Treasure Cove. I almost asked him, but then decided to leave it alone. If you were still here, I'd see you at church or something."

"You weren't even going to call?"

"I thought about it, for a long time, in fact. Then I decided against it."

"Well, thanks," she sulked. "Hope I haven't been too much of an inconvenience for you?"

"You know you haven't. I've begged you to eat with me for three meals now. If the banquet weren't tonight, I'd be begging for a fourth."

"Then why weren't you going to call?"

"Rejection isn't something I could have faced right now. I've lived with it for so long it seems."

"Why would I have rejected you?"

"The first thing I did when I saw you on that sidewalk was look at your left hand."

"My left hand? Why?"

"You don't ever do that? Look at guys' left hands?"

"No." She wasn't getting it at all. "Why would I look at a guy's hand?"

"A ring, Meg? A wedding ring?"

Now she got it. She never did that. She never cared. She never really thought about marriage. But then, she hadn't met anyone in years that she would have considered marrying. "You thought I'd be married?"

"Not thought, was convinced you would be. A casual meeting of you and Mr. Right would have been hard enough. But to call you up while he was in the background, probably reading the latest bestseller to you over cappuccino, would have been a bit too much right now."

"No one's ever read to me but you, Phillip."

"Whew ... 'cause that was one scary picture. I knew you never liked cappuccino, and if this guy had forced that on you, then that would have meant you lost your backbone."

They laughed. It was so good to laugh, to really laugh. To laugh at humor that started from the belly, then grew until it couldn't be contained. That seldom happened to her anymore. She suddenly found everything funny. The kid on the playground who could only get halfway through the monkey bars. The mother chasing her two-year old around with a sandwich trying to get him to eat between rides on the slide. The skinny man with the long beard roller-blading down the sidewalk. She laughed and laughed until tears were coming out of her eyes relentlessly.

"You've got to stop. I can't take too much laughter at one time anymore!"

"Get used to it," he replied with a charming smile.

"Everyone, excuse me, please," Phillip said as he scooted back his chair and stood up, suddenly somber after a meal of laughter and foolishness. "I need to prepare for my speech. I've very much enjoyed dining with all of you."

Meg followed and pulled him aside.

"Are you all right?" she asked him.

"Would you be if you were in my shoes? Until three days ago these kids were expecting Max Caldwell. Now, they get me."

"Well, you've made a great impression on them already. The fact that this is a proper banquet and you caused our table to be called down three times places you right up there next to Mr. Caldwell."

"Thanks. I need all the encouragement I can get right now."

He walked through the door to the foyer of the gym. She felt sorry for him. It was a big job to pull off. Years ago she would have thought Phillip Barton would be just the guy to do it. He was so good with teenagers—his evening at the table had proved that. By the time everyone had been sitting for three minutes, he had them all in stitches, along with nicknames for each kid. Ira even came over and spoke to him, much to the dismay of all the kids.

"Wow," Brandon had said. "I didn't even think Mr. Epstein knew how to smile."

"He doesn't," his twin, Brett, followed. "It was painted on."

Phillip laughed, but immediately let them know that Ira was his new boss and there would be no more jokes about him, unless they were made by Phillip himself. More laughter followed, in fact, that was the first time they were called down.

Mr. Roberts came up to the stage and tripped across the platform, a feat which he did on purpose every year, except for the first, which was quite by accident. It had loosened up the whole stiff evening so appreciatively that he promised to do it every year afterward, much to the chagrin of several board members. Meg found it cute, and always laughed hard when it happened. In fact, she had gotten into the habit of judging his falls. The first year was a ten, and it had gone down from there.

As Mr. Roberts came to the podium, he looked at Meg and asked, "Well, Miss MacAllister?"

She held up six fingers and the place went wild. Last year he had only scored a two.

"It's my pleasure to welcome all of you to our End of the Year Banquet. First, thanks to all the residents for going along with our need to educate you in etiquette. However, I am a little concerned with some of the adult influence we've had this year." He looked directly at Meg's table. She shrugged in innocence.

"Thank-you, board members, for all the work, planning, decorating, and such that went into this."

At this, all the children clapped.

"But now, we need to thank our speaker for tonight who swung in at the last moment to fill a very important need. He's Phillip Barton, from north Florida. He serves as minister of youth and music at..."

Suddenly Mr. Roberts grew quite pale as a man entered from the door of the gym fully dressed in Max Caldwell's uniform. All eyes turned to see what was happening. Gasps came from several kids, and most adults looked shocked.

"Continue, please," yelled the football suit.

Meg grinned. It was Phillip's voice. Mr. Roberts grinned. He obviously had figured it out too. Even Ira was chuckling. All the kids, however, were totally perplexed.

"As I said, Mr. Barton ... uh ... is ... uh ... a former resident of the Treasure Cove Children's Home. He lived here for five years, but that was long ago."

"It wasn't that long," yelled the football suit again, taking its place next to Mr. Roberts with one huge leap onto the platform. "I'll take it from here, sir. You may be seated."

The football suit guided Mr. Roberts back to his table. On his way to the podium, Phillip stopped, frustrated, next to an unsuspecting girl, and exclaimed, "Well, if you insist! But I will only sign one autograph before the show."

He grabbed a marker from his pocket and proceeded to sign *Max Baby* on a linen napkin she was holding. The gym went wild, and the girl played along by screaming when he handed the napkin to her. When he finished, everyone began waving their napkins at him.

"Please! Please! Control yourselves! This is why I hate to speak at places! The crowds are so uncontrollable!"

The kids roared with laughter. Meg couldn't believe it—Ira Epstein was laughing out loud. He waved a hand at Phillip in approval. Mr. Roberts even acted giddy about it all. The kids that had spent the evening sitting with Phillip were now yelling a cheer, and Phillip was swaying to the rhythm. The man was gifted, no doubt about that.

After an amazing talk encouraging the kids to dream big and believe in themselves, he stepped back from the podium and the crowd clapped wildly. Some kids were in tears. Others were whistling and whooping. Adults were drying their eyes, and brothers and sisters found each other to hug. Phillip came back to the microphone and made one final announcement.

"I will be free to sign your napkins now."

Kids grabbed their napkins and ran to form a long line to get Phillip to sign them. Ira Epstein walked over to Meg.

"That is some guy, is he not?" he started, never making eye contact, just continuing to stare at Phillip.

"That he is," she agreed.

"You be careful with him."

"Excuse me?"

This time he looked at her. "I know you guys had a thing in the past. Just be careful with him. I kind of think he's damaged goods right now. It's a pity, because what he just did was astounding. But if his heart's not in it, then he needs to find his heart again."

She was stunned. Ira had a soft spot? He cared about Phillip? She was even *more* stunned that he was being civil to her.

"Don't look at me so strangely," he said. "I'm not saying we have to like each other. I'm just saying that I believe we have a commodity in common that we need to take care of. We think alike, Meg, just on different terms. We both know what we believe to be right, and we go after it with unleashed vigor. We move the world, you and I."

"You're putting me on your team?" she asked in disbelief.

"No, just in my league." He smiled and walked off.

Meg took Phillip's arm as they walked out to the parking lot later that night after helping to clean up. "You're really good at this kind of stuff, you know. You always were. The youth ministry is going to miss you."

"Maybe, but I'm not going to miss it."

"Yes, you will," she countered. "Maybe not right away, but you'll miss it."

"We'll see."

She opened the door to the Porsche and looked up at him. "Thanks for what you did. Those kids will never forget tonight."

"I hope not."

Chapter Six

Meg finished the offertory at the piano and then sat down next to Phillip on the front seat at Treasure Cove Community Church. He had tears streaming down his cheeks.

"You okay?" she asked quietly.

"Just fine," he responded as he leaned in to her. "I had forgotten what it was like to go to a church and actually enjoy the worship. Last Monday morning, the pastor called me into the office and went over the entire bulletin with me—notes included—and explained everything I did wrong. Hymns too fast, introducing them wrong, choir special had too much of a beat, and a teenager's dress was too short."

"You're lying," she whispered back.

"If I were lying, I wouldn't have a brand new job waiting here for me."

David Dewey, the minister to single adults, and his wife Cindy invited Meg and Phillip over for lunch. They had been very close to Phillip when he was a member at the church during his college years. David was also the minister that married Craig and Janet. They were probably Meg's closest friends in Treasure Cove, but they were very different from her. They had married right out of high school, gone to college together, and now were the parents of four animated children. Meg wondered how she managed to homeschool them and still keep her sanity. The only consolation Meg had at the end of some days was to know she could go home and get away from it all.

"You've changed so much, Phillip," Cindy said as they sat down after lunch.

"Hasn't he?" Meg agreed. "He's so thin."

"I wasn't talking about weight," Cindy explained. "I meant your drive. You seem so defeated about things, yet at the same time you're still very confident about your abilities. It's not like you to be beaten down."

"I know exactly what your problem is," David joined. "You were never told that to be in the ministry you have to have the heart of a lamb but the hide of an elephant?"

Phillip shook his head. "No. But I don't believe that's possible. You either have one or the other. At least all the pastors *I've* worked with have forgotten the lamb's heart part."

"Not this pastor."

"Come on, David. What problems have you ever had? You're this wonderful guy that everybody loves."

After that comment, Cindy let out a loud snicker. "Right! We could tell you stories you wouldn't believe! We've had to learn how to turn a deaf ear to some things and some people."

"You see, Phillip," David explained, "in every church there will be those who love you and those who hate you ... and I don't mean just a little bit. I get my job threatened by people all the time telling me if I don't change something or start something, I'll be out of here so fast I'll see my head spin."

Phillip stared in shock. "What do you do?"

"I tell them if that's what God wants, then I'll be the first to start packing. But if God isn't through with me here, they can bring the forces of hell against me and things won't change one bit."

"We also had a problem when we were first married," Cindy broke in. "David was a part-time youth pastor at this small church near our college. Some of the mothers got upset because we would hold hands on youth trips, or kiss goodnight before we went to our own rooms at camp. They said we were bad influences on their children and were tempting then with sensual thoughts."

Phillip laughed. "I can't believe that! I get in trouble because I'm single! I can't tell you how many times I've had parents tell me they would send their child to camp if I were married because then I would be more trustworthy."

"See, Phillip, it's not just you. We've all been christened into this thing. The church is full of wonderful Godly people, and it's full of miserable, bitter people," David continued. "And I've found that for every one person who thinks I'm the worst minister that ever worked at their church, there are twenty who think I'm wonderful. However, the one often speaks louder than the twenty ..."

"And more often," Cindy added with a laugh.

"You guys are depressing me," Meg said slouching down on the couch.

"Why don't they have a class about this in seminary?" Phillip asked.

"Good point," David agreed. "Why don't you write them a letter and suggest it?"

"They could call it *How to Survive Your Own Crucifixion 101*," Phillip said bitterly.

🏝 🏝 🏝

As Meg's phone chirped, she glanced at the display. The number wasn't one she recognized. "Hello?"

"Meg? It's Phillip."

"Phillip! How did it go?"

"Well, pretty much as I expected. The first thing the pastor told me was that I was a quitter and that this church didn't need quitters. A few of the girls cried. Several of the parents have already formed a committee and are fielding resumes'. Some of the parents are actually upset—I didn't expect that—some of the choir members too. It's just like David said, for everyone who hates you, there's about twenty who don't. Why didn't they say so, Meg, any time during the past year?"

"I don't know, Phillip. I guess we members-at-large tend to take our ministers for granted. I've learned one thing through all this … I'll let everyone at our church know how much they're appreciated from now on."

"You do that. It means more than you know."

"So when do you leave?"

"Would you believe they demanded six weeks?"

"Six weeks! That's preposterous! Is that in their constitution?"

"No, the constitution only calls for a two weeks' notice. The pastor said I did all this sneaking around and that the church deserves at least six weeks so they can find a replacement. Whatever. You're the one who told me to handle this responsibly."

"Responsibly, but not ridiculously! You should have gone with what the constitution said. They don't deserve you another six weeks."

"Some of them do. I'll do it for them. I want to leave the ministry believing I gave it my best shot."

"You're not leaving the ministry, Phillip. You're taking a break."

"No, I'm leaving the ministry. I don't want to do this again."

🏝 🏝 🏝

Summer passed quickly. Meg's parents and youngest brother, Andrew, eighteen, had come down for the entire month of July. For one-week, her oldest brother, Herbie, and his wife and children came to the beach. Meg enjoyed Susan and the kids, but Herbie was dark and brooding. He was pushing forty, and obviously facing some kind of midlife crisis. Susan believed he was seeing a younger woman, but she wasn't worried. It had happened before, probably several times. As long as they stayed married, she didn't really care. Meg felt sick at the thought.

Craig and Janet had been unable to make it this year. Craig felt he needed to plan more activities with the youth since summer was the only time most of them weren't busy. The few times she had talked with either of them, however, they seemed tired and stressed. Janet was naturally bubbly and optimistic, and Craig was always a dreamer with plans. It sounded as though they were running on very little, just barely getting by. She needed to talk with them face to face—she knew they'd never tell her anything over the phone.

Mitch, twenty-six, the brother just younger than Meg, had managed a visit also. He had recently divorced his wife of three years, and was happy to be a free man again. He brought his three year old son with him, but did absolutely nothing with the boy the entire week. He had partied all night at clubs and slept all day at the house. Meg spent a lot of time with Michael, his son—such a lost little boy. His mother had gone back to college to get her degree, and Mitch had him on weekends, but usually dropped him off at the MacAllister's while he worked or played.

The only bright spot of all the siblings was Andrew. He had just graduated from high school and was preparing for college with plans of becoming a lawyer. His once bright orange hair had faded to a light auburn. He was the most vibrant of all the MacAllisters, and the most personable. While in Florida, he spent most of his time at the children's home playing, working, and enjoying life with the kids there. He had several guys from the home spend the night from time to time. Meg was glad about this. She often had girls over, but never boys. This gave them a much needed chance to see normal family life.

As the MacAllisters drove away the first morning in August, Meg felt both alone and relieved. Change, no matter how wonderful, was always somewhat stressful and draining for her. She welcomed the quiet, and looked forward to reading a few books and going a few places alone before the grind of school began again. She loved teaching, but it took so much out of her. She refused to just teach—she wanted to inspire. She wanted to educate her students not only about her subject, but also teach them to love it. That was a big task. Some she never reached—others tolerated it, but there were always those surprises, those few who glimpsed the vision and grasped it wholeheartedly. She wondered who those few would be this year.

Phillip had moved to Treasure Cove on July fifteenth. He had been so busy training with Stan that she had seen very little of him. Her family loved Phillip, and used to refer to him as their *fifth son*. He managed to come over a few times while they were there, but not near as often as she had hoped. She was proud that her mother never made mention of him except to say how wonderful it was to see him again and that she hoped happiness would find him somehow. Her mother had been very upset over their break-up years ago. To Meri MacAllister, Phillip had almost been a savior to her daughter. The two years that followed their meeting had transformed her into a young lady with vision and purpose, such a contrast from the girl they had brought to Florida after graduation that summer.

Before the family left, her mother did pull her aside to make a few simple requests—*Take care of Phillip for the present. Make sure he eats. Make sure he plays some. And make sure he hears that he's doing a good job when he takes over for Stan.*

Meg smiled at her. "For the present, Mom?"

"That's all I'm asking, Meg. Yes, I'd love to see something develop between you two again, but I'm more concerned with seeing him pick himself up right now. See if you can get him to come with you to Houston for Thanksgiving. I think being with a family would be good for him."

Her mother was heading for the car after all the *goodbyes* when she turned around one last time. "I'm really worried about him. You'll watch after him, won't you?"

"Yes, Mom," she nodded. "I promise I will."

🌴 🌴 🌴

Meg sat on the glassed-in back porch and closed the thick book. How refreshing to have finished a novel in only four days. She would need to go to the library in the morning for another one. She glanced down at her watch, but it wasn't on her wrist.

"Now that's relaxation," she said to Spiro, asleep next to her in the recliner, "to be free of time completely."

As she walked to the kitchen to put up her glass, she pulled out her phone to check the time—five seventeen. She would need to have dinner soon. Should she cook? Perhaps she should go out.

"I wish I could have something delivered. Some shrimp with lobster sauce! Yum!"

She decided to head out to Fang's for Chinese food. She then thought of Phillip. She hadn't seen him since her parents had left on Monday. He hadn't even been in church, except for one service, since he had moved back. She had made a promise to her mother and knew her mother would ask when she called. She'd better do something, at least attempt some kind of contact. She picked up the phone and punched in the station's number, still remembering it from years ago when he had worked there.

"WJBA," said the receptionist in a cheery tone.

"Hello, is Phillip Barton there?"

"Yes Ma'am. I'll transfer you."

Meg listened as the radio played on hold. She'd really expected to see more of him than she had. Perhaps he didn't want to spend much time with her. She could understand. Being friends after being so much more was hard. They would have to work through this new arrangement slowly.

"Phillip here," came the voice on the phone.

"Hey, Phillip, it's Meg."

"Meg! How are you?"

Well, that was cheery, she thought. "I'm hungry. I was thinking about Fang's. Want to join me?"

"How 'bout you join me here? I need to stay until ten o'clock. Grab something for me and come on by."

"Will you get in trouble for having company?"

"Trouble? No! I'm in charge, remember?"

"Well, I never know with Ira. He might walk in while we're eating egg rolls or something and throw me out—then he'll fire you for consorting with me."

"Egg rolls! Hey, get me an extra one, will you?"

"What do you want for an entrée?"

"You know what I like. Just surprise me."

"Okay, then. See you in a few minutes."

Meg walked into the foyer of the station with two bags full of food. She nearly fainted at what she saw—the place was a complete dump. Wallpaper was peeling, the carpet was heavily stained and still a sickly pink, paint was faded, and a hole was in the wall behind the doorknob. The old windows actually rattled when she closed the door. The receptionist's desk belonged in the 1960's, and the ceiling tiles were no longer white, but a sickly yellow.

She moved on down the hallway trying to find Phillip's office. Apparently the receptionist had left for the evening, and the only ones there were Phillip, the DJ, and a technician. She didn't want to yell, because she knew from the past they often left the broadcast booth open during the evening hours, and even when closed, it was hardly sound proofed. She snooped around quietly, peeking in doors that were ajar, gently tapping on others that were closed. She had forgotten how big this place was.

"Gotcha!" squealed a voice from behind along with two firm hands grabbing her arms.

She screamed.

"Shhh!" Phillip motioned as he led her to an office at the end of the hallway.

"Don't ever do that again!" she said sternly, yet still in a whisper.

"I couldn't help it," he grinned as he shut the door and took the bags from her. "You looked like some sort of spy creeping around like that."

"I was trying not to be disruptive."

"Well, you failed. Your scream was just heard over three counties away."

"Not my fault. That was your scream, in reality."

"Yeah, you tell that to Ira when he comes running in here after fielding a bunch of calls over it."

He began pulling food and condiments from the bag. "How many people were you planning on feeding tonight?"

"I'm hungry, what can I say?"

"Did you bring Spiro? We'll never eat all this ourselves."

She helped her plate, adding two egg rolls at the end. Sitting back with her Coke, she opened some duck sauce and began to dig in.

"This place is a dump, you know?" she said with a mouthful.

"Oh? I hadn't noticed."

"You're kidding, right?"

He glared at her. "Of course—it's horrible."

"What happened?"

"*Pink carpet* is what happened. After that receptionist fiasco, Ira swore that no funds from him would ever refurbish this place again. If the employees wanted it fixed up, they'd have to raise the money and do it themselves."

"He's a jerk," she mumbled, taking a huge bite of egg roll.

"A successful jerk, nevertheless. Do you even take time to breathe between bites, much less chew?"

"I can breathe and chew at the same time. I thought everyone could."

Phillip, just getting started with his food, sat back in his chair and glanced around his spacious, though extremely shabby office.

"Why don't you fix it up?" she wondered. "Get a contractor in here and get a price for a total face-lift. I'm talking from the carpet to the paint to new windows … everything. Then I'll give you ten names you can call and you'll have the money for it in one afternoon."

"No thanks."

"What?"

"No, but thank-you for the offer."

"No? Why? This place is depressing. If you'd fix it up right away, I'm sure Ira would be impressed."

"Remember me telling you that Ira had me brainstorm about things I would do?"

She nodded as she licked a trail of duck sauce from the side of her hand.

"Well, the last thing I said was, *And I'll make this place look like it wasn't transported from ancient history.* He then looked at me and said, *Not with my money, you won't,* to which I replied, *No problem. I'll get it from somewhere.*"

"So, let me get the money for you."

"Meg, please. I appreciate the thought, but let me do this on my own. One of the people I might call could possibly have the last name of MacAllister. But that's as far as I want you to be involved."

"I know lots of people with money, Phillip. I could make this very easy for …"

"Meg!" He had stopped eating and closed his eyes. "No … thank … you."

"Just let me help you."

"Why do you always have to be in control of everything?" He tossed his fork onto the plate. "Can't you let other people do their own thing sometimes—make their own successes?"

"I'm not trying to *control* anything. I saw an area I could help with and was just trying to fix it."

"See, you even have to control what you call your controlling! Sometimes people don't want or need you to fix anything! This world won't fall apart if you mind your own ..." He stopped.

She backed down as she watched him just sitting there, staring out the decrepit window through broken blinds.

"I'm sorry, Phillip."

"I'm tired of people trying to help me, Meg. Every idea, every plan, everything I've tried to create for the past seven years has been helped by *well-meaning, concerned* people. I am the boss. Ira has given me free reign here. In two months, my training will be over, Stan will be gone, and *I* will fix this place up with funds that *I* have raised."

She felt horrible. She had a tendency to overstep her boundaries often, but people usually gave in because she was right. She kept forgetting how sensitive he had become. It was almost as if his self worth was on the line with every conversation. She kept seeing glimpses of the old, carefree Phillip, but the new, beaten-down man always seemed to win out.

"I'm really sorry, Phillip. I came over here to cheer you up and get you to eat, and it appears that I've been unsuccessful at both." She paused. "Do you want me to leave?"

He shook his head and gave a small laugh. "Any normal person would have already left after my yelling at them. You ooze with such confidence—I wish I could just have a smidgen of it."

"So you *do* want me to leave?"

"No, just don't try to *help* me anymore."

She grinned, and he finally began to smile also.

"Agreed." She pointed toward his plate. "Now eat. I'm only trying to be a good friend."

"With friends like you, who needs enemies?"

They both laughed after that statement, but inside she didn't find it funny. She had the feeling this couldn't be an open, honest friendship. She would have to watch herself and her words carefully, or at least until he regained whatever it was that he had lost.

Chapter Seven

Meg enjoyed spending the rest of her summer mostly alone. She read several more books, wrote an article for the local newspaper, took Spiro for his immunizations, bought a bicycle and began riding at the park. She even went camping one weekend with two girls from the home. As the first day of school grew nearer, she began to feel the excitement that always emerged at the thought of new opportunities and students—the excitement that was absolutely drained by the end of the school year.

She was thrilled when she could finally get her classroom ready for the first semester. She hung her pictures of Shakespeare, Tolkien, Lewis, Thoreau, and Hawthorne, made a nice bulletin board for the parts of speech, created book reading charts, and began to assign books for rosters she had already obtained. She remembered so clearly where every student had sat last year and found herself feeling a little sad over the ones who had graduated and wouldn't be back.

Suddenly, Spiro began to bark.

"Shh! Quiet, boy! If you start that they won't let me bring you here on work days."

He didn't let up. He barked at the door as though Meg was about to be mauled. She went to it to prove that no one was going to burglarize her classroom, only to be startled with a *Boo!* from Phillip as she opened it. Once again, she screamed and Spiro went crazy.

"You've got to stop that!" she yelled.

"Yes, teacher," he teased, reaching down to pat Spiro's head. "Are you the teacher's pet?"

"Cute, but I'm still having a coronary over here."

"Here," Phillip pulled out a single yellow rose and handed it to her. "This is for your desk. I thought you might enjoy something fresh for your fresh year."

"How thoughtful," she said as she took the rose in its petite ceramic vase to her desk. "Thank-you, very much." She paused a moment, then wondered, "I don't suppose you remembered that I love yellow roses. It was just a fluke that you picked up yellow?"

"They were on sale today," he smiled, with that silly twinkle in his eyes again. He looked around the room with approval. "I love what you've done with the place. I was thinking about putting Shakespeare on the walls at the station too. Thought it might add some class to that hole in the wall. What do you think?"

Meg got stiff and said her words in a robot-like manner. "What - ever - you - think - boss - will - be - ac - cep - ta - ble."

"I deserved that," he said, blushing a bit. "I haven't seen you since that night at the office. I was wondering if you hated me."

"No, I don't hate you. I just don't like you anymore."

"Well, I feel so much better now," he mumbled sarcastically. "Look, I need to apologize for that whole thing."

"Forget about it, please. I'm over it. You were right, though. You had a plan already, and I came sticking my two-cents in as though I could change the world. I really need to stop that."

"Let me make it up to you—let me take you to lunch."

"I've got Spiro."

"Okay, we'll pick something up and go to the park."

"What do you think, Spiro?" she said looking down at the little dog whose tail had not stopped wagging since Phillip's appearance.

"You know," he mused, "he likes me better than you now."

"He does not. He's just being polite."

"I love hot dogs," Meg said taking a big bite of her foot-long beneath a large oak tree.

"Do you know how much fat is in a hot dog?" Phillip asked her as he put mustard on his grilled chicken sandwich.

"No," she said quickly, then added "and please don't tell me."

She fed Spiro a hot dog of his own, and added some salt to her onion rings. Phillip worked on his sandwich and salad, and for a while, neither said anything.

"Why haven't you been to church?" she broke the silence.

"Hmmm … good question."

"I'm being nosey again. You don't have to answer that."

"No, you deserve an answer."

He ate another bite, took a drink of his Diet Coke, and then threw the rest of his sandwich to Spiro. She felt horrible—he had eaten so little of it. She was going to starve him to death if she didn't learn to keep her mouth shut.

"I am such a jerk!" she blurted out.

"No, you're not," he said quickly. "You have a right to know that. I mean, for heaven's sake, I quit the ministry and then don't show up at church for a whole month. Any friend would have asked the same thing."

"You gave your sandwich to Spiro! You stop eating every time I'm around you. Obviously, I keep making you lose your appetite."

He laughed. "I didn't like the sandwich. It was horrible! The salad is good, though."

She smiled, a tad relieved, but then wondered if he was being serious or just trying to make her not feel so rotten.

"Church is hard right now. My last Sunday up there, a few of the parents had a little going away party at a choir member's house. It was small. The pastor never said *goodbye*, there was no mention of it being my last Sunday or anything. This small group just wept, and then pled with me to pray for the church when I left. They wanted God to work, but it seemed impossible. *Don't forget us*, they begged, but I have to confess, that's exactly what I intend to do."

He put his salad down now, and leaned back against the tree.

"I can't pray for them, Meg. I hate that church. I hate the pastor. I hate those people and how they treated me. I told the folks at the party to leave the church. I told them there was no hope, and they should go somewhere where God is." He paused. "I had no right to do that. That wasn't my place."

"Don't you think *hate* is a bit of a strong word?"

"I think it's the only word that adequately describes my feelings. Would you like me to sugar coat it ... or be honest?"

She needed to channel this in a more positive direction. "But *this* church isn't *that* church."

"Believe me, I know. Treasure Cove Community Church is wonderful and has always been so good to me. Did you know there were three families that sent me $100 a month each while I was in Seminary? Because of them, I made it through. I couldn't have handled anymore work, and I sure didn't want to go into debt very deeply with a big student loan."

Spiro came crawling into Phillip's lap hoping for another sandwich. He pulled him close and gave him a cube of cheese from his salad. "I just can't seem to let go of the bitterness enough to be able to worship. I don't know that I'm mad at God. Sometimes I think that—then I weep. I know He loves me and is in control. It's just His people that I can't stand."

"Oh, Phillip," she said reaching over to pet Spiro, "I wish I could say the right things to help you over this. When I think of what you've been through, it nearly kills me inside. You deserve so much better."

"I don't know, Meg. Maybe I needed to be knocked down a notch or two. All I've ever wanted was to be in the ministry. Maybe I thought I was better than I really was. Maybe I confused *calling* with *desire*."

"No, you are most definitely *called*. But I think you've been knocked down more like nine notches."

"Nine?"

"Yeah, and there's only ten."

"So, I'm way down there, huh?"

"Way, way down there."

She watched him as he gazed off into the distance somewhere, his blue eyes still gleaming, even in distress. His thin body concerned her. She could have never imagined him so skinny had someone told her.

"Do you exercise at all?" she asked.

"No, I don't really enjoy it anymore. When I was here, I used to work out with other guys. That was lots of fun. Now, exercise is just another form of loneliness."

"Not anymore, it isn't," she declared.

"What?"

"Starting tonight, you and I are going to play tennis at least three nights a week."

"We are?"

"Yep. Now," she paused slightly, "I jog every morning at six a.m. I don't suspect that you could keep up with me right away, but I'll go slowly with you at first."

"I don't want to jog. I hate jogging."

"Fine, but just so you know I jog at six o'clock sharp. Just drive your little Durango over and you're more than welcome to join me. I'll feed you breakfast whenever you choose to come. If, however, you don't jog, don't show up at my door for breakfast."

"What do you usually eat for breakfast?"

"Whatever I feel like eating."

The next morning Meg pulled on her jogging shoes after dressing and put her hair up in a pony-tail. Spiro began to bark.

He made it, she smiled. She was going to get him back into shape if it was the last thing she did.

"Good morning," she said opening the front door.

"You know, this is really too early to run," he grumbled walking in.

"I don't run. I jog. And it's addictive, you know?"

"No, I don't know. I've never jogged or run in my life. I know why you run, though."

"Why's that?"

"To burn off all that food you eat."

He followed as they left through the French doors of the back porch and went out onto the deck.

"We need to stretch a little before we start," she said as she walked down the stairs.

"Whatever you say, coach."

They did some stretching and then began their jog. She went miserably slow, but he seemed to be doing fine. She sped up a little bit, and he stayed right with her. It was only near the end of the jog that he began to get overly winded.

"Do you want to walk the rest of the way back?" she asked.

"No, if we can just slow the pace a little bit, I think I'll be all right."

She slowed, and he was fine.

"Bacon and eggs, huh? It's a good thing you run."

She ignored his comment. In the past, he had always picked on her about something. She realized it would now be her eating habits. She placed his plate down, and then hers, then she prayed.

"You did pretty good last night at tennis considering you haven't played in years," she told him.

"I'll beat you one day. You do know that, don't you?"

"I look forward to it," she said, always ready for a challenge.

He ate several bites heartily. She was impressed. He actually had an appetite this morning.

"You know, I hate to admit this, but I actually feel pretty good after that jog," he confessed.

"I told you it was addicting."

"We'll see. I may be dead tired by tonight, though. I'm a night owl and do my best thinking then. What if you've just ruined my whole bio-process?"

"Poor thing. You'll just have to start doing your thinking in the morning. I bet this brain food ought to help. What do you usually eat for breakfast?"

He smiled and shook his head. "I don't want to tell you."

"Why not?"

"Because, teacher, you will reprimand me."

"I promise not to reprimand you, no matter how horrible it is. Is it like sprouts or something?"

"Coffee ... black."

"And ..."

"More coffee ... still black."

She acted as though she were zipping her lips. She absolutely could not skip breakfast. The more she thought about it, she didn't think she could skip any meal.

"Is it that you don't like cream and sugar ... or is it the calories that you don't like?"

"Hmmm ...," he mulled. "I guess it's probably the calories, because I used to drink it with cream and sugar."

She shoved the sugar bowl toward him, then the creamer. "If you're going to be jogging and playing tennis, the extra calories won't hurt your lovely figure."

"That's okay."

"Phillip, if it makes the stuff taste better, why not put it in?"

He surrendered again and put in a teaspoon of each. She watched carefully as he drank.

"Well?" she asked.

"I don't want to tell you how good it is, because you'll gloat."

"Enough said. And I'm not gloating either ... nor am I controlling."

Chapter Eight

"Welcome to your junior year of literature and composition," Meg said with enthusiasm to her first period class. A hand went up immediately.

"Yes," she said as she looked down to her seating chart. "Mr. Wallace, I believe?"

"Yes ma'am," he replied. "Bryson Wallace. I think I'm in the wrong class. I'm supposed to be in English III."

The class laughed.

"Bryson, you're in the right class."

He was embarrassed.

"But never mind about the mistake. In my mind, *English III* sounds boring and mundane. *Literature* and *Composition*, however, have a ring of excitement to them. Don't you agree?"

He shrugged his shoulders—okay, one she would have to work on. It didn't help that his first experience in class made him seem like a buffoon.

She continued, hoping to inspire future writers and readers on to their destinies. She explained the topics they would cover and the wonderful assignments and projects they would have the *privilege* of completing. Very few were as thrilled as her, most were nervous at the amount of work, and others were completely bored. *Typical.*

Class after class came through. Fourth period brought Alissa and several other seniors she loved, then came last period—Carmen. She hadn't seen her since she had left at the beginning of summer. The fact that she was back indicated she wouldn't be living with her mother this year. Carmen's hair had grown even longer. Her bangs, now down beneath her nose, hung over her eyes. Meg hated that. She knew the girl was desperately trying to hide.

After class, she made sure she spoke with her before she left.

"I'm glad you're in my class this year. I know you like to read. I bet you'll be a good writer too."

"Don't count on it," she said gloomily, never looking up or even lifting her head.

"Bad summer?" Meg found herself asking then wished she would have kept her mouth shut.

"Wretched."

"Now there's a good word. See, I told you you'd be a good writer. The average kid would have said *bad, rotten,* or *miserable.* You come up with *wretched.*"

"Yeah, well how about I write you a little essay about my summer vacation," the girl mumbled unenthusiastically. "I'm sure you'd love it."

"You do that—extra credit right off the bat."

She actually looked up, peering through her hair. There was way too much hurt in her eyes for someone so young. "I might."

She left, but Meg actually felt hopeful. The fact that she might write the story meant that she might open up to her. This would be a first, not only for Meg, but toward anybody. Whenever Carmen had been discussed, either at school, at the home, at church, or with other girls, the response was always the same—she never talked to anyone. Having her in class this year, and teaching something Carmen actually enjoyed, reading, might build a bridge for someone to be a part of her life. Meg said a quick prayer, and then began to prepare her room for the next day.

When sixth period rolled around the following day, Meg waited anxiously for Carmen to enter class. Just as the bell rang, the girl walked through the door. She was wearing the same type clothes she as yesterday— black jeans with a black t-shirt. Meg couldn't tell if she was looking at her or not through the bangs. She called roll, then asked the class to open their grammar books and begin working. She called Carmen up to her desk. She hesitated, painfully aware of all the eyes on her. Meg should have done it differently.

She leaned over to her and whispered so that no one could hear. "Did you do your extra credit?"

Carmen nodded.

"May I have it? I would really like to read how you elaborated on *wretched.*"

She went back to her seat, ripped out several pages from a spiral notebook, and gave them to Meg. A few in the class were staring still.

"It's never too early to start earning extra-credit," Meg offered. "Some of you may need to think about that seeing as you don't care for doing your class work at the moment."

There were several giggles, but Meg's eyes were on Carmen. She went back to her desk, sat down, and began her work. It was all she could do to not to read the *report* immediately. She made herself place the paper in her satchel, and was determined to ignore it until she was home.

Meg quickly changed, and then sat down in the large, blue recliner on the back porch. She opened the French doors for the breeze from the ocean could blow through and so Spiro could run in and out if he wished. He wished not. He jumped up onto her lap and curled into a ball. She opened her satchel and took out the papers Carmen had given her.

What I Did For My Summer Vacation by Carmen Delancey. Meg smiled. The title was typically cynical. She realized the girl must have a sense of humor in there somewhere.

I went back to Carole's, my mom's. I can't call her Mom anymore because she doesn't like it. She wants us to be pals instead. I had the honor of meeting Chad, her boyfriend. I could have called him Dad if I wanted. I didn't. Carole really wanted things to be great this summer. I would have settled for good.

She cooked this big meal the first night I was home. It was really good, too. They grilled steaks, with baked potatoes, and had a huge, delicious salad. Carole had even bought the big cheesy croutons that I like so much. In years past, those croutons had actually been my supper. That was the last meal she cooked. Good thing she bought those croutons, huh?

The first weekend we were together, she had promised a movie and dinner out at this big, fancy restaurant. Carole told me how great it was going to be. I could even order lobster if I wanted because she had a great job now and Chad did too. Friday night came, and Carole nor Chad were home. Saturday came, and Carole was home for a couple of hours, then had to go somewhere important. Chad came home around supper time. He wanted to take me out for dinner. I told him Carole was doing that. He told me she wouldn't be back until Monday. We went to dinner, and I had lobster for the first time. We came home and Chad had me for the first time. Chad was right. Carole didn't get home until Monday.

We never went to any movies. We never went out to dinner, at least Carole and I didn't alone. Chad took me out all the time. One morning, sometime shortly after July 4th, Carole decided we should have a family picnic since she had been gone for the holiday. We went to a lake with a bucket of chicken. Carole lit up a joint and got high. She downed a fifth of liquor and fell asleep. Chad and I took a walk in the woods and went skinny dipping near a waterfall. We came back and found Carole still asleep.

At the beginning of August, Carole's company had a luau at her boss's big house. We all went. One big happy family. As soon as we got there, Carole shot up something into her arm while we were in the car. She offered me and Chad some. We didn't want any. We got inside, and everyone was having a wild time. I tried to drink a beer, but got really sick and threw up by the pool. Carole yelled at me in embarrassment, calling me some pretty nasty things in front of everybody. Her boss kept saying it was okay. Chad kept saying it was okay. But she kept right on yelling at me. Chad took me home. Carole came home about three days later.

I had two weeks left at Carole's. She didn't say much after the luau. Chad suggested we go out to dinner and see a play at the auditorium. Carole agreed. I ate lobster again. We never made the play because Carole got a call and had to be taken home so she could go to work. She would be back in two days. Unfortunately, she came back a day early and found me and Chad asleep together in her bed. She packed her clothes and left. Chad brought me back to the home in two weeks. What a wretched summer.

Meg sat stunned. She didn't know whether to feel appalled or honored. This was a sixteen-year-old girl, not a twenty-five year old out on her own. The information she had just received could put both Carole and Chad in jail, yet it had been shared, probably for the first and last times, to her in confidence. She had no idea what to do with it. As bitterly depressing as it seemed, it was also a step in a direction that might build a bridge. She took her red pen, made a few grammatical marks on the paper, and changed a couple of sentences, showing how they could have been better written. At the top she simply wrote, *Very well expressed. I look forward to reading more class work from you. Twenty extra-credit points.*

Spiro jumped up from his sleep as the phone chirped. Meg reached over to the small table next to her chair and pressed the accept button.

"Hello?"

"Hello yourself," came the reply.

"Mr. Barton, what are you up to … calling me at this hour?"

"It's four fifteen. What's wrong with four fifteen?"

"You've never called at four fifteen so there must be something up your sleeve."

"I want fried chicken tonight."

"Excuse me?"

"I want fried chicken, but I don't want to order it out. I want real, homemade fried chicken, and you're the only person I have enough guts to ask to cook it."

She was floored. He actually wanted to eat something fried, and he was inviting himself over. These were two new steps in his life. She had to comply.

"I'll run to the store right now," she told him.

"I promise I'll make it worth your while."

"I doubt that, but I'll do it anyway."

"Oh no, it'll be worth it. I have some great news."

"What?" He had her curiosity going now.

"No, no, no. Chicken first—news later."

"You know, Phillip, I get enough stress working with immature teenagers all day. I don't need it from you too when I get off work."

"But isn't surprise the spice of life?"

"Right."

🌴 🌴 🌴

"Come on in!" Meg yelled as the doorbell rang.

Phillip made his way to the kitchen after greeting Spiro and lingered over the stove for a moment. "Ahh … now that is the heavenly smell I have craved all day long."

"Let's see, you've had breakfast here, now dinner. Perhaps you should move in?"

"Oh no!" he said backing up. "You had your chance to marry me years ago. Don't think bacon, eggs, biscuits, or fried chicken will win me back. Besides, I have news to tell. It'll be worth your slaving over the stove."

That's right—his news. He seemed excited to tell her, but she decided to turn the tables and put him off for a change. "It can wait until after supper," she said glibly.

"No, I want to tell you now," he insisted.

"Well, I need you to take Spiro out for a little walk. I haven't had the chance because I had to rush out for groceries and start cooking right away."

"It won't take long."

Boy, was he ever eager. She held back her smile. "Later, Phillip," she said pointing toward the outside.

"Okay, okay. But I'm letting you get by with this only because you're frying chicken."

He devoured his meal. Meg hadn't seen him eat like this since their meeting in June. He ate three pieces of chicken, two helpings of mashed potatoes and gravy, a big pile of green beans, a salad with the dressing doused over it, not on the side, and even dessert. He said very little as he ate. Occasionally he would give Spiro a bite of chicken, despite her protests. Her dog was getting too fat.

When they finished, he cleared the table as she loaded the dishwasher, then he sat with Spiro in the living room. The dog curled up next to him and when Met glanced over, his eyes were closed. He'd been getting up early with her every morning to jog, and then he worked late nights at the station. He was probably worn out, but that was good. Keeping him busy would keep his mind from dwelling on the past. The sooner he healed, the sooner he could get on with life.

"You're not going to drift off now, are you?" she asked as she sat across from him in an overstuffed chair.

He came to, smiled, and jumped right in with his news. "I approached

Ira today with my contractor's bid on all the improvements the station needed. It was really expensive. At first he sort of looked at me funny, and then he said, *Didn't I make it clear that I would not fund such a project?* I looked him squarely in the eye and said, *Very clear.* Then I handed him the sheet with all the donations promised, plus photocopies of the checks I had already received."

He was beaming just like the old Phillip. His cheeks were rosy, his posture high, and it actually seemed as though he had put on a little weight.

"And what happened next?" she asked bursting with excitement for him.

"He shook my hand, then he turned around, three hundred and sixty degrees, and he said, *Now, you shake my hand.* So I did. He said he needed to be congratulated also for making an excellent choice in station manager. He believes he has the best in the country."

He smiled as he let it all sink back in. Suddenly Meg felt she wanted to do more than just shake his hand. Everything within her wanted to climb on the couch next to him, put her arms around him … she had to make herself stop. She literally shook the thought out of her head.

"Are you okay?" he asked.

"It's nothing—I'll get over it."

"Can I get you something?"

"Nope. I'll be fine. Tell me when you start."

"Monday—the sooner, the better."

"Well, that was fast. When it's all finished, I want to see it. Until then, I have no desire to step into that place again."

"I'll be sure to let you know," he smiled.

"Just curious, do any donors on your list happen to share my last name?"

"Do I look stupid? Your dad is the richest man I know personally."

She got up from the chair and held out her hand. "Let's walk the beach."

He took her hand and made her pull him up. "You're a slave driver, you know? First, you make me run with you in the mornings. Now, I have to walk with you at night."

"Don't forget the tennis."

"Please, let me forget the tennis. My ego can't take much more of the tennis."

"After today, your ego should be fine for awhile."

Phillip began attending church again faithfully. He went to Sunday school, morning worship, Sunday evening small groups, and even joined the choir for Wednesday night practice after services. He was beginning to be his old self again. They ran together most mornings and continued playing tennis a couple of evenings each week. Occasionally they would play doubles with David and Cindy Dewey, or a couple of teenagers from the home. He was beginning to fill out also. The muscles that had been non-existent when she first saw him in June were now slowly popping out again. His eating had returned full force, and she was thrilled to get him back to the Crab Shack so he could have a plate piled full of crab legs also.

"These are so good," he said with a smack of his lips as he stuffed another morsel of crab meat into his mouth.

"You're embarrassing me," she teased as she slid her own chunk through a saucer of melted butter.

"Yeah, right. You don't appear to be slacking up any."

"I have to confess, it's a lot more fun being with you here now than it was in June."

"I was so nervous that night—you have no idea how nervous. It's a wonder I ate anything at all."

"Why were you nervous?"

"Why?" he repeated as though it were the most preposterous question ever asked.

"Is that a hard question?"

"Gee, the girl, or should I say, woman of my dreams, suddenly re-appeared back into my life. I definitely didn't want to blow it."

She was startled. She thought this whole thing was about friendship now. When did the dreams suddenly appear?

"Don't look weird at me. I'm not saying I was still in love with you. It's just that's who you had always been to me. I didn't want to come off as the loser I really was. I wanted to try and present myself with some dignity."

"So, you're saying you don't see me as the girl of your dreams anymore?"

He laughed, all the while trying to break a small crab leg apart. "You're the girl of every man's dreams," he said, pulling the string of meat out. "You're gorgeous, smart, talented, have a real cute little dog, and drive a hot car. What more could any man want?"

"Obviously something more because I don't seem to have a man, and I'm twenty-nine years old."

"Well, you are a bit intimidating. You're better at everything than anybody, and your dad's a millionaire. I mean, what can anybody do to impress you?"

"I don't need to be impressed. It would be nice to be loved, though."

"Good luck."

"Good luck? So, you would never date me again? I can cook for you, but that's all, huh?"

"I can't date you again. We're friends now, remember?"

"And there's no chance of that ever changing?"

He now grew still and somber and stopped eating. Meg wanted to panic again.

"Meg, I don't know if you're serious or not, but I probably need to lay all this out on the table anyway."

Her heart began to pound. Was there someone else? She must have wrongly assumed that things were possibly beginning to move in a new direction with them.

"I don't think I could ever have a relationship like we had again. Every day of my life I've felt like I was being rejected again. You have no idea what it's like to wake up as a four year old and wonder why there's no mommy or daddy to hold you. I'll never forget when I was around eleven boasting one night in an orphanage that when I turned eighteen, I was gonna find my parents, hunt them down, and beat the blank out of them for what they did to me. The RD, a really heartless guy, laughed out loud. He said, *Kid, have you ever wondered why you get shuffled around to a different place every few months? Whoever your parents were, they made the trail so hard you'll never find them. Somebody doesn't want to be found. Maybe they knew you were mean from the beginning.*"

"Phillip, no!" she exclaimed. "He couldn't have meant that!"

"He did, and I checked. Would you believe there isn't a valid birth certificate available for me anywhere? I don't even know where I was born."

"That's impossible! There have to be records somewhere."

"Yeah, maybe, but I'll never get a hold of them. Don't you see, now? I thought at one time that maybe I could get married. Have a wife … you, of course … and a bunch of kids, and live happily ever after. But what if you left me? What if something happened to a child? What if you died? I couldn't live with that loss on top of everything I've gone through. I just couldn't. And as for parents, I don't ever want to know who they are. If they went to this much trouble to make sure I was put away for good, they're more heartless than the churches I've been in these past years. I guess I hate them more than I hate anybody. I was an innocent baby, not even an obnoxious child yet. How could they?"

She shook her head. There had to be people who could dig through this red tape. There had to be someone who could find his parents. She almost insisted, but remembered how offended he got when she offered help.

"Meg, if I could have ever married anyone, it would have only been you. But, because I care so much, that's the reason I can't. I just can't let myself be rejected again."

She was crushed, not just for herself, but because he was closing himself off to possibly the best kind of love he could know on earth. No wonder he was so self-protected. No wonder he closed himself off when he became too vulnerable. Would he have married her nine years ago had she not rejected him then?

"Meg! Phillip!" boomed a robust voice from across the deck outside the Crab Shack.

"John Mason!" Phillip yelled back, recognizing the man first.

"The one and only," he said coming over and hugging them hard.

"The beach bum entrepreneur himself," Meg greeted him warmly.

"How are the *Mason Mon* beach shops doing? I haven't seen you since I moved back," Phillip wondered.

"I'm in the Bahamas now—got five shops down there."

"So, you've gone totally tropical now?" Meg smiled.

"Totally and to the max, man ... or should I say *mon*!"

John Mason was the oldest beach bum alive. At sixty-four, he had huge success by having his beach shops become the famous icon up and down the Florida coasts. When someone left Florida after a vacation, they had to bring back a *Mason Mon* t-shirt. His bushy gray hair and beard were still hideously shaggy, and his dark skin had begun to wrinkle years ago. There was never a freer spirit created, and sometimes Meg hoped never would be. He was a church member, however, and very vocal about his beliefs, but if she could only turn his volume down by half, she could have fared being around him much easier.

"Hey, Meg," he said loudly, turning to her, "there's this dude I hired down in the Bahamas a few months ago from Houston at my newest shop. I asked if he knew the rich MacAllisters, and he says he knew you."

"Really?" She tried to imagine who she knew that lived in the Bahamas. "What was his name?"

"Bummer," he said scratching his beard. "I can't believe it. I have no idea! I hired about thirty-five personnel, and his name just slips by me."

"Ok, Dad. Thanks a million. This means a lot." Meg circled the number on her notepad several times as she balanced the phone between her shoulder and her ear.

"Why do you want a private investigator? Are you in some kind of trouble?" her father asked.

"Nothing like that. I just need to find out some information, and I knew you could give me the name of really good one."

"He's good, Hon. The best."

"I hope so. Take care of yourself, and tell Mother *hello*."

"She says it back ... and wants to know how Phillip is."

"He's doing just fine. Bye, Dad."

She immediately dialed the number and held her breath as she counted the rings.

"Hello?"

"Yes, I need to speak with Kevin Morris."

"Seeing that you've got my private number, that'd better be me."

"Listen, I don't want to give you my last name or any other information unless necessary. Money is no option, and you'll be paid in cash for all your services."

"Okay, I understand. What do you need?"

"I have a contact in Houston who you can go through. His name is Micah Speers. His number is 555-6146. He'll pay you in advance if you need it."

"No problem, lady. Just tell me what you need."

"I need you to find the birth parents of a Phillip Barton."

"Birthplace?"

"No idea."

"Okay. Middle name?"

"Doesn't have one."

"Is this an assumed name or an alias?"

"He's thirty-two, is an orphan, and has never been able to get close to tracking them down with regular search agencies."

"Hmmm, sounds as though someone doesn't want him to be found. This could get costly."

"Money is no option."

"But, I may need cash to just open some doors with this case."

"Micah Speers will take care of what you need."

"Okay. Do I get your first name?"

"Margaret."

Chapter Nine

"Achoo! Achoo!" Meg couldn't stop the sneezing.

"I take it you don't like hayrides," Phillip said as he balanced himself on the huge trailer.

"Actually, I love them," she countered as she pulled another piece of straw from her hair. "They're probably the only things I like about Halloween. It's my sinuses that are complaining."

The annual fall hayride for the church youth group was in full swing. The tractor meandered through the pasture, swaying constantly toward its destination. Meg could finally see the bonfire in the distance.

"Ahh," she sighed, "hot dogs are on the way," and then she sneezed again.

"You really shouldn't ride in the hay." he scolded her. "I understand allergies can get quite irritated if you don't take care of them properly."

"I'll take some antihistamine when I get home." She motioned toward the front of he trailor. "Look at Alissa and Brandon. They're having too good of a time, I'm afraid. We need to make sure one of us sits near them on the ride back to the church."

"And spoil all their fun? What kind of chaperone are you?"

"The kind that gets asked back every year."

She did love hayrides. They reminded her of growing up in Texas. Although she hadn't lived on a ranch, many of her friends had. Everyone looked for excuses for hayrides, and fall was the time of year to have them. Hiding in hay, throwing hay, wrestling in hay were favorite activities of younger and older children alike. The biggest difference between those hayrides and this one was that the breeze blowing through the trailer was warm here, not crisp and cool as it was in Texas by this time of the year.

"A million dollars for your thoughts," Phillip said as he dropped down beside her. The swaggering ride had finally gotten to him.

"A million dollars? That's pretty steep."

"I offered a penny one time, but you said it was too cheap and never told me anything. So, I'm offering a million. Do I get lucky?"

"Sure, but remember money can't buy you everything. I'll let you in on this one though. I was thinking about how much I miss the change of seasons living here. It's like we have this long, hot summer, then we get a few months where things cool down, but never really get cold. Then, before you know it, it's hot again, and you wonder what happened to winter."

"I thought you liked it here."

"I do. I like the people, the place, the church, the kids at the home, my school—I just don't like the weather."

"Now, that's a revelation. I always picked you to be the typical island babe. Nice tan, hair bleached out just a little, always walking around in sandals and tank tops."

"I like it sometime. It's great during the summer when there's no school, but take right now, for instance. We should all be wearing jackets. That fire in the distance should be a welcomed relief from the chilliness we'd be feeling. We should be putting an extra blanket on the bed at night. Parents ought to be wondering if the kids will need a heavy jacket or a light windbreaker. At home they're stacking firewood near the back door and have already had to use the fireplace once or twice. And then you can always wish for snow, doesn't mean you'll get any, but at least you can wish."

"Hmm," he sighed. "I don't ever remember seeing snow. It seems like one of the orphanages I was at we had snow. I was really young though, like a preschooler. I remember bigger kids coming in all wet and cold, others begging to go out and play, but I was too small to see out the windows. It may have just been a dream."

"Do you think you were up north?"

"I can't remember. Everything runs together in my mind. I can only pick out bits and pieces of my past, at least until I came to Treasure Cove. From thirteen on, I'm clear. Before that, it's all foggy. The one thing I do remember is moving around a lot."

Meg thought of her secret mission with Kevin Morris. She actually felt guilty about going behind Phillip's back to locate his parents, but she knew he would never do it on his own again. She had weekly updates from her *contact*, Micah Speers, but they were always the same—*nothing has turned up yet, but there are a few new leads to follow, and he needs more money.* She smiled at herself for the espionage game she was playing right now. Micah wasn't even a close friend, just someone who worked for her father that managed to hunt her down at every company Christmas party. He was a computer programmer and did whatever IT stuff her father desired—at the company or at home. From her yearly conversations with him she had discovered he was huge into mysteries and science fiction. She figured he would be the perfect guy to help her pull this off. Mr. Morris would have to dig deep to pin Meg to Micah. And no matter how hard the detective pressed, Micah would play the game to the hilt.

"I would love for you to explain the expression on your face right now," Phillip said, leaning over to her in the trailer, at which point the whole procession came to a lurching halt.

Kids screamed as several fell back in the hay after having stood in anticipation of roasting hot dogs. Others scrambled to get off their trailer first before the other two trailers stopped. Phillip quickly backed against one of the sides as a near stampede ensued.

"All this over hot dogs?" he muttered.

"Hey, some of us really like hot dogs," she defended.

Meg ate three hot dogs and stopped keeping count of the marshmallows. After the eating was done, she stood up and began her traditional scary story. This was really the highlight of each year's party. Loving to read, she would research several ideas from already written stories, and then casually discuss events in the lives of the kids over the past couple of months. When it came time for her version, she would weave the biggest concoction of mixed up plots she could imagine, and have the group on the edge of their seats by the end. Every year, there were always a couple of girls who preferred riding back with the other adults in vehicles rather than try to venture through the dark unknown pulled by a tractor.

"You'd be a horrible mother," Phillip said as they settled back onto the trailer for the ride back. "I can see it now, *Kids, would you like for Mommy to tell you a bedtime story?* And the little tikes are screaming, *No, Mommy! Not tonight, please!*"

"Yeah, but it'd be great for teenagers who were my kids. You find out they've done something they don't want you to know, and whammo, you weave a story that will have them confessing before you can even finish."

She pondered the idea of motherhood. Now *that* was a thought that never crossed her mind. Of course, it would be nice to be married before entering into the role of mom, but that was looking bleaker each year. She hated having these thoughts. She had been content with her life until Phillip came back. It was as if she now regretted ever letting him go. She wondered how different things would have been had she not broken off the relationship. They would have married when he graduated from seminary and she from college. She could have been a support for him during the tough churches, and could have been a wonderful help. She was an excellent pianist, and worked well with teenagers. They would have probably had children by now, a home of their own ...

"What on earth are you thinking about tonight?" he asked her again.

"You know what?" she said, immediately changing the subject. "I really need to go over by Alissa and stop that before it gets started. I'll talk to you later."

She wobbled around the trailer until she got to Alissa and Brandon.

"Mind if I join you?" she asked.

"Not at all, Miss Mac," Alissa said. Of course, to make room for Meg meant Alissa had to scoot over closer to Brandon.

"I was wondering," Meg began, "do you ever get to talk to Carmen?"

"That, Miss Mac, is like a total impossibility."

"She doesn't talk to anyone?"

"Not a single soul. And you know me—I can carry on a conversation with a rock. I've tried to get her to say anything, but she never says more than one or two words."

"Is she moving into the new dorm now that she's a junior?"

"I don't know. The RD was showing her around this afternoon, but she was saying things like, *This would be where you would wash your clothes. This is the kitchen and you would be responsible for helping prepare a few meals a week. This would be your private room … if you come.* It was all iffy sounding."

Meg had an idea. "If I had her over to spend the night, would you come too?"

"Miss Mac, don't put that on me. I love staying at your place, but just me and you and Carmen. You could tell that story at the campfire next year!"

"Alissa, it wouldn't be that bad."

"Yes, it would. I couldn't do it. It would be like waiting to go to the dentist. Yuck!"

"Ok, you can bring someone else. We'll have another girl too."

"Miss Mac, now you're asking me to torture not only myself, but bring in a friend for the fun and games also?"

"Alissa, please? This girl needs help. Maybe you and I together can be her help."

"You can bring a horse to water, but you can't make him suck it up."

Meg rolled her eyes at the misquotation. "So, be Carmen's water."

"Oh, there's a word picture I don't want to visualize."

"Do it for me … please?"

Alissa had obviously been distracted from Brandon as she imagined an evening with Carmen. Meg could tell she was weighing the options.

"Okay," she finally agreed grudgingly.

"Yes! Thank you!" Meg hugged her tightly.

"You will owe me big after this, though."

"You name it! Whatever you want, I'll do it. I promise."

🏝 🏝 🏝

Meg was in the thick of grading papers when the phone rang. Spiro jumped up immediately and began to bark at it.

"Spiro," she moaned in exasperation, "the tiny phone won't hurt us!"

She pressed the button and answered with "Hello."

"Meg, this is Micah," came the voice in a half whisper. He was sounding sneaky and suspicious as usual. She played along, talking softly even though the only one in earshot was Spiro.

"How are things?"

"I have news—real news."

Her heart began to pound. She had hired Mr. Kevin Morris over six weeks ago—she had stopped counting at six—and all he could come up with were dead ends each week. Now there was real news?

"He says he's found a big link, but he needs to talk with you directly."

"Really?" She played along with him a little longer. "Do you think he's on the up and up, Micah? Can we trust him?"

"He has a good rep, Meg. If we can't trust him, I don't know who else there is."

"I can't thank you enough. You know that, don't you?"

"Glad to have been a help. Let me know what our next move is."

"Will do," she assented.

"Okay, over and out."

"Roger that," and she pressed the end button.

So, something had come up. If Kevin Morris hadn't come so highly recommended by her father, she would have fired him some time back. She wondered if he'd actually found Phillip's parents. Imagine telling Phillip the news. Would he thank her? Would he hate her? Would this help resolve some issues, or would this bring even more questions worse than before? She decided to finish her grading, make supper, and then place her call to Kevin Morris, P.I.

"The Margaret?" Kevin Norris replied.

"Yes," she told him. "I understand you have something for me … finally." She felt she should add a hint of disapproval so he wouldn't think her the amateur she actually was.

"You have no idea the wild goose chase you've sent me on, ma'am. I've done many investigations in my life, but never one that took me all over the place like this. Would you believe I ended up in Australia at one point?"

"Australia?" She was more intrigued than anything else, but felt she should sound a bit alarmed at the idea of him traipsing around the world with her cash. "Are you squandering my money, Mr. Morris?"

"I would hope you should know better than that."

"I'm hoping. Now, what do you have?"

"Of course, you should expect that I know everything there is to know about Phillip Barton by now. Station Manager at WJBA in Treasure Cove,

Florida. I know his ministerial disappointments, his education, and his five years at the Treasure Cove Children's Home. Prior to that, his life was extremely unusual. He never stayed in one place more than eighteen months, which is highly irregular, because you would think a kid would need some kind of security. I've traced his travels back to a place where he apparently lived the first nine months of his life. It's not actually an orphanage. It was a lady who sort of took care of abandoned babies before they were adopted—only Phillip was never adopted."

"Where is this lady?"

"Minnesota."

"Minnesota! How did he end up in Florida?"

"By a fluke probably. I talked with the coordinator of the orphanage he was placed in after he left this lady's care. They have extremely incomplete records—the man was rather embarrassed. He said something had been tampered with, and that he would get to the bottom of it. He has the name of a nurse who apparently had to give Phillip some kind of medical care regularly. But as far as I can tell, Mr. Barton is the picture of health. Do you know of any health problems he has today?"

"None," she replied, wondering what could have been wrong with him as a toddler.

"Apparently, someone didn't want Phillip Barton to ever find his birth parents. He went from Minnesota to Washington State. From there to Arizona, from Arizona to Australia, from Australia to Hawaii, and then to Massachusetts, Georgia, Arkansas, and then somehow to Florida. He was deliberately being shuffled around to avoid finding or being found. It seems that when he ended up in Florida, the director at the home, a George Estes, refused to pass him around again. He tried to find several foster homes, but Mr. Barton was a bit of a disturbed lad by that time. Finally, they just let him stay at the home."

"Thank goodness," she said more to herself. "It appears it was the only thing that was ever stable in his life."

"And I imagine that would be important to you seeing as you had a serious relationship with him during your first two years of college."

Meg felt the heat rise in her cheeks. "What? What do you know about my past? What do you know about me period?"

"Miss … *Margaret*, if that's what you continue to insist I call you, did you think I would just take all this anonymity lying down? I'm an investigator. When someone tells me money is no object, I want to know who said it and why."

"So, how long have you known about me? *What* do you know about me?"

"It didn't take long to put it all together. I guess I had your identity pegged for sure in under an hour."

"Are you kidding? How?"

"Your area code for starters. I immediately found out it was Florida. You obviously had some kind of connection to Houston with the Speers guy. It took about five minutes to discover he works for your father. You had money, so obviously you had some connection with MacAllister Oil. Within a few minutes I was Googling your beach house in Treasure Cove, summer property of Herbert MacAllister, present address of his only daughter, Margaret, aka. Meg." He paused. "Do I need to go on?"

She was embarrassed big time. "I guess it's comforting to know that you're good at what you do, Mr. Morris."

"Indeed—that's why I do it. Now that we've cleared the air of all the secrecy, can we get rid of Micah Speers and just let me report to you directly. I've had your phone number in my contacts since that first call and your name with it since that first hour."

She was blushing again and very thankful the competent Mr. Morris couldn't see her. "Sure. I guess now that things are moving along there will be more reporting than previously."

"I sure hope so. This has been one wild case."

"What happens now?"

"I need a ticket and a hotel room. I'm going to Minnesota to talk with a nurse and a babysitter."

"Get what you need," she told him without a second thought. "How soon will you leave?"

"As soon as possible." He paused a moment. "I've never in my life seen anything like this. I've investigated many cases, but this one has gotten me totally perplexed and intrigued. I haven't taken another case for a month now ... don't have the time, but also don't have the interest. Chasing cheating husbands is boring next to this stuff."

"You'll let me know as soon as you find out anything?"

"Yes, ma'am, *Margaret.*"

She smiled at her silliness. "*Meg* will be fine. I believe I'm about as intrigued as you are. If I didn't have a life to carry out, I might join you for that trip to Minnesota."

"If I thought I could actually meet you in person, I might beg you to come. I would love to see the face of the name I'm working for."

She felt a slight twinge. Was he flirting with her? "I'm surprised you don't have pictures of me pinned to your detective cork board, Mr. Morris."

"Who says I don't, *Miss MacAllister*? The truth is I'd like to know if your eyes are really that deep of an emerald green."

Again she flushed. "Emerald green?" She swallowed. Was she really going to ask this? "And what color might your eyes be, Inspector Morris?"

"Plain brown."

Meg stayed awake in bed a long time thinking about her conversation with Kevin Morris. She knew absolutely nothing about him other than he was very good at his job and he had brown eyes, yet she was drawn to him. Perhaps it was his confidence, and maybe even his audacity. She had so skirted around Phillip and his beaten down nature the past few months that to talk with a man so sure of himself was … refreshing. Her face warmed again.

The truth is I'd like to know if your eyes are really that deep of an emerald green.

And I, Mr. Morris, would like to know if your eyes are just plain brown.

Chapter Ten

Meg tried to put last night's phone conversation with Kevin Morris out of her mind. Alissa, Lana, and Carmen were now on her back deck and would be spending the weekend with her. Alissa and Lana were doting on Spiro while Carmen stared out into the Gulf. Meg brought out a tray of Cokes and invited them to sit. To everyone's surprise, Spiro chose Carmen's lap as the spot to plant himself. Meg realized that he was ready to be noticed by the one who had ignored him from the moment she had walked in. She was startled at first, but then placed her drink down and began to pet him gently. Meg, not wanting the new visitor to feel self-conscious, but free, immediately tried to start some conversation.

"So, what are your favorite classes this year?"

"Definitely *not* lunch!" Lana began. "This year's food is absolutely horrible. They should let us make our own lunches or something."

"Our own lunches aren't free," Alissa reminded her.

"Still, you would think with all those grandmothers working back there, they could come up with something decent."

"I like the food," Meg put in. "See, food that someone else has cooked always tastes good when you're used to cooking for yourself all the time."

"I wish I could cook for myself," Alissa said. "No problem."

"Okay, we're off the subject," Meg said, stealing a glance at Carmen, who was now cuddling Spiro as he nuzzled closer to her. *Good boy.* She moved the conversation back on track. "I don't want to know your worse subject. I want to know your best.

"Oh, gee," Alissa started in with dreamy pretense, "mine would have to be English IV with Miss MacAllister. She's the best."

"Stop that," Meg scolded. "Okay, you can't include my classes. It has to be something else."

"Well, that's not fair," Alissa pouted. "I really do like your class best."

"Yeah, but I bet it's not for the subject matter," Meg replied. "It's because I let you get away with anything."

"Whatever the reason, I like it best, and that's my final answer. You can't make me change it."

"Okay, you can keep it since I didn't qualify my question right off the bat. Lana?"

"So I can't pick your class?" Lana asked.

"No. It's a given that I'm the best teacher and have the best subject, okay?"

"Well, at least you're modest about it," Alissa mumbled.

"Okay, my favorite subject," Lana mulled the thought around. "I guess it would be Art. I like it a lot."

"I've got it!" Alissa jumped up. "I write the stories, and you draw the pictures! Then we can make a lot of money, buy a beach house here next to Miss Mac, get a little dog, and all live happily ever after!"

"Would I have to live with you?" Lana asked.

"Not necessarily. Miss Mac will probably still be single and you can move in with her and Spiro."

"Oh, please," Meg moaned. "I won't always be single."

They all stared at her, even Carmen.

"What? Do you girls think all I ever do is tote you around from place to place?"

"Yes," Alissa and Lana said in unison.

"Forget it," Meg went on. "What about you, Carmen? What's your favorite subject?"

The quiet girl looked out toward the beach, her hair actually blowing out of her eyes for a change. She thought hard, or at least it appeared so. Then she turned, looked at them all, and said, "Lunch."

Meg sort of nodded while Alissa and Lana stared at her for a moment. Then, ever so slightly, one corner of Carmen's mouth turned up. It was the first almost smile they had ever seen her make. Suddenly, Alissa burst out laughing, followed by Lana. Meg didn't know whether she should panic or not. Had it indeed been a joke? Then Carmen gave a full smile. Meg breathed deeply. Carmen had actually related to the three of them for the first time. Meg tried to laugh, but the truth was she was hiding tears of joy on the inside.

The rest of the evening was wonderful. Carmen didn't actually participate fully, but she was a part of all they did. They cooked spaghetti for supper. Meg showed them all how to make meatballs. This was exciting because they would be able to do this at the dorm. They cleaned up after supper, played a few board games then settled into *Spin the Bottle* because Alissa insisted they play.

"Okay, on this spin, whoever the bottle points to, you have to tell us how many guys you have kissed, and give us their names," Alissa explained.

"Whatever," Meg said, bored with the whole game. It had been fun as a teenager, but as a twenty-nine year old it was rather draining.

"Ooooo! Miss Mac!" Lana yelled, indicating that the bottle had landed on her. "Tell us everything, now!"

Suddenly Meg blushed. She hadn't counted on having to tell her secrets.

"You're blushing!" Alissa blurted out. "This ought to be good!"

"I have no secrets," she tried to say matter-of-factly. "There are only three guys."

"Three?" Lana said. "I don't even have one! Three sounds incredible."

"Yeah, but I'm twenty-nine. Most women my age would ... well ..."

"Go on," Alissa urged.

"Never mind." She sighed. "Okay ... well ... there was this guy I went to my junior prom with. His name was Greg. We dated a few months then he moved before my senior year started."

"What did he look like?" Alissa quickly asked.

"I don't have to give details, just names, remember?"

"Okay, okay."

"Then there was Alan," Meg went on. The thought of him almost made her sick to her stomach. "He was a guy I sort of dated my senior year."

"What did he look like?" Lana tried.

"No, no, no. No details. Then last, was a guy I dated in college." Meg stopped.

"His name?" Alissa drilled.

"Is it important?" Meg asked her. "You haven't known the others."

"That's the rules of the game," Alissa insisted. "We at least get the names if you won't give us details."

Meg seriously considered lying. If Phillip only had an inconspicuous nickname.

"You're holding out," Alissa said with a suspicious grin.

"His name was Phillip." She tried to sound nonchalant.

Alissa and Lana screamed again. They stood up and started dancing around the couch.

"What are you doing?" she asked them.

"It's the beautiful, blonde buck, isn't it? Mr. Barton! What a babe!"

"I didn't say *Phillip Barton*."

"Okay, deny it then," Alissa challenged.

Meg closed her eyes. She could lie now, but there would be no stopping their investigation after this. They would learn they had dated in college, and it would be all over. She would be branded a liar.

"I really hate this game, you know," she said. "Can you believe they're doing this to me, Carmen?"

"You did agree to play," was all Carmen said. At least she spoke.

"Okay. Yes. I dated Phillip for a couple of years back in college."

The dancing started again. Meg was glad when her phone chirped. She desperately needed a diversion.

"Hello?" she answered.

"Meg MacAllister?"

"Yes, it is."

"This is Kevin Morris."

"Just a second." She told the girls she had a private call and would be outside for a while. Of course, they made assumptions and accusations that Meg denied. She walked out the French doors, shut them behind her, and put the phone back to her ear.

"I'm assuming you have some information for me." She was rather excited to hear from him again, not sure if it was the investigation or Mr. Morris himself.

"Do I ever. I'd like to meet you in person to sort through all of this. We need to seriously discuss the next steps. They could be dangerous, for both you and me."

Meeting him actually seemed a bit bold, and she was uncomfortable with that. "I'd rather not. Can't we just talk over the phone?"

"Meg, someone, I'm not sure who, has put out a lot of money, time, bribery, black mail—I mean, you name the dirty description and that's what's been going on here for many, many years. I'm leaving Minnesota tonight, mainly because I don't trust myself being here. Too many weird things have happened to people who got too close to Mr. Barton and the truth. I would rather not talk over a telephone to you about this."

"Okay. We'll meet. Do you know who his parents are?"

"I know the name of one parent. The other is the one I'm concerned about. There is no record of a father, just a bunch of shuffled around information. I'm surprised I found the mother. It took quite a bit of bribing."

"How do you know it's really her?"

"Well, that's something we'll have to talk about. Contacting her may put her in danger. It may put you in danger. It may put Phillip in danger."

"My goodness," she was taken back. "Do you think we should stop?"

"See what I mean? We have a lot to talk about. I'll call you when I get into town."

"Okay. Do that."

She turned off the phone and tried to steady herself. What had she gotten herself into? She was just trying to help a friend and had apparently uncovered something dastardly. She began to fear for Kevin Morris, as he was the one doing all the tracking. If it were as serious as he claimed, he could be in trouble. Should she call her father? Should she warn Phillip? Should she call off the investigation? Had they already gone too far? She had forgotten all about her guests until a squeal from Alissa brought her back.

"So, do you have a date?" Lana asked as she walked back in.

"I'll never tell," Meg said trying to lighten her mood."

"We need to finish our game," Alissa said.

Meg moaned. No more personal questions, please, but then that's what the game was all about. She plopped back down onto the couch and braced herself for more intrusion.

"Okay, you make up this one, Lana," Alissa told her.

"How about, the person you admire the most?"

"Boring!" Alissa said.

"I like boring," Meg commented.

"Let's ease up the pace a little, Alissa," Lana explained.

Alissa, grumbling, spun the bottle again. This time it pointed toward Carmen. Meg was now very glad that Lana's question was simple. Carmen deliberated.

"Nobody," she finally said.

"You don't admire anybody?" Alissa questioned her.

"No. Nobody comes to mind," she said again.

"You listen to music all the time," Lana tried to help. "Isn't there a musician you admire?"

"Nobody," she repeated.

"What about Miss Mac?" Alissa asked her. Meg wanted to shrink and disappear. This did not need to be happening. "She's done a lot for you."

"Nobody."

"Yeah," Lana came in to agree with Alissa. "You don't even admire Miss Mac?"

"Why should I? What does she have in common with me? A rich girl moves into her rich daddy's beach house and shares her abundance with us thrown away kids. Yeah, that's my goal in life. I wanna grow up and be just like her."

At this, Lana and Alissa became infuriated.

"You can't talk about her like that!" Alissa shouted.

"Sit down, Alissa," Meg commanded.

"Why can't I talk about her? Because I don't let her buy my affections like she's done with you two!" Carmen was yelling now too.

"That's about the lowest thing I've ever heard anyone say in my entire life," Alissa continued. "She doesn't buy anyone. She cares about us."

"Alissa! Sit down!" Meg demanded this time.

"But she ..." Alissa tried to speak, but Meg wouldn't let her.

"Alissa! Enough!" She breathed deeply, calming herself. "Carmen, you don't have to like me. That's not why I do this. It's okay. And please feel free to speak your mind however you want."

"Sure," Carmen said, surprising them all. "Everyone always wants me to speak my mind. I hear it all the time. *Let it out. Share your emotions. Just let it all go. You need to talk more.* Blah, blah, blah. Why? Can any of you change my life? Can any of you go back in time and undo all that's happened to me? So what if I tell you my life's story? You can't fix it, so what's the point?"

"You can't bottle bad things up inside you," Lana said. "They'll come out eventually."

"Well, let them come."

"What on earth is your problem?" Alissa asked, still showing contempt.

"Here's my problem, if you really want to know. I remember my father molesting me when I was three. I remember my mother beating me because I complained about it at six. When my parents divorced, my mother had boyfriends over all the time. Only they weren't boyfriends, I eventually figured out. They paid her good money to either be with her or me. At eleven, I got sick of being a whore, so I told the guidance counselor at school. My mother was arrested, and I was sent to live in a foster home. Three nights after being there, my foster pop raped me. I ran away for awhile … until the cops found me. I spent a little time in a detention center. Then mom was out, claiming I was lying for attention. They had no proof, so I was sent back to live with her. Mom beat the crap out of me more than I can remember, never for anything I was doing in the present, but for giving away *our little secret* and ruining her lucrative career. She was now stripping at a bar and didn't make near as much money. I took it as long as I could then, finally went to the emergency room one night because I knew she had broken my arm. I was taken away from her, and sent here." She paused then sarcastically added, "Gee, I feel so much better now."

Lana went over to her and slowly stuffed her hair behind her ear, revealing the long scar on her cheek. Meg and Alissa watched, but said nothing.

"My father gave me this. He abused me too, for six years. I thought it was over when I turned eleven. I didn't realize he had started with my little sister, who was six." Lana choked up for a moment. It was hard for her to tell this. "When I realized he was abusing Lacy, I told him he had better stop, or I would tell the authorities. He backhanded me against the wall. He had this huge jeweled ring on, and it gashed open my face. He left me there, hoping I would die. He had no use for me anymore. He then took Lacy and left. When I came to, I was in a hospital. I explained everything to the cops. They found him and Lacy three states over the next day. They sent us here to live."

Nobody expected a response from Carmen, but she suddenly lit up.

"Where was your mom?" Carmen wanted to know.

"She died two months after Lacy was born—a car accident."

"What a jerk," Carmen muttered. "You'd think guys could at least have some sense of decency, you know? Like, why children? Why their own kids? Why?"

Carmen now had tears in her eyes. She was beginning to shake. Meg, not really sure how to handle the situation at this point, was preparing for anything. Suddenly, Lana threw her arms around the shaking Carmen and held her tight.

"I know you don't believe me, but if you will let it out, you will feel better," Lana insisted.

Carmen grasped Lana's arms as if clinging to life itself. She began to shake even more. Then Alissa moved over to her and joined the hug. Meg didn't want to interfere. This girl needed this. She didn't trust adults, and she didn't know how to express anything. Meg just prayed that somehow God would perform a miracle in this room tonight. Carmen suddenly burst into sobs. She cried uncontrollably for close to ten minutes. Lana and Alissa cried with her. Meg got tissues.

"I'm sorry," Carmen finally managed to say. "I didn't mean to do that."

"No problem," said Alissa. "We all have to do that, you know?"

"Until we can let it go, it kills us," Lana said.

"I must have been about to die, then," Carmen said, with half of a smile forming.

"You were dead," Lana told her. "You had already lost your life. You were just breathing as a matter of habit."

Meg smiled. No trained psychiatrist could have done better, although many had tried. Meg didn't want to interrupt the moment. She knew the girls needed time to help heal now.

"I need to make a phone call," she said as she stepped back out onto the deck. She closed the doors so the trio could have their privacy. She watched for a few minutes as the three of them talked. Carmen seemed almost like a normal girl. Lana and Alissa sat on either side as the conversation continued. Meg would have loved to have heard it, but this was not the time.

She dialed the phone and waited for the ring.

"Hello?" answered Phillip.

"Hello yourself."

"Hello, Miss Mac. Wanting some adult conversation tonight? Are the teenage natives getting restless?"

"Sort of." She explained what had happened.

"You know," he told her, "that is so typical of girls that come to the home. I used to want a family so bad, but after hearing some of the stories there, I was sometimes glad. Having no family can be better than having a bad family."

"I need a vacation," she said, realizing she was feeling rather stressed.

"Thanksgiving is only a week and half away," he said cheerily.

"Oh rats!" she exclaimed. "I forgot!"

"You forgot about Thanksgiving?"

"No, I forgot to ask you to come with me to Houston for

Thanksgiving."

"How nice," he said sweetly, "but the Deweys have already offered and I've accepted. Everyone else at the station will be gone anyway. Since I've got nowhere to go I may as well work."

"You could cancel," she suggested.

"I could, but I think I'll stay. Thanks anyway. Maybe I can make it out there one of these days."

Her duty was done. She had fulfilled her mother's request by asking him to come. She was actually a little relieved that he wouldn't be there. She wanted to work with Kevin Morris on figuring out what to do about Phillip's parents. Working behind his back while he was actually waiting at her house would have been too underhanded for even Meg.

"Okay," she said. "Well, I probably need to go in and lighten things up. I'll see you Sunday."

Chapter Eleven

The next afternoon, Meg left the three girls watching an old movie as she drove toward a small truck stop just outside of town. Kevin Morris had called from the airport in Tampa to let her know he had arrived. She suggested a place she had never been hoping only people she had never seen would be there. When she had asked Kevin how she would recognize him, he told her not to worry—he would know exactly who she was.

"That was a no-brainer," she said to herself. "He's probably seen pictures of me from birth until this morning by now."

She pulled into the truck stop and was glad to see the parking lot nearly empty. Only a few semis were running whose drivers were dining, resting, or doing whatever they did at truck stops. She parked behind the building and walked around to the front entrance. As she made her way through the front door, she began scoping the premises for Mr. Kevin Morris. She had envisioned the typical fictional investigator person, complete with trench coat, hat, and pad and pen in hand. She knew it was ridiculous, but her imagination had a tendency to get carried away on occasion. So far, no one was matching her vision.

She walked to the back toward the small seating area for the restaurant. *This must be what they call a greasy spoon,* she thought. The smell of grease was strong, and many of the tables still had grease spots, crumbs, and dirty plates left over from the lunch crowd. She was about to think that Mr. Morris had not arrived yet, when she saw a man wave toward her from the farthest booth in the back corner. He was much younger than she had imagined and looked as though he had just stepped off the golf course. His dark hair was slightly long, and his brown eyes danced as she approached the table. A big smile began to appear beneath a thick mustache as he stood and reached out his hand.

"Mr. Morris, I presume?" she said as she shook his hand.

"Alive and in person," he responded. "Have a seat, please. Can I order you something?"

"I don't think so," she replied as she sat down in the slippery booth, trying to hide her disgust.

"Lovely smirk—you know places like this serve the best food."

"I'll take your word for it, Mr. Morris. Shall we get down to business?"

"Well, I can see it's gonna be all work and no play with you. And can we drop the Mister? Just Kevin, please."

"All right, *Kevin*," she complied. "Let's talk. What have you found?"

He took a sip of his coffee and pulled out a small note pad from his golf shirt pocket. He flipped through several pages until he found what he was looking for. She smiled. At least she had the note pad right.

"What I've found, Meg, is a big, nasty, ugly, messy can of juicy, slimy worms," he began. "When I got to Minnesota, I talked to the babysitter lady first, a Mrs. Louise Williams. Apparently, Phillip's mom lived with Louise during the latter months of her pregnancy when she began to show.
"

"Was this Mrs. Williams a relative?"

"No, just a lady that the father contacted to do this. It seems that her job back then was caring for newborns prior to placing them in their adoptive homes."

"Never heard of such a job."

"Me either," he agreed, looking up at her for a moment with a doubtful look. "Then, when the baby was born, he was never adopted. She just kept him until he was put into an orphanage of some kind. Let's see," he glanced down through his notes, "that was for about nine months. Shortly after that, he was diagnosed with some kind of severe health problem that required treatments once a week. They called her in to be with him since she was the only familiar person to him."

"She was his mother, at least to him," Meg said trying to hold in her anger. "Why did they take him away from her in the first place if they didn't have a home for him? And what was the health problem? Did Mrs. Williams ever notice anything wrong with him?"

"That's where it starts getting weird. She said he was as healthy a baby as she'd ever seen. After a couple of months of these weekly shots, he'd just start screaming when he saw her because that meant, you know, another injection. So they asked her to stop coming after that. That was the last she saw of him."

"Did she know the mother's real name?"

"Yes. It was Clara James." He turned another couple of pages in the note pad. "Then I go to see the nurse who attended him at the orphanage. Fortunately, Mrs. Williams knew her name, or I would have never found her. Nurse Nancy was one wired-out woman. When I first mentioned the orphanage, she denied having ever been there. I threw out a couple of lies about certain fabricated documents that proved otherwise, and she suddenly regained her memory. I mentioned a baby boy, a little over thirty years ago requiring weekly injections. She had no memory of that either.

Then I mentioned Phillip Barton's name. She flinched. I knew she remembered, but she swore she didn't."

She was leaning forward, not wanting to miss a word.

"I realized I had to play her game. Someone had paid her off big to keep this a secret for thirty-something years. I asked her how much it would take for her to remember the boy, the medicine, and the condition he had. She flatly told me she needed enough to get her out of the country for good if she were to say anything."

"You agreed, of course," Meg butted in.

"You bet I did. I figured if you wouldn't pay the money, I was willing to just to get to the bottom of this. She gave me a steep figure."

"No problem. Did she give you any answers?"

"Oh yeah," he said, turning another page. "First of all, the baby wasn't sick. The father, she didn't know his name, never wanted anyone to be able to trace the baby back to him. But he also never wanted the baby to remember where he came from. She was injecting him with an experimental drug that would cause lapses in memory. If it worked, he would never have clear memories of any time in his life that he was receiving the medication."

"No way!" she exclaimed. "That's sick! This was a baby! The father must have been a monster."

"She said she was paid a huge chunk of dough to never utter a word of it … ever. She's been ridden with guilt all these years. She hated what was happening, but soon the baby was shipped out somewhere, so she tried to put it out of her mind. Never could."

"I should hope not."

"I went and got the cash, gave it to her, and she said not to come back—she wouldn't be there."

Meg sat back to try and take all the information in. Phillip had been ripped from the only person he knew at nine months, been given mind altering drugs, and then hauled off somewhere new every once in a while to protect some man's reputation.

"What do we do, now?" she asked him.

"I go to South Dakota," he replied, turning another page in the note pad.

"Why South Dakota?"

"Because that's where Clara James is, now known as Clara Anderson, Phillip's mother."

"I'm going with you," she insisted.

"Don't. Let me finish this," he tried to discourage.

"I'm paying your ticket out there and back. I'm going."

"Okay, when?"

"I leave for Houston to spend Thanksgiving with my family a week from Tuesday. We'll go the Friday after Thanksgiving. I'll book two tickets in my name from Houston to South Dakota. Okay?"

He sighed for a long moment. "I'd rather you let me do this on my own."

"I want to be there to meet his mother. I'll know if it's her, or if we've been led astray on some wild chase again."

"How will you know it's her? Women's intuition?" He was almost sarcastic.

"No sir. I know Phillip better than anyone in this world. If this woman is really his mother, I'll recognize her, somehow, I will."

"Sounds spooky to me, but it's your money. Besides, I'd be a fool to pass up a trip with a dame like you."

"Dame?"

"Sounds real Sam Spade-ish, doesn't it?" He grinned big and waved his eyebrows. He was rather a handsome man beneath the massive mustache. "You know, lots of investigators' clients fall in love with them."

"Is that so?" she smiled. "Is that in fiction or reality?"

"Does it matter?" he smiled back.

"I believe you're flirting with me, Mr. Morris."

"I'm glad you caught on early, Miss MacAllister. That will make this whole affair so much easier."

"Affair?" she asked cautiously.

"Oh, that's just an expression. Don't take it too personally."

Sunday morning with three teenage girls was almost impossible. They did each other's hair, changed shoes, changed clothes, and even went through Meg's closet a few times. Spiro seemed to enjoy the excitement, whereas Meg was becoming a nervous wreck with each passing minute. Just when she thought everyone was ready to leave, Alissa came up with one more modification that had to be done. By the time they reached Sunday School, they were ten minutes late. The pastor passed the rushing crew as they headed toward their classes. He glanced at his watch, and then back at Meg. She smiled and mumbled something about not being cut out for motherhood.

She managed to make some sense of her lesson, and then rushed to the sanctuary to begin the pre-worship music. When she finally finished the offertory, a slightly modified, or as Phillip always said, Megified, version of a Handel piece, she sat down to relax and enjoy the sermon.

She hadn't even noticed that Phillip was to do the special music that morning. This was his first solo since returning to Treasure Cove. He had left the choir loft during the offertory and removed his robe. He then plugged in his acoustic guitar and began to play. Meg was still impressed by his ability. He had been good in college, but now he was incredible. Then he began to sing. She felt her heart swell with emotion as his tender, perfect voice melted into a beautiful melody. All she could think was what a waste for him not to be in a church somewhere working. After hearing him speak at the home last spring and now hearing him sing, she couldn't figure out why any church couldn't see the jewel they had received. How could he have been so rejected? Why was there such impatience?

He finished singing, gently ending the song with his guitar, and then came and set down by her.

"That was beautiful," she whispered. "You're an excellent musician."

"Thanks," he whispered. "I'm honored that you would think so."

After church, Meg took the girls back to her house and had them help her finish preparations for a delicious Sunday meal that had already cooked in the crock-pot overnight. When they finished eating, she cleaned the kitchen as they packed to go back to the home. Carmen had lightened up significantly over the weekend, and Lana and Alissa had talked her into definitely moving into the older girl's dorm-house with them. Before now, she had confessed that the whole idea of working with others, as far as cleaning and cooking were concerned, had really bothered her. Now she had made friends, and was looking forward to making more. As Meg deposited them at the home, she thanked God for her house, her position, and her status, which allowed her to do exactly what she had done this weekend.

I know, Father, that it wasn't me who brought the healing, but Alissa and Lana. But I thank You for letting it be possible for me to get them all to my place so it could happen.

She didn't feel like going back to her own house just yet, so she decided to drop by and see Phillip for a while. She had only seen his condo once, and that was while he was moving in. She almost hated going by because she had really wanted to buy one of the Treasure Homes, but her pride had gotten the better of her. The location was perfect. It was still on Gull Island, very near her parents' house, and the facilities were gorgeous. They had been available in one, two, or three bedroom models. She had wanted a three bedroom one so that she could still have girls over. Phillip's had two bedrooms, and it was so nice. The foyer opened up into a living room with a beam-exposed vaulted ceiling. To the right of the foyer, also open to the living room was a spacious kitchen. Off the back of the living room were sliding glass doors that led to a large deck on the beach. The bedrooms and two full baths were upstairs, with the master bedroom having its own small, private deck. As she pulled into the lushly landscaped lot, she felt a twinge of disappointment. This was not the first opportunity she had missed because of her stubbornness.

She walked up the steps and knocked on his door. She heard a yell, but wasn't sure what was said. Was he asking her to come in or had he yelled at someone else? She waited, but no one answered the door. There came the yell again. She assumed he was busy doing something and had yelled for her to come on in. Slowly, she opened the door and peeked through. More yelling.

"Hello?" she said timidly as she crept into the living room. She still went unnoticed. Then she discovered the culprit—a football game.

"You're ignoring me over a stupid game?" she teased as she walked next to the couch with her hands on her hips.

"Meg?" he said startled. "Why didn't you knock?"

"I did. All I heard was yelling. I didn't know if you wanted me to go away or come on in."

"Well, by all means, always come on in," he motioned for her to sit.

"This place is so nice," she said as she looked out onto the deck. She did feel it could use a woman's touch. A few plants here, a framed picture there, a throw-rug or two strategically placed, and this place would be magazine ready. Of course, she knew better than to suggest anything, especially with all that she had done behind his back as recently as yesterday. She knew what was right, to face him with the truth now, but what if it were a dead end? What if Clara James Anderson was a decoy and Kevin had been led down a wild path? It would be worse for Phillip to get his hopes up, and then have them dashed yet again.

"I'm glad you're here," he said suddenly, turning off the television.

"The game isn't over—you don't have to stop on my account."

"I wanted to show you something today. I was going to ask you after church tonight because I knew you'd be busy with the three musketeers this afternoon."

"The three musketeers and I had a great weekend. Carmen finally let go."

"That whole story is incredible! I don't know what these girls would do if they ever lost you, Meg. You mean so much to them."

She smiled. That was a compliment coming from one who knew how they felt.

"What's the surprise?" she asked.

"Let's go," he said taking her hand and leading her out the front door.

The drive led to the radio station, where he insisted she close her eyes before going through the front door. She heard the music being piped in from somewhere as they entered the building, eyes still closed.

"Okay," he said. She could tell he was grinning from the sound of his voice. "You can look now."

She opened her eyes and was amazed. The remodeling had been completed, and it was classic. The new carpet was textured to discourage traffic wear, with specks of blue and teal and rose. The walls were teal, and the chairs in the reception area were a dark rose. The desk, the very new desk, was a lightly stained wooden masterpiece.

"This is beautiful, Phillip," she breathed as she looked at various framed scenes taken at local places in Treasure Cove.

"That's not all," he said as he led her down the hallway.

He showed her each office, completely redone in the same colors, with new furniture, replaced windows, new blinds, and classy valance curtains. He then guided her to the broadcast booth. The shabby wall had been replaced with a huge glass window so all passing by could see the DJ hard at work. Phillip gave the man on duty a thumbs up, and he responded with a wave. He then proudly opened the door to his own office. It was breathtaking. Everything in the entire building was brand new, from the furniture to the computers to the phone system. Phillip had done well.

"Okay," she said. "I'm impressed. I'm very impressed."

"Isn't this great?" he said proudly. "It was really hard getting the work done because we broadcast twenty-four hours a day. I had them do the booth first, making it completely sound proof, much to the disappointment of the rest of the employees. But that gave the construction crew freedom to work after that. It looks like a whole new place, doesn't it?"

"It *is* a whole new place. The colors are wonderful. Did the receptionist pick them out?"

He laughed. "Actually, she did in a way. I had an interior designer come in and look at the place. I asked her to give us three different schemes, and then we, as a group, would choose what we liked best. Of course, everyone was so awed by the prospect of something other than pink carpet, we immediately agreed on these colors. When it all came together, we were speechless."

"Has Ira seen it?"

"Oh yeah! He was funny about the whole thing, though. When I told him the remodeling had started, he said he wasn't stepping foot in here until it was finished. It was finished Friday. I called him up and said to come for inspection."

"Oh, boy," she mumbled.

"Don't you know it? He tried to be grumpy as he came through the door, muttering about he was glad his money wasn't used for such vanity. But when he saw it ..." Phillip paused.

"Yeah? Go on! Don't leave me hanging!"

"He actually yelled in delight."

"You're kidding? Ira showed a positive emotion?" She was stunned.

She went over to him as he stood next to the window, opening and closing the blinds that now worked perfectly, not to mention, matched perfectly too. She put her arms around him and looked up into those dreamy, smiling, turquoise eyes.

"You done good, home boy. You done real good." Then she hugged him for a long time.

"Thanks," he said, as they broke apart. "If I remodel something else, will you hug me like that again?"

"How about I do your place?" she said, without thinking … again.

"What's wrong with my place?"

Will I ever learn to think before I speak?

Chapter Twelve

As Meg walked into the greeting area at the Houston Intercontinental Airport, she immediately spied the bubbly red-head waving frantically. Beside Janet was Craig, and she was comforted that they seemed happy and relaxed. Whatever the problem had been, perhaps it was solved now. Janet ran up to her and hugged tightly, followed by Craig, who waited his turn and then warmly held his younger sister. She grabbed her carryon bag, and they made their way through the airport to the limo with Janet talking the entire time. When the car pulled up to the gatehouse at the MacAllister estate, the security guard opened the massive iron structure and waved them through. Many memories flooded over her as they drove down the shaded drive to the mansion. Some were wonderful, some were dreadful, but then *all of life was really like that*, she told herself.

She was immediately welcomed by her parents as she walked into the house. The massive greeting room was home to her yet it would seem impersonal and ornate to a stranger. To the right was a formal dining room, and to the left was a study. She walked through the dining room and into the kitchen, a place where she had seldom actually cooked a meal. Marguerite, their cook for as long as Meg could remember, was working her magic on something that smelled too good to be true. Meg hugged the Spanish woman as though she was a part of the family—for all practical purposes, she was.

She then made her way up one side of the stately staircase, newly carpeted with the same maroon color it had always been. She opened the third door on the right, her room. Not a thing had changed. The queen sized bed with its white posts and billowing baby blue canopy brought a warm smile to her face. Her dolls were lined on the shelves against one wall, her trophies on another. A white baby grand piano on a powder blue rug still stood in the center of the room. She put down her bags and played a quick three octave scale with one hand. Her parents still kept it in tune.

"Bring back memories?" Janet asked as she joined her. "Am I interrupting?"

"Not at all," she sighed, turning around and smiling. "Please rescue me from all this sentimentality."

"You can be so funny some times. If I get sentimental, please don't rescue me. Just let me wallow in it."

"Eek. The very thought is close to disgusting. Both wallowing and sentimentalism."

Janet hugged her again. "It is so good to see you, Meg. I miss you so much."

"I hate to say this, but I tend to miss you too ... occasionally."

She set her bag on the foot of the bed as Janet described their trip to Houston in detail. They only lived three hours away, but got caught in a traffic jam because of a bad wreck. This, of course, upset Janet severely, and she couldn't get her mind off the tragic scene when they finally passed. Meg half listened, knowing that Janet would talk about anything that came to her mind just to keep conversation going. She nodded and gave a few monosyllabic responses so Janet would know she was listening, but mainly she kept inspecting various aspects of her room as she drifted in and out of daydreams. She opened the double doors to her balcony and walked out, Janet following right behind talking the entire time.

"This is my favorite place in the whole house," Meg finally said.

Janet stopped talking and eagerly picked up on her thought. "It is beautiful here."

"It's more than just beauty. It's the whole feeling that comes from being out here. I remember as a child looking down on the pool house and listening to Craig and Herbie's parties. Teenagers seemed so wild and scary to me because they were loud and silly to be such big people. I used to watch the gardeners work relentlessly on the landscaping and wonder why they would do so much for a place where they didn't live. I didn't realize until years later that we paid them. I thought they just liked us a lot. From up here, I would see certain ones that were really nice to me, and then I'd run down to talk to them and help them plant or mulch or water. I just thought we were all great friends. When I realized they were hired help— that they just did what my mom told them to—I was so hurt. I began assuming then they were only my friends for the same reason."

"How sad. Sometimes you can be so depressing."

"Me?" Meg said turning to her. "What about you last Christmas? Apparently, whatever it was that had you down and out is over with now."

Janet sighed. She gazed out onto the gardens as she appeared to collect her thoughts. "That was such a hard time for me. I guess it was a turning point. All I ever wanted out of life were three things—a wonderful husband, a bunch of kids, and a house of our own."

"One out of three ain't bad," Meg smiled.

"Not when there isn't anything else you really want. I've got a wonderful husband. I mean, my goodness, I was so in love with him years before he ever noticed me. When he married me, I couldn't imagine ever being unhappy. I just assumed everything else would fall in line, but it never did."

"Hey, at least you've *got* a husband. At the rate I'm going, I'll miss that one all together."

"If that's all I ever have, I'll be happy and content. That's what I've finally come to this year. I mean, if I have to live in a rented apartment for the rest of my life with no kids at all, but I have Craig, I will be happy. It's just ... well ... I never imagined that we wouldn't have children."

Meg didn't want to pry, but evidently it didn't bother Janet to discuss it. "Are there some problems ... I mean ... health-wise?"

"Not that anyone can find. We've been to doctors and had all these crazy tests, and, as Craig puts it, we're both batting a thousand."

"What's the problem?"

"I don't know!" she cried with frustration. "Timing, maybe? Stress? I can't figure it out. But it really started getting to me last year."

"And now?"

"I guess I had to come to the point where I believed God was in control. It's like Craig finally told me, *God could make Mary pregnant without sex; and He could make me not pregnant with it.*"

Meg laughed. Only Janet could take that statement as a *word from the Lord.* "Okay ... wonderful husband, no kids, but what about the house? You guys talked last Christmas like you were thinking of building."

She just shook her head and shrugged.

"What happened?" Meg asked her.

"Craig doesn't want to build until he feels we're going to be somewhere permanently."

"Good luck," she said sarcastically. "After spending time with Phillip, I wonder if anyone can stay at a church very long."

"Oh, you get over that after awhile. And then, not all churches are buildings of brutality. We're at a wonderful place. The people are supportive, the pastor is so compassionate, and the youth are very responsive."

"Then why don't you want to stay permanently?"

"Craig wants to move in a different direction ministerially. He's leaning more toward young adults. He thought about looking into college campus ministries."

"I could see that. Something kind of like David Dewey?"

"Yeah. He's talked to David quite a bit this past year. Maybe something will open up soon. But I can tell you this—it'll be very hard to leave this church."

"Maybe," an idea came to her, "you guys could recommend Phillip when you leave."

🏝 🏝 🏝

Thanksgiving dinner was definitely a feast. Marguerite had prepared a luscious turkey with cornbread dressing and all the trimmings imaginable. Herbie and Susan and their children came for dinner, but left shortly after the meal to go visit with her family. Mitch was there also, but Michael, his son, had stayed with the mom. Andrew was in full form, talking non-stop about how wonderful school was, how interesting the classes were, and how enchanting college women were. He hoped, one day, to catch one of his own. Everyone laughed and enjoyed the refreshing spirit he always managed to bring into a place.

"I will be taking a little trip in the morning, so I won't be able to join you all," Meg tried to say matter-of-factly as they began to make plans for Friday.

"A trip?" her mother asked. "Where?"

"It's no big deal," she said nonchalantly trying to downplay any questions that might arise.

"So, where are you going?" her father asked.

"South Dakota," she mumbled.

"South Dakota?" Craig blurted out. "A *little* trip?"

"Why on earth would you be going to South Dakota?" her mother wanted to know. "I don't like the idea of you traveling that far all alone. Take one of us with you, if you have to go."

"I won't be going alone," she hated to admit because now more questions would ensue.

"Who's going with you, then?" her mother continued to drill. "Do we know her?"

"Dad does," Meg said looking at her father hoping for some help. "His name is Kevin Morris."

At this, her father looked sharply at her.

"Herbert," said Mrs. MacAllister, "who is this Morris fellow?"

"A guy who does some work for me occasionally. He's very responsible, Meri. Don't worry about her."

Meg sighed. She knew she would have to answer to her father later. As expected, shortly after retiring to her room for the night, a light rap sounded on her door.

"Come in," she said rising sleepily from beneath the covers and turning on the lamp.

"Are you already asleep?" her father asked as he closed the door and approached the bed.

"Not yet, but I have a big day tomorrow."

"That's what I wanted to discuss with you. Why are you going to South Dakota with a private investigator?"

"It's just some research I've been doing for a friend. We're right near the end, and I wanted to be there when it happened," she tried to explain simply.

"When *what* happened?" He wasn't going to be dissuaded.

"Daddy, let this go."

"No. You can choose not to tell me, but I would really rather you did."

"It's not all that big of a deal, and I don't want the whole family to know, okay?"

"Fine ... tell *me*." His stern expression indicated he wasn't convinced this was a wise idea.

"I hired Kevin to find Phillip's parents. He's tried in the past with a couple of search agencies, but they all came up empty. I thought I'd give it a try."

"Does Phillip know about this?"

"No sir. That's why I'd like to keep it quiet."

"What's in South Dakota?"

"His mother, we think."

"You think? This must have been one humdinger of a search."

"You have no idea, Daddy."

"Be careful, will you? I trust Kevin. He's very good at what he does. You, I never know whether to trust or not."

"Thanks a lot—love that vote of confidence."

"Well, what can I say? Every time I talk to you, you've got your hand in some new project. Your mother thinks you really need to settle down."

"With a man, I suppose?" she asked snidely. He just nodded. "Daddy, I can't marry a man if he's not interested in me. It's not like I've put a sign up saying *Keep Off*. It's just there's been no one in my life."

"*I'm* not complaining about your marital status—that's your mother's territory. I'm not a big fan of men anyway ... especially where my daughter's concerned."

"Hmm," she sighed.

Meg found her gate at the airport and began to search for Kevin Morris. She looked for a well-dressed, preppy man with an uncomfortably thick mustache sitting or standing somewhere in the waiting area. He would be quite handsome without the caterpillar over his lip, but it was just too hard to get past. She giggled at her thoughts. Perhaps he hadn't arrived yet. She took a seat near the windowed wall where several were watching planes land and take off. A woman with a small child was trying to read a thick book, but the child kept wandering off, interrupting her leisure. A young couple sat staring at each other, holding hands and gazing at what must have been a brand new engagement ring. A seemingly impatient businessman stood, tapping his foot and glancing at his watch every few seconds while sipping a cup of cappuccino. And what appeared to be a farmer, a man dressed in old jeans, faded boots, a flannel shirt, topped off with a John Deere cap, was sitting in a corner reading a magazine with cows on the front cover.

"Flight nine-two-seven to Rapid City is now boarding," came the announcement from the intercom. People began to gather their belongings and move toward the walkway. Meg anxiously looked at her watch and wondered if Kevin Morris would make it on time. The lady managed to gather her carry-on bags and her child, though he was hardly cooperative, and load the plane. The businessman quickly grabbed his briefcase and drank down the last of his cappuccino. The farmer stood up, adjusted his hat, tucked the magazine into a beaten up leather backpack, and pushed his wire-rimmed glasses up on his nose. He then looked straight and Meg and waved. He was a rather familiar farmer—Kevin Morris.

"You are a man of many faces," she said as he approached her. "You should have told me we were dressing extremely casual." She looked nice—wool pants, silk blouse, with a cashmere sweater around her neck for the cooler weather in South Dakota.

"I prefer the element of surprise," he said smiling beneath what looked like a three day beard … and no loathsome mustache. "Shall we load?"

She picked up her overnight bag, just in case they needed to stay, and followed farmer Kevin onto the plane. They found their seats, buckled up and prepared for take-off. When the plane was in the air and on its way, she stared at him with raised eyebrows.

"What?" he asked defensively.

"What's with the getup?"

"We're going to a ranching community. I'd rather fit in than stand out."

"So, the whole golf look down in Florida?"

"Fitting in," he smiled.

"Do you even play golf?"

"Nope," he grinned at her. "Never have, and never will. Too slow paced for me."

"And the … uh … massive mustache?"

"Nice touch, huh?"

"Depends. What *touch* were you going for?"

"Did you not like my handsome mustache, Miss MacAllister?"

"No comment. And I suppose the longer hair was a wig?"

He looked around carefully then leaned into her and said, "I'm wearing the wig now—the longer hair is the real deal."

"I see." She bit the sides of her cheeks to keep from smiling. "Is the scraggly beard today real or painted on?"

"Oh, most definitely real … took me a whole week to get it to look like this."

She was actually impressed and relieved that the mustache was not his normal look. And she had been right—he was dashingly handsome, as far as she could tell. Then she wondered why that even mattered.

"I suppose this is an unusual venture for the English teacher," he said as he stretched out his legs beneath the seat in front of him.

"Yep. Just give me the conventional eight-to-three and I'm a happy girl."

"I bet you're good at it, too. Do your students love you?"

"Only the ones who like to work. The rest? It's doubtful." She pushed the bill of his hat up so she could see the brown eyes behind the tiny wire-rimmed glasses. "So, Farmer Kev, you know everything about me, and I only know that you're a grown man who likes to play dress-up. I feel I'm at a disadvantage. Tell me at least something about you."

"The long or short version?"

"It's a lengthy flight to the great, white North."

And what a story it was. He had been raised all over Central America by missionary parents. He had two sisters, one older and one younger, who were both married and had children. He had begrudged his parents because his only dream in life was to play football, but being raised out of the states he never had the opportunity to train during his younger years. They insisted he go to the same college as they because of free tuition. The football team was minimal at its best. He played all four years, but had no chance at the pros. After college, he began working at an investigator's office until he could decide what else there was in life besides football—he discovered it there. The man had a heart attack and was told to slow down. He began to do all the legwork, and his boss did all the paperwork and brain work. It wasn't long before he found he had a real knack for the detective business.

"And the rest, as they say, is history," he finished.

"Are your parents still missionaries?"

"Still *a-preaching and a-reaching*, as they always said."

"Does this make you a religious person, then?"

"Yes, and no," he tried to explain. "Yes, I'm a Christian. No, I'm not very good at it. It seemed as though I never had a choice about God. I had to do religious work while growing up. I had to go to an extremely fundamental Christian college, ties and black pants to class, the whole route. So, when the *had to's* were over, I sort of stopped."

She nodded.

"I suppose you disapprove," he commented.

"I didn't say that," she responded quickly. "Look, I think everyone has to make their own choices. I made some bad decisions when I was young, but it was a group of really caring, really transparent Christians that pulled me up and got me back on my feet. I was blessed to be in a church where I was loved and nurtured … a place I couldn't wait to go whenever the doors opened … not a place I was forced to go. And then I know others who gave themselves to the church and were run over by hate and misplaced authority." She smiled at him. "Your journey's not over yet. Maybe you just needed time to heal and discover who God really is, not who others say He is."

"So you don't think I'll get struck by lightning or something for being a wayward son?"

"I doubt that, but if you do, I hope it's after we get off this plane."

Chapter Thirteen

The drive to Edgemont, South Dakota from Rapid City was a nice break from the bustle of the MacAllister Thanksgiving. Kevin had managed the *borrowing* of an old pick-up for the trip and knew exactly where they were going. He made every turn perfectly, as though he had grown up there. He was a thorough and competent man when it came to details. Meg felt her heart would leap from her chest when he finally stopped the truck in front of a quaint log cabin overlooking a beautiful river.

"Here we are," he announced.

"I'm so nervous." She bit her lip and rubbed her chest to calm her pounding heart. "What if this really is his mother?"

"It better be, or you and I have wasted a whole lot of your money and my time."

"You don't understand, though. *This could be his mother.* I mean, he has been a nobody in his mind all these years because there was no one who claimed him. This could change his life."

He smiled and took her hand. "Calm down. All my instincts tell me this is the lady." He paused. "This is what you wanted, right?"

She looked up at him and his expression was full of compassion. She managed a smile as she thought how good it felt to be the one comforted for a change. And she couldn't deny that when he took her hand, her heart stirred for just a moment.

"Do you mind if I pray?" she asked, removing her hand from his. "Nothing fancy, I just need to settle down."

"The peace that passeth understanding?" he acknowledged. She nodded. "Have at it."

After a short prayer they left the truck and approached the house. He pushed the doorbell as she stood back to observe the place. It was beautiful and tasteful. The cold air was beginning to burn her eyes, and she tried to wipe them without smearing mascara all over her face.

"You okay?" he asked.

"The wind."

"It is cold up here."

The doorknob began to turn, and then the door opened. Meg couldn't help but gasp at the sight. A small framed woman in her early fifties stood there. She was the opposite of anything Phillip was—short and brunette with small wisps of gray flowing through various spots—but there were those eyes.

"Mrs. Clara James Anderson?" Kevin asked.

"Yes," she said smiling.

Oh my, there was that smile. Meg had never in her life felt such emotion. If she had tried to speak, she would have burst into tears. Those turquoise eyes were gleaming as Clara greeted her unknown guests.

"You don't know us, Mrs. Anderson," he continued, "but we're here with some information about your son."

"Which one," she said, still smiling. "Matthew or James? They're both here now if we need to talk with them."

"Neither," he said gently, obviously knowing this might be a hard blow to her. "Your other son—the one you gave up for adoption thirty-two years ago."

Her demeanor changed immediately. She stopped smiling and came out into the cold for a moment, barely leaving the door open behind her.

"I don't know who you are, or what you're up to, but I have no other son."

This time Meg spoke up. She felt desperate. "You didn't have a baby thirty-two years ago?"

Clara Anderson's expression changed again. This time she motioned them in and led them to a small study off of the entrance to the cabin. She said she would be right back, and then left for a little over a minute. Neither Meg nor Kevin said a word. She knew this was Phillip's mom, but she feared that convincing Mrs. Anderson might be difficult. She seemed adamant about not having another son.

"Now," Clara said, closing the door. "Who are you, what do you want, and what is this about a *son*?"

"Were you not pregnant thirty-two years ago, and did you or did you not stay with a Mrs. Louise Williams in Minnesota?" Kevin asked her, a bit too coldly for Meg's preferences.

The stunned woman stared in disbelief, her eyes flooded with much emotion. "Yes," she agreed. "I was pregnant, and I stayed with Mrs. Williams."

"Did you or did you not have a son?" he continued.

"No," she said, taking both Kevin and Meg by surprise. "No," she repeated, slowly shaking her head. Tears welled up like pools of liquid turquoise. "I had a baby girl." She paused. "But she was never adopted. She was stillborn."

Meg shuddered. What was going on here? This had to be Phillip's mom—those eyes had to belong to his mother.

"Did you ever see the baby, Mrs. Anderson?" he asked her. Meg was about to scold him for such a cold question, until Clara answered.

"No, I didn't. They said she was badly deformed, and if she had lived, it wouldn't have been for long. It was best if I just lived with my own idea of her than to see her lifeless body."

Meg was confused and Clara obviously was too, but Kevin didn't seem disturbed at all by the news. It was as if he had figured out exactly what had happened and continued questioning her.

"Mrs. Anderson, I know this may be difficult, but I need you to tell me about your delivery. What happened that day?"

Clara sat down for the first time and tried to pull the thoughts back up. They must have been pushed deeply away for many years.

"It was one week exactly before she was due," she began. "I started having severe cramps. Mrs. Williams immediately took me to my doctor who said there were some major complications. He had to do a c-section right away or both myself and the baby would be in danger."

"Were you awake for the surgery," he prodded more.

"No—it was an emergency. They didn't have time for anything other than just putting me asleep. When I awoke, they gave me the news. It was horrible—I lost my baby girl."

Clara was choking up, but Kevin seemed to pay no mind. He scribbled down a few words on his note pad then turned back to her.

"They lied to you, Mrs. Anderson," he said calmly. "You didn't have a baby girl—you had a boy. He's alive and well today, and his name is Phillip Barton."

At the sound of Phillip's name, she jerked her head up. Her eyes changed, and she actually went into hysterical laughter. Meg and Kevin looked at each other, baffled by the sudden outburst.

"He made a mistake." Clara now wore a triumphant grin. "He thought he had covered his tracks. He thought he had the perfect plan. He thought he was so smart, but he made a blunder ... a big blunder."

"Who?" Meg asked her. "Who and what?"

"I was just about to throw the two of you out of here," she said, still smiling, practically beaming. "The whole story of a baby boy, the fact that he was alive, it was tearing me apart. I thought someone was playing a cruel joke on me. But that name—now *that* has significance."

"I don't get it," Meg said, wanting to understand whether this lady believed she was indeed Phillip's mother or not.

"Only I would get it," she said. "His father was an up and coming politician. I worked for his campaign that year. We got very close ... too close. I ended up pregnant. He was married with two children. He wanted me to get an abortion, privately of course, because his platform was dead against it. I couldn't do it—I couldn't have my baby slaughtered. I told him it didn't matter if he wanted the child or not, I did. I was so young, only nineteen. He convinced me I should let someone adopt the baby who could give it the best possible chance in life, and that I should finish my education so I could have a good future. I gave in. He found me a place with Mrs. Williams and even a wonderful family for the baby. When the baby died, that ended it. I grieved, blamed myself for the whole ordeal, and tried to push it out of my mind. But now ... this whole story is unbelievable."

"What about the name?" Meg wanted to know. "Why is Phillip Barton so significant?"

She laughed again. "He always called me *Clara Barton*. He never used my real last name, James. In fact, it got to be such a habit, that when he introduced me to people, he always said *Clara Barton*, and I would always correct him and say, *Clara James*. He would laugh and say I was the nurse that healed all the hurts in his campaign—thus the significance of the last name. But, it's even more than that. This man's middle name is *Phillip*. He wanted to name his own son after himself, but his wife didn't like it at all. Thus, *Phillip*."

Kevin explained the great goose chase he had been on, the covered tracks, the moving around, the injections, the tampered files, and then Phillip's own failed attempts to find her. Clara's expression grew more excited with each new detail in the story.

"He didn't win," she said with a grin that seemed unstoppable.

"Who was his father?" Kevin asked the question Meg was dying to have answered.

"Back then he was just running for a representative position in the state house. You would now know him as Senator George P. Evans."

She let the name sink in. The two gasped with the realization of what that meant. Sen. Evans was the leader of the moral and family values group in Washington D.C. He had made this his platform and was so vocal about his stand that even some conservatives found him obnoxious. It would have reeked major damage on his political career had the fact ever leaked out that he had an illegitimate child.

"I just saw a documentary on him last week," Meg suddenly remembered.

"Saw it too," Clara laughed. "What a bunch of baloney! It would almost be worth dragging the whole thing up just to see his expression!"

"Mrs. Anderson," Meg said softly, finally coming back to the reality that she was sitting here with Phillip's mother, "would you like to see a picture of your oldest son?"

She nodded tearfully and sat down next to her. Reaching into her purse, Meg pulled out a snapshot someone had taken of her and Phillip at the hayride. It was a perfect picture of his face—beaming smile, glowing blonde hair, and beautiful blue eyes that Meg, for the first time, had finally seen in another person. She gave it to Clara.

The woman immediately began to sob as she stared at the picture. Through her sobs she managed to say, "He has my eyes. He has *my* eyes."

"And your smile, too," Meg added.

It took her several minutes to get her emotions under control. When she finally could speak again, she asked Meg, "Who are you?"

"He's a dear friend. We've been close for many years."

"Does he know what you've done?" Clara asked her.

"No, he doesn't. And I know this may be hard for you, but you need to let me tell him in my own time. He's had a rough several years, and this information needs to be given to him at the right time."

"I've waited this long, I can wait a little longer. What's wrong with him? What does he do?"

"He was in the ministry for several years," Meg began, but Clara jumped up and clapped her hands before she could continue.

"He's a Christian, then?" she wanted to know.

Meg smiled and confirmed, "A wonderful Christian man with talent beyond description. He's had some rough experiences at churches and is now a station manager for Christian radio."

"Near here?" Clara asked, excited.

"No." She suddenly realized that Clara had no idea where Phillip was. "We live in Florida."

"Please invite him to come here for Christmas," she begged. "Please let him see his whole family."

"I will," she promised. "I'll do everything I can to see to it that Phillip Barton is here for Christmas with his mother, his stepfather, and his brothers and sisters."

Clara brought Meg and Kevin into the living room where the rest of the family was sitting. She very carefully explained the details of what she had learned today. Apparently, from her husband to her youngest child, a twelve year old girl, she had already spoken of her pregnancy, the still-born birth of a baby girl, and her grief and guilt that followed. When she finished the story, her family embraced her, and then they embraced Kevin and Meg. Clara showed them the picture of Phillip, and they all were amazed at the resemblance.

"Honey," her husband said, as he looked down at her, "you finally have a child with your eyes." Her brown-eyed husband and their four brown-eyed kids all laughed in agreement and cried with joy.

Meg felt as though she would rapture on the flight back to Houston. She talked non-stop to Kevin about everything. He mostly just smiled, and she found pleasure in how attentively those brown eyes took in her every word. She had no idea how she would keep this news from Phillip, but however she told him, it had to be special.

"I'm sure you'll come up with something very appropriate," he said to her. "Promise me you'll tell me how you did it."

"I will."

"He's a lucky guy, you know—having someone as wonderful as you care so much about him."

"I told you ... it's not like that. He's a dear friend."

"And he's okay with that? I mean, have you looked in the mirror lately?"

Her cheeks warmed—she so hated doing that. "If I didn't know better, I'd think you were trying to compliment me," she said trying to gain control of herself.

"And I believe you are blushing. Surely you receive compliments regularly on how attractive you are. "

"Actually ... no. Seldom does anyone say anything about my ... *attractiveness.*"

"I guess that shouldn't surprise me." He tugged his cap down and narrowed his eyes at her. "You are quite an intimidating woman."

"In what way?" She was dumbfounded.

"You're educated, you're competent, you're outspoken, and you have access to any amount of money you need to make sure you move the world in your direction. All those things would make the average male think twice before commenting on your beauty. If he's gonna flirt with you, he'd better have enough confidence to think he can handle you."

Her mouth fell open. "Uh ... okay." Shaking her head slightly she asked, "And so you have an abundance of confidence, I suppose?"

"I wouldn't say that ... exactly. I've just been around long enough to know that when I find something that's worth pursuing, I'd better jump before the chance is gone. I believe our deal here is done, but I don't believe I'm ready to just have you walk out of my life."

She stared at him for several moments. His expression remained serious, his eyes hoping. He removed the thin glasses and stuck them into the pocket of his flannel shirt.

"I'm not really sure what I feel about you ... Kevin," she said honestly. "I mean, I barely know you, and most of our conversations have been about all this business."

"Let me take you out to dinner tomorrow night. We'll talk about everything except business."

"I can't do that," she protested. "I need to be with my family. What will they think? I've already left them for an entire day to be with you ... or so they imagine."

"Let them think what they will. Do you believe it would concern them that you were spending time with a successful businessman slightly older than you?"

"Just how old are you?" she asked. "You've never told me."

"Ask me tomorrow."

Later that evening, she heard her father's familiar, rhythmic tap on her door.

"Come on in, Daddy," she called out wearily.

He opened it and then gently shut it behind him as he looked around the room. "A lot of memories in here," he said nostalgically.

"Yep ... kind of gives me a warm, fuzzy feeling every time I come home. Do you think Mom will ever change it ... you know ... decorate it ... spruce it up?"

He shook his head as he grinned tiredly and sat on the edge of her bed. "I doubt it. She wants to leave all your rooms like they were when you were growing up."

"Why? To torture us when we have children so they can come back and see how goofy we were as teenagers?"

He chuckled. "Oh, I'm sure—that's exactly why." He gave her an odd look. "You planning on having children in the near future?"

"That's doubtful, and I'm beginning to get the idea that perhaps marriage isn't in my stars at all."

"Marriage is tough, baby girl. It's a good thing, but it's a hard thing. Not everybody's cut out for it."

"And you don't believe *I'm* cut out for it?"

"I'm not saying that. What I am saying is that people that like control—people like you and me—we've either got to learn how to compromise in life or we have to marry some spineless, patient, worm."

Her eyebrows flew up. "Mom is not a spineless worm!"

"Of course, she isn't—I learned to compromise. And that's all I'm telling you. You're a very self-reliant person, kiddo. You're also self-made. You see a goal, a project, a dream, and you go after it with gusto. Marriage is about learning how to merge your goals and dreams, which means giving up some things and taking on others."

"And you're telling me all this because ...?"

"Because you're twenty-nine and you're restless. It can be a great thing to share your life with someone, but it's more than just finding that someone. It's a lot of sacrifice, a lot building, a lot of rebuilding."

"You and Mom have done okay."

Another chuckle. "Again—a lot of sacrifice, a lot of rebuilding. You only see the destination with a few glimpses of the journey. There's been a lot of heartache, a lot of frustration and a lot of anger over the years. We had to chose to work through it and move beyond it."

"Gee, Daddy, you almost sound poetic. I didn't know you had it in you."

He took her hand. "Baby girl, you've gotta decide if being with someone is worth the change, worth the compromise, and frankly, worth the fight. Are you willing to sell out wholeheartedly and build a life with someone more than you need to be in control?"

"What is the deal with people insisting I have *control* issues? I do not have to control the world!"

"No, but you do insist on controlling *your* world. I'm not saying that's a bad thing, just that it's a bad thing in a marriage. You can't invite someone into your life and then demand they conform to *your* ideals. You have to take them for who they are … appreciate them for who they are … and then love them completely for who they are."

She sighed. "I'm still confused, though. Why are you giving me this little speech? Do you see someone in my future that's about to propose?"

"I see a man from your past who asked you not to meddle in his life anymore, yet you cared so much for him that you've gone and gotten the most precious gift a person could give him—a mother, a family, a legacy, when before there was none. He's a gentle spirit, Meg, and he's been broken to pieces. You tell him what you've done and he's either gonna love you or hate you … and if he loves you, are you prepared to bend enough to let him heal without you forcing your *fix-it* mentality on him?"

She smiled a sleepy smile and shook her head. "It's over between Phillip and me. What I've done is simply for a friend. Besides," she raised an eyebrow and peeked mischievously at him, "I'm having dinner with Inspector Morris tomorrow evening."

This definitely took him by surprise. "Wow. Business dinner?"

"He said we won't discuss a lick of business the whole night."

He nodded and scratched his head thoughtfully. "Kevin Morris." Now he mulled the name. "That's a horse of another color, kiddo. That boy just might have what it takes to keep a handle on you."

"I do *not* need to be *handled*! I'm not a circus animal!"

He stood and laughed. "Close to it." He started to walk to the door but turned back toward her. "I never would have pegged you being taken with someone like him." He nodded again. "You sure wouldn't have to treat him with kid gloves, that's for certain."

"Is that an approval?"

"No … just an observation. Like I said, I'm not a fan of men—especially where my daughter's concerned."

Kevin picked her up from the MacAllister house, and received both warm and cold stares from various family members. Meg assured them it was a *thank-you* dinner for all the work he had done for her, but suspicions were high. Her mother and Janet were unusually solemn and silent about it. She knew they both adored Phillip, and with him being back in Treasure Cove, they assumed there would be a rekindling. The prospect of another man took a bit of wind from their sails. For Meg, however, this was the first breeze she had felt in many years, and she found it quite refreshing.

He took her to a cozy Cajun restaurant, and she figured he must have researched that too—Cajun food was one of her favorites. There was nothing remotely Cajun near Treasure Cove, and she griped about it often. The atmosphere at the Bayou Lagoon was rather formal for Cajun, and the band was too advanced to be called the *Swamp Stompers*, but the food was marvelous.

"You really enjoy eating, don't you?" he asked her as she continued to sample various dishes from the buffet.

"If I talk too much during a meal, you'll know it's lousy," was her reply.

"This must be great food, then," he laughed.

"Hey, if you really want to talk, dinner with me isn't the way to go about it."

"I'll be patient—you can't eat all night." His eyes teased her with a wink.

After dinner, they did finally talk, and they laughed about various cases he'd had, or certain students she'd taught. They shared a few deeper things, like her senior year, and his rebellion toward his strict parents. She enjoyed watching his eyes light up with animation as he described his life, and she felt relaxed and relieved that there was probably nothing she could say to this man that would cause him to emotionally crash. He was stable, sure of himself, and extremely handsome without all the disguises. She even found his slightly long hair to be attractively unique. As he contorted his expression she couldn't help but laugh.

"You find me funny?" he asked with mock hurt.

"Adorably so." She blushed yet again. *She* was most definitely the one flirting now.

He stopped talking, and his expression changed. His eyes grew soft and his smile tender. "Come on, let's dance," he said as he stood up and reached for her hand.

"I can't dance," she said stunned. "I mean, I haven't danced in close to ten years."

"Then it's time you picked it up again. All you have to do is follow my lead—if you can let yourself. I won't tell anyone if you're not any good."

"I'm good at everything," she defended.

"Prove it," he said, still holding out his hand.

She took his hand and followed him to the dance floor. As they swayed with the music, she allowed herself to lean in on him, to relax, to let him lead. The smell of his cologne or soap, or perhaps just him, and the gentleness of his hands on her waist touched a longing deep inside that she had hidden for many years. She let her fingers softly caress the hair falling on his neck and hoped he couldn't tell what she was doing. Slowly she moved one hand down his shoulder to his upper arm. Strength. Unexpectedly, she realized that she felt very comfortable being held by this man.

"Just how old are you?" she asked as she pulled back a moment to see his face.

"Thirty-seven," he replied, brown eyes narrowing at her question. "Is that old enough to take care of you, Meg MacAllister?"

"I didn't know I needed to be take care of. I thought I was doing just fine."

He wrapped his arms tighter around her waist and pulled her in closer. He then whispered in her ear, "Then you have no idea what you've been missing."

Indeed. Perhaps it was time for her to rethink some things. She placed her hand on his neck again and gently threaded his silky hair through her fingers. *What am I doing?* He pulled her closer and she smiled as she laid her head on his shoulder. *Just dancing—that's all—just dancing, and it is glorious.*

Chapter Fourteen

Before returning to Florida, Meg had been drilled by her mother and Janet, still fans of Phillip. She thought back on a particular conversation as she prepared for school that Monday morning after Thanksgiving.

Meri had complained, "I don't know why you would come up here and start traipsing around with some strange man when there's a perfect one waiting for you in Treasure Cove."

"Because the one down there has made it clear, twice, in fact, that he wants no relationship with me."

Janet jumped in. "He's lying then."

"Really?" Meg had responded sarcastically. "You know this because you've talked with him recently? According to Phillip y'all haven't spoken in years."

"I know his heart. He was like a brother to me. Your breakup devastated him, and he was determined to give you all the time you needed to sort through your feelings."

"See," Meri said as though ten years hadn't passed and this was the most obvious conclusion. "He still loves you."

"Whether he loves or doesn't love me isn't the point. What he told me leaves no room for interpretation or open-endedness. He doesn't want a relationship with me—that's the bottom line."

"So you just turn up in Texas and start seeing some strange man that none of us have a clue about." It was hard to have a discussion with a mother convinced her daughter was on the wrong track.

"He's not strange, and Daddy knows him."

Her father glanced above his paper for the first time. "Don't bring me into this, baby girl. You're on your own with your mother when it comes to romantic affairs."

"This is not an *affair*!" Meg couldn't believe her family was so exasperating about this. "All I did was have dinner with the man!"

"And invite him over here for dinner tonight," Janet reminded her. "Seems to me you want the family to get to know him better."

"A decision I'm seriously reconsidering at the moment ... believe me."

🌴 🌴 🌴

She remained on an emotional high quite some time after returning to Treasure Cove. Between finding Phillip's mother and getting to know Kevin Morris better, even if only over the phone, it was hard to imagine life being much sweeter. Things were great at the home, and Carmen had done a total turnaround. Meg managed to grade all the midterm papers and tests before Christmas vacation started, and she had partied herself to oblivion with every Christmas event from school, church, and the children's home.

There was a serious matter hanging over her head, however. She had to tell Phillip about his mother. She had tried several times, but it always seemed to be wrong. Christmas vacation was quickly approaching, and she needed to do something. As weird as Phillip's mood swings were, she had no idea how he would respond. Would this throw him over the edge, or would it be the missing piece he had been searching for all his life? She needed some no-nonsense advice, and as much as she hated to, there was only one person she felt would be scathingly blunt enough to offer that.

"Ira, I've either done something wonderful, or something horrible, and I'm not sure which," she confessed to her nemesis. She couldn't believe she had come to his office to discuss it.

"This should be interesting," he replied. "Exactly what have you done, Meg?"

"I've found Phillip's birth mother."

He was silent at first as he processed the information. He breathed deeply, rubbed his scraggly black beard, stared out the window a bit, and then finally brought his gaze back toward Meg. "I take it he didn't commission the search?"

"No. In fact, it was when he said he didn't want to find her anymore that sort of prompted me to do it."

"I see," he pondered. "And what do *I* have to do with this thing *you've* done."

"His mother wants him to spend Christmas with her and her family. If he agrees, would you give him some time off to do that?"

"And if he disagrees?" Ira asked her.

"Then you may have my head on a platter, Ira," she said directly.

He laughed at her candidness. Standing up, he walked over and shook her hand. "I may still never agree with you," he said, "but I am afraid that I will always like the way you do business. How does ten days sound?"

"You'll give him ten days off for Christmas?" she asked in unbelief.

"Why not? We ran this station without him once, we can do it for a few days again."

This time she shook his hand. "I may not always agree with you, Ira, but

I'm afraid that I am beginning to think you're a decent person after all."

"Please don't let that get out," he winked. "I have a nasty reputation to uphold."

🌴 🌴 🌴

She took Phillip to a state park where they could picnic and relax for a few hours. Spiro played ball as long as they would throw it, and Phillip ate more chicken than she thought humanly possible. She, on the other hand, being a nervous wreck, hardly ate anything. After a few trails and a snack of homemade chocolate chip cookies, they sat down by the river and relaxed. Spiro immediately fell asleep, and she wished she could join him. Why was this so hard? Maybe it was because she knew this information had the power to destroy their relationship forever, a betrayal even deeper than when she had broken up with him years earlier. He had made it clear he didn't want to find his birth parents.

"Would you please tell me what's going on?" he broke in on her thoughts. "You've been quite the stranger since coming back from Houston, and suddenly today we're out frolicking in the warm Florida winter."

"A lot happened that week," she managed to say. "Quite a week."

"You want to tell me about it?"

"I suppose," she stalled. "I have a Christmas present for you."

"How nice," he said with a hint of scathing. "It took an outing for you to give it to me?"

"Oh, it's quite a humdinger."

"What on earth have you done, Meg?" He was almost indignant.

She shrugged as she realized there was no turning back now. The truth was about to be revealed.

"That's not fair," he said as he softened. Again, his emotions were like a roller coaster. "You should have told me we were exchanging gifts here. I've got you something too, but it's wrapped up at home. I even got something for Spiro."

At the mention of his name, the pup looked up, wondering if he would get a morsel of a cookie that he so desperately wanted but Meg had insisted he couldn't have.

"Well," she tried to explain, "this needs to be done on its own. Nothing competing with it."

They sat in silence a moment, Phillip staring expectantly, Meg biting her lip and twisting her fingers.

"Phillip," she finally broke the silence, "I've done something really, really ... uh ... *big* here." She looked over at him, now nauseous from nerves.

"What have you done exactly, Meg?" he asked cautiously.

"Oh, Phillip, I care about you so much. And this whole thing with you being rejected and everything, it was hard for me to sit still and just let you stew in it."

"What have you done, Meg?" he asked again, with a more serious look.

"Here." She handed him an envelope.

He opened it up to find a round trip ticket to Rapid City, South Dakota. "What on earth is this? You want me to spend my holidays at Mount Rushmore or something?"

"You're either going to love me, or you're going to never want to speak to me again."

"Would you get on with it!" he shouted. "What's going on?"

"I found your mother!" she finally blurted out, then said more tenderly, "I found your birth mother."

He stared at her in unbelief saying nothing, just shifting his eyes back and forth from the ticket to her.

"She's wonderful, Phillip. She has your eyes, or should I say, you have hers. She's a beautiful Christian lady, and you have two brothers and two sisters."

He still sat silently, but now looked out over the river. She continued to explain the whole story. She told of the closed doors, the medicating, the switching from place to place, and then revealed his father, Sen. George P. Evans, with the *P* standing for Phillip. He just sat there, motionless and silent. Finally she broke in.

"Say something!" she pleaded. "You hate me? You're thankful? You're disgusted? What, Phillip? Please say something."

"I guess I need to talk with Ira," he said.

"I already did—he's giving you ten days."

"Wow … it looks like you've thought of everything." He was still registering no emotion.

"Okay, so you're mad at me. That's fine," she resigned. "I suppose I deserve that. But please, give your mother a chance. She's so wonderful."

"You've met her?"

"Yes, after Thanksgiving I flew up there."

He finally stood up and walked over to lean against a tree. Cautiously she joined him.

"Do you hate me?" she asked, trying to read his eyes.

He put the ticket into his shirt pocket, put both of his hands on her face, and pulled himself unusually close.

"How could I hate you when I love you so much?" he asked just before he kissed her. She knew she should pull away, but she had longed for this too many times the past six months. Everything about it was familiar and right, but she wasn't free to kiss him now. How could she tell him she had given up and finally moved on? The longer he kissed her, the more confused she felt. This might seem right at this moment, but it wasn't.

"Phillip, stop!" she finally pulled away. "I can't deceive you about this."

"No, I'm sorry," he immediately apologized. "I ... I shouldn't have done that."

"You don't understand — I didn't mind! In fact, I've waited and I've wanted ... it's just ..."

"I shouldn't have done that. I was way out of line."

"No, it's not that," she tried to explain. "I'm ... well ..."

"You're what?" His face was pink from embarrassment.

"I'm seeing someone," she finally said with tears and much regret.

He stepped away from her quickly. "I didn't know," he said shaking his head gently. The hurt showed in his eyes.

"I never told you. I didn't know if I should. I didn't really know how you felt about me."

"Yes, you did, Meg. I told you I didn't want a relationship with you. I made it really clear how I felt—I just wasn't honest with you."

"Why didn't you tell me?" She threw her hands up in frustration. "Why did you tell me you didn't want anything more than friendship?"

"Because I didn't want to be rejected again. It was hard enough losing you once. I couldn't do it twice in a lifetime. I just got carried away in the moment. What you've done for me ... finding my mother ... I mean, that's more than anyone could ever ask. I'll always treasure that."

"Phillip, don't give up on me. Not yet. Let me work this out with ... with him. Let me see where things stand. I have to tell him about you, you know. To have these feelings for you, but be dating another man ..."

"No," he quickly interrupted her. "Work things out with him. I can't do this with you and try to process a relationship with a family I've never known I had. If you've got a chance with someone else, take it. He may be the one for you, Meg—the one I've always been afraid you'd find. And if he is, then you deserve him, because you are too wonderful for words ... and for me."

They said very little to each other the last few days before Christmas vacation. They were awkward as they passed at church, but remained cordial. She did ask if they could talk once, but he preferred they wait until after Christmas—he only wanted to work on one relationship at a time, and building the one with his mother was more significant at the moment. She understood and complied although she didn't want it to be like this. What was worse, she was going to Houston and would be with Kevin for two weeks, but was now unsure as to how to deal with him.

For nine years, I have nobody, Lord, she prayed as she prepared to leave for the airport on the morning of December twentieth. *Now, you bring two incredible men into my life at one time. If there's anyone out there who doesn't think You have a sense of humor, just send them this way. I'll help clear that right up.*

She had washed and scrubbed Spiro well for the trip so he wouldn't offend other passengers too badly. She found his travel cage and packed his favorite toys. She wondered how people with children ever managed to make a trip anywhere with everything intact. She thought of Susan, her sister-in-law, a wonderful mother—that was her total life. She even looked over the infidelities of Herbie just to keep the family together for the sake of her children.

I would probably be a horrible mother, Lord. I would never be as patient, or indulgent, or compassionate as Susan. In fact, if my husband ever looked at another woman, I'd hit him over the head so hard his eyes would probably never work again anyway.

Spiro barked in agreement.

"It's scary, Spiro, but I think you really do understand every word I say."

She checked in her luggage, and then went to find Phillip's gate. Her plane left about thirty minutes after his. She had deliberately planned this because she hoped to see him off to South Dakota whether he wanted her to or not. She saw him standing nervously outside a coffee shop nibbling a cinnamon roll. Stopping for a moment, she allowed herself time to take in the sight. He was going to see his mother for the first time. He looked so handsome in his starched jeans and red long-sleeved polo. She saw he had a colorful sweater in his hand to don when he reached the cold. He never saw her approach.

"Nervous?" she asked putting a hand on his shoulder.

He turned with a jump. "Am I ever."

Spiro immediately jumped up toward him, and Phillip welcomed the affection. He handed the roll to Meg and reached down for the little dog.

"I figured you might be. I hope you don't mind me seeing you off," she said, petting Spiro as he licked the glaze from Phillip's fingers.

"I've never flown before, you know," he told her. "This is like a double whammy for me. Seeing my mother and being subjected to unearthly altitudes both for the first time on the same day." He paused, then looked at her and said, "You should be coming with me for this."

"Now you tell me," she smiled. "I would have in a minute, but I didn't think you wanted me too."

"Well, as usual, you listened to my words exactly, but they weren't conveying what I really felt."

"And they say women don't speak frankly …"

"She's wonderful, just like you said she was," he said as he let Spiro down.

"You've spoken with her?"

"Just briefly — I needed to make arrangements about getting to the house."

"Are you renting a car?"

"No. She insisted on picking me up. She and my…" he paused, almost teary-eyed, "my step dad."

"I'm so happy for you," she said reaching up to caress his cheek.

"I owe this all to you," he said, taking her hand. "Thank-you for seeing past my stubbornness to what I really needed."

"I'm very familiar with stubbornness," she laughed.

"That you are."

The last call for his flight sounded.

"It's really not fair," he said as he picked up his carry-on bag. "You've got Spiro to fly with you."

"Call me in Houston," she told him as he walked toward the gate. "Please let me know how things are going."

"If you're lucky," he waved back.

She watched him disappear then went to the window to see his plane off. She prayed for him earnestly, that God would heal many wounds during this trip, and that Phillip Barton would finally have a sense of belonging to a family for the first time in his life.

"It's our turn, Spiro," she said, picking up the pet carrier and putting down the happy dog. They walked to her gate, she put Spiro into his cage, and then they boarded the plane. It was only ten forty-five in the morning, but she was already exhausted.

"I can't be overextended today," she told Spiro. "I haven't done anything."

Chapter Fifteen

As Meg walked through the hallway leading from her gate to the waiting area, the only face she noticed was Kevin Morris. The welcoming smile, mischievous brown eyes and strands of brown hair sticking out from behind his baseball cap reminded her why it had been so easy to forget Phillip during Thanksgiving break. He moved to her immediately and she put Spiro's carrier down. Reaching out to her, he hugged her tightly for several long seconds—it felt good to be held by him again. Her anxious pup's bark, however, broke up the reunion.

"So, you're the famous Spiro," he said, leaning down to introduce himself.

"He doesn't care for traveling by plane," she explained as she let him out and connected the leash.

Spiro cowered from the new man slightly, not comfortable with a stranger being so close to his Meg, but Kevin let the dog smell his hand and approach him when he was ready. He pulled out a piece of cheese from his coat pocket and offered it—that was all Spiro needed. They were friends for life.

"It's good to see you," he said as they moved toward the luggage area. "I was beginning to forget little things about you, but they're coming back now ... really fast."

"Oh, yeah? What kind of little things."

"Certain expressions ... the way you hold your head to the side when you're tired ... that one strand of hair that always falls down into your face ... your slender fingers, and your beautiful green eyes."

Good heavens—she was blushing again.

"I can go on if you like," he told her.

"That's enough," she said curtly. "Much more of that and I might start putting on airs."

🌴 🌴 🌴

At the MacAllister house, the decorations were more beautiful than Meg

114

remembered. Meri always saw to it that Christmas was celebrated in full form. Every window had a lighted wreath, and every room had its own decorated tree. The house smelled of cinnamon and pine, and something was always baking to be offered to the many guests who were invited over during the season. As Kevin walked in with the luggage, he stopped to breathe in the heavenly aroma.

"My goodness," he said as he closed his eyes. "Where am I? This is like I've stepped into Christmas itself."

Meri walked by and clapped in delight when she saw her daughter had arrived. She rushed to her and hugged her warmly. "It's so good to have you home, dear!"

"Good to be home, Mother. You remember Kevin?" She pointed a thumb toward him.

"Oh yes." She was polite and offered a gracious smile. After shaking his hand, she gave her attention to the small dog that was jumping endlessly around her feet. "Shall we go to the kitchen, Spiro, and see if Marguerite saved something wonderful for you?"

Kevin followed Meg upstairs with the luggage while Meri took Spiro to the kitchen for a snack.

"Unbelievable," he sighed as he glanced around the room. "Was this where you grew up? I mean, was this your own personal little palace of a room?"

She nodded. To her it was just home—secure, familiar, and comfortable. She imagined it must be awesome for a man who had been raised in dirt-floored houses in Central America.

"This was my own personal palace," she admitted.

He walked over to the piano, and picked out a few notes.

"Do you play?" she asked in surprise.

"Only *Heart and Soul*," he sighed as he turned back to her with a silly grin. "But," he continued, "it is my understanding that you are quite the accomplished musician. After seeing this in your room," he stroked the baby grand, "either that is true, or you were way overindulged as a child."

"I'll say it's probably a little bit of both," she smiled, suddenly realizing she was cocking her head to the side, just as he had said.

"Play something for me. Anything. Impress me again."

"Again?"

"You never cease to impress me, you know?"

She smiled and sat down on the bench. "Any requests?"

"Okay, for starters ..."

"Starters?" she exclaimed.

"Of course," he said motioning her to scoot over so he could sit beside her. "You have to show me the entire spectrum of your talent. For starters—play something really ... oh ... deep."

"Deep?"

"Yes, you interpret that anyway you like."

She thought a moment and then began the first movement of Beethoven's *Moonlight Sonata*. She knew he wasn't watching her fingers, but her face. She could feel her cheeks warm again, but didn't mind. She knew she was in her element, and she knew she was very good. She let herself get lost in the haunting melody as she played on.

"That was delicious, Marguerite," Herbert MacAllister said as the cook brought out a dessert. "How do you manage to come up with unique, delicious meals every single day?"

"You pay me too good," Marguerite teased, still having a thick accent after all these years. "I can't afford to cook you something nasty."

They all laughed, and Meri began to cut the pie and serve slices to each one.

"If I ate here often," Kevin said, taking his slice, "I would get huge."

"You are kind of small for a football player," Andrew commented.

Kevin raised his eyebrows in wonder. "Football? How did you know about my football aspirations?"

Herbert jumped in. "They all grilled her about you—she told 'em everything she knew."

Kevin narrowed his eyes toward Meg. "Everything?"

She shrugged. "I didn't know a whole lot—I just pulled out anything I could think of to make them stop."

Meg's family interacted with Kevin really well. Perhaps this was a sign. Andrew was fascinated with his line of work and spent a lot of time talking about the various aspects of investigating. Herbert knew he was a shrewd businessman who was worth his word in gold. Meri said very little, but she remained gracious throughout the meal. After supper, he settled easily onto the couch next to Meg to continue conversing with the family. Spiro jumped into his lap, always happy to find a new friend, and the banter continued.

"So," Meri finally asked, having held her tongue and curiosity at bay since meeting Kevin at Thanksgiving. "Would someone mind telling me how the two of you met?"

Meg told the story, and though everyone was initially interested in their budding relationship, the process of finding Phillip's birth mother changed everyone's focus. Tears formed in Meri's eyes as she imagined how wonderful this must be for him—a mother, a father, sisters and brothers. It would be like the biggest dream in his life coming true. Herbert then thanked Kevin for doing such a fine job, and wanted to know if there was any organization that gave awards to private eyes for exceptional work.

"I've been paid well, sir," he said. "And I don't need a trophy to tell me I've done a good thing. Just hearing your conversation, meeting his mother, and finding Meg, have been reward enough."

She blushed … again.

🌴 🌴 🌴

Craig and Janet came to Houston on the twenty-second, then Janet, Susan, Meg and Meri all went shopping the following day. Most of them, except for Meg, had finished their buying already, but they were indulgent as she dragged them from place to place trying to find the perfect gift.

"How old are your kids now, Susan," Meg inquired. "I mean, are we at the *clothes* stage yet, or are we still enjoying toys?"

"Hal is sixteen," Susan said.

"Any suggestions?"

"He loves his Auntie *M*," she smiled. "You could get him a bag of sticks and he would receive them proudly."

"Okay, next, although you're not being much help."

"Hannah is now fourteen, and loves to read. You take it from there, literature teacher."

"That should be easy then—I can fill that bill well." She made a few notes on her list and asked about the next child.

"Heather, ten, is still into Barbie and anything to do with her. Good luck, though, on finding something she doesn't already have."

"You better shop with me there. And next is little Heath. I need no help for him."

Heath was an eight-year-old bundle of joy and energy. Meg had bought his gift already last summer—a remote controlled model of the Mayflower. Heath loved ships and sailing. He had models hung all around his room of boats he had built himself. When she saw the Mayflower at a hobby shop, she purchased it immediately and hoped for strength to save it until Christmas.

The four ladies sat down for lunch at their favorite sandwich and salad place, a tradition they had come to look forward to. This was really the only time of the year they spent together alone anymore. Each year also brought new changes and directions for all of them, so catching up from a *woman's view* was always refreshing. Meri talked of her projects, Janet talked about moving up to teach second grade instead of first after all these years. Susan talked about the changes in her children. Then it was Meg's turn.

"So," Janet started in on her, "tell us all about this fling you're having with the mysterious P.I."

"It's about time you flung with someone," Susan added, eliciting embarrassing laughter which drew attention from other tables.

"Yes, Meg," Meri agreed. "Please shed some light on this, will you."

Meg knew she was blushing again.

"Oh my," Janet said softly. "It's more serious than we thought—she's actually turning red."

More womanly giggles.

"Okay, all of you," she wanted desperately to diffuse the direction this was heading. "It's not near as serious as you're trying to make it."

"Who said it was serious?" Susan piped in. "We're only calling it a fling."

"We would never get our hopes up," Janet agreed with her.

"Go on, Meg, and you girls stop teasing her," Meri said in mock reprimand.

"We met while he was working on Phillip's case for me."

"How romantic!" Janet breathed.

"I had no idea," Susan commented.

"You guys," Meg said, looking at them sternly. Both ladies put their fingers to their lips indicating they would hush from now on.

"We just took a liking to each other, and have been talking over the phone occasionally. There's really nothing more to elaborate on."

Janet and Susan stared at her, and then at each other, and then allowed big smiles to spread with no words following. Her mother, however, tried to appear unresponsive, but Meg knew she was still voting for Phillip. Janet's mind had apparently been swayed by the idea of new romance.

"You guys better mind your own business," Meg warned them. "Don't create something that's not there. Oh, look! Our delicious lunches are here!" she exclaimed, changing the subject quickly and speaking in high, silly tones. "I guess our talking is all over."

"At least yours is," Janet finally spoke. "You never talk when you eat, especially if the food is good."

"Yum," she said as the waitress placed her shrimp salad in front of her.

That evening, Meg walked Kevin to his green Jeep after supper and another leisurely visit with the family. She grabbed a sweatshirt on her way out and pulled it on as they stepped into the chilly December air.

"Meg," he said, stopping to look at her beneath a harvest moon. "I hope you haven't minded me horning in on your time with your family during the holidays."

"Mind? Are you kidding? This is the best Christmas I've had in years."

"I was wondering," he continued, "if I could steal you away for lunch tomorrow on Christmas Eve. I know you have a big get together tomorrow night, with extended family and all, but I wanted just a little time alone with you before the big day."

"You know you're invited tomorrow night."

"Really?" His eyes lit up.

"Of course. That ought to set up a family rumor mill for a few weeks—*Meg brought a date.*"

"I love the thought of being a source of gossip." His familiar mischievous look made her chuckle. "I'll be there for sure ... but I'd still like lunch ... alone ... if that's okay."

"I'd like that too." Ugh ... blushing again.

The next morning he picked her up and took her back to the same Cajun restaurant.

"You're not as creative with your eating as you are with your disguises," she noted as they read over the items on the buffet.

"When I find something that works, I stick with it. You loved this place last time."

She breathed in the Cajun aroma and smiled a nod of agreement.

He had become more predictable with his clothes, however, since his perceived need of pretending was no longer deemed necessary. She discovered he seemed to prefer comfortable jeans, worn sweatshirts, tennis shoes, and a Houston Astros baseball cap. For Christmas, she had bought him two new sweatshirts feeling that wouldn't be too personal, but simply a nice gift.

After ordering drinks, they discussed a few quirks he had picked up on from being around her family, and she filled him in on the strange characters he would meet tonight at the party. When they filled their first plates, Meg, as usual, ate in silence as he continued to converse. He ordered a special dessert for them to share, and then his expression became unusually serious.

"What are you thinking about?" she wondered as she shoved a piece of deliciousness into her mouth.

"How best to do this."

"Just stick your fork in and eat the best parts before I get to them."

"No, not that," he shook his head, still solemn. "How best to give you your Christmas gift."

She stopped eating. "Today? Christmas is in the morning. You promised you'd be there."

"I know, and I will, but I wanted to give you this while we were alone."

He reached into his pocket and pulled out a small gift, all wrapped up in glittery green paper with a shiny, red bow. She smiled.

"The wrapping is quite cute. Do it yourself?"

"One of my many talents," he said more nervous than humorous. Suddenly he addressed the issue. "Meg, I'm getting old."

She snickered.

"Don't laugh," he said quickly, "you are too."

She stopped, glanced over at him a moment, then took another bite.

"What I'm trying to say," he hesitated, "is that I've come to a place where when I see what I like and what works, I go after it."

"That's why you're good with your job," she noted as she took another mouthful.

"Yeah, I suppose that's true." He paused. "Open it."

"Okay." She took the small gift and tore into it. She had never been one to savor unwrapping. Her motto was to get to the good stuff as quickly as possible. The paper gone, she now held a small white box. She opened it to find a small green case inside.

"Is there actually a gift in here somewhere, or will I find yet another container when I open this?"

He just smiled and watched as she opened the small case. Her eyes grew wide at the contents.

"Kevin," she whispered. "It's beautiful." She removed the ring and examined it closely. It was a single, large diamond surrounded by two small emeralds on either side.

"The emeralds are for your eyes," he explained. "I've never seen anything like them."

She didn't take it from the case yet—still unsure about such an expensive gift so soon in the relationship. Her two sweatshirts seemed very inappropriate at the moment.

"This isn't just a ring, Meg," he said as he took her hand. "It's a *sort-of* engagement ring."

She now stared at him with an utter loss for words.

"Ah," he nodded. "Something other than food can shut you up. Before you say anything, I don't want you to answer right away. We work, Meg, we really do ... this thing we've got going on here. I've thought about nothing but you since Thanksgiving, and I'm not getting any younger. For that matter, neither are you."

She furrowed her brow — this was the second time he had referred to her age. She wasn't *that* old.

"Take all the time you need. If you're not ready to marry me, then this is just a friendship ring."

"Some friendship ring."

"If ... or when ... you decide to accept. Then, *poof!* It transforms immediately into a full-blown engagement ring."

She hesitated to put the ring on her finger, but finally gave in. It was a perfect fit and looked lovely on her slender hand. She wished she could be as certain as him, but she had to be honest.

"Kevin," she began, "you need to know that I'm sort of struggling with feelings for someone else right now, too. We aren't dating, and probably never will, but until I can figure out my heart where he's concerned, I can't commit to you … as tempting as it is."

"Phillip?"

"Yes," she admitted. "Call it unresolved or unrequited, or whatever, but I can't pretend the feelings aren't there, and I can't agree to marry you while I'm dealing with this. I mean, part of me is saying throw caution to the wind and say *yes* right now, forget Phillip, start a life, and get on with living."

"I like that part of you a lot," he smiled, although there was a hint of hurt in his eyes.

"But," she went on, "there's this other part that needs to be sure. And in reality, we don't know each other that well."

He said nothing, but took her hand and looked at the ring. He then stood up and pulled her up with him.

"Where are we going?" she asked.

"To the dance floor."

"But no one else is dancing," she protested.

"I need a good excuse to hold you right now."

As he held her while they swayed to the music, she was almost ready to just give in and accept. This was her first proposal ever, and this was an incredible man. Did she love him? Maybe. Love wasn't always enough. She had seen that with both Herbie and Mitch. As he held her tenderly, the image of Phillip began to fade again. Was she really that fickle, or was it possible to be in love with two men at the same time?

Lord, she prayed softly, *please give me wisdom.*

Chapter Sixteen

Meg turned her eyes toward the front door each time it opened. It wasn't like Kevin to be late. She felt silly worrying but couldn't help it. He had more or less proposed at lunch—*that is what he did, isn't t? Propose?* She glanced down at the ring as her Great Uncle Bob explained the results of his latest colonoscopy. The thought of a possible marriage to help remove her from extensive contact with Uncle Bob was appealing in itself. The door opened again. No Kevin—just a recently married cousin. *She's seven years younger than me,* Meg thought. *He was probably the first proposal she ever had. At what point in a relationship do you know someone well enough to determine marriage is the obvious next step?* Uncle Bob moved on to his heart cath. Finally, *finally,* Kevin arrived. She immediately excused herself from a detailed description of the uncle going off blood thinners for the procedure, and went to greet her guest.

He had dressed surprisingly appropriate for the occasion—khaki pants, a Christmas sweater, and no cap. Why it surprised her, she wasn't sure. She knew so little about him on one hand, yet felt as though she'd known him all her life on the other. She'd never seen him in a formal social setting and wondered how he would blend. At the moment he looked lost standing in the foyer and smiled when he finally spotted her coming from the large room toward him.

"You had me scared for a moment," he confessed as she took his hand. "I was afraid I was going to have to face all these people alone."

"I wouldn't wish that on my worst enemy," she assured him.

"I see you're wearing the ring," he whispered into her ear.

"Of course I am. It's quite beautiful—a Christmas present ... a friendship ring, sort-of."

"Good. It's very becoming." He held up a flat paper bag. "Later tonight, when we get a chance, you've got to steal away with me for just a few moments. I looked all over town for this."

"Is that why you were so late?"

"Why? Worried I might not show?"

"Yes—I didn't want to spend the entire evening engrossed in

colonoscopies."

He shot her the strangest expression. "Is that why you invited me?"

She introduced him to only the important relatives, the ones who actually cared, and definitely avoided Uncle Bob. After all the formalities and greetings, they migrated out to the pool house where some of the younger relatives had congregated. Janet and Craig were there, and that made for a more fun night. After a couple of hours of eating and laughing, Kevin asked if they could go to her room for a short while. She gave him a strange look, wondering if that were an appropriate request, but he assured her everything was above board and proper. Why should she doubt? He had proposed but not even kissed her yet. Whatever he wanted with her bedroom surely must be trustworthy. Once there, he took out the flat paper bag he had stuffed inside his sweater and handed it to her. She opened it to find a piece of sheet music.

"*I'll Be Home for Christmas?*" she read.

"Can you play this for me?"

"Of course. However, I notice there are words here. I can't sing at all, so don't expect me to do a double performance, okay?"

"No problem," he said as he sat down with her on the bench. "I'll sing."

"Do you sing?"

"Not worth a pig's paw," he winked, "but I can't play even worse. So, you play, and I'll sing."

She began, and he was right—he couldn't sing, at least not well. She figured she wasn't much worse, so she began to harmonize with him. They sang and laughed at certain parts they absolutely couldn't get right, and then sang it again.

"Should we take this downstairs and perform it for your family?" he asked after the third try.

"You're joking, I know, but they would love it and ask for more."

He chuckled lightly then took her hand, tracing the outline of the ring on her finger. "Thank you—I've always wanted to do that."

"Was singing a tradition for your family growing up?"

Now he laughed as he shook his head. "There's a thought. We didn't even celebrate Christmas in my family."

"Christian missionaries don't celebrate the birth of Christ?"

"I tried to tell you how ultra-fundamental they were. My sisters couldn't wear pants, no make-up for Mom, no eggs or bunnies at Easter, absolutely no mention of Halloween, but we did celebrate Thanksgiving."

"Well, I don't know that some of their ideas aren't all that bad. We have religious holidays but they've totally lost their meaning. Perhaps if we ditched some of the tradition, we might have a greater appreciation of the true purpose of the celebration."

"Yeah, you can tell it did wonders for me."

They were silent for a little while, so Meg began to gently play the song again.

"Did you know I've started going back to church?" he suddenly interjected.

She stopped abruptly and turned to him. "No. When? Where?"

"After Thanksgiving. I just felt like I needed to make good on my decision to follow Christ years ago. You got me thinking about making right choices for the wrong reasons. I was sincere when I became a Christian, but ... I don't know ... it's like I wanted Christ, but I didn't want my parents' religion along with Him."

This surprised her. She hadn't realized his growing up was quite that miserable. It was nice to know he was back in church, but that was an issue they would need to discuss if there were to be any future in their situation. Her life was built around her relationship with Christ. A marriage without Christ at the center of both partners would be impossible for her. She knew he was a Christian. He had been firm and convincing as he shared his conversion experience, but he had grown bitter at the hard rules to which he was made to conform.

She silently prayed, *Why do you keep bringing people into my life that hate the church? Is there a message I'm supposed to be getting or giving here, Lord?*

"So," she asked, "where've you been attending?"

"I called and told your dad that I needed to go to church. I asked him where he thought I should go. He said his church, of course, so I went."

"And ..."

"I like it," he smiled with a nod. "It's nice. It's big ... I actually like that 'cause I can sort of get lost there ... nobody breathing down my neck. I'm not ready to join my parents in mission work, yet, but at least I'm closer to building my own faith than I was this time last year."

"There you are!" said Janet, out of breath as she burst into the room. "Everyone's trying to find you. You left your phone in the pool house and it's been going off like crazy."

"Sorry," Meg apologized. "We were just singing Christmas songs."

"I'd love to have heard that," Janet said sarcastically.

"Hey—he doesn't sing any better than me!" Meg protested as she reached for her phone.

"Now I know why y'all are hiding out up here," Janet continued jeering.

Meg punched in her code to unlock the phone and checked her recent calls. Phillip. Her heart began to race. "Um ... I need to return this call. Janet, can you keep him company ... and away from Uncle Bob while I go to the study?"

"Hello?" Phillip answered

"Oh, my gosh! I'm so glad you called me! Sorry it took so long to call back … I had left my phone … doesn't matter. It's been killing me to know how your visit's going."

"Beyond description. I can't thank you enough, Meg. I have a family—I have a real family. And they are wonderful."

"Isn't your mom great?" She was so excited it was hard to contain herself.

"She's perfect. She's what I always dreamed a mom would be. And Thomas, my step-dad, he's the best. My brothers are these wonderful guys with humor and life just oozing out of them. My sisters are gracious and warm. I'm even an uncle!"

"Phillip, I'm so happy for you!"

"I've gone from being a nobody all my life, to being a son, a brother, an uncle, and even a brother-in-law. I am flying high, Meg," then he paused, "and I owe it all to you."

She sat back in the large, leather chair and pulled her knees up to her chest, listening to him talk about all the wonderful family traditions he had the privilege of experiencing. He told her every present he had bought for each person, and how they had already placed gifts beneath the tree for him even before he had arrived.

"I held a three week old baby, Meg. I've never held an infant in my life. I've bounced toddlers, and chased children, but I've never held a baby—I never could. I'd just look at them and wonder how a mother could ever let one go." He paused again then said, "She didn't know, Meg. She didn't give me up. She told me that she had to go along with the father until the birth, but that she had already decided to keep me after I was born. She was gonna tell the agency *no* and take her baby and go home. But she thought I was dead."

"Phillip, I can't tell you how much it means to me knowing that you have a family."

"Enough of me. How's your vacation gone so far?"

"Pretty good, although we're having the annual MacAllister Christmas party right now."

"Oooo, I've heard way too much about those reunions. I pity you."

"Thanks. Remember me tonight as you bask in the glow of the fire in your snug log cabin."

"Meg!" he blurted out. "It snowed today! We're gonna have a white Christmas! My first snow ever and it's at Christmas!"

"I'm jealous now. You can stop anytime."

Suddenly there was silence as the excitement faded and he asked, "Have you seen him?"

"Yes," was all she could say. She knew he was referring to Kevin.

"Are things going well with you … and him?"

She paused. This wasn't something she wanted to discuss with him.

"Yes."

"Now, I'm jealous," he teased.

They were both silent a few moments, then he said, "Well, don't forget about me altogether during the holidays. Okay?"

"How can I? You still haven't given me and Spiro our presents."

"If you're a good girl, maybe Santa will have something special for you back in old, hot, Florida."

"Merry Christmas, Phillip."

"Merry Christmas to you, Meg … and thank you again."

"You're welcome. See you in a few days."

Christmas morning was wonderful as usual. All the children and grandchildren of Meri and Herbert MacAllister had gathered in the family room, the only truly informal room in the house, with a fire going and Christmas music playing softly in the background. There was much laughter and levity with the opening of presents and passing around of pastries. Meri and Meg kept everyone's coffee cups filled, and all the ladies were looking forward to making Christmas dinner. Mitch had brought Michael over to spend the night on Christmas Eve, and he was awed by the whole event. Mitch seemed to sulk, but he still couldn't help but enjoy his gifts. Susan's children were gracious and pleasant, and Janet and Craig were in much better moods than the year before.

Kevin was supposed to come, but he had told Meg it wouldn't be until around noon. He had so enjoyed spending time with her family, but it was her family, and she should have the privilege of spending Christmas morning alone with them. She insisted he should come early, but he refused. As the gift giving ended, the ladies made their way to the kitchen to begin the preparations, while the men cleaned up the incredible amount of trash and boxes and junk that had been dropped around the room. Meri, of course, prepared the turkey, while Susan made her special dressing. Janet and Meg worked on everything else—vegetables, a casserole, various salads. Marguerite had already baked some desserts, insisting that she must contribute to the family meal or take the chance of being fired with all the rest of them cooking so well in her absence.

The doorbell finally rang. Meg immediately excused herself amid jeers from the kitchen crew, wiping her hands on her apron as she approached the foyer and opened the door.

"Merry Christmas," said Kevin, handsome as ever with a red sweater, black jeans, and a Santa hat.

"A mutant elf," she said shaking her head.

He came in and glanced around the room carefully.

"What are you looking for?" she asked.

"All these decorations and no mistletoe," he commented as he handed her a carton of eggnog. "Makes one think you come from a staunch, unaffectionate family."

"Well, if the shoe fits ..." she let her voice trail off. Her family was definitely on the unaffectionate side.

"Love the apron."

"I suppose you have several for when you need to pose as cooks, housewives, etc."

"Ha, ha," he mocked. "You go finish your duties. I'll follow the laughter and join whomever I find there."

🌴 🌴 🌴

After a delicious dinner, everyone relaxed. Meg gave Kevin his shirts, and he immediately put one on. The kids wanted to go to the pool house and swim, so Meg, Kevin, Janet and Craig agreed to watch them. Even though Meg was having a wonderful time, her thoughts kept drifting to Phillip. What was Christmas like for him this year? What was he doing right now? Was he holding the baby again? Was he stoking the fire in the log cabin? Was he enjoying a Christmas gift that someone in his family had given him?

"You're far away," Kevin told her as Janet and Craig went to give towels to the kids.

"Yes, I am. I'm sorry."

"No problem. Love the ring you're wearing, by the way."

She smiled and looked at her hand. "This has caused way too much speculation among my family, you know?"

"Good," he grinned, brown eyes dancing with pride. "I like to be the cause of speculation. I just hope one day the speculation will be gone, and we'll have something more permanent to talk about."

🌴 🌴 🌴

The visit in Houston had been wonderful, but Meg was anxious to get back to Treasure Cove, and Spiro was anxious to get off the plane. As soon as they made it into the waiting area, she leaned down to unlatch his cage and let him out. He took off instantly.

"Spiro, no!" she yelled, immediately jumping up to run after him. As soon as she popped up, however, she bumped into someone. She rushed to apologize, only to hear laughter and spot Spiro in Phillip's arms.

"In a rush?" he asked. "I understand the holidays can do that to people."

He looked so good and refreshed. His cheeks were red from windburn, but his eyes were glowing like never before. He held out his open arm to her, and she responded with a warm hug. He put down Spiro, attached the leash, and walked with Meg to baggage claim. He asked about her vacation, and she asked about his. They made small talk and then made their way to the Porsche.

"Come by my place before you go home," he said. "I never gave you your presents."

"Don't think I've forgotten about that either," she said, opening her trunk.

"So, you'll come by?"

"Well, seeing that you actually greeted me at the airport, I suppose I could oblige."

"This," Phillip said handing her a beautifully wrapped package, "is for you. And this," he said handing a smaller package to Spiro, "is for you."

"Who goes first?"

"Spiro, of course," he said, unaware how his gentle smile unnerved her. She unwrapped the package to reveal a brand new ball. He sniffed of it, sat and stared at it with his head cocking back and forth to each side, then growled at it. Finally Phillip picked it up and threw it into the kitchen, at which the dog tore out after it.

"One satisfied customer," he said then turned to Meg. "Your turn."

She opened the package but took her time with this one. Once the paper was off, she carefully un-taped the nondescript box. Looking in, she was overwhelmed at the contents. First she removed the two porcelain busts, one of Beethoven and one of Chopin. Then she pulled out a collection of CD's of the two composers. They were encased in a golden container with ivy leaves painted around the sides. She looked up at him and smiled.

"You remember way more than you want to let on," she told him. He just shrugged his shoulders. "Beethoven and Chopin, my favorites. How did you find this?"

"Well, when you're Christmas list is only two, and one of them is a dog, it makes shopping a little easier."

"I take it your list won't ever be a mere two again."

He shook his head and grinned. "Never again. Let me show you what I got."

He began with trivial stuff.

"Every year, they give the kids the same things that they open at the same time." He pulled out three pairs of tube socks, a package of chocolate covered cherries, and a carton of Whoppers from a large box. "We had to open them at the same time. Everyone acted so surprised and shocked. Of course, I was surprised, then I was let in on the joke."

Next he pulled out a thick jacket. "This was from Mom and Dad. They assumed that living here in Florida I wouldn't have a good coat while up there. They were right. So, each winter when I go visit, I'll have a coat.

"This is one of my favorites." He held up a photo album. "Mary Ann, she's my 16 year old sister, is really into fancy photo albums. She made copies of pictures of all of them over the years and created a history of the Anderson clan." He excitedly flipped through pages for a while and proudly showed Meg his family. He described each one in detail and told of their interests and pursuits.

He showed her the rest of his gifts and explained what happened as he opened them, and in turn told what he had given each in his family.

"But this," he told her as he handed her a large envelope, "is by far the best."

She opened it up and began to read the contract. Her eyes grew wide as she looked over the papers. "These are adoption papers," she said astonished. He smiled and nodded. "They adopted you?" He smiled and nodded again. "You're no longer Phillip Barton?" He shook his head this time. "Phillip Anderson ..." she said softly, letting the name move around in her thoughts for a moment.

"Phillip James Anderson," he said proudly.

Meg reached over and hugged him tightly. This truly was a new man, and the new name fit the occasion. She would have a hard time remembering it for a while, but she knew it would grow on her.

"I'm so happy for you, Phillip."

"I owe it all to you, you know?" he said, keeping his arm behind her on the couch. "I was so miserable and stubborn about the whole thing, refusing to even think about trying to find them anymore. Then you go and sneak behind my back, even after I was flat out ugly to you, and you do this thing for me. How can I ever pay you back?"

"You can't," she said standing up. "You can't ever pay me back. For the rest of your life you will owe me ... big ... and I will never let you forget it."

He helped her put her gifts back into the box and rounded up Spiro who was begging to go out onto the beach and play ball. She loaded even more into her car, and prepared to leave.

"You do know about the big New Year's Eve celebration at the church tomorrow night?" he asked her.

"Yeah—not my favorite holiday. It's always such a letdown after Christmas."

"But, you will be there," he wanted to know.

"Of course," Meg said, starting the Porsche. "If you can't beat 'em, join 'em."

Chapter Seventeen

New Year's Eve was turning out to be wonderful. Meg had the chance to reacquaint with everyone and hear about various Christmas gifts kids had received at the home. She played several games too silly for a woman her age, but even the pastor and his wife were participating, and after all, this was a celebration. Phillip wore a Minnesota Vikings football jersey he had received for Christmas with the name *Anderson* written on the back. He took great pleasure in explaining to anyone who asked exactly who *Anderson* was now.

They had a small concert with various people singing or performing some kind of act or another. Phillip sat next to her, leaned over close, and whispered into her ear.

"Nice ring," he noted.

She blushed. She assumed he had never noticed. "Thanks," she replied calmly.

"Christmas gift?"

"Uh huh."

"From ... uh ... parents?" he wanted to know.

"No."

"Brother?"

"No."

"Sister-in-law?"

"No."

"Nieces or nephews?"

"No."

He stopped asking. "I thought so," he nodded knowingly. "Any significance attached to it?"

"No," she told him a half truth. At this point, it had no significance. She smiled at the remembrance of Kevin telling her *poof* and then it would become an engagement ring.

"Wow." He raised his eyebrows. "Some ring for no significance."

"Would you like to go outside to talk, or can I listen to the rest of the program in peace?"

He held up his hands in innocence. "My lips are zipped." He lied. About a minute later, he asked her, "Is he loaded?"

"Phillip! Be quiet!"

He promised to stop again. Another lie. "Is he good-looking?"

"I'm going to move somewhere else if you don't stop," she warned.

"Well? Is he good-looking or not?"

"Phillip!"

Several turned around to stare. She pointed at Phillip, and he shrugged and said, "It wasn't my voice that yelled out." They turned back around.

"You're going to get me into trouble," she said sternly.

"Me? I am *not* a trouble maker at all—that's your area of expertise." He grinned.

"Yes, I know. I'm a 29-year-old Old Maid school marm who is still getting stared down by grown-ups. It's not comforting."

"So … is he good-looking?"

She just glared at him. He hushed at last.

The program ended with a silly skit designed to take them to the final countdown. As the actors began to count, everyone jumped to their feet and started counting down with them.

"Ten! Nine! Eight! Seven! Six! Five! Four! Three! Two! One! Happy New Year!"

A recording of Auld Lang Syne began to play, and couples began to wish each other a happy New Year with the traditional kiss.

"I love New Year's parties, don't you?" he said grinning at her.

"Whatever," she mumbled, and started to head to the concession area for something else to eat. But Phillip pulled her back and kissed her right in the middle of the gym in front of the entire church, although thankfully, not the entire church was watching.

The new year was proving to be more hectic than any prior, and the added stress of trying to figure out her sudden love life wasn't helping. As she sat on the back deck cradling her morning coffee, she considered how ridiculous all this was. Up to this point in time men had never mattered. She had always been so busy that she told the Lord if marriage was in her future, He would have to bring the man around and make it clear to her. Her life was full, busy … and yes … overextended. Right now her head was spinning with all she had to do, but ever at the front of her mind was the dilemma of Kevin and Phillip.

Lord, I don't even want to dwell on this! I've got too much to do to just sit around and contemplate men.

She took a quick swallow to empty her mug and glanced at the time on her phone. "Holy moly! I'm gonna be late! Spiro! Let's get you tied up now!" *See, Lord, I can't keep doing this!* After she attached Spiro beneath the deck, she scrambled up the stairs and grabbed her satchel. *No more*, she determined. *I'm tired of thinking about men. I'm not doing it anymore. I've got too much on my plate already to get over occupied with all this mess. Enough with it—I'm done!*

She tackled the duties of her life with full force. There were weekly papers to grade for each junior composition class, tennis was starting up again and she coached the high school girls' team, fundraisers were in the planning for the children's home, and then there was the myriad of questions she had to field concerning her new ring and the kiss at New Year's. Meg plopped onto the couch after school one Friday, ready to take a leave of absence from everything. Papers were piled on the floor, her tennis bag near them, Spiro was barking from the back wanting to be let in, and she had a meeting at seven o'clock with the board at the home to discuss the final preparations for Saturday's fundraiser. She had just about decided to sleep the rest of the afternoon away when the doorbell rang.

"What now?" she grumbled as she slowly got off the couch, hearing Spiro barking profusely at the fact that he was not there to guard her from whoever was at the door. The bell rang again.

"I'm coming!" she yelled, Spiro getting crazier. "Spiro! It's okay! Settle down!" He probably couldn't hear her.

She tucked her hair behind her ears and opened the door. What she found shocked her so intensely that she literally felt her knees buckle.

"Alan," she whispered, both in disgust and surprise.

"Hello, Meg," he said smiling. "I need to talk with you."

She couldn't believe Alan Parsons, the guy who had ruined her life over ten years ago, was standing at her door, her paradise, and somehow invading her life again.

"I don't know how you found me, in fact, I don't know how you managed to get through the gate out there. I don't want to talk to you. Please leave." She tried to close the door, but he gently pleaded with her to stop.

"Just hear me out. Please?"

"This is not the day, Alan," she said, still shaking from the shock. "It's already been horrible, and it's not over yet. In fact, my weekend is going to be unbearably long. I don't honestly think I can handle you right now on top of all that's already happening."

He looked away extremely dejected, nodded in understanding, put his hands in his pockets and turned to go. He turned around briefly to say,

"Just please let me talk to you sometime." Then he started walking away. She knew she should probably stop him, but she had no desire. Spiro was going full blast at this point, and she needed to grade papers, and she had to get ready for tonight's meeting.

"Wait!" she called after him. "I don't know what you're doing here, and I don't know what you want. It's not money is it?"

He turned around, hands still in his pockets, and shook his head. "I want your forgiveness."

She was shocked again. He wanted her forgiveness? She had forgiven him, or so she thought, years ago. But to actually have to absolve him of everything face to face made her realize perhaps she never really had.

"Next week" she finally said. "We'll meet sometime next week. How can I get in touch with you?"

He smiled. "At church."

🌴 🌴 🌴

After the meeting that night, Meg found herself knocking on Phillip's door. She didn't want to tell him about Alan, who had totally monopolized her thoughts for the rest of the day, *as if I didn't already have enough to think about with men*, but she desperately wanted to be with a real friend for a while. She was already burdened under the load of everything she had to get done, but now she felt she would explode emotionally if she didn't find a release.

"Hey!" he said opening the door. "What a pleasant surprise!"

"Hello." She forced a smile. "Can you cheer up a miserable soul for a few moments?"

"I'd love to." He welcomed her in and closed the door. They sat in the living room as the breeze from the beach blew through the open doors to the deck.

"What seems to be the problem?" he asked her.

"I think I'm overextended."

He burst out laughing. "You're just realizing this?"

"I guess so," she told him, nearly in tears. "Maybe that's not it, though. I've always been this busy—it's just getting to me this year, I guess."

"You're not as young as you used to be, you know?"

She glared at him. Kevin had told her the same thing last month.

"Well, you're not!" he emphasized.

"Okay, I'll buy a wheelchair then, and start drinking *Ensure!*" she burst in anger as she jumped up.

"Hold on," he said soothingly as he followed her onto the deck. "I wasn't trying to be mean—just trying to lighten your mood. You're very dark tonight."

133

"That's why I'm here. I don't like being dark, and I can't seem to break out of it."

They stood on the edge of the balcony, Meg leaning with both hands on the rail facing the water, and Phillip with his back on the rail watching her. She glanced over at those blue eyes and saw them filled with compassion and concern. That was all it took—her defenses melted and she began to cry. He immediately took her in his arms and just let her sob. Neither said a word. When she felt she was through, she pulled away, wiped her eyes, mascara running everywhere, and tried to regain some composure.

"Do you want to tell me what that was all about?" he ventured.

"I wish I could. If I understood it all, I probably wouldn't be feeling this way."

"You want to take a stab at it? Try to just talk it out. Start putting your feelings into words, and maybe it'll begin to make some sense."

"I'm frustrated," she began, though not really knowing how to start. "I have so much to do, but I am so sidetracked by this whole … this bit of … well …"

"What? Just say it."

"You and Kevin!" she finally blurted out.

He nodded in acknowledgement. "So that's his name."

"See," she said, showing her frustration. "I need to be able to talk about this with my best friend. I need to say, *Hey! I think I'm in love with two men at the same time! What in the blazes do I do?* But I can't! Because one of them *is* my best friend!"

She glanced up at him—he wasn't smiling.

"You're my best friend, Phillip. How do I tell you that I care for Kevin and that he's wonderful, and older, and secure and settled in his life … that he makes me feel taken care of and is ready to settle down with me and make a permanent life together … that he laughs at all my jokes, thinks I'm the greatest musician in the world, and sits with me at the piano and laughs as we sing out of tune together."

"Just like that," he said to her. "You just sort of blurt it out in a moment of emotion." He paused and then released his hallmark smile. "Do I get equal billing, except for the part about singing off key?"

She smiled and reached for his hand as she softly said, "And you make me laugh—you make me enjoy life. You make me take notice of everything that's good and wonderful. You make me want to take care of you."

He nodded as he thought on what she had said. "Two very different feelings," he deduced.

"Two very different men."

"But only one incredible woman who has captivated them both. Do you want my advice?" he chuckled.

She smiled. In the midst of life-changing competition he could still remain winsome. "Sure, give me some advice, as a friend, of course."

"Of course," he mocked. "Decide which one you want to build a life with. Of course, one hasn't proposed."

She looked away. "I know. That's what makes it even harder. Do I take the best offer I've had yet, or do I hold out for something better?"

"Hmm, that's a tough spot you've been put in, isn't it?"

"So, do I deserve my frustration?"

"Do you ever!"

"You're not making this any easier," she pouted.

"I sort of excel at that, don't I?"

She breathed out a long, exasperated sigh. "Do you ever ..."

"Carole wants me to come live with her again—permanently this time," Carmen divulged after school on Monday.

"Oh, great," Meg blurt out sarcastically without thinking. "I mean ... well ... I don't mean that's bad, I was just thinking that ..."

"It's okay, Miss Mac—it is bad. I don't want to go back anymore. She seems to think that since Chad is out of the way, we can sort of make up and go on with life as normal."

Meg nodded, knowing it was impossible, but she had learned that no matter how some children had been used and abused, most of them still adored their parents and wanted that dream of a normal life.

"You know, and I know, that it's stupid for her to say that. Right?" the girl asked.

"Carmen, I don't know your mother. All I know is what you've told me about her, which is pretty rotten. Do you think there'll be a difference this time?"

She gave a sardonic laugh. "Right. Just like last time, and time before, and time before, and time before, and time before ..."

Meg believed she would have kept going had she not stopped her. "I get the point. I'll talk with Mr. Roberts and see what I can do. I can't make any promises though. You understand that this is a legal matter, don't you?"

She nodded.

"You understand that the authorities make the rules and we have to abide by them?"

She nodded again.

"Okay then, I'll do everything I can, but without your testimony of what happened last summer, they'll probably send you back to her."

"I just can't tell anybody else." She looked defeated and beaten down. "I'm sick of having this stigma attached to me everywhere I go. I just want to be ... well ... good, I guess."

"That is a legitimate and worthy goal, Carmen—good. There's nothing wrong with wanting to be good and to live a good life. I promise I'll do my best."

"Thanks."

Chapter Eighteen

Meg finished tennis practice and set out to the park to meet with Alan. After talking with Carmen, her anxiety about seeing this dreadful man again had faded somewhat. No matter how hard things may seem at times, there were always those who had it worse. Alan had been at church yesterday, just as he said. She only spoke with him briefly about a place and time to meet then abruptly left him alone. She almost had a twinge of guilt over being so rude, but a few choice memories flushed the guilt right down the drain. She saw him sitting beneath the tree where she and Phillip often picnicked. She would most definitely not talk to him there.

"Let's sit over here," she motioned to him as she found a bench.

"I liked the tree better—it's so peaceful," he told her.

"I like the tree better, too, but I have really nice memories of that tree, and I'd rather not have you louse them up for me."

"I deserve that—I know I do."

"Okay, let's get on with it. I've had a really long day." She wasn't even going to attempt civility.

"Fair," he replied. "If you don't mind, just let me talk through all this, telling you my story. It's hard. Then you can yell or hit or do whatever you want when I'm through."

"Whatever," she said smugly. "Just make it quick, please."

"I'll try. The summer after we met, when you graduated, I had to quit college—no money."

"Drugs will do that to your pocketbook."

"Yeah, well, I was in pretty bad shape. I did all these pitiful odd jobs for a couple of years, thinking I would eventually get back in school, get my degree, and get a life. But I never could. I'd save my money, then go on a binge, lose my job, my place—I mean it was really bad.

"Then I started painting houses for this guy named Bill Bennett. He was a great boss—lots of fun, real good to his employees. He was big time religious, though, which grated on me. He was always praising God here, praising God there, praying for us on the job, even praying for the people we were painting for, saying that God had let our paths cross for some reason. Despite his over-zealousness about God, I liked him. He was a good man, and he rewarded you for hard work."

Meg smiled to herself because she knew how Alan had hated religion. She would have loved to have watched him squirm working for this man.

"All this time I'd been driving a motorcycle. I finally saved up enough to put a down payment on a car. I was so glad to finally have a car, my first ever, and I was twenty-three. One week to the day after I got it, someone stole it. I didn't have insurance or anything, so the whole thing was lost. I was so mad that I skipped work. I wasn't as stupid as I used to be, so I did go back the next day. Bill asked me what the problem was, and I told him. He then proceeded to tell me that God must be working somehow.

"Well, I exploded. How dare he try to turn my tragedy into one of his praise sessions! His response was for me to go to church with him that Wednesday night. I was like, *No way, man.* But he made me a promise. He said, *Alan, if you go tonight, and God doesn't do something profound for you, I'll leave you alone about Him for as long as we work together.* I made him a promise, and then I went.

"So, we're at church, and Bill stands up and begins to tell everyone who I am, the guy they've all been praying for. I'm sinking in my seat, ready to die. He then tells then about my car being stolen, and how I needed something big from God that night, and he wasn't just talking prayers, he said. So, the pastor tells everyone to bow their heads, and he starts praying for me."

Meg was about to burst. She could just imagine the whole scene, and of all people for it to happen to.

"The pastor says, *Amen,* and so do about twenty other people—scared me to death. Then this one guy stands up and comes over to me. I'm thinking they're gonna start doing weird stuff and I'm getting ready to bolt, but he holds out his hand with a hundred dollar bill in it and says to take it. I look at Bill, and he just nods. So I took it. Then a little old lady comes up and hands me a twenty. Then people just start getting in line to hand me money. I left that night with three thousand dollars. That's more than I'd spent on the car I had. As I'm leaving, this guy comes up and says he owns a used car lot. If I come by tomorrow, he'll set me up in something at cost."

He sat back for a moment and shook his head—then he laughed. "What else could I do?" She shook her head. "I bought a nice car, kept working with Bill, kept going to church, and got saved three weeks later."

"I don't believe it," she said, still not putting it past him to have made the whole thing up.

"I wanted to tell you first. You were the first person who came to mind. You'd been really faithful to church and all before I stepped in and messed up your thinking. I owed you an apology. That's when I found out you'd moved to Treasure Cove. I figured to leave you alone would be best."

"Smart choice. So why in heaven's name are you here?"

"Well, I worked for Bill up until last summer. Our church took a mission trip to the Bahamas. Bill paid my way to go. He's so great—such a man of God. I fell in love with the islands. Bill told me stay and keep doing mission work. So I got a job at a new Mason Mon beach shop that was just opening."

"John Mason," she whispered, remembering him telling her he had hired someone from Houston.

"Yeah! John. Nice guy too, but a bit hard on the ears."

She smiled, but wouldn't give up to laughter. She was still suspicious. "So, how did you end up here?"

"God is calling me to minister, Meg. I've been doing a lot of preaching and teaching down there. I started praying about God giving me some direction, and making it clear … and He did."

She'd been praying the same thing lately and nodded in understanding.

"Then John Mason comes up to me after I got to preach in church one Sunday night, and he says, *Dude, you need to be preaching.* I told him I was thinking about it. He told me to stop thinking and start preparing. He knew a college in Treasure Cove that was great, and that he'd pay my tuition if I'd go."

She stared in unbelief.

"So, here I am," he smiled.

She stood for a moment. This was too much to take in. Knowing he was saved, that was tolerable, almost believable. Hearing about the mission work, that was harder, but she could swallow it. But to find he was here, in her town, at her college, preparing for the ministry was just too much.

"You're lying," she finally said.

"I'm not, Meg. That's why I'm talking to you now. Can you see why I need your forgiveness? Do you understand why I needed to talk to you?"

"Why here?" she asked angrily. "Why not somewhere down the road, or upstate? Why Treasure Cove?"

"I have no money. I don't even have a car. There's my bike over there."

She assumed he meant motorcycle, but indeed it was just a bicycle.

"How did you get to my house?" she wanted to know. "How'd you get through the gate?"

"I parked my bike and climbed over."

"Oh great! The neighbors will love that!" she fumed. "I don't want you here, Alan. This is my place, my part of the world, my haven. I want you to leave."

He sat quietly for a moment—brown eyes sad, hands rubbing his trimmed beard, and his dark hair barely moving in the breeze. She knew she was destroying every hope he had in life right now. She didn't care. He had destroyed her life once too. Her feelings were valid.

He stood up, nodded his head, and placed his hands in his pockets. "Okay," he agreed. "You're right. I don't deserve this, and I know I don't deserve your forgiveness either. But thanks for at least hearing me out."

He walked toward his bicycle, and she could tell he was wiping tears from his eyes. She had just destroyed possibly his only chance at a decent life. He may have destroyed her once too, but she had a family and plenty of money to pick her back up. She had gotten a Porsche for all her destruction. He was riding a bicycle in his early thirties.

"Alan," she called as she ran after him. He wouldn't turn to her. "I'm sorry. That was a lot to ask from me in one meeting."

He still didn't turn to her. He merely nodded.

"I do forgive you," she finally said. "That's hard for me. You know that, don't you?"

Still he only nodded. She made him turn around. His eyes were already red and swollen. If she had wanted to break him, she had succeeded. He tried not to look at her, but she forced him to make eye contact.

"Look at me, please," she said. "I have to tell you this eye to eye."

He looked, but his expression was pitiful. He was worse than an abused, whipped dog, she thought.

"You ruined me, you know?" she told him. "I met a great guy years ago, but I couldn't marry him. Do you know why?"

He shook his head, tears welling up in all corners.

"Because I wasn't pure," she said, remembering the real reason she had broken up with Phillip. Tears began to form in her eyes. "He was going to be a minister, and I just couldn't face him at an altar of marriage and defile him. How could I tell the teenagers he would work with to wait when I didn't? How could I be this scarlet letter in his life?"

He cried again, almost sobbing, as if he was bearing all her guilt and shame. She felt horrible, not so much for him, but for the reason that her impurity was still a factor. Although it had been eleven years since she had been with Alan, and there had never been anyone else, that didn't erase the fact that she wasn't a virgin. She was still in the same boat as before. Suddenly, her choice in a husband was clear.

"Alan," she finally said. "Look, go to school, go to my church, do what you need to do. It's okay. Be a minister. Work hard. I forgive you."

"Thank you," he managed. "I would hug you, but I would never dream of touching you again. I'm very, very sorry."

"It's okay. I've done well for myself in spite of you. God wiped your slate clean, and so will I."

She started to leave when he called out her name. She turned around.

"I know this sounds petty," he called, "but God wiped your slate clean too."

She nodded and headed back to her Porsche. *No, He didn't*, she said to herself. *All things can be forgiven, but they can't all be undone.*

🌴 🌴 🌴

Meg enjoyed Sunday night services at church the most. They were usually informal, with plenty of opportunities for members to share. They sang choruses as well as hymns, and had other instruments besides just organ and piano playing. Tonight, so many shared that the pastor didn't even preach. As the time for the service neared the end, John Mason, who spent about half of his year in Treasure Cove and the other half in the Bahamas, felt compelled to introduce Alan to the church and explain his situation. He gave all the details, just as Alan had told Meg, only with a few *dudes* and *unreals* thrown in. He also told the church that Alan was a friend of Meg's from Houston. Several people who knew Meg well immediately looked at her with raised eyebrows as if to ask, *Is he the one?* They knew the name *Alan* well. She wouldn't respond, but when she happened to catch Phillip's glance, she nearly broke. He was obviously upset, and he must have known from her reaction that this was indeed *the Alan.*

She thought the service couldn't get any worse, and would have left had she not needed to play something peppy after the dismissal. The pastor stood and said David Dewey had something to share before they dismissed. David made his way to the platform. As she looked at Cindy for some indication of what might be happening, she saw her crying. *Oh no.* What was this all about?

"I love this church," he began. "I can't imagine ever having a life anywhere else. You folks took Cindy and myself in fourteen years ago and loved us more than I ever thought a church could. You have supported my ministry here with your single adults whole-heartedly. You have embraced my children and helped us raise them to love and honor God."

He paused, looked at Cindy then returned to his written speech.

"Because of all that, it is extremely difficult for me to say the following. Tonight, I am turning in my resignation as Minister to Single Adults here at Treasure Cove Community Church. I will be leaving in two weeks for Mississippi where I'll be serving as pastor of a new church that has just recently been started. Cindy and I thank you all for your love, and we covet your prayers as we journey into this new venture with God."

There were gasps and sighs across the sanctuary. Several had already begun crying.

Meg was floored. Other than Phillip, these were her best friends. How could she get through this whole ordeal with Alan being here if Cindy weren't two miles away? And what about Phillip? She glanced over at him, his face and eyes red, and knew she would need to speak with him tonight.

How do I play something peppy after that? Perhaps a funeral dirge is more in order.

After the service, she was again suffering from extreme frustration as she had several things on her mind at once. First, there was the church greeting Alan and promising prayers and support as he attempted to follow God's will. Then there was all the emotion being displayed toward David and Cindy's leaving, with many trying to get to them and express their feelings. Then there was Phillip, whom she couldn't find. His Durango was still in the parking lot, but he had disappeared. She asked several people if they had seen him, but no one had.

"I think he's in the gym," one teenager finally told her. So she made her way there quickly. Sure enough, he was shooting baskets … all alone.

"So, how was your night?" she attempted a start at a discussion.

"Like a dream," he responded as he kept shooting. "A nightmare."

"It's amazing, isn't, how one man's blessing is another man's curse?"

He stopped shooting and held the ball, but never looked at her. "He's the one, isn't he?"

"Alan?"

"Yep."

"He's the one," she confessed.

"Did you know he was here?" he asked her.

"Yeah, I found out Friday, a week ago. He showed up at my house."

"Tell me you didn't let him in!" he said turning to her in anger.

"Of course not!" she defended. "I'm not a fool!"

"I can't believe he's here! Why didn't you tell me? Why did you keep this from me?"

"Excuse me?" She was now getting angry herself. "I don't have to answer to you about anything. Since when do I need to report to you about who is in and out of my life?"

"Obviously never, I suppose!" he yelled as he began shooting baskets again.

"You don't own me, Phillip," she said as she stopped the ball and took it from him.

"I never have, and I never will," he told her solemnly.

She just stared at him for the moment. So, he had no intentions of marrying her. She had been right at the park. Phillip needed someone other than her, and Alan was the reason why. She hadn't seen Phillip this upset in years, not even over the churches he had served. In fact, he wasn't just upset, he was angry. She gave him the ball and turned to leave. After a few steps, she turned back around and said, "I don't want him here anymore than you do, but I'm not God. I'll learn to live with it, no matter how much it hurts. I suggest you do the same."

She left to the sound of the ball being dribbled then swooshing through the hoop.

Cindy found Meg as she was about to get into her car.

"Meg!" she yelled from across the lot. "Wait!"

She stopped, put her Bible onto the seat, and waited for her friend.

"Was that the one?" Cindy asked as she came near. Meg nodded. "I'm so sorry. I can't believe this happened. Of all the people in the world for him to work for and impress, it had to be John Mason."

She found herself smiling. "And some people think God has no sense of humor."

"Well, I'm not laughing right now. I feel for you. Are you going to be okay with this?"

"Cindy, do I have a choice?"

She shook her head. They stood in silence.

"Why didn't you tell me you guys were leaving?" Meg asked her.

"David didn't want to. He wanted the whole church to know at once. He felt it would stop any rumors that might start if he could just explain before speculation set in."

"I understand. You know that I'm absolutely miserable tonight, don't you?"

"Gee, I can't imagine why. Why don't you come over and we'll have some coffee or something. I have the makings for root beer floats. How does that sound?"

She thought for a moment, but decided against it. She had something else she needed to do.

Opening the door to her house, Meg sighed in emotional exhaustion. She stepped out onto the deck as she let Spiro in and then took a deep breath of the salty air. Even the familiar sounds and smells of her beach couldn't calm her nerves this night. The little dog was a burst of joy in the midst of the turmoil as he hopped endlessly around her feet. She went back inside and sprawled out on the leather couch trying to snuggle with him as much as he would let her. He was ready to play. She let him down and he immediately began running through the house at top speed. Pulling up her hand, she stared at the ring on her finger. She traced the outline of the two emeralds and thought of Kevin. He had felt sympathy for her when she explained the story of Alan, but he never condemned her. At this moment, she was tired of being lonely. She was tired of living her life for everyone else. She honestly believed she was ready to settle down with someone who would take care of her for a change. She was tired of handling everyone else's problems. She picked up her phone and pressed the contact that had become more familiar with each passing day.

"Hello," came the voice of comfort she needed to hear. Kevin. "I was hoping you'd call."

"Hey," she said softly.

"I thought about calling earlier but I'm never sure when you get in on Sunday nights."

"You would have missed me—I just walked in."

"I miss you anyway." There was silence.

"I need to see you, Kevin. I need to be with you."

"What's happened?" he asked with concern.

She explained the story of all that had occurred that evening. She cried on and off, and included events from the past week that only added to the overload of the night. By the time she had finished, she was even more miserable.

"I'll come down tomorrow," he said.

"What?"

"If that's okay?"

"It would be wonderful!" She actually felt a surge of hope. "You would come here?"

"In a moment—all you had to do was ask. We'll spend some time together and see if we can pull you out of the gloom. That's the beauty of being your own boss—your time is your own."

"I can't believe you'd do this for me."

"Why not? I'm in love with you. I'd follow you to Borneo if I had to."

"A tropical island? Now that sounds nice," she mused as a smile began to grow.

"But you live in the tropics already. Are you seeking a change of residence? If so, I have a wonderful suggestion."

"I think I might be. One thing I know for sure—I'm definitely seeking some type of change."

"Again, I have a wonderful suggestion."

Chapter Nineteen

Meg held tightly to the leash as she waited for the plane to land. Spiro wasn't sure if he was happy to be at the airport or not. He knew there was the obvious absence of his pet carrier, but he still refused to be jumpy. He stayed close to her and wagged his tail only slightly when she would speak to him.

Kevin's plane taxied into position for the ramp and it seemed forever before people began appearing. She watched carefully for her knight in shining armor and wasn't disappointed. There he was, confident as ever, in his faded jeans, a sweatshirt she had given him for Christmas, and worn tennis shoes, all topped off with strands of hair sticking out behind his Astros cap. She walked over to him slowly, waiting for him to see her. When he finally did, there was his smile, his dancing brown eyes, and his arms outstretched toward her. She ran to him and nestled in the comfort of his being here ... for her, and her alone.

"Take me to the nearest hotel, first," he asked her as they loaded into the Porsche. "Let me check in, and then I'm all yours."

"You're not staying at my house?" she asked in surprise.

"Not yet. You have to marry me first."

She drove to the only hotel in Treasure Cove just off of the interstate. She helped him check in and find his room, then they got back into the car. She was surprised that he had said nothing about her Porsche yet. Most men drooled over it before even speaking to her.

"Where to now?" he asked.

"I need to take Spiro home, and then we can either go out to eat, or I can cook something at home. What do you want to do?"

"How about we go out tonight," he suggested. "No responsibility for you except to show me around."

"What do you feel like eating?"

"Let's see," he mulled, "we're in Florida, on the coast ... hmmm ... how about seafood?"

"I know just the place."

They arrived at the Gull Island gate and she punched in the combination, then drove on down the road and pulled into the driveway. He got out, holding Spiro, and followed her to the door. He remained quiet, but observed details all the while. She put the pup on the back deck with fresh food and water and then went to freshen herself up a bit also. When she returned, Kevin had his notepad out and was looking behind the curtains in the living room.

"What are you doing?" she asked him.

"Just a minute," he said as he wrote something on his pad.

He then went to the French doors off the glassed in porch. He opened one and observed the lock. He ran his hand around the perimeter of one door and made a few more notes. Spiro ran in. Meg caught him and put him back out, closing the door. Kevin then checked out the glass on the back porch. Again, he made a few notes.

"Please tell me what you're doing," she pleaded.

"Well, this is an old house."

"Thank you," she said. "It's even older than I am."

He looked at her and smiled briefly, then went back to business. "It's very unsafe. That little gate up there wouldn't stop anyone who seriously wanted to do some harm. You could break into this place easily without anyone ever knowing."

She shrugged her shoulders.

"Do you realize," he went on, "that the crime rate in Florida is astronomical?"

"It's not too bad here in Treasure Cove."

"I'm going to have a hard time sleeping tonight knowing that you're staying here in a place so vulnerable like this."

"I told you that you could stay here with me," she teased.

"Meg, you've got to let me install some security devices tomorrow," he said sternly.

"Oh," she smiled. "I get it! You're whole take on being here is to install security at my house. Good idea."

"What?" he asked. He looked somberly at her. "I'm here to visit you. I just happened to notice that your house is completely vulnerable, and I can't have that. I'll install security hardware while you're gone to school tomorrow."

"You didn't plan this?"

"Are you kidding?" he said, almost in shock. "I assumed your father would have had this place as secure as the one in Houston. I'm a little upset, to be honest."

"No problem. It's okay. Install whatever you want tomorrow. I'll give you a key and the combination to the gate."

146

Meg took Kevin to the *Crab Shack*. It was too chilly to sit on the outside deck, so they managed a table beside a window. He observed all details with a keen eye.

"Are you checking out the security here too?" she asked.

"No," he smiled at her. "I love architecture. This place is wonderful—exposed beams, wood siding and walls, huge windows. Would make a nice house, don't you think?"

She agreed. She probably loved the Crab Shack as much for the atmosphere as for the food, although the food was excellent. He obviously enjoyed it too. They piled a plate full of crab leg shells between them, and then ordered another round.

"You know what I like about you?" he grinned. "Well, one thing, at least."

"My singing?" she giggled.

"Not quite," he smiled back, "although it is better than mine."

"Barely."

"True—you eat well."

"Thank you," she said laughing. "You're not hard to please, are you?"

"Well, think about it—you spend a lot of time thinking about a place to take a lady that she'll really enjoy. You go there, looking forward to the experience, order a huge meal, then she says, *I'll have the grilled chicken salad with a mineral water, please.*" He used a high-pitched voice for the latter.

She laughed—it was all too true.

"Now you," he continued, "I just try to keep up with you. You challenge my manhood, you know?"

"Good—everyone needs a challenge in life."

They enjoyed their evening. She forgot about her trials and tribulations for awhile, and he apparently forgot about the unsecured house ... for awhile. She took him back to the home and they sat on the back deck with light jackets and enjoyed the gentle breezes from the Gulf.

"The waves are huge tonight," she said after they sat a long while in silence just listening. "I'm gonna miss living here."

He looked at her strangely. "You're moving?"

"It looks like it," she nodded. "I figure ... sometime this summer most probably."

"Really? Where to?"

"I suppose that's up to you," she smiled.

He stared at her for a moment then he smiled, understanding what had just occurred. "You're not kidding me are you?"

She shook her head and then held up her ring to the light. She waved her hand over it and said, "Poof! Oh look—it's an engagement ring!"

She had never seen him smile so big. He stared at her in amazement for a little while, just shaking his head off and on.

"Does the offer still stand?" she asked him.

"Does it ever," he said finally coming over to her. He took her in his arms and looked down into her eyes thoughtfully. "What about Phillip?"

"Phillip who?" she asked as he leaned in to kiss her for the first time. Yes, her troubles were melting quickly.

Meg had a hard time keeping her feet on the ground during school the next day. She wanted desperately to let the world know she was engaged to Kevin Morris. Several students asked about her happy mood, but she just smiled and went on. She felt a sense of comfort whenever she thought of him at her house installing security equipment. She had offered him her Porsche to drive around while here saying she would take the van to school. He refused. It would be easier to load equipment into the van he had reasoned with her.

She wanted to call off tennis practice so she could get right home, but knew that could be fatal to the team. She trudged on, working with backhands and placement. She discussed strategy as they prepared for their first meet coming up the following week. Her energy and spirits were higher than they had been in a long while, and it didn't go unnoticed. One girl even told her that whatever she had for breakfast, she needed to have it again every day. Meg grinned at her and said she hoped to do just that.

As she finally drove home, there was the van, side doors opened, parked in the driveway. Also, the sawhorses had been pulled out of the shop, along with power tools galore. She parked the Porsche and began to look for Kevin. Hearing the drill from the back of the house, she opened the gate of the fence and was met by Spiro running to greet her.

"Hello, baby," she cooed to him as he jumped into her arms. "Have you had company all day?"

She spied Kevin up on the deck, drilling in toward the house.

"Hello up there!" she called. He stopped drilling, removed his safety glasses, and waved down at her.

"I'll sleep better tonight!" he called back then immediately returned to his work.

She climbed the steps of the deck and observed him from a distance. His t-shirt was dirty and worn, but his handling of the drill was done with expertise. She watched him stuff several small wires into the drilled hole, and then he puttied it over. He then went inside and attached the wires to something on a window.

"The back is secured, miss," he said as he stood up.

"Wonderful. I feel so much safer now."

"You ought to. This place was scary. Not only is there that pitiful gate up front, you have free access from the beach."

She glanced out to the water and sand. It had always been her friend, she thought. How strange to see it as a threat. She had to confess, however, it was comforting to know someone was taking care of her for a change.

"You're quite the handy man," she said as she took his hand and ran her fingers over calluses she had never taken the time to notice before.

"And your dad is quite the tool collector," he said leaning in to give her a small kiss. "I saw the shop and thought I would take a peek at it before I left. I was going to rent all the tools, but ..."

"Hey!" she blurted out. "How did you get in? There's a pad lock on the door!"

He made her follow him out to the shop. He took the lock off a table, removed a small metal device from his pocket, locked the lock and then reopened it within a matter of seconds. She just smiled sheepishly staring at the lock.

"Either you're a great thief, or I'm sort of naïve," she grinned.

He nodded.

She went inside to change clothes and start dinner, but was sidetracked by her phone. Spiro barked, and she giggled at him.

"Silly dog," she said. "Who needs security when you're around?"

She read the display—Cindy. "Hey, girl. Packing already and need my help?"

"Not yet," Cindy confessed, "and I'm dreading it."

"I don't envy you."

"Look, we know next week is going to be hectic, so we wanted to spend at least one evening alone with you and Phillip before then. Could you make it for dinner tonight?"

Meg was silent.

"Meg? Is that okay?"

"Goodness," was all she could manage.

"Is there a problem?"

"Sort of," she said slowly. "Kevin is here right now."

"Oh." Silence. "Is he staying with you?"

"No," she quickly told her. "He's staying at the Ramada."

"Well, he's welcome to come too. We'd love to meet him."

She was quiet for a little while longer. "I've agreed to marry him."

"Meg, that's great. I'm happy for you. Bring him over and we can all meet him tonight."

"Why not?" she found herself saying, but not feeling really comfortable with it.

"Is six thirty okay?"

"We'll be there."

⚓ ⚓ ⚓

As Meg turned onto the street where the Dewey's lived, she spotted Phillip's bright red Durango immediately. She heard herself gasp slightly, but managed to keep her emotions under control. At that moment she wished she had declined the invitation. After parking, she just sat still.

"Is there a problem," Kevin asked her.

"Sort of." She just stared at the Durango.

"Well?"

"Phillip's here," she told him.

"I see," he nodded. "Was that a surprise to you?"

She shook her head.

"Were you going to tell me sometime before we entered the house that he was here?"

"I didn't know how I would tell you, or how I would feel for that fact," she mumbled.

"I have no problem with this, but you look miserably uncomfortable."

"If I stop and think about it, I won't do it." She opened the door and got out quickly.

"What are you doing?" he asked, running to catch up to her.

"I can be too rational," she explained as she rang the doorbell. "You'll learn that about me. I can reason the spots off a Dalmatian if I'm not careful. I could give you a hundred reasons why I should never face this moment right now, but in my heart, I know I've got to … so let's just get to it."

"Yes, Ma'am," he said as David answered the door.

"Meg!" David greeted her with a hug. "You must be what they call a long, tall, Texan," he said, reaching his hand out to Kevin.

"Well, not so tall, but I suppose compared to Meg it could seem that way." Kevin said, shaking his hand.

Meg punched his arm slightly. "I never realized my height was an issue!"

"Hello, Kevin," said Cindy as she took his hand. "I'm Cindy."

Meg ignored them as she spotted Phillip standing up from the couch. He smiled at her and gave a little wave as he came toward the group.

"Hi, Kevin," Phillip said, extending his hand. "I'm Phillip Anderson."

"Yes," Kevin greeted him, "Meg told me you had changed your name."

"Not just changed, adopted," Phillip explained. "It seems that I owe you a whole lot. You're responsible for finding my family."

"Yes," Kevin agreed. "You owe me, all right. I've had a lot of cases over the years, but nothing that took me off the beaten track as far as yours did."

"Well, Kev," Phillip began teasing, "I'm a complicated person. It would

150

only be right for anything having to do with me remain complicated."

"Then you have lived up to your reputation, sir," Kevin told him.

Meg sighed with relief. The exchange had gone well between the two of them. She had always thought Phillip to be tall, but next to Kevin he towered.

After dinner, Meg helped Cindy with the kitchen while the men moved into the back yard to watch the kids.

"He's really wonderful, Meg," Cindy said. "I didn't want to like him ... I have to confess that to you. I thought that you would marry Phillip, have a lot of kids, and get him back into the ministry—because you could most definitely handle those ornery pastors and church members."

"Phillip doesn't want to marry me, you know?"

Cindy smiled as she put away dishes and said, "He doesn't know what he wants. I just hope you do."

"I do," she held confidently. "I'm not getting any younger, you know?"

Cindy laughed at her as the men came back in. It was starting to rain.

"So you guys can't weather the weather?" Cindy teased.

"We're wimps," David confessed easily.

"I noticed you guys had your house up for sale," Kevin said. "Any takers?"

"Fat chance—it's only been up for two days. I have a feeling we'll be waiting months before we get any buyers."

"Well, you're in a nice neighborhood. From the looks of the cars and the toys, I'd guess mostly young families, probably middle income. You could rent it easily in a week," Kevin noted.

"I don't even want to go there," David said as he held his hands up. "No way. I'll deal with the extra payments before I deal with renters. When we leave, I want to leave. I can't come back down here and check up on it every few months."

"How about I buy it from you and rent it out?" At this statement, everyone turned and looked at Kevin. "I have several rental houses in and around Houston. It's kind of a side job. Why not have one down here too? It would give me and Meg a good excuse to come back every now and then."

"Wow," said Phillip. "Several? I guess the P.I. business does pretty good."

"Let's just say I've had some rather lucrative cases over the years and a few wealthy clients. I don't like putting my money in places I can't see, so I've invested a lot of it in real estate."

"Let me get this straight," Phillip leaned toward him. "You have income coming in from several rental houses monthly?"

"I have fifteen right now."

"You're welcome to sixteen, if you want," David butted in quickly.

"Well, show me around then, and let me get a good look at the place," Kevin said, standing.

"It's a mess back there," Cindy warned.

"No problem," Kevin assured her. "Your mess will be long gone before someone else moves their mess in."

Kevin, David and Cindy began touring the house, leaving Phillip and Meg alone.

"What a guy," Phillip said.

"I'd like to think so," she replied.

"Cindy tells me you've agreed to marry him."

She nodded.

"What made up your mind?"

"A combination of a lot of things," she said plainly. "I'm tired of this limbo I've been living in for the past couple of months. I needed to make some choices, so I made them."

"Well, that's Meg for you. I wish I could have your resolve about life. I'm never sure about any decision. What if the other choice I didn't make was the better option?"

"Sometimes, Phillip, it's not about better or best. Sometimes it's just about good. If we linger over what could have been, we'll spend our whole lives spinning our wheels. I've seen a good choice here. I've made my choice, and I'm not going to look back and wonder if there was anything better."

"That's fine—as long as you know it's good enough. A couple of weeks ago, you weren't sure."

"A lot of things can happen in two weeks … in one night for that matter."

He nodded in acknowledgement. "Obviously."

"He's very good to me, Phillip. He can take care of me."

"I know," he agreed. "That's why I'm not complaining. I told you someone better than me deserved you. He's the one."

"He's not better," she said curtly. "He's just ready."

"I can see that. I didn't realize you were so ready though."

She chuckled. "I didn't either until I saw him at the airport after that horrible Sunday night. I'm tired of living in the past and that's what Treasure Cove is full of for me. Bad past, good past, missed opportunities past—all of it. I need to move on and make a future for myself. I'm not getting any younger, you know? If I'm going to have kids or travel or build or do anything, I need to get started."

"Tick, tick, tick, I suppose. The old biological clock giving you fits?"

"More like the old psychological clock. I've needed a change for a while. It's just taken the events of the last week or so to make me realize how much."

She heard the laughter in the back and wanted to join them, but felt compelled to stay with Phillip. He didn't say anything for a long while.

"I suppose this kind of cuts in on our friendship," he finally said.

"I guess. It'll be hard for me to see you as just a friend. You know that you've always been more to me than that."

"Until today."

"No, until Sunday night," she replied sternly.

"You do realize we have a lot to talk about," Kevin said as they got comfortable on the big, white, leather couch back at the beach house.

"Like what?" she asked as Spiro jumped over and around them.

"Oh, things like, when ... where ... home ... children."

"Oh, little trivial details like that."

He smiled at her and pulled her next to him. She laid back against his chest and let the sense of security melt through her. From the first time he had held her while dancing, she could never get away from the comfort she sensed.

"So," he went on, "when do we set the date? Or would you rather wait a while first?"

"No more waiting," she insisted. "I would say at spring break, but then we have to deal with all the problems of school not being over yet. Probably the smartest thing to do would be to wait until summer. I can resign, move, and get married all in the same month. How's that for efficiency?"

"Very adventurous. A June wedding, perhaps?"

She nodded.

"I take it you want to get married in Houston then? Not here?" he asked her.

"No, not here. Houston is ours. Treasure Cove isn't ... at least not yet."

"I understand. Next on the list is where ..."

"My parents' house, in the garden, at the gazebo—how does that sound?"

"Beyond wonderful. I'll get married in the sewer as long as it's to you," he said, stroking her hair.

"Oh, that's romantic," she mumbled in contentment.

"Okay, where will we live?"

"At your place I guess. Where do you live?" she asked, suddenly realizing she had never seen his home.

"It's a loft."

"How cool." She sat up and turned to face him. "You live in a loft?"

"Yes. I didn't realize it would elicit such a response. I would have told you earlier."

"We'll live at your place," she settled. "We can build later if we want."

"Well, that leaves just one more question ... children."

She leaned back against him and thought about that one. Children. She was twenty-nine, he was thirty-seven. "What are you thinking?" she asked him.

"Well, finally a question that stumped you," he chuckled. "I knew it couldn't be that easy."

"I don't know, Kevin." She was definitely unsure of the topic. "Should we be married awhile, or should we just let happen whatever happens? You know, Craig and Janet have tried for years to have kids and haven't been able to."

"I'd like some," was all he said.

"Well, we'll think about that one. We've got about five months to make the decision."

"Fair enough," he agreed. They enjoyed the moment in as much silence as Spiro would allow before he spoke again. "There's something really important that I feel we need to do, Meg."

"Sure, what is it?" she asked curiously.

"Let's pray about this. If this is God's plan for us, we need to seek his blessing."

She smiled, nodded in agreement, and said, "Absolutely."

For the next three days, Meg enjoyed Kevin's company. She kept looking for reasons to convince herself she had made the right decision— she found plenty. He was a dream come true. Once you got past the rugged good looks and the playful eyes, there was a warm and compassionate man who adored her. He did several fix-up jobs around the house that she kept meaning to hire out but never managed to get around to. She struggled learning the security system, but he refused to let up until she had it down perfectly. In fact, everything had been perfect except for one small detail. He had asked her several times to walk the beach with him, but she just couldn't bring herself to do it. She didn't want to speculate why. Perhaps it was just that the wind was too cold in January for a good brisk walk. It was great, however, for her morning jogs, which she had taken alone for quite a while now.

As she watched his plane leave, she felt alone again. The reality of all she still had to do in the real world of Treasure Cove set in. She took Spiro for a walk at the park, and then went home ... alone. It was going to be a long, miserable, and lonely five months.

Chapter Twenty

It had been one week since the Deweys left and two weeks since Kevin left. Meg sat alone grading papers as she occasionally looked out onto the beach. She should probably get up and move around, but the big, fluffy recliner was just too warm and cozy. It was the coldest day yet by far, which wasn't saying much in Florida, but she found herself longing for the cooler winters of Houston. She tried to imagine Kevin's loft. She had made him describe it to her in detail, even to the placement of the Oriental rug. She longed to see it … and to see him. She found herself beginning to drift when the phone startled her. Spiro began barking.

"Spiro!" she yelled. "The phone doesn't hurt us!" It was useless. Why did she even try?

It was Craig. "Hello, big brother."

"Favorite brother, isn't it?"

"Absolutely," she said warmly. "What a nice surprise."

"How does it feel to be someone's fiancé'?"

"Right now it feels rather lonely?"

"Believe me, if anyone understands that, it's me," he laughed. He and Janet had been engaged for two years while he was in New Orleans and she still in college in Treasure Cove. A twinge of guilt ran through her mind. She could have done that for Phillip.

"I have some good news and some bad news," he went on. "Which do you want first?"

"Oh, great," she mumbled. "Bad news."

"It appears that when you move up here this summer, we will be far away from you. We, as in Janet and I."

"Okay," she said cautiously. "Now for the good news."

"It appears that Treasure Cove Community Church is interested, very interested, in having me as their new singles' minister."

"You're kidding!" she yelled in unbelief.

"We'll be coming down in two weeks in view of a call."

"You've just made my day. Shoot! You've made my week!"

"Glad to hear it. Janet and I have been thinking about living arrangements ..."

"Well, of course you'll live here," she assumed.

"For starters, we'd like to, but then we want to build. Dad said if we wanted we could have the lot north of the beach house."

"That's a beautiful place," she said as she walked out onto the deck and glanced at the property. "That would be perfect."

"Yeah," he said dreamily, like the old Craig again.

🌴 🌴 🌴

The two weeks before Craig and Janet arrived seemed like an eternity. Meg tried to busy herself with tennis matches, papers, fundraising plans for the home, and even planning the wedding in June. No matter how hard she tried however, she was lonely and miserable. As she stood at the front of her senior literature class trying to explain Shakespeare's *Julius Caesar*, she wondered why she bothered. Even her best students today were totally uninterested. To be honest, so was she.

"Miss MacAllister," came the secretary's voice over the intercom.

"Yes," she replied.

"Could you please come to the office for a minute?"

"I'll be right there."

The class began to *ooh* as they always did when someone was called to the office. She assured them she was not in trouble and that she would return to torture them with the rest of Act II when she finished. She made her way to the office leisurely, enjoying the break from Julius. As she walked inside the office, solemn looks reflected from everyone's faces.

"Phillip Anderson wants you to call him immediately," said one of the secretaries as she handed her a slip of paper with his name on it. "He said you should have his number but made me take it down just in case."

"What's going on?" she wanted to know.

"Call Phillip," she insisted without saying more.

Meg reached into her pocket and nervously punched his name fearful of what she would find.

"Meg," he said, "you need to get over to the hospital right away."

"What's happened?" she asked, beginning to panic.

"They didn't tell you?"

"If they had told me, do you think I'd be asking you?" she said angrily, tired of the runaround.

"It's Carmen," he said. "She attempted suicide a little bit ago. She's in a mess. They keep trying to sedate her, but she refuses to cooperate. She won't see anyone or talk to anyone but you. Can you get down here?"

She didn't even answer. She shut down the phone and yelled, "Get someone to take my class for the rest of the day! I don't care what they

156

study!"

She sped and prayed all the way to the hospital. *Funny, Lord, how all your own problems disappear when someone else is in trouble. I can't believe how I've gotten so caught up in self-pity. I've neglected everyone lately.* Then she whispered, *Especially Carmen. Forgive me, Lord. Forgive me. And let me help her—somehow, help me to help her.*

She parked, ran from her car to the receptionist who was waiting with information, and then ran to find Carmen. She could hear her yelling from the stairwell door. Meg made her way to the room and slammed open the door.

"Carmen!" she yelled out. "I'm here!"

"Miss MacAllister!" the girl screamed back. "Tell them to stop! Tell everyone to stop! Please tell them to all go away!" Her arms were bandaged from her elbows down, and she was extremely pale and exhausted from screaming.

"Everyone, please get out and give me a few minutes with her alone," Meg pleaded.

"I'm not allowed to leave, Ma'am," said one nurse. "She's a suicide patient. Twenty-four hour care is demanded."

"Then I'll give her some care," Meg insisted. "Leave the door opened and stand right outside if necessary, but nobody's going to accomplish anything as long as she's like this."

The nurse, Mr. Roberts, a cop, a paramedic, a doctor, and Phillip all exited the room. Meg went over to Carmen who grabbed her and sobbed.

"I can't go back to her, Miss Mac," she cried. "I just can't do it. I'd rather die than go back to her."

"I'm so sorry," she tried to soothe as she held her tightly. "I tried my hardest to get them to let you stay, but they couldn't find a legal reason. You've got to tell them, Carmen."

The girl pulled back and shook her head. "I can't tell them. I can't tell people what I've done. I want to be new. I want to be good. I want to be different, but I don't want to start anywhere else again. I want to start here with you and Alissa and Lana. Please don't let them send me back to her! Please! Please!" She began sobbing again.

Meg wasn't sure exactly what she could do, but she assured her she would work everything out and there was no need to worry. She finally calmed her down enough to let a nurse sedate her. When she fell asleep, Meg went out into the hallway to talk with Mr. Roberts, the cop, and Phillip.

"What's going on?" Phillip wanted to know.

"The authorities, that's what's going on," she said with disdain.

"We're just upholding the law, ma'am. She's required to return to her mother today. I was just obeying orders," the officer tried to explain.

"Meg, she has to go back," Mr. Roberts said. "First, it'll be recommended that she be released into the custody of a mental hospital for treatment—then she'll have to go home."

"She'll try it again," she told him. "But this time it'll work."

"Why doesn't she want to go home?" Phillip wondered.

"Because!" Meg yelled and then quieted down, "because her mother is a dope addict and a whore."

"We don't know that," Mr. Roberts quickly interjected. Meg glared at him. "Well, we don't. She's been investigated, and she comes out clean."

"Okay, then Carmen is the biggest liar in the world," Meg sarcastically consented. "Whatever the problem, this girl doesn't need to be with her mother. Look how she's improved the last few months. Her mother didn't do that!"

"Our hands are tied," Mr. Roberts said helplessly.

"This is ludicrous! You can't send her to a psych-ward—she doesn't need that. She needs a stable, comfortable, environment where she is safe and free from things a sixteen-year-old should never have to even know exist."

"We don't have a choice in any of this," the older man tried to explain.

"Okay, then," she was getting angrier, "who makes the choices here? I'll move heaven and earth to see to it that this girl is done right by the authorities."

Mr. Roberts gazed around, obviously not wanting to answer this one.

"Who!" Meg demanded. "Who determines what happens to her?"

"Her mother has legal custody at this point, which means she has total freedom to do with her whatever she wants. If she wants her to go to the psychiatric hospital, then off she goes. If she wants her home instead, then she goes home. Again, our hands are tied."

She shook her head. It seemed hopeless, but she had promised Carmen, and this time she would *not* fail her. "What if her mother agrees to another arrangement?"

"What kind of arrangement?" Phillip asked.

Mr. Roberts scratched his head, nodded, and said, "If it was in a legal contract and signed by the mother and a lawyer, I suppose something else could be worked out."

"I'm going to see my lawyer," Meg said turning to leave.

"What are you going to do?" Phillip asked as he ran after her.

"Just move heaven and earth, of course," she replied resolutely, pushing her way through the hall.

🏝 🏝 🏝

"Hello?" Carole Delancey's voice was raspy and tired, as though she had just awakened.

"Mrs. Delancey?" asked Meg.

"Ms. Delancey," Carmen's mother corrected.

"I suppose you've heard about your daughter?"

"Yeah, she's one messed up kid."

"I'm going to get straight to the point, Ms. Delancey. How much would it take for you to sign legal custody of Carmen over to me for say … two months?"

"What, sell you my daughter? What kind of warped pervert are you?"

"I'm not a pervert, Ms. Delancey. I'm someone who cares about your daughter and would rather pay through the nose to see her anywhere but at your house."

"What kind of idiot are you? Are you trying to steal my kid?" Carole yelled out using several expletives. She was slurring a little bit so Meg figured she must be strung out on something.

"How much, Ms. Delancey? I'm serious now—you name your price."

More swearing from Carole, then a simple statement—"For two months, how about five hundred bucks?"

"No problem. My lawyer and I will be there tomorrow morning with a contract and a check."

"No checks!" she quickly countered. "Cash only!"

"I'll see you tomorrow, Ms. Delancey, with cash in hand. I'll be in touch with the details."

"Whatever, lady."

Meg then went to the children's home and found Alissa and Lana.

"Get a change of clothes and your pillows," Meg told them.

"What's going on Miss Mac?" Alissa asked.

"Carmen," was all she said.

"She went home today," Lana said confused.

"No, she didn't," Meg told them. "Get your stuff and I'll explain on the way."

When Meg got to Carmen's room, she had the girls stand outside while she went in. Carmen was watching television while the nurse sat in the corner of the room.

"Excuse me," Meg said to the nurse. "I'll need an extra bed in here tonight, perhaps a roll away."

"Just use the empty bed," the nurse pointed. "Nobody will be allowed to room in here tonight anyway."

"I still need another extra bed."

"I don't know what you're planning, miss, but I can't allow it."

Meg pulled a hundred dollar bill from her pocket and gave it to the nurse. "This is not a bribe—it's a reward. I don't know what all the rules are in this hospital, but this particular wing bears the name *MacAllister Children's Ward*, does it not? Do you know what my name is, ma'am?"

The nurse shook her head.

"MacAllister—Meg MacAllister. I founded this ward for children who needed things to be done differently while hospitalized. Do you know why I did that nurse ... uh," Meg read her badge, "Nurse Nancy."

The nurse shook her head again.

"Because children are fragile. They aren't emotionally mature enough to handle a lot of the bad things that have to happen to them in a hospital. Unfortunately, this young lady you're so concerned with right now has had a hard time handling the bad things that have been forced on her while out of this hospital. What she needs right now is not a staunch nurse in a starched uniform who knows the rules. She needs two friends in jeans and pony-tails who can relate to her. Do you understand what I'm saying, Nurse Nancy?"

The nurse nodded, put the money in her pocket, and said, "I'll speak with the doctor. I'm sure something can be arranged."

Carmen looked over at Meg and smiled. "Thanks, Miss Mac. You sure know how to make things happen."

"I'm working on it," Meg told her as she set on the edge of the bed. "How are you doing?"

"Okay, I guess. They want me to go to a loony bin."

"I know. I'm working on that too."

"They say if I don't go, I have to go back to Carole's."

"I know." She didn't want to talk of the arrangement she was trying to make with Carole Delancey because it would be just like the woman to back out at the last minute. "I'm working on that too. In the meantime, I have a surprise for you."

Carmen smiled bigger with anticipation. Meg left the room and came back with Alissa and Lana. They ran to her and hugged her and immediately began to talk. It was the best therapy she could have at the moment.

🌴 🌴 🌴

Meg and her lawyer, Stephen Adams, stepped off the small private plane into the biting Tallahassee wind. They quickly made their way inside and hurried toward the gift shop area. Meg looked around for the woman that Carmen had described in one of her papers. There she was, dressed in a slinky black dress with a thin, short jacket wrapped around her. Her curly hair stuck out wildly with more gray than Carmen had described. Meg motioned for Stephen to follow her.

"Ms. Delancey?" Meg asked as they reached the woman.

"Yeah," she said. "And you would be who?"

"Meg MacAllister. This is my lawyer, Stephen Adams. Where would you like to make this transaction?"

"Somewhere away from this door," she said shivering with a strong expletive.

They followed her farther down the hallway and sat on a long, padded bench. Carole was still shivering.

"Would you like some coffee or hot chocolate or something, Ms. Delancey?" Meg asked her.

"Coffee. Black." She replied.

"You go over the contract with her, Stephen. Can I get you something too?"

He shook his head and opened his briefcase.

When Meg returned, they were finishing. Meg handed Carole her coffee and sat down with them.

"I want to see the cash before I put my John Peacock on anything," Carole told them.

"Your John what?" Stephen asked.

"You know, John Peacock! The guy who wrote the Constitution," Carole explained as though he were an idiot.

Meg and Stephen nodded. Meg then reached into her coat pocket and produced an envelope. She pulled out five one hundred dollar bills and gave them to Carole. The frail woman felt them with shaky hands and then smelled them.

"Why are you doing this, lady?" Carole asked her.

"Because I care about what happens to your daughter. That's it."

"Whatever," she mumbled adding some more profanity, "Give me the pen and let's get this over with."

She signed her named, Meg signed hers, Stephen signed his and then notarized the document. Meg tried to hand her the envelope the money had been in, but she said she didn't need it. She stuffed the bills down her bra then turned to go.

"Just for the record, Ms. Delancey," Meg said to her, "I got off cheap. I would have gone up to five thousand."

Carole stopped, turned around, and cursed at her.

"I'd love to stay and chat with you, but I've got a plane to catch," Meg mocked.

🌴 🌴 🌴

"Miss MacAllister, this is highly irregular," the doctor said as he looked over the papers.

"I assure you they're completely legal," Stephen told him.

"Mr. Roberts?" the doctor looked to the director.

"It's legal," he agreed. "Carmen is to be released into the custody of Meg MacAllister for two months as of this past Thursday."

"Okay," the doctor smiled. "Go get your girl."

Meg walked into the room to find Carmen packing her bags slowly. She looked up as Meg came in. Her dark eyes were red and brooding.

"I've got some good news for you, at least I think it's good news," Meg told her.

"It's gonna have to be pretty powerful," she said, continuing to pack. "I'm going to the loony bin, you know? At least it'll buy me some time before having to shack up with Carole again."

"You don't have to go to either for awhile."

Her eyes lit up. "I'm going back to the home?"

"No."

Her head drooped again. "Where are they sending me now?"

"You're going home with me ... at least for two months."

She spun around and looked at her. "You're kidding me, right?"

Meg shook her head.

"I'm going to live with you?" She was shocked, excited and beside herself.

"For two months."

"Yahoo!!" the girl yelled as she flung her arms around Meg and hugged her. "How did you manage that?"

"You don't want to know," she told her. "Are you ready to go home?"

"Like never before," Carmen smiled.

Chapter Twenty-One

Living with Carmen was wonderful. The next week flew by. Carmen started jogging with her in the mornings, helped her grade papers when she finished her own homework, cooked supper with her, and watched old movies with no complaints. They even discussed some of the shows afterward. Meg discovered this girl was extremely bright. Had she been raised in a normal home environment, she would have been tested long ago for giftedness. Carmen even kicked in big time to help prepare the house for Craig and Janet's arrival. They dusted and vacuumed and cleaned windows and scrubbed the stove and prepared the master bedroom for occupancy.

When Craig and Janet finally came, they were floating with emotion. It was good to be back in Treasure Cove, Janet's hometown. Her mother and brother had been killed in a car accident when she was fifteen, and her father had died of heart complications when she was a senior in college. When she left, she had hoped it would be for good, but now she was ready to return—she was ready to come home.

Craig immediately called the pastor and began meetings that very evening. Janet stayed home with Meg and Carmen and visited.

"This is so unbelievable," Janet said as she rubbed Spiro's back. "I can't believe I'm sitting here, in this house, in Treasure Cove, with the possibility of moving back. Pinch me, Meg."

Meg got up to oblige.

"I'm just kidding," she protested. "You need to lighten up."

"Impossible," Carmen mumbled. "It's part of that high school teacher thing."

They all laughed, except Carmen of course, who always tried to be the straight man.

"Tell me about the wedding!" Janet asked excitedly.

"Goodness," Meg sighed. "I haven't thought about the wedding in days. I'm ready to just hand it all over to Mother and let her have it."

"Ooooo," Carmen moaned. "I wouldn't."

"My mother is most definitely not your mother," Meg told her.

"Wouldn't matter. My wedding, my big day, my once in a lifetime—I'm gonna plan it."

"Well said," Janet agreed. "What do *you* want, Meg?"

"I don't know. I just want to get married and live happily ever-after."

"Good luck!" Janet snickered.

Sunday morning was nerve racking. Meg tried to concentrate on her lesson, but she fumbled and bumbled through the whole thing. Her girls just stared at her, wondering what would cause such a loss of control in the always together adult.

"Did you have a fight with the old man?" Alissa asked in the middle of class.

"What old man?" she asked, looking up from her notes.

The girls laughed.

"Your old man, you know, your fiancé'," Alissa explained.

They laughed again.

"The old man and I are fine," Meg told them. "My brother is up for a big job this morning. I can't help but be a little worried."

"Tsk, tsk, tsk, Miss Mac," Alissa spoke up again. "Be anxious for nothing … just pray."

"Good point, Alissa. Girls, why don't we just pray?"

Craig had to preach that morning. Meg tried to be objective and critical, but it was impossible. She thought he was great and encouraging and wonderful and handsome and witty. Janet, who sat next to her, squeezed her hand several times during his sermon and commented that this was the best he had ever done. After church, the singles had a big banquet for them where they had a question/answer time after eating.

"Would you expect us lonely singles to baby sit your children for free?" asked one girl.

"Absolutely," Craig responded. "All ten of them!"

"When we go on retreats, can we have coed rooms?" asked a guy.

"Absolutely," he said again, but added, "as long as you're married first."

The men booed, the women cheered.

"Will we take a mission trip to Europe this year?" another asked. "France and Italy in particular?"

"Absolutely," Craig told them, "as long as somebody pays my way."

The questioning went on and on with a few serious questions thrown in between the silly ones.

"He's gonna be great," Phillip leaned over to tell Meg. "It's really gonna be nice having him and Janet here again."

"Yes, it will," she agreed glancing up at him hoping for a glimpse of those blue eyes. She got it. He stared at her for a moment, and then they both turned away. She felt herself blushing yet again—she so hated that.

"I think it's great what you've done for Carmen," he tried to divert the awkwardness.

"She's such a neat girl."

"These two months may be a life changing point for her."

"At least part of it. Maybe she'll get a glimpse of what life is supposed to be like."

"I had a foster family like that," he said. "They were wonderful."

"What happened?"

"I was a rebellious jerk," he shook his head.

"Well, at least you're not rebellious anymore," she said flippantly.

He just laughed.

Craig was called to Treasure Cove, and he and Janet would be back in two weeks. The plan was for them to store their furniture and belongings in the basement beneath the MacAllister beach house. It was the full length of the house, but unfortunately it was full of over thirty-five years of accumulation. The privilege of rooting through it fell upon Meg and Carmen with some volunteered time from Phillip. Their first Saturday, the girls decided to tackle it with a vengeance.

"If I ever have to run away again, this is where I'm coming," Carmen said as they tried to pilfer through old furniture and stacks of boxes.

"You'd never make it," Meg told her. "Great security system."

"Thanks for the tip. How old is some of this stuff? I think I've read about couches like this in my history book."

"Ah, I remember that couch," Meg smiled. "Lime green was really big at one time."

"I like the white one upstairs. You don't need another one—let's get rid of this one."

"It holds so many memories," Meg deliberated.

"Well, one thing is for sure, you can't keep your junk-filled memories and Craig's furniture in here at the same time."

"True. Okay, let's move the couch out."

Phillip walked up as they were trying to get it out the door.

"Ladies, let me help you," he offered. Then he proceeded to tell them where to place it once they got it outside.

"I thought you were going to help us," Carmen said a bit agitated with him.

"I did," he grinned. "I just told you where to put it."

That set the tone for the rest of the day. They worked and moved and cleaned and went through the entire basement. Phillip picked up some Chinese food for lunch after a run to the city dump, and Meg grilled steaks for dinner. After a few minutes of sitting on the deck, Carmen excused herself.

"Mom, Dad, I'm pooped. You've worked me like a dog all day, and then you forced me to eat all that food for supper. I'm just worn out. You kids stay up and have a good time, but I'm gonna hit the hay."

She left with a yawn.

"She's a real joy," Phillip said once she had left.

"You have no idea how much," Meg agreed. "I only wish her own mother could see what she's really like."

"Do you ever wonder why some people have kids?"

"All the time. Mitch with Michael is one of the most pitiful situations I've ever encountered. People would think that somehow the money that's available to both of those parents would make up for the lack of relationship. Mitch could care less. He's partying every night, staying high or stoned or whatever. He shows up at work with Dad for a couple of hours to make it look official, then he's gone. He gets Michael every other weekend and every other holiday, but just dumps him off at Mom and Dad's, and then goes his merry way."

"What about Michael's mother?"

"She despises Mitch for getting her pregnant, marrying her, dumping her and then going right back to being an irresponsible teenager at age twenty-seven. She's back in college trying to recapture some of her youth too from what I hear. Michael's in day care when he's not at my parents."

"Let's see," Phillip mulled, "we've got Carmen right now, why don't we adopt Michael too, and then we'll be one, big, happy family."

"I know you're joking with me," she said turning to him, "but I can't tell you how often I've thought about adopting so many of these kids. That's one reason why I'm so active in the home. I can't adopt—I'm not married, but I can try to give them the best life possible while they're there."

"I've often wondered if I would ever even have kids of my own. I sometimes think I should just get married and start adopting kids every year. Brothers and sisters that no one else will take because there are too many of them. Four year olds that are a little rambunctious and not near as adorable as newborns, and teenagers that have been so thrown around they have no idea what a normal life is like."

"You've got to have at least one of your own," Meg insisted.

"Why?"

"Those blue eyes have got to be passed on to another generation."

Craig and Janet finally moved down. There was barely enough room to fit all their belongings into the basement, but they managed to cram them in. Janet immediately began mothering Carmen, Craig set out to start planning things at the church, and Phillip spent a lot of time at the beach house because of being so close to Craig and Janet. Meg was happy again after living alone for so many years. It was almost like having a family, though in a different way. She tried to place everyone into roles, but it never came out even. Finally she decided to just enjoy the time together while they had it. Carmen would be going back to somewhere in a month, Craig and Janet would be building their house soon, and she would be leaving them all to marry Kevin.

Valentine's Day struck Meg in the middle of explaining the proper use of adverbs to a junior composition class. Things were not going well. She had never had such a hard year at teaching. Perhaps it was time to retire, for more reasons than just getting married. As she tried to explain to Bryson Wallace ... for the third time ... that adverbs modify verbs, adjectives and other adverbs, he stared blankly.

"I don't get it, Miss Mac," he said frustrated. "How can it describe another adverb if it is an adverb. I mean, how do you figure out which one is the first adverb?"

"It doesn't matter right now, Bryson. We'll diagram later. You just need to understand where the adverbs are and then ..."

She was interrupted by a knock at the door.

"I'll get it!" about six students yelled.

"No, I'll get it," she said, heading for the door, welcoming the relief.

She opened it and was greeted by a dozen red roses.

"What's this?" she asked the secretary who was delivering.

"Beats me," she responded, but I'm guessing it has something to do with Valentine's Day."

She carried the roses to her desk amongst cheers and whoops. She took out the card and read silently, *To Meg: Happy First Valentine's Day. I look forward to next year's. All My Love, Kevin.* Meg smiled and blushed.

"Who's it from, Miss Mac?" yelled a girl from the back.

"Her fiancé, stupid!" a boy countered.

"I wish I could get just one rose," said another girl.

"Perhaps Miss Mac will hand some out to you lonely girls," a boy suggested.

"Bite your tongue," Meg said turning to him. "Let them get their own fiancés!"

She replaced the card and tried to get back to explaining adverbs. Now, not only was Bryson lost, but half the class had suffered a memory lapse. She patiently went over the process again, writing example after example on the board. The same students kept raising their hands to answer her questions.

"Could someone else please try and identify the adverbs?" she pleaded.

"But we don't know what they are," Bryson insisted.

Another knock.

"I'll get it," came about ten voices this time.

"No," Meg said again, "I'll get it."

She opened the door to be greeted with a dozen yellow roses.

"What's this?" she asked the secretary again.

"I have no idea," the secretary told her. "I just deliver what they bring to the office. I can tell you this though, you have received more roses today than the rest of the entire faculty put together."

Meg blushed. She dreaded taking them into the classroom. Her dread was valid. The class made more noise than before as she sat them on the desk and searched for a card. There was none. Her heart skipped a beat. She knew only Phillip was aware of how she loved yellow roses. Surely he didn't send them.

"I want a fiancé like that," said the girl from the back again.

"No card," commented a guy. "The yellow ones are from a secret admirer."

The class *ooed*.

"Really? Miss Mac?" The girl's eyes grew wide. "You're engaged, but you have a secret admirer? Does Mr. Fiancé know about this?"

The bell rang. *Yes!* Meg was saved by the bell. *At least once I've managed a stroke of luck*, she thought as her class eagerly collected their things and exited the classroom.

"How beautiful!" Janet exclaimed as Meg and Carmen brought in the roses from school. "Two dozen? Kevin must be really in love. Why didn't he put them both together? The red and yellow mixed would have been so pretty."

"They're not from the same guy," Carmen mumbled as she set the yellow ones on the table.

"What?" Janet asked in shock.

"We don't know that," Meg was quick to explain. "One came with a note, and one didn't."

"I see," Janet said seriously. "Which came with a note? Red or yellow?"

"Red," Carmen mumbled out again.

"Oh," was all Janet said. She then looked at Meg with one eyebrow raised. "Gee, I wonder who would know to send you yellow roses?"

"Don't go there, Janet," she warned. "I think you're mind is overreacting."

"I'm lost," said Carmen as she went to her room to change clothes.

"Hello?" came Kevin's voice from the other end of the line.

"Happy Valentine's Day!" Meg said cheerfully.

"Back at ya! So, how was your day?"

"Except for having adverbs interrupted by roses, fine."

"I apologize," he said, "but I thought it would be great fun to have them delivered to the school."

"Oh, the students did think it was great fun! I'm thanking you on their behalf. Of course, you realize you will be responsible for their educational delinquency concerning adverbs?"

"There's always tomorrow."

"No," she corrected him, "tomorrow is participles. Today and yesterday and the day before were adverbs."

"Should I contact my lawyer?"

"Maybe."

"Speaking of lawyers, how's Carmen doing? Is the custody thing working out?"

"She's doing great. It's like she's this normal girl now. She went for a psychological evaluation last week and passed with flying colors."

"Does this not give proof that she needs to be away from her mother?"

"That depends on who reviews her case. For some, yes—for others, no. We'll have to see."

"Do you think her mother will want her back?"

"Not really. But she'll probably want some money again. I could keep paying her off, I suppose, so Carmen could go back to the home, but that's not fixing anything. Besides, it's sickening to think I'm supporting a prostitute's drug habit. I wouldn't mind at all if it were something respectable."

There was silence and then Kevin said, "I want to come see you. Is that okay?"

"Okay?" she said. "Please, come see me! I miss you!"

"I was beginning to wonder, seeing that you have all that company now."

"I'm not lonely, but I do miss you still."

"How about this weekend?" he asked.

"Perfect! Now that Craig and Janet and Carmen are all living here, you can actually stay at the house."

"Not yet," he disagreed. "We'll be married soon enough. Let's keep all appearances above board, Meg. Remember what the Scripture says: *Avoid the very appearance of evil."*

"When did you get all religious on me?"

"When I realized God had blessed me with a wonderful gift."

⚓ ⚓ ⚓

Kevin's visit was a breath of fresh air. Phillip continued his regular visits for the three days Kevin was there. Phillip even invited them all over to his place to grill out one evening and play games. They had a wonderful time. Meg was settling into her new decisions, and was feeling secure about her future for a change, at least until the Monday evening of Kevin's last day in Treasure Cove.

"Let's go for a walk on the beach," he suggested.

"Not tonight," she yawned. "I'm kind of mellow. Let's just sit out here on the deck."

He sat quietly for a little while and then asked her, "Why?"

"Why what?"

"Why won't you walk the beach with me? You tell me over the phone how wonderful it is when you go out on the beach at night. You either just walked the beach or are about to walk the beach or are gloomy because it's raining and you can't walk the beach. You describe these dreamy moods it puts you in, and then when I've suggested going out there together each night, there's always some reason why you don't want to. I'm jealous of whatever it is. I want to enjoy those moments with you."

"I'm not trying to keep you from it," she said, taken back by his assessment. "I'm just not in the mood."

"Why are you always in the mood when I'm away, but never when I'm here?"

"I don't know," she began to defend herself. "Bad timing, I suppose."

"I hope so."

"Are you trying to get at something?"

"I'm not sure," he said. "It's just weird."

"You're being too sensitive." Then without thinking, which she was prone to do often, she finished up with, "Just get over it."

She knew it was harsh, but she was tired of his trying to make something out of nothing. He sat still for a moment and then stood up.

"I need to get to bed. My flight is very early in the morning," he told her.

"Okay. You'd probably better go."

And that was that.

I think there's trouble in paradise, she said to herself as she dropped him off at the hotel.

"We need something big, someone big," Mr. Roberts explained to the board of directors. "We keep getting more and more children, and we just can't afford to house them, feed them or clothe them."

"I'll step up my contributions," Ira offered.

"We can't do that," the director explained. "You're at your legal limit—you and Meg. We've got to have some kind of constant funding coming in from other sources."

"Let me make some calls," Meg suggested.

"You guys don't understand," he tried to explain. "In order to fund what we're proposing here, more children basically, that means we need more housing, more staff to run the housing, a new and larger cafeteria with more workers, and more office personnel to handle the huge amount of paper work that will come with each child. We're talking a significant increase in donations."

The board members all looked at each other in silence. Their ideas were depleted.

"What do we need here?" Ira finally asked him. "Do you have any ideas?"

"I have an idea," Mr. Roberts said, "but it's a long shot. We need a big name here. We need someone who will take us on as a charity. A celebrity, a big name Christian musician, a rich politician, an actor ... someone who's in the spotlight and can drum up a lot of money year round. Someone who will promote our cause every time he or she is in public."

"I get it," Meg announced. "Kind of like the game show host telling everyone to get their pets spayed or neutered at the end of his show each day."

"Exactly," Mr. Roberts clapped his hands together. "The problem is finding someone who hasn't already got three or four of these going on."

"How about Max Caldwell?" suggested a lady. Everyone glared at her. "Okay, bad idea."

"Any singers you know, Ira?" suggested another.

"I may own the station, but I never cared for this pop-Christian stuff. I'm blank. I could talk to Phillip about it though."

Everyone sat in silence again trying to come up with a name to approach. Several more were thrown out as possibilities, but most were dismissed as not wanting to have their names associated with the home. Then, as if Meg had been in a cartoon, a metaphorical light bulb went on above her head.

"Wait a minute," she said slowly, eyes growing bigger. "I believe I have just the person in mind."

"Oh great," mumbled Ira. "Here we go again."

"I don't think so, Ira," she smiled at him. "I think you're going to love this."

Meg told them her idea, and they gave her the go-ahead to give it a try.

Chapter Twenty-Two

One month later, it was time for Carmen to leave. Meg and Janet helped her pack, while everyone helped ease Janet's tears. Meg had taken her to get her driver's license the week before, so Carmen drove the Porsche back to the home. They had heard nothing from Carole, so all fingers were crossed that she would leave her alone and let her live her last year and a half in Treasure Cove. Of course, she could call tomorrow and end that dream. Meg thought about continuing to pay her off, but hated the idea of Carole gleaning anything positive from selling her daughter yet again.

She parked the Porsche and turned off the key then handed it to Meg with a *thanks*.

"No problem," Meg told her. "I'll come get you every now and then and let you get in some driving practice."

"No, not for that. Thanks for taking me in for two months."

"You don't have to thank me for that."

"Of course I do." She looked up at her astonished. "What you did for me was ... well ... awesome. How could I not thank you?"

"It was my honor ... and my privilege."

They got her bags and went into the girl's honor dorm. As soon as Carmen opened the door, everyone screamed, "Surprise!"

There were streamers and banners everywhere and a big poster that said *Welcome Home, Carmen* on the far wall. Everyone was throwing confetti and laughing and yelling. Carmen just stared in silence, and when everyone got quiet, she said, "All right, who's going to clean this up?"

With that, laughter abounded. They encouraged Meg to stay and enjoy the party, and she obliged. She felt good about leaving her there. When she finally decided to go, Carmen gave her an envelope and told her to read it later when she had some free time. They hugged and she left, feeling a twinge of sorrow at losing her houseguest. She had truly been a delight.

As soon as she got back home, she went out onto the deck, opened the envelope and began reading.

Miss Mac, I don't even know how to put into words the way I feel. You've done more for me than any other person ever in the world. I just need you to know that no matter what happens after today, I know I can handle it. If Carole calls tonight and makes me go back with her, it will be okay. Because, for the first time in my life, I know that I am important, that I am somebody, and that I am free to decide who I am. It doesn't matter what my father's done to me, and it doesn't matter what my mother is. I can be whoever and whatever I want to be.

You've shown me that God really did make me special, and that no matter how much my parents screwed up, that doesn't mean I have to too. You've taught me how to cook, how to dust, how to do laundry, how to iron, and how to love other people even if they don't love you back. I know that Carole will probably make me come back soon, if for no other reason than to get more money out of you (yes, I figured that out ... why else would she have given you that kind of power?). If she tries to get money again, don't do it. Let me go. I'll be all right because of what I've learned from you.

Love, Carmen

She put the letter back into the envelope and stared out at the water. The sun was setting, and the afternoon was fading, but for the first time, she had hope for Carmen.

God, she prayed, *please don't let her mother ask for her back.*

🏝 🏝 🏝

Craig and Janet had gone out for the evening, so Meg decided to vacuum. She went through the entire house, getting every corner and stooping under every piece of furniture. She threatened to put Spiro outside several times if he didn't stop attacking the machine hoping he would back off for awhile. As she finished up with the dining room and began cleaning the back porch, she was startled to find Phillip staring at her from the deck through the French doors. She waved and smiled, but he didn't wave or smile back. *Oh, no.* What had she done? She turned off the vacuum and opened the door.

"Is there a problem?" she asked as he came in sweating and huffing from the jog down the beach.

"You bet there is!" he said as he took a piece of folded paper from his pocket. "What is this, and what in heaven's name do you think you're doing?"

It was a flyer announcing that Sen. George P. Evans would be speaking on behalf of the Treasure Cove Christian Children's Home in two weeks.

"Put on the brakes for a minute," she told him as she watched him seethe inside. "I am most definitely up to something, and if you'll hear me out, you might agree with me."

He collapsed onto a chair, folded his arms and blew out a deep breath as he glared and waited.

"We needed a big name to help raise some cash for the home," she began. "We went through tons of names trying to find the right one, but nothing worked. Then it hit me! Why not have the biggest proponent of family values and morals be our spokesman to the world?"

"Stupid idea! He's a hypocrite!"

"Ah," she said putting up a finger to correct him, "don't misjudge me yet. See, I figure it this way—he sits at a special table with several special people from the home—me, Ira, Mr. Roberts, a couple of others, and of course, an alumnus from the home itself ... you."

She was smiling—he still wasn't.

"You don't understand," he said disdainfully, "I don't *want* to sit with him. I want nothing to do with him!"

"Now, now, Phillip, you keep butting in. I have a plan." She used her best school teacher voice.

"Go on, then."

"See, the rest of us suggest to him he make our home his special charity."

"He won't!" he argued, getting more disgruntled with each sentence she spoke.

"Of course, he won't. We know that! But see, you don't say much of anything throughout the whole dinner. You're just kind of there ... sitting next to him. We make the proposal about two minutes before he's to speak. About one minute before, Mr. Roberts excuses himself to get up and introduce our honored speaker. It is at that time that I say, *Oh, Senator Evans, I don't believe I properly introduced you to the man sitting beside you. His name is Phillip Barton, former resident and orphan from the home.*"

She smiled as she waited for the idea to sink in. He stared at her a moment then shook his head. "You are wicked—very wicked, and in a scary sort of way. How did you manage to get Mr. Roberts to go along with it?"

"Well, he doesn't know George is your dad."

"He doesn't? No wonder he complied."

"Ira knows though," she smiled.

"You and Ira put this thing together?"

She nodded.

"You and Ira actually agreed on something?"

She nodded again—proudly

"Miracles never cease." He shook his head swallowed hard. "I sure hope I can pull this off."

🌴🌴🌴

March had arrived and preparations were in full swing for the

175

fundraising banquet. They had booked the most expensive and largest banquet hall nearest to Treasure Cove, with Ira footing the bill for the whole affair. Meg had agreed to pay the fee asked by Sen. Evans, which all thought was too steep for a charity function, but because Meg insisted, they went along with it. This was the biggest thing to ever happen in the history of Treasure Cove.

"What if it doesn't work?" Phillip asked Meg as she helped him with the tie on his tuxedo.

"Then it doesn't work and we try something else."

"That's a lot of money spent to see a Senator squirm."

"I couldn't think of a better use for it." She smiled as she surveyed her handiwork. He looked handsome in his black tux and blue eyes. The last time she had seen him dressed like this was at Janet and Craig's wedding. At that time, she assumed the next would be at their own nuptials.

"So, I just play the quiet boy and don't say anything through supper?"

"Pretend you're my date," she told him. "We'll talk a lot. I'll make some idle chit chat with the senator now and then. He knows I'm footing the bill for him, so he'll be polite and obliging."

"You're not nervous about this at all are you?" he asked as sweat began to bead on his forehead. "In fact, I think you're rather enjoying the whole thing."

"I'm afraid so," she said matter-of-factly. "Phillip, there are few things that money can actually buy, but this is one of those moments my money has made possible—you bet I'm enjoying it."

They entered the banquet hall and began to mingle with other guests. She kept an eye on Phillip to make sure he didn't back out—he was a bit too nervous for her comfort. He began looking paler as the evening wore on.

Finally, the Senator entered along with Ira and several secret service men. The crowd applauded and then Mr. Roberts asked them all to find their places at the tables. Meg escorted Phillip up to the front, round table where he took his seat next to Senator George P. Evans. He had lost all color by now.

Ira, catching Meg's attention, mouthed to her if Phillip was all right. She shrugged—she honestly didn't know. She made him drink some iced tea and told him to get a hold of himself. He managed a faint smile.

Mr. Roberts said the blessing for the food and then the fun began.

Ira introduced everyone at the table except for Phillip. "This is Meg's date," he said simply. "He is the station manager at my WJBA."

As Ira and Meg had predicted, the Senator could care less. A lowly station manager dating a millionaire's daughter. Good for him. Mr. Roberts joined them and Ira introduced him and his wife. Meg and Ira were animated with their conversation. She so enjoyed the game she was playing that she began to wonder if maybe she shouldn't get into politics herself. She caught Ira winking at her several times as she complimented the exemplary work the Senator had done over the years. Phillip, however, did not appear to be faring well at all.

"Are you going to pass out?" she whispered discreetly to him once.

"I hope not," he mumbled from the side of his mouth. "This is a bit hard to swallow, you know?"

"Pretend you're in my shoes. Pretend he's not your father who sought to murder you while in-utero, or drugged you for years as a child to mess up your mind, or packed you around the world insisting you never be adopted into a lovely home."

"I'll try," he managed, taking another sip of his tea.

Things kept rolling along. The Senator was in top form as he cavorted with his best personality to the wonderful people at his table who were doing sacrificial things for these poor, innocent children who had been so rejected by unfeeling and self-centered adults. Meg and Ira winked. It was almost time for the final show.

"So, Senator," Ira began. "You can see the fix we're in. Just like with your campaigns, Miss MacAllister and myself can only give so much money. We need someone who can get to the public and make our desperate needs known."

"I understand. I really do," he nodded with concern. "I will try to think of someone who could help you with this mountain you're facing."

"Well, Senator," Meg said, "we were hoping you would do it."

He smiled one of his politically ingratiating smiles and said, "Oh, my dear folks, if I didn't have so much on my plate right now, I would love to help you and to help these children. It's such a worthy cause."

"We thought, Senator, being the proponent of all that is right in this world," Ira continued urging, "that surely you would consider this more seriously. You're not just giving us a flippant *no* are you?"

The Senator adjusted his collar and managed the same facade of a smile. "Of course not, Mr. Epstein. I intend to get some people on this immediately and see what can be done."

"Excuse me, folks," Mr. Roberts said as he pushed back his chair. "I have a few announcements to make, and then it will be your turn Senator."

"Should I come with you?" the Senator asked.

"No, that's fine," Mr. Roberts said. "Just sit comfortably until I introduce you ..."

"Of course," he agreed.

As Mr. Roberts walked up to the platform, Meg leaned toward the Senator and said, "If there were just some way to urge you more strongly to take part in this. We believe, Senator, with your record and high values you could do a lot for these children."

The Senator smiled, fixed his hair and adjusted his tie again as he prepared to face his public. Mr. Roberts began his announcements. Phillip grew paler. Meg's heart pounded. She and Ira exchanged knowing looks, then she said to the Senator, "Senator, excuse me one last time."

"Of course," he said giving her his full attention.

"It just occurred to me that I've been terribly rude about my date here tonight. I never properly introduced the two of you."

The Senator looked obligingly to the menial station manager and smiled.

"This is a former alumnus of the children's home here," she told him.

"How wonderful," George said rather hurriedly. "That's just great."

"His name is Phillip Barton."

For the first time that evening, Phillip genuinely smiled. He reached out his hand to a now paling senator and flashed those blue eyes.

"Howdy, Dad," he said as the Senator froze.

"And now," Mr. Roberts continued from the platform, "our honored guest and speaker, Senator George P. Evans."

It was amazing. Not only did the Senator promise to elicit contributions for the home around the country, he agreed to a sizeable yearly contribution himself. The look on Mr. Roberts's face was priceless.

"What did you guys do to him when I left the table?" he asked.

"I'm sure we don't know," Ira told him. "We're just nice guys appealing to another nice guy to do something nice in our part of the world."

"You certainly look better than a few hours ago," Meg told Phillip as they sat on his back deck.

"I can't believe you pulled this off," he said, shaking his head.

"I've done a lot of crazy things in my life for no reason other than fun, but this had to be my most fun moment ever."

"It was a moment all right. As for the fun, I don't know."

"So, did the Senator have any fatherly advice for you before he left? He seemed to be in an awful hurry."

"Actually, he did say something—he said he'd call me sometime. Maybe we could have lunch."

She laughed. "Right—like I can see that happening."

"I need to wind down," he told her. "Walk the beach with me for a while."

"Sure," she said, taking off her high heels and dropping them onto the deck.

Chapter Twenty-Three

It was getting close to Easter, which meant a week-long spring break from school, and a whole week to spend with Kevin and the rest of her family in Houston. Meg was close to floating again as Monday of the last week rolled around. She prepared her papers for the last class of that day as students began to flow in. The excitement had spread to them also. She knew there was no sense trying to cram anything deep into them for the week, so the plan was for them to finish their books by Thursday, and give three minute oral reports on Thursday and Friday.

Class went well. Most of the students read, a few spaced, and only one fell asleep. That was better than usual. After class, she noticed Carmen dragging around, waiting for the others to leave. When all had left, she approached her desk.

"What's going on?" Meg asked her as she collected a few of her things.

"I needed to say goodbye."

"What?" She stopped everything and whipped her head around.

"Carole wants me back … again." Carmen was actually smiling.

"Oh, Carmen," she moaned as she felt anger begin to rise.

"It's okay, Miss Mac," she assured her. "It really is. I can handle this now. I can handle her now."

"Are you sure?"

"I am. If it looks like it's gonna be permanent, I'm just going to settle in. I really think she wants more money …"

"I can do that," Meg interrupted.

She shook her head. "No, please. I need to face this once and for all. I've tried to run from it, and it always sneaks back up. Thanks to you, I really think I can handle it. I've got a plan."

"Tell me about this plan of yours then," Meg said, admiring her for such strength and resolve.

"Well, she promised me a car. Maybe I can bank on it, maybe not. But if so, the first thing I do is find me a church. Now, I know the girls there may be snooty, and no one may want to be my friend, but I don't care. God loves me. I know that, and that's just fine.

"Then I get a job and start saving for college. I am definitely going to college, Miss Mac. I have one more year of school left, and I intend to study as hard as I can."

"I'll see to it that you get into college," Meg assured her.

"No," she said firmly. "I've got to do this on my own. It may take a lot of work, and I'm sure it will, but when I get out there ... in the real world ... I'll know it's because I did it. And then I can help others do it too."

Meg took Carmen in her arms and hugged her tightly, tears spilling out. "And you will make it. You're the oldest sixteen year old I've ever known."

Carmen smiled, and wiped her own eyes. "I'll always have one regret though, Miss Mac."

"What's that?"

"I won't be a virgin like you whenever I find that right guy and get married. I really do regret that."

She took Carmen's hand and had her sit down. She looked her in the eye and said, "I have a story to tell you—I didn't realize no one had."

Meg was feeling weary and lonesome again that night. She finally decided to call Kevin. They didn't usually talk on Monday nights, but she needed to hear his voice and find his reassurance. She punched his name and lay back in the blue recliner on the glassed-in porch.

"Hey," he answered.

"Hey," she said. "It's me."

"I was just thinking about you. I was even about to call."

"You should have. I needed to hear your voice."

"Why is that?"

"Carmen's moving back with her mom, and she's not fighting it anymore. She seems to think she has the strength to stand up to her now."

"Sounds like a good move to me."

"I suppose," she sighed. "What's up with you?"

"Well, I was just thinking that maybe we ought to postpone the wedding for a few months."

The words hit Meg like a brick. She sat up quickly in the chair scaring Spiro off.

"Why?" she wanted to know.

"I don't feel like things are quite right between us. There's a distance that I'm not comfortable with."

"Of course there is! Several hundred miles worth of distance!"

"I'm not talking about that kind."

"Well, Kevin," she began to reason, "this is a long distance relationship. I can count the periods of time I've seen you on one hand. Of course there's going to be distance. When we get married, and things settle down, that distance won't be there."

"I certainly hope not, but I don't want to take that chance."

"What exactly are you saying?" She could feel her heart in her throat.

"I said exactly what I meant. I think we should postpone the wedding, that's all. We'd be able to spend regular time together for a couple of more months after you move up here. Then, when we're both comfortable with the relationship, we can move on."

"I can't talk about this over the phone. I'll be up there Friday evening— let's talk about it then, face to face."

There was a long pause. "I won't be here for Easter. That's another reason I wanted to talk to you."

"What!" she exploded. "What are you doing? First you say we need to be together then you say we won't be able to!"

"Hear me out before you embarrass yourself," he warned. "My mother called me today from Ecuador. Dad's got cancer and it's spreading quickly. He only has a few weeks to live, perhaps a few months, but not long."

"Let's get him to a clinic then," she insisted. "There are all kinds of treatment options for cancer now."

"Meg, this is my father. He refuses any medical help on that level. He believes God will do what God will do and that we should let it lie." He paused again. "Mom has never asked me for anything since I've been back in the states, but she asked if I would buy tickets for myself, my sisters and their families and come down for Easter."

"Okay," Meg shut her eyes and shook her head, "I am embarrassed. I can be a real selfish jerk sometimes."

"I'm not trying to make you feel guilty," he told her gently. "I just feel like I need to do this, and perhaps get some things right with my dad."

"Of course you do. I understand."

The silence was long.

"You don't want me to go with you?" she asked.

"No," he said more comforting than condemning. "This is going to be hard. I know you could hold your own, but I'm not sure I could. I need to face this alone."

"Okay. But please grant me this?"

"Anything."

"Please don't postpone the wedding right now. Let's have our Easters, and then we'll get together and talk."

"Meg ..."

"Please?"

"Okay," he agreed softly.

Meg struggled through Tuesday's and Wednesday's classes. It was hard trying to deal with everything Kevin had told her, but it was hard facing the last class of the day without Carmen there. She enjoyed Wednesday evening services, and was glad for that bright spot in the week. She had decided not to go to Houston at all for spring break because she would be going up sometime shortly afterward to see Kevin.

While driving home after choir practice, she had a long talk with the Lord.

God, why am I on such a roller coaster? Why is it that I seem to be able to control other people's lives so easily, but manage to be so out of control with my own? I was beginning to think that maybe it was because I needed a husband. But even that appears to be going nowhere now. Is he not the one, Lord? I was so sure he was. Everything was pointing that way, and he even has gotten close to you again as a result. I thought for sure that was a confirmation.

She breathed a deep, long sigh.

Give me wisdom, Lord. But more than that, give me the strength to deal with whatever that wisdom may show me.

Shortly after she made it home, Phillip came over. He greeted Craig and Janet and then asked to speak with her alone. She led him to the deck outside.

"Is this a long talk or a short talk?" she asked him.

"Middle-sized," he smiled.

"You never let me off the hook, do you?"

"Not after that stunt you pulled with the senator. Let's take a walk down the beach."

"I could use that."

They pulled off their shoes as she called Spiro and the three of them headed out.

"I understand you're not going to Houston for spring break," he began.

"No. I'll go down sometime later. Kevin is going to Ecuador to see his parents."

"I heard. How sad for him."

"Yeah. I guess I'll never get to meet his father," she said with melancholy.

They walked a little while longer. The breeze was beginning to warm up now, and it felt good to be barefooted in the surf.

"I have a huge, really big, humongous favor to ask of you, Meg."

"Sounds serious," she said as she stopped to look up at him. "What on earth is it?"

"Well, my family is coming down for Easter—all of them—Alex and Clara, Matthew, his wife and baby, James and my two sisters."

"Phillip, that's wonderful!" She was so excited for him that she forgot

182

her own troubles for the moment.

"But ... I want to do things right ... really right."

"You will! How could you not?"

"You don't understand. I want to show them the perfect time while they're here. I want to cook for them, show them around, boil crab legs and shrimp, grill snapper, make gumbo ..."

"You don't know how," she laughed.

"Ding!" he smiled. "Has that little bell gone off inside your head yet?"

She stared at him and then understood. "You want me to cook for your family?"

"More than that," he said, pleading with those blue eyes. "Just be with us. Act like you're supposed to be here. Could the girls stay with you?"

"Wait. Slow down." She tried to collect her thoughts. "You want me to spend Easter with your family?"

"Yeah," he nodded, "and cook too. And keep my sisters."

"What would they think? Wouldn't it be weird?"

"Meg, I've never needed you more."

"I doubt that," she muttered. She looked out to the ocean and thought about her miserable plan to spend the week alone and mourn her possible failing engagement. "I'll tell you this—it sounds way better than what I had on the schedule."

"What was that?"

"Spring cleaning."

School was out for spring that Thursday. Good Friday was a holiday, but not because it was Good Friday, just because it was the Friday before Easter. And Easter wasn't recognized by the school board as a religious holiday but rather a celebration of spring. Meg always rolled her eyes when the principal would explain the rules at the beginning of each year and discuss the importance of separation of church and state ... to which Meg always gave the unwanted response explaining how that phrase wasn't even in the Constitution.

She woke up Friday morning all alone in her house again, except for Spiro who was fast asleep on the foot of her bed. Janet and Craig had left for Houston the previous afternoon, and the house was unusually quiet for the first time in weeks. She wondered how Kevin would adjust to Spiro sharing their bed. He had slept with Meg since the day she had brought him home. Now, however, she was wondering if she and Kevin would even make it that far. He would be leaving Houston today for Ecuador without her. She would fly up for a weekend in two weeks so they could discuss the seemingly surmounting problems with their relationship.

"I hope he's not going to be one of those men that makes mountains out of molehills," she grumbled as she sat up in bed. Spiro stirred and opened his eyes. She reached over to pet him as she got out of bed and tried to untangle her Miami Dolphins jersey after a night of fitful sleep. He didn't move as quickly as usual.

"I'm feeling slow too," she said as she left him on the bed. She readied herself for her jog and called for the little dog to join her. He slowly made his way to the living room, but he refused to go outside.

"Are you okay?" she asked as a knock came from the French doors. She turned to see Phillip waving his hand at her. She picked her pup up and went to the back door.

"What are you doing?" she asked him.

"Hopefully going for a jog. May I join you?"

"Yeah, just a minute though," she said as she examined Spiro. "He's not very peppy today. He doesn't even want to go out this morning."

"Let me see him," he said as he took Spiro in his arms. "What's the matter, boy? Has she been treating you badly?"

He examined him also but couldn't find anything obviously wrong. "Maybe he's having a bad day? It happens to all of us."

"Not to Spiro, it doesn't," she said worried. "I need to call the vet after our jog."

"Ms. MacAllister, it's Good Friday," said the vet. "Can't you at least wait until Monday morning?"

"He's sick," she told him, "and he's never sick … at least not like this."

"If this is the first day he's acted like this, there's no need for concern. Bring him in Monday morning and I'll look him over—perhaps keep him overnight for some tests or something. He won't die over the weekend."

"That's pretty heartless," she protested.

"It's seven forty-five in the morning on one of my few days off for the entire year. I don't feel very light of heart right now."

"Okay, Monday morning," she regretfully agreed.

She clicked off the phone as Phillip toasted frozen waffles. Spiro was still laying by the French doors in the warm sunlight. She reached down to pet him, and he just looked at her, never moving.

"Are you okay, baby? Are you in pain?" she asked him. He only closed his eyes and went back to resting.

"Breakfast is served," Phillip said setting down their plates. "What did the vet say?"

"Take two aspirin and call him Monday morning," she replied mournfully.

"He'll probably be okay. He's just a hyper dog and he's getting a little older. It happens to all of us eventually."

"I guess so. I've never seen him like this though."

Meg joined Phillip at the table, he prayed for the food and for the week, and they ate.

"My family will be here at 4:00 this afternoon. I need you to help me make a grocery list, and then we'll go shopping after breakfast."

"Have you planned my entire day?"

"Close," he said, excited about the week to come, "and your week too."

"Okay, what do you want to eat tonight?"

"Well, I'm sure they'll be tired and won't want to go out. I thought about the Crab Shack, but decided to wait until later in the week. Then I thought about your fried chicken, but thought that would be too much for the first night. I don't know, Meg! I'm a mess! What do you suggest?"

"I suggest that you calm down first," she smiled. "How about we grill steaks, have baked potatoes and a salad? That will be simple, but filling."

"Can you bake cookies too—chocolate chip?"

"Absolutely, I am at your disposal this week, although I'm not sure exactly why I agreed to do this."

"Because you got me into this," he quickly reminded her with a grateful smile.

While shopping, Phillip was close to being manic. This whole experience had brought out sides to him she had never seen before. His behavior at the banquet where his father, the senator, spoke was unprecedented. And now he was acting as if his whole acceptance from the family was based on how well he fed them while they visited.

After shopping, they went back by her house to get the van for his family and to pick up Spiro, who was still not himself. Then they went to Phillip's where she helped him organize and put away groceries as they planned the events for the day.

"Okay," he went over the plan again, "I pick them up at four. You'll stay here and have iced tea and cokes ready for them when we get back. I'll help everyone settle into their rooms, and then we'll walk the beach. At six, we start the grill ... wait! When do we start baking potatoes?"

"I'll put them on at five thirty," she assured, making him sit down and breathe. "Phillip, I'll take care of the food. All you need to do is grill the steaks when it's time ... and I'll tell you when that is."

"Oh no!" he suddenly remembered. "I didn't put that baby bed thing together! I need to get it up! What if he's asleep when they get here and he needs to be put down right away?"

He jumped up and ran upstairs to start on the Pack-n-play. By the time he left to get his family, he was a nervous wreck. She assured him everything was ready and he had nothing to worry about, but he fumbled around for ten minutes trying to locate the keys to the van.

"Is it possible you left them in the van?" she asked him.

"I never leave keys in a vehicle," he assured her as he continued to search. Knowing where his mind wasn't today, she checked the van. Sure enough, there they were. He thanked her and took off.

The house was ready for the guests and the food was ready for cooking, so she had a chance to relax while he was away. She picked Spiro up and held him in her lap as she sat on the couch looking out over the deck at the seagulls. He lay motionless rather than watch the birds. He hadn't eaten breakfast or lunch, but he was drinking. She tried not to worry, but she had never seen him so still or quiet.

Chapter Twenty-Four

"We're here!" Phillip announced as the family began to pile into his living room. Meg placed Spiro down gently on his little cushion and went to greet the rest of the family.

She found Clara first and hugged her tightly.

"I will always owe you so much," Clara whispered to her. Meg smiled and then greeted Thomas, the stepdad. She remembered vaguely having met Matthew and his wife Terri, who had been pregnant at the time, last Thanksgiving. Baby Nathan, who was almost five months, was wide awake and smiling.

"Oh, my gosh!" she said as she took the baby. "Look at those beautiful eyes." He had the same blue as Phillip and Clara. She looked up at her old friend and smiled at his expression. He had never seen her with a baby before and was evidently shocked at the sight. James, a college student, was tall like Phillip, but with the dark brown eyes like the rest of the children. Mary Ann, sixteen, hugged Meg also, and then Julie, twelve, shook Meg's hand and then headed over to Spiro.

"He's so precious," Julie said as she stroked his back. Meg returned Nathan to his parents and joined Julie next to Spiro.

"He's normally very excited," she told her. "There's something wrong with him today. He's never been like this before."

"What kind is he?" the girl asked.

"A Cairn Terrier."

"Just like the dog on the Wizard of Oz?"

"Yep. He's a sweetheart. I wish he were feeling better."

"Me too. I would love to play with him."

"Julie wants to be a vet," Thomas explained as he came over to them.

Meg shook her head and said, "I hope she'll be better than the one I called today. I can't see him until Monday morning."

"He'll be all right," Julie told her. "Look at his eyes—he's smiling."

Meg looked at Spiro, and sure enough, his eyes were happy for the first time that day.

"Let's see if he'll eat something," Meg suggested, picking him up and taking him to the kitchen.

She had Julie pull out a baggie of cheese cubes to feed him. He ate one and then another.

"You must be his good luck charm," Meg said as she watched the gentle girl feed him by laying the cheese on her hand and then offering it to him.

The afternoon was wonderful. Phillip settled Matthew and Terri into his bedroom, Clara and Thomas into his spare room, and then he and James would stay on the couch bed. After settling, just as planned, the family walked the beach, except for Julie, who stayed at the house with Meg and Spiro. After walking, they grilled the steaks, ate dinner, and then sat back for some wonderful visiting. This was the first time in Meg's life that she could remember being a part of a family get together that didn't surround her family. She felt uncomfortable at first, but began to loosen up as the evening wore on.

When it was time to think about bed, Meg gathered the two girls and their belongings and packed them into the Porsche.

"I can't believe I'm riding in a Porsche," said Mary Ann as they left Phillip's.

"Don't be too impressed. It's eleven years old."

"Good cars are like fine wine," the older sister grinned, just like Phillip, "they only improve with age."

"This from the expert on wine," Julie moaned sarcastically.

"This house is wonderful!" Mary Ann exclaimed after unpacking and joining Meg on the couch. "I could get used to this kind of life."

"And what is this kind of life?" Meg wondered.

"The beach, the city, the warmth!"

"Funny," Meg told her, "I think your log cabin is just adorable. And you get the change of seasons and snow."

"It gets old," she moaned desolately.

"So does this."

Julie came back in carrying Spiro. She had kept the bag of cheese with her, and was pulling out another piece for him. He ate it gratefully.

"I do think he's feeling better," the serious girl said as she sat in the fluffy, peach chair.

"I know he is," Meg agreed.

They talked about this and that for quite a while. Meg learned that Mary Ann had stars in her eyes and loved the theater. She was into anything to do with drama and actually enjoyed Shakespeare. She was fun-loving, easy to get along with, and ready to try anything, at least once. Julie was quiet, loved to read, but the thought of acting on a stage petrified her. Her dream was to grow up, live alone, and have a house full of pets. Meg laughed to herself at both of them. By the time they were her age, they would most probably be far from those dreams.

Saturday passed quickly. After touring the radio station and Treasure Cove, watching Shrimp boats dock for the weekend, and flying kites in the warm breeze on the beach, everyone relaxed on the deck or in the living room. Meg got up to begin preparing the pot for the shrimp boil. Spiro followed her into the kitchen, feeling better, and sat up on his hind legs for a snack. She obliged with more cheese.

"Can I help?" asked Clara as she came into the kitchen.

"Not really. I've got it under control."

"Okay," said Clara, "*may* I help then?"

"Sure," Meg smiled as she handed her a knife, three oranges and three lemons. "Quarter these, squeeze them into that large pot on the stove, and then drop them in."

"Put them in the pot after I've squeezed them? The whole thing?"

Meg nodded. "Every bit of it. You know Phillip is so proud to have you all here. It's still strange to see him with a family. He's always been the orphan boy to all of us."

"I wish I'd known about him—I would have never abandoned him."

"You didn't abandon him, Mrs. Anderson."

"Please call me Clara," she insisted. "Mrs. Anderson sounds so formal. And after what you've done for me, you'll probably always be my best friend."

Meg laughed at her.

"What's so funny?"

"Phillip is my best friend, I guess, in a way."

"He told me that the two of you used to date."

"Yes—years ago."

"He never told me what happened. He said you just went your separate ways."

"Well, more or less, I guess that's what happened. I was very young when he left for seminary, and was afraid to make a serious commitment. I broke it off." She stared out the front window onto the landscaped lot for a few moments. Was that all? She was too young?

"Meg?" Clara brought her back. "Are you okay?"

"I don't really know sometimes." She looked back at her. "I've begun to think recently that maybe there was more to it than just that. Maybe it wasn't just because I was young."

"What else?"

She stopped slicing the onion and celery and stared past Clara this time, thinking deeply about what she should say. "He was going to be a minister … and a great one. You have no idea how good he is. He's a wonderful teacher and musician. He has a beautiful voice."

"I didn't know he sang," Clara lit up in surprise.

"Beautifully! And he plays the guitar too. He's wonderful."

"Wow—any other surprises up his sleeve for us?"

"Probably. He's a remarkable man."

"Then why did you break it off with him?"

She stared into Clara's blue eyes and drank in the whole reality of the fact that she was talking with Clara James Anderson, the mother of her dearest friend, Phillip.

"I wasn't a virgin," she said plainly. Even saying it this day, years later, cut her deeply.

"And neither was I," Clara reminded her softly. "But that didn't ruin my chance for happiness. Thomas knew all about my pregnancy and my affair with George. I was frank with him from the beginning."

"But how could I marry a minister … a youth minister no less … and drag that around with us to every church?"

"Think about it this way—what might have happened had you married Phillip? You're a very strong woman. I assumed you loved him at that time."

"Very much."

"What would have happened when his ministry was challenged had you been beside him all those years?"

She thought of the beaten down man that she had encountered last June. He hardly ate or slept. He was destroyed and hopeless, and had given up on the only real dream he ever had. A lump began to grow in her throat as she thought of how she might have spared him some pain, encouraged him when no one else had, and even insisted that those who had degraded him make it right.

"Dear God," she said looking at Clara, "how did you know?"

"He's my son. He's still in love with you, and your promise to this other man is killing him again."

Hot tears began to form in the edges of her eyes. "Why doesn't he tell me?"

"Because he's a man," Clara said, putting down her knife and putting her arm around Meg. "All he knew was that you rejected him once. How could he put himself through that again? He had to be strong, pick himself back up, and move on with his life," Clara paused, "in radio."

That stung, but if Clara was right, she deserved it. Had she really been protecting Phillip, or just herself from the humiliation of being open and honest with all she would come in contact with over the years that would follow?

"Meg," Clara said, turning her face to meet her blue eyes, "can you honestly say that you don't love him any longer, and that this man you're pledging your life to is more worthy of your love than Phillip? You went out on a limb to find *me*. That's more than just a good friendship. That's a commitment to something deeper."

Julie came in and interrupted them by accident. When she saw Meg's face and her mother embracing her, she awkwardly asked if she could take Spiro to the beach for a short walk. Meg nodded, and she left quickly.

Drying her eyes Meg asked, "Do you think she'd buy that it was just the onions?"

"I doubt it," Clara smiled. "She's a very perceptive child."

After dinner they visited shortly, but then everyone wanted to make it an early night because of Easter morning the next day. Meg and the girls said their goodbyes and then headed back for her house. They each showered, dried their hair, and laid out their clothes for the next morning. When Meg came into the living room, being the last to finish, she found Julie and Mary Ann sitting on the couch rather somberly.

"What have we here?" she asked them. "You guys look miserable."

"What were you and Mom talking about tonight in the kitchen when Julie walked in?" Mary Ann piped out quickly.

"Mary Ann!" her sister cried out.

"Well, I want to know!"

"It's none of our business," Julie insisted

"It's okay, Julie," Meg said. "You might as well know." She leaned back into the softness of the peach chair and closed her eyes.

"That serious?" Mary Ann asked.

Meg chuckled. These girls were just plain fun to be around. "Not really. It was just an emotional moment. I don't know if you knew this or not, but I used to date Phillip."

Mary Ann and Julie's brown eyes grew wide with wonder.

"It was a long time ago. The relationship ended when he graduated from college and left for seminary."

"Did he dump you?" Julie asked with a touch of disgust.

"I don't care if he is good looking ... or even my brother," Mary Ann groaned. "He's scum if he dumped you."

Meg nodded and then carefully said, "What if I dumped him?"

The girls looked at each other, eyes still big, then Mary Ann said, "Good for you, Meg! Always let a guy know who's in charge! That's what I say!"

She laughed with the girls and then told them she regretted breaking up with him only because she was going to miss being a part of this family.

🌴 🌴 🌴

Easter Sunday was wonderful. Meg awed the Andersons with her piano playing, and then Phillip brought them to tears with his solo in the choir's Easter special. Meg and Clara prepared a big dinner of ham, yellow rice, potato salad and green beans, topped off with Key Lime Pie. Poor Terri ended up taking a long nap after dinner from being up so much through the night with Nathan. He had been sleeping well at home, but the new environment had messed up his pattern. There was no church on Sunday night, so Alex suggested they have their own service. They all went over to Meg's so she could play the piano, and they heard Phillip play guitar for the first time. They each were asked to share something meaningful to them about Easter, and then Thomas closed in prayer. Meg could never imagine her family having any kind of Christ-centered happening. Her parents were Christians, and Craig also, along with she and Andrew, but she believed that if they ever tried to pull off an event like this, Herbie would dismiss himself from the family, and Mitch would probably take a machine gun to the place.

🌴 🌴 🌴

"He's had a heart attack," the vet explained to Meg and Julie.

"What?" Meg asked wanting to make sure she heard correctly.

"He's had a heart attack," the vet repeated.

"Dog's can have heart attacks?" she asked him, still not believing what she'd heard.

"Miss MacAllister," the young man said as he removed his glasses and looked at her with disdain, "you are paying me an exorbitant amount of money to give you a professional diagnosis of your animal. Yes, dogs have heart attacks, and yes, again, your dog has had one."

Before Meg could respond to his insolence, Julie spoke out. "You're a real jerk."

"Thank you, little girl," was all he said to Julie. He then turned back to Meg and handed her a bottle of pills. "This should help—it's heart medicine. He needs to take it every day, and you need to lay off of the cheese with him."

"What about fat-free cheese," Julie asked with a snarl. "Or are you aware of such things."

"Sure," he said snidely. "Don't bring her back with you next time, please. What is she? One of those orphans you lag around all the time."

"I won't be back," Meg said as she picked up Spiro. "I'll drive the 50 miles to Tampa for my next visit."

As they got back into the Porsche, Julie said, "Wonderful bedside manner."

"Yeah, well, I don't know if he's like that with everybody or just me."

"What on earth did you do to him?"

"Do you understand much about politics, Julie?"

"A little bit. I know you've got democrats and republicans and independents. And now the reform party is beginning to make a name for itself."

Meg looked at her in surprise. "You know more than most adults. He was campaigning to be on our city council. I didn't like what he was promising, so I heartily endorsed his opponent. His opponent won."

"And you're rich, aren't you?" she asked with a smile.

"Rather."

"Good for you. We need more women in politics," she said in all seriousness, but Meg couldn't help laughing.

When Meg and Julie got to Phillip's, he shushed them as soon as they walked in. Nathan was asleep on his shoulder, Terri and Matthew were napping upstairs, Thomas had gone with James to find some antihistamine, and Clara was walking on the beach with Mary Ann. Julie left to find the other girls while Meg said she would stay with Phillip. She watched as he held the baby tenderly and walked and rocked him around the room. He had always been a gentle soul, but to see him in this new light was overwhelming. She said she was going to the kitchen to get lunch started, but she watched him from afar for a long time. He never stopped rocking and swaying. He would nuzzle his cheek next to the baby's and whisper words she wished she could hear.

"He's asleep, you know," she said, coming up quietly behind him.

"I don't care," he whispered back. "He's precious. I want to be a dad, Meg. I want to have a family. Know any prospective brides?"

"I'll see what I can find," she smiled. "Any qualifications?"

"I'll be thirty-three in two weeks," he told her. "Just female and breathing at this point would be nice. I'm not getting any younger, you know."

She smiled and ran the back of her fingers over his blond hair. "Neither am I."

"Yeah," he told her, "but you've got a man."

☀ ☀ ☀

Meg went with Phillip to the airport to see the Andersons off. It was rather emotional. Seldom did Meg get picked up or dropped off by her family. Unless Craig or Janet happened to be in Houston, or now, Kevin, a car was usually sent for her. Her heart actually began to ache, just as it had when Carmen went back to the home, as she said goodbye to Julie and Mary Ann. She promised the younger sister she would send updates on Spiro, and Julie promised to research heart attacks with dogs and give her some information. Mary Ann cried as she told Meg goodbye, and asked her secretly to reconsider marrying Phillip so they could be sisters. Clara then pulled Meg to the side.

"Think about what we talked about," she told her. "I know what it's like to be in love with the wrong man, and I know what it's like to make a life with the right man."

"Thank you, Clara. I will think about it."

🌴 🌴 🌴

Meg and Phillip went back to her place so he could return the van, then she took him home.

"Stay and eat some of these leftovers with me," he pleaded. "You've got Spiro with you. I'm totally alone … again."

"I was really hoping to get some spring cleaning done."

"I'll help you clean tomorrow," he said sadly. "I don't want to be alone quite yet. It's a bit of a letdown to be with so many and then go back to being just one."

"I understand," she said nodding.

They ate leftovers, looked at pictures, talked about his family, and listened to some music.

"You want to go for a walk?" he asked her as the sun began to set. "I'll hold Spiro."

"Sure, but I think he'll be okay. Aren't heart attack victims supposed to exercise?"

They walked, but talked little. Phillip was unusually quiet. She knew he was missing his family. They were all wonderful people. She had absolutely fallen in love with his sisters, and was dreading the fact that she would be in Houston when they came down to spend some of the summer with Phillip. Spiro began to drag a bit, so Phillip picked him up and cradled him the rest of the way.

As she prepared to leave, he took her hand and melted her with his eyes, yet again. "I can never thank you enough for this week. For as long as I live, I'll always remember what you did."

"Consider us even," she smiled. "Let this be the make-up deed for all the misery I put you through with the senator."

He smiled and looked back at her. "No," he shook his head. "I'm afraid I will always owe you for this week."

"Okay," she granted doubtfully. "Have it your way, but I can be cruel with a life debt, you know."

"I look forward to it," he told her as she opened the door to go. "By the way, what time do you want me over for spring cleaning?"

"I jog at 7:00 sharp on Saturdays."

Chapter Twenty-Five

Craig and Janet returned, school began, and life went back to the same routine as it had been for years. Meg tried to prepare herself for the trip to visit Kevin, but she had a hard time concentrating. She knew she needed to discuss their future, but she couldn't think of what to say. He wanted to postpone the wedding—she didn't. He wanted to work through problems—she couldn't figure out what they were. She didn't hear from him until the Thursday after Easter, and she was to fly in on the next Friday. He had a good, but difficult visit with his father. He had just returned, staying longer than planned, to help his mother work out details that must take place after his father's death. They discussed things she didn't want the girls to worry about, and his father was able to discuss things with Kevin that he felt he ought to know.

Kevin picked her up at the airport, but the greeting wasn't what Meg had expected. He had been interviewing clients all day, so he was in a dress shirt and tie. But his greeting was formal also. He hugged her, but not like before. She didn't feel the security and warmth that had always flooded over her when he held her. They made small talk until they reached his loft. She noticed a Porsche with a *P EYE* on the license plate. It was much newer than Meg's. No wonder he hadn't been impressed with hers.

"This is magnificent!" she exclaimed as she walked through the huge apartment. "What a place! You're quite a decorator for a man. I'm impressed."

"I must confess," he told her as he brought her a cup of coffee, perfectly fixed, "I hired a decorator. I have a few things I've collected that I put up, but the classy stuff, she did it."

"Well then," she said, "I admire you for having the sense enough to get someone else to do it."

"Here are some pictures I took of the family," he said as he sat next to her and pulled out his phone. "Here's Mom and Dad. He looks really bad. Mom looks old. This is Karie and Kristie, their husbands. Here are the kids. Great kids, all of them."

He showed more pictures and talked of his family. He and his dad parted on civil terms, but not good terms. His dad was disappointed in him and wished he would leave the sway of the world to follow the call of God. Kevin insisted that he was following God's call on his life, and that he had helped many people in the process. His dad was afraid that helping a man's mind was not helping his soul.

"I wish things could have turned out better," she told him as she took his hand.

"This was better—better than it had been … and better than it might have been. He was actually being gentle with me."

"How did you turn out to be so gentle with a father so unmoving?"

"Sandpaper," he replied. "My father was the sand that rubbed the rough off of me."

"It's not like that with all men, you know." She thought of Herbie. "Some men with hard-minded fathers become hard-hearted men."

He just smiled. Meg knew he loved her—she could see it still in his eyes. As she sat with him, she knew he was the right man for her to marry. He would love her, take care of her, and make a good life with her. She just had to convince him somehow.

"You know that I love you," she finally said out of the blue.

"Always to the point," he smiled. "That's what confuses me about you."

"Being to the point is confusing?"

"In this case, yes," he said as he stood up to move away from her, as though he needed to put physical distance between them. "I can't figure it out."

"Figure what out? Please tell me what on earth you're struggling with."

"The beach."

"What?"

"The beach—why won't you walk the beach with me?" he asked her.

She shook her head in disbelief. He was basing the future of their entire relationship on whether or not she would walk the beach with him? "This is crazy!" she exclaimed. "You've had bad timing!"

"I won't accept that."

"Then you're crazy! I don't know what kind of answer you want from me."

"I want to know why you will never walk the beach with *me*."

"I told you," she tried to reason with him, "sometimes I like to and sometimes I don't. You've had the misfortune of being with me when I don't."

"Consistently."

"Ok, yes—consistently."

"But yet, when I talk with you over the phone, you're sad, so you walk the beach. You're thrilled, so you walk the beach. You're lonely, so you walk the beach. You're frustrated, so you walk the beach. You're miserable, so you walk the beach. You're thinking of me, so you walk the beach. But when I'm there, suddenly you're just not in the mood." He paused, then looked at her and asked, "Now tell me—why won't you walk the beach with *me?*"

She was furious. She stood up from the couch and began to pace. "I can't give you any answer because there is no answer!" She looked over at him and threw her hands up in frustration. "I'm in love with you! I'm ready to spend the rest of my life with you, and you're asking me about the beach when the beach isn't even a part of our life together!"

"There!" he yelled as though a great discovery had been made.

"What?" she screamed back.

"It isn't a part of our life together. It is just yours and yours alone!"

"That's ridiculous. I've walked that beach with everybody!"

"Everybody but me. And I want to know why," he said quieting down. "Why is it that you absolutely refuse to share that with me? Whether you realize it or not, you've shut me out there and have done so rather rudely. What else will you shut me out of, Meg? When we're married, what little compartments will I discover that are also off limits?"

"You're making too much out of this," she insisted, trying to calm down.

"Why won't you walk the beach with me?" he asked again.

"Stop it," she said through gritted teeth.

"Why won't you walk the beach with me?"

"I said stop it!" She was getting angrier.

"Why won't you walk the beach with me?"

"Do you want to marry me or not? Just make it plain! Stop with the run around!"

"The only thing I want to know at this moment is why you won't walk the beach with me."

"You're being ridiculous."

"Then give me an answer." He was resolute.

"There is no answer!"

"I won't leave this alone!" his voice was rising again. "For once be honest with me about the stupid beach! Why won't you walk the beach with me?"

"Because it's not our beach to share!" she yelled one last time as she burst into sobs. "I can share everything else with you, okay, but not that ... not that." She cried harder than she had ever remembered crying in her life. She was shaking and sobbing and couldn't gain control no matter how hard she tried. She hated the confession she had just made. "That belonged to me and Phillip," she finally admitted. "I can give you every part of me, but I can't give you that."

He sat down and put his head in his hands. She managed to stop crying but couldn't control shaking. She still didn't understand what had happened. Why hadn't she known this until now? How had all this emotion for Phillip been masked? How could she have been so in love with Kevin, yet still be so tied to Phillip?

"That's why I can't marry you," he finally said.

"What?" She was stunned.

"I love you with all my heart and soul, Meg, but I can't be a second choice."

"You're not," she told him. "I never agreed to marry Phillip. Never. Not even years before. He never asked—I never said *yes*."

"Not agreeing and not wanting to are totally different things," he said as he pulled her down onto the couch beside him. He held her hand tightly and tried to comfort her again.

"I told you how I felt about Phillip when you proposed," she reminded him.

"Yes, and you promised to work through it. When you accepted my proposal, I assumed you had thought it out and that I had won."

"I had and you did," she said, still hoping this wasn't happening.

"Meg, I know that we could go ahead and marry, and that I'd be the perfect man to take care of you. I would be everything you ever needed … but I would never be everything you ever wanted. And that would break my heart from the beginning and would one day catch up to you too."

She stood back up and wiped her eyes. "I really do love you."

"I believe you," he smiled, brown eyes no longer dancing. "But I'm not *Mr. Right*."

She was so confused she couldn't figure out what to do next. She had thought her choice was the right choice. Phillip had told her he didn't want a relationship with her then he had kissed her and told her he had lied. Then he told her he couldn't handle a relationship with her. Kevin had proposed and agreed to marry her. She was leaving Treasure Cove and marrying him and living the rest of her life with him. Then Clara told her Phillip still loved her. As though controlled by some force beyond her reasoning, she took the ring off her hand and offered it back to him.

"That's your ring, Meg," he shook his head. "You keep it."

"I can't. The only other man in this world that I would marry could never afford a ring like this. If I kept it, it would be one more thing to discourage him."

He took the ring, but then he took her in his arms. She cried again as she realized she would indeed miss him and miss what could have been. She wished she could have let go of Phillip somehow, but she realized now that it was never going to happen. She was too in love with him to ever fully love anyone else. And she had to face that … whether Phillip ever did or not.

🏝 🏝 🏝

She stayed the rest of the weekend at her parents. Surprisingly, her mother was distraught over the break-up, and wanted to know why, but Meg wouldn't give any details. This was her personal disappointment, failure, misery, whatever, and she wanted to seethe in the hurt alone. Susan cheered her up some as she talked about her children, but depression always followed because Herbie was still doing his unattached thing, whether with another woman, or just alone. Maybe marriage wasn't all it was cracked up to be. Meg knew that wasn't true. Kevin would have been a dedicated, loving, doting and wonderful husband. Herbie was merely the world's greatest jerk.

She stuck to her schedule and didn't return to Treasure Cove until Monday afternoon. As she pulled into the driveway, she noticed that Craig and Janet's house had begun construction. Janet was all excited when she met her at the door, but Meg's face revealed there was trouble in paradise. She explained the wedding was off but gave no real details.

"I can't believe this!" Janet exclaimed, immediately bursting into tears.

"Don't cry, Janet," Meg begged. "I've done enough of that this weekend for both of us."

"But I don't understand. I thought everything was perfect between the two of you."

"Yeah, me too. I guess perfect is relative, huh? I'm going to get a shower."

🏝 🏝 🏝

Meg trudged through school the next few days. She expected someone to notice the ring missing from her left hand, but no one said a word about it. The workload was very high at this time of the year. She had her junior classes reading some difficult literature, and her senior classes writing essays each day. She knew to expect, at this period in the school year, not to be the favorite teacher.

Her mind, however, was far from school. She kept thinking about Kevin and how sure he was that she was still in love with Phillip. She knew it was true, but she had come to the point where she believed she could live her life without him. Now she was wondering again. Should she tell him? Should she meet with him and explain the situation? Should she let him know that she'd never marry another man, or more aptly, another man would never marry her because he is her only true love? Or should she go on with her life, as mundane as it was beginning to seem, and pretend that she wanted no husband, no family, and no change? She had done it before and been just fine. Of course, before, she had actually believed it. Now she knew it wasn't true. She had tasted the possibility of a *happily-ever-after* and its absence had left a bitter taste in her heart.

"Miss MacAllister?" came Bart Marcum's voice ringing in the midst of her thought.

"Yes, Bart?"

"Why do we have to dig deep stuff out of this book? I mean, *The Great Gatsby* is a good book. I admit I like it. But can't we just like it and not have to pull its guts out?"

The class laughed, and Meg found herself smiling.

"Bart, you have to dig the guts out because there is a deeper meaning to the story than just what you've read on the surface. What does it say about the American dream?"

"That it's a real nightmare," he responded.

"Aha!" she said, waving a finger in the air. "You're not as confused as you thought you were."

Meg sat in the blue recliner with Spiro as she graded essays and tried to focus on something other than her miserable twist of fate. Each sentence, however, reminded her that this time next year she would be doing exactly the same thing instead of cooking dinner in Kevin's loft and waiting for the impending arrival of her husband.

Suddenly Janet burst through the front door, frantically waving an envelope back and forth, and significantly bringing a change of focus for Meg's melancholy mood. "I got a letter from Amy!" she yelled.

"The mean blond we used to know?" Meg grumbled looking back down to her papers.

"She wasn't mean. She was just a little more serious than you or I."

"Now, *that's* an understatement."

"Anyway," Janet continued, "she and Nickos have moved to a small town in north western Alabama where he is pastoring. She says it's beautiful up there and they are enjoying the life of a small town for a change. She's homeschooling her kids, and the kids love living out in the country. They're hoping to have enough money to buy bicycles for all of them at Christmas."

"Kids?" Meg said looking up. "Amy's a mom? Poor kids."

"Meg, stop being so hateful! Amy's a wonderful mom. You've got something awful stuck in your mind about her. She's really a wonderful person."

"I think she thought I was a bad influence on you," Meg told her as she added another graded paper to the endless pile.

"You were!" the redhead laughed. "You were horrible for me! You talked me into things that I would have never done in my entire life! But it was incredible fun …"

Meg smiled. They had indeed had some great times during those college years, much to Amy's dismay and judgment.

"Amy is wonderful," Janet continued. "I wish you could have had a chance to really know her. You two are more alike than you'd like to admit."

"No way!" Meg said with emotion for the first time. "Not one iota!"

"You'd be surprised."

"I'd be scared to death if she were my mom. How many kids does she have anyway?"

"Five."

"Five? You've got to be kidding! They have five kids? How does she homeschool five kids?"

"Only three of them are in school," Janet began to explain, but Meg cut back in.

"Two of them are preschoolers?" Her eyes were wide with shock. "Unbelievable! How does she teach school with two preschoolers running around?"

"Well, one of them is a baby, so it doesn't run yet.

"She's a better woman than I am."

"Wow—there's a statement I never thought I'd hear from you."

Meg thought about how imperfect her life seemed compared to Amy's. She slowly got up from the chair, reached for her phone and excused herself to the back deck. She was struggling with pure jealousy at hearing about Amy. Why did she deserve a husband and a family … a big family? *Why*? And why would Meg never have either? She stared at the phone in her hand. What if Phillip loved her still too? Clara had said as much. What could it hurt to ask? It was obvious to her that she would never marry anyone else, so why not just let him know how she felt? She'd always been up front and honest about everything. Why not now?

"Because," she told herself, "if he doesn't want anything more than friendship, I've struck out completely."

She walked down to the beach and let the warm sand sift between her toes. This beach had either been the ruin or the blessing of her life. It had caused her to lose Kevin, but perhaps keep Phillip. There was only one way to find out. She stared at the phone, pulled up her contacts, and finally punched in the station.

"WJBA, may I help you?" came the receptionist's voice.

"May I speak with Phillip Anderson, please?"

"Just one moment."

Her heart pounded as she listened to the hold music. What was she doing? She could hang up now and think this through more thoroughly. She needed a better plan than just telling him flat out.

"Phillip here."

"Phillip," she said, trying to collect her thoughts and her emotions. "It's Meg."

"Hey! How are you? I haven't talked with you since Houston," he said cheerfully.

"I know. I was hoping we could talk. I have something fairly drastic I need to speak with you about. Are you free this afternoon?"

"Wow," he said slowly, "not too free. This has been a hectic week. We're doing our annual fundraiser right now."

"I forgot," she said disappointed. "Maybe another time."

"No. I need to hear about something *drastic*. I have forty-five minutes coming up for supper but will have to be back by six."

"Okay," she said, trying to drum up her courage. "How about meeting at the park?"

"Sounds good," he said. "Could you bring me a sandwich or something?"

"How about Fang's?"

"Wonderful."

She hung up and took a deep breath. Did she have the courage to deal with this once and for all? She sure hoped so.

Chapter Twenty-Six

Meg watched the clock and felt her heart would never stop pounding. What was she doing? She had to be crazy to think this was going to work. She ran through every possible scenario in her mind, but she knew nothing could prepare her for the actual confrontation.

"Where are you going?" Janet asked her as she prepared to leave.

"I'm meeting Phillip at the park with some Chinese food."

"Really?" A broad smile formed.

"Really," she confirmed with no emotion whatsoever as she left.

She drove to Fang's and picked up some food. She knew she was early and that the food would be cold, but she needed to collect herself away from all of Janet's recent emotional mayhem and settle down before he arrived. She was a wreck. She left the food in her car and went to sit on a bench awhile. She stared out at the children playing in the park and felt that twinge of disappointment again. She had honestly envisioned herself on the way to motherhood by this time next year. Now everything seemed so dismal. She never even knew she wanted to be a mother, but when the prospect presented itself, she liked the idea.

"Meg?" She turned around to see Alan Parsons standing next to the bench. "I thought that was you," he said with a smile.

"Yeah, so what are you doing here?"

"I like this place," he told her, still standing. "This is where you forgave me, you know. It has a special significance for me. It's kind of peaceful."

"I suppose," she mumbled.

"You look ... I don't know ...down. Are you okay?"

She was indeed miserable. Why hide it? "No, I'm not okay. I'm struggling pretty strongly with something right now."

He sat down beside her, his eyes full of compassion. "Tell me, Meg," he pleaded. "I'm not trying to intrude. Just let me help, or at least pray for you."

"Why not?" She told of her trip to see Kevin and how he had interrogated the truth out of her. She explained her feelings for Phillip, and how it was difficult for her to realize that if he didn't want to build a life with her, there would probably not be anyone. She was here to spill her heart out to the one man she obviously loved, but only had a few minutes to do so, but had to do it now because she may never have the nerve any other time. Alan listened intently as she went on. When she finally finished, he smiled. He had changed so much. He was humble and kind and gentle now, so far from the arrogant, self-absorbed man she had known years ago.

"Meg," he took her hand and put his arm around her, "Phillip is a good guy, and you two would make a wonderful couple. Let me pray for you. Let's ask God to guide you. He gives us the desires of our hearts, you know? If this desire is that strong, it must be from God. Can I pray?"

"Please do," she replied through small tears.

As he prayed, she really did feel a peace. She felt relief from the bitterness she had felt for Alan since he had been here, she felt relief from the hurt she had been feeling over Kevin, and she felt peace about telling Phillip how she felt. When he finished, he reached over and kissed her cheek gently.

"You're a wonderful person, Meg," he told her. "I hope and pray God's best for you. I want nothing more in this world than to see you happy. You've given so much to others—it's time for you to receive something in return."

"Thank you, Alan."

"God bless you," he said as he got up, went over to his bike, and left.

She felt better. At least one healing had taken place today. She waited for five fifteen to roll around. It did, but no Phillip. He must have gotten tied up. She went and got the food from the car and waited some more. Five thirty came, but still no Phillip. She wondered if he had been delayed. She would now only have fifteen minutes with him. She was starting to lose her nerve. Five forty-five. If he did come, it would be too brief. She couldn't tell him in this short of time. She would just explain the break up with Kevin and leave the other for another time. When six o'clock rolled around, she gave up. He obviously wasn't coming. Something must have happened. She cleaned up the cold food, half eaten, and left.

When she walked into the house, Spiro greeted her. He was almost back to his old self again. He seemed to be the only bright spot in her life at the moment.

"Did you see Phillip?" Janet asked.

"As a matter of fact, I didn't."

"That's funny. He called here right after you left to say he had more time and would be there earlier than he thought."

"Well, he never showed," she mumbled. "Something must have come up."

"I guess. They're doing that fundraising thing now, you know."

"Yeah."

Meg felt like a complete idiot. She was sitting in her room, all alone, except for Spiro, listening to her Chopin CD from Phillip, and pouting. Janet had eagerly read Amy's entire letter to Craig making Meg even more miserable. It was ten fifty-seven p.m. Normally by this time, she would have already had her evening shower, put on her Miami Dolphins jersey with a pair of shorts, and been ready for bed after reading a couple of chapters from her latest novel selection. Instead, she was sulking. She knew in reality she had nothing to be unhappy about. She had a wealthy father who could make anything at all possible for her. She was intelligent with a wonderful job that gave her the possibility to shape young minds for the future, thus she was shaping the future. She lived in a beautiful house on the beach in Florida. She was young and attractive, her light brown hair now reaching past halfway down her back. She was shapely, in great health, with much to live for and look forward to. Yet here she was mooning over a man. She could probably have any man, if she wanted. But she only wanted one—at least that much was clear to her now.

In a moment of crazy fury, she put on her running shoes and headed down the hallway in a huff. As she passed through the living room, Craig immediately asked where she was going.

"To jog," she said resolutely.

"At ten thirty at night?" he asked concerned. "Are you crazy?"

"Hey, life is full of little surprises isn't it?" she retorted as she opened the French doors to the deck.

"It's thundering, Meg," Janet called after her. "Maybe you'd better not go."

"Maybe I'll get struck," she muttered under her breath so that no one could hear.

She left the deck and began running down the beach for a change. She never ran down the beach. She always ran north, but tonight, she ran down. She ran faster and faster, hoping to somehow run the self-pity and self-doubt away. It wasn't working. Soon it began to sprinkle, and the thunder was growing louder. She knew where she was as she looked up at the condos all lit up in the night. There was Phillip's place. His light was on, so he must obviously be home. Because of the rain beginning to fall, she felt she probably should stop in until it passed over.

She ran up the back steps to his deck as the sprinkles began to get heavier. She could see him watching television through the glass doors. She knocked. It startled him. She knew he was probably wondering who would be at his back door at this time of night. As he came closer, he recognized her.

"What do you want?" he asked rudely as he opened the door.

"Excuse me?" she replied.

"I said, what do you want?" He was cold and hateful towards her. At any other time, she might have thought this was a joke, but she could tell he was serious.

"I was jogging, and it started raining," she explained as she panted for breath. "I saw your light on and thought I would drop by until the storm passed."

"You don't jog at night, and you never jog this direction," he said suspiciously.

A crack of lightening followed by a huge boom caused them both to jump.

"Come on in then," he said, still detached.

She didn't move. She stood outside the back door as big drops began to fall.

"Are you coming in or not?" he yelled at her.

"Not," she said, confused about his whole mood.

"Suit yourself," he said as he turned around, but not closing the door.

The rain began to pour, but she neither went in nor left. She just stood there staring at him. Something had happened, something horrible, and it had to do with her, and he was thoroughly disgusted. He turned back around to see her still standing in the pouring rain.

"For heaven's sake," he yelled at her, "come on in until it stops!"

"I think I'll just stay here," she yelled back. "It fits my mood!"

"Your mood? What on earth is wrong with you? I thought you had the world by the tail!"

"What is wrong with you?" she screamed out. "What have I done?"

"Would you get inside! You look like an idiot standing out there!"

"No! As long as the earth is mourning, I may as well mourn with her. Ever heard of the song *Cryin' in the Rain?* Well, that's me right now!"

"What are you crying about?" he said with contempt. "You're a big girl! You make your own decisions!"

"What are you talking about?" she yelled over the rain. "And where were you today? You didn't show up, and then you didn't bother to call!"

He came outside and got right up into her face. "Oh, I came all right, and I was thoroughly disgusted! That was some drastic news you had to share!"

"What?" She was stupefied. He had come? "If you were there, why didn't you stop? I had your dinner!"

"Because what I saw turned my stomach!" he replied, letting the rain splash onto his face. "I couldn't have eaten if I was starved!"

"What are you talking about? I called you down there to share something really important, and you just drove on by?"

"You could have told me over the phone, thank-you! I didn't need to see it up close and personal!"

"See what?! What is going on?"

"Your drastic news!" he said, getting angrier and angrier. "You broke up with Kevin, you come back here, and then you hook up with that good-for-nothing jerk that nearly ruined your life years ago! Did you think I really wanted to hear about that?"

"What are you talking about?" she asked in tears.

"Alan! Do you think I'm stupid? I saw the two of you huddled up together on the bench!"

"He happened to be there on his bike while I was waiting on you," she explained in exasperation. "He said I looked miserable, and so I told him the whole story. Kevin wouldn't marry me because he knew I was in love with Phillip. I realized Kevin was right, so I was at the park preparing to spill my heart out to Phillip, only Phillip never showed!"

"But he kissed you!"

"Holy cow! He prayed for me! He took my hand and prayed for me then he kissed me on the cheek and said he hoped everything would work out for us!"

There was silence except for the sound of rain and thunder.

"Come out of the rain," he urged her, softly this time.

"No!" she resisted. "Do you understand what has happened yet? I was there to tell you that you're the only man I'll ever fully love. If you won't have me, then I'm ruined for everyone else." Drenched with rain, she paused and closed her eyes. "Do you understand?"

He took her hand and made her come inside. He went to the bathroom, brought out two towels, and handed one to her.

"Do you understand, Phillip," she asked again.

He looked at her for a long while, then said, "Do I ever."

He went to a shelf in his living room and took down a box that Meg recognized from a play they had been in at church back in college. He had played a wise man, and it was the box he had used to carry the myrrh. He reached in and took out a small package. He handed it to her.

"What's this?" she asked as she put down her towel and took the little box.

"Open it," was all he said.

She opened the container, and there sat a ring with two beautiful, small diamonds placed in a setting so they looked like a heart. She gasped and then looked up at him. "What's this?"

"I had it made that summer before I left for seminary. I was going to propose."

"Oh, Phillip," she said wearily, "I'm so sorry."

"No," he stopped her. "No more apologizing about the past ... or the present, for that matter. If you're saying what I think you're saying, then it's time for us to think only about our future and move forward."

She looked up at his eyes. They were warm and tender, finally the disgust and resentment of the evening gone. "I want to spend my life with you, Phillip, and not just as a friend." There—she said it clearly and plainly ... no mistake could be made about her intentions.

"I was hoping that's what you meant," he said, trying to smile, but beginning to be overcome with emotion. He looked down at her as tears began to shine like beautiful turquoise pools. She reached up to wipe one as it began to streak down his cheek. He quickly took her in his arms and held her tightly. She began to cry again as she felt a security and comfort that she never thought she would know.

"I can take care of you, Meg," he told her. "You may not think I can, but I can and I will."

She looked up at him and smiled as she said, "And I can take care of you too."

"Do you want to stick with a June wedding in Houston," he asked.

"Are you kidding?" She took his hands and gently rubbed them with her own.

"Too soon? We can wait ... I mean ... we've waited this long."

"Wait?" she exclaimed. "I'm over here wondering if this weekend is too early, trying to settle on perhaps next Friday, and you're wanting to wait until after June?"

"Next weekend?" he asked in surprise. "You want to get married next weekend?"

"Phillip, if we don't, something will happen and we'll never get married! We've had the worse luck in the world apart. I don't want to wait unless you can give me some really valid reason why we should."

"Next weekend sounds great!" he smiled with a twinkle in his eyes again. "Here?"

"Definitely—Treasure Cove is ours. We belong here."

"At the church?" he asked. She shook her head. "Where then?"

"Our place," she responded with a smile. "The beach."

"You want to get married in the sand?"

"Most definitely. And not only that, I will find a dress so long that I can go barefooted!"

"You wouldn't. '

"Wouldn't I?"

They stared at each other for a moment as they let it all sink in. For both of them, this was their deepest dream come true. Meg could hardly contain herself. She was going to marry Phillip Anderson in one week. Suddenly, she just jumped up and screamed with delight. She ran out the back door and into the rain again and let it wash away every fear, tear, insecurity and pain that she had felt the last week. He came back out and insisted she come in.

"It would be just my luck," he said as he pulled her close, "for you to get pneumonia the week before our wedding."

"You can't get rid of me that easily."

"I hope not," he said as he kissed her forehead, then her cheeks, then her nose, then at last her lips.

Meg melted. *This* was so right.

When Phillip drove Meg home that evening shortly after midnight, Craig and Janet were waiting. When the lights of Phillip's Durango shone in the driveway, the front door was flung open.

"I'm okay," Meg told them as she and Phillip approached the house. "I ended up at Phillip's and everything is fine."

"Whew," said Janet as she led Meg inside. "You're drenched! Come inside and get dried off. You're wet too, Phillip. Don't you guys have enough sense to get out of the rain?"

"Thanks for bringing her home," Craig said, assuming that Phillip was just making a delivery and leaving. Instead, he walked inside too. Meg had to keep herself from smiling as she watched Craig and Janet both shrug their shoulders at each other. She had been horrible to live with the past week. Well, actually, she had been horrible since they had moved in. For all of her life she had been stable, sure, directed, and competent, but the last few months her entire life had been turned upside down. She felt an apology was in order.

"Craig and Janet," she began, "you'd better sit down."

They sat and glanced at each other, then at Phillip, then toward Meg.

"First, let me apologize for the past couple of months. I know you probably assumed you were moving in with the old Meg for a little while. Unfortunately, she left a while back. I can't explain all that I've been through this past year, except to say that thirty is climbing up on me fast. I was seeking something, although I don't know that I was totally aware of this search. When Kevin broke up with me last weekend, I was mortified. I thought all my hopes for change and purpose and moving on were gone."

"I didn't know you wanted to move on," Janet said. "I thought you loved your life."

"I did too, at least until something new presented itself. Suddenly, everything I had worked so hard to be and do seemed insignificant and temporary. I knew there were reservations in my heart about Kevin, but I didn't know what they were … he did, however."

"What?" Craig asked. "Are you about to explain the breakup to us?"

Meg reached over and took Phillip's hand and held it up to her heart. Both Craig and Janet grew wide-eyed.

"Kevin knew I was still in love with Phillip. He knew that I cared for him too, but he also knew that it wasn't the same love I felt for Phillip. He told me he couldn't settle for second place."

Everyone was quiet. Janet and Craig sat stunned. Meg waited for a response, but they remained silent.

Phillip finally broke in. "Well, I for one think Mr. Kevin Morris is a really smart guy. Meg and I are going to be married next Friday."

Still no response. Meg expected a jump and a squeal from Janet, but she just stared.

"Phillip and I are getting married," she repeated, "next Friday ... here ... on the beach."

Janet began to smile, then to giggle, then to cry, and finally she got up from the couch and embraced Meg as she sobbed.

"You're one for surprises this year," Craig managed to say. "Please tell me that this will be your final engagement and that the marriage will take."

"It better be," she told her brother. "Why do you think we're doing it so soon?"

"You know Mom will have a fit when she hears this?" Craig told her.

"For just a brief moment," Meg said with certainty. "As soon as she finds out I'm marrying Phillip, she'll be here on the next plane."

"Don't you know it!" Janet beamed. "Phillip, Meri MacAllister is more in love with you than Meg!"

"I doubt that," Meg said as she pulled Phillip to her.

"None of that!" Craig piped in. "You have to wait until you're married before you can kiss or hold hands or anything like that, you know."

"And this would be following your example?" Meg mocked.

"Oh, my gosh!" Janet exclaimed again. "Look at your ring! Where did you get it?"

"Phillip," Meg replied.

"It's beautiful," Janet said as she held the hand up to get a closer look.

Phillip beamed. Meg adored the fact that he was proud of his gift and that he never once mentioned it in comparison to Kevin's.

"Meg!" Janet finally began to squeal. "Oh ... my ... gosh! We've got so much to plan in just one week! How could you do this? You can't make a wedding in a week!"

"I can do anything in a week," she assured her. "Remember—I am the queen of overextension."

"Now there's an understatement," Craig bumbled out.

Chapter Twenty-Seven

Meg woke up late the next morning—it had been a long evening. Phillip hadn't left until the early morning hours, and she couldn't remember when she actually fell asleep. The last time she glanced at the clock it had been four fifty-three a.m. She was feeling it now, however. No matter how elated she was over the fact that she was actually marrying Phillip Anderson one week from today, she was completely exhausted. Even Spiro wasn't moving fast.

"I'm gonna be late, Spiro," she mumbled, "if I don't get with it. No jog this morning, baby. I hope you don't mind. Janet will take you out for me, okay?"

She had showered the night before, or sometime in the morning—she couldn't remember—when, so she dressed quickly, grabbed her papers and headed out the door.

"To say I'm a little disappointed in your reports is putting it mildly," Meg said sternly as she handed back the papers.

"We just don't get it," Bart blurted out in exasperation. "We read a book and then you make us dig out things that just aren't there!" He was being rude, not cute. He had made it known he hated this class, and he hated reading and writing.

"You don't get it, Bart?" she asked with exasperation and sarcasm. "Gee, what a surprise. I would have never guessed from your report." She handed him his paper, a failing grade, and put her hand on his shoulder. "That is why we have convenience stores—to employ people like you on a rotating basis. People who can't think for themselves. People who can't express themselves creatively. People who have the attention span of a fly."

He shot up. "You're trying to make us into something we're not!"

"You bet I am!" she retorted, sending him back down immediately. "I'm trying to teach you to be thinkers, to see beyond your own limited world. Each of you has incredible potential in this life, but it doesn't just happen by accident. You have to grow in every area. Look at you … you look like adults. Some of you think you are adults. But you're not!"

She walked to the front of the room, went to the board and wrote the word *RESPONSIBILITY* in huge, capital letters. Then turning around, she threw her hands into the air.

"Do you even know what this word means?" she asked. "Right now, it simply means you read a book, think about it, and then turn in a paper. For some of you it means working a part-time job to help pay for a car or gas. For some of you it means making your bed in the morning or doing laundry. For some of you it means absolutely nothing!"

She sat on the front of her desk and continued the rant. "My job is to teach you how to be *responsible* in this world. Reading and writing are just the tools I have the privilege of using. Mr. Wood uses science. Mr. Williams uses algebra. Mrs. Pearson uses history. The bigger your mind becomes, the more you are capable of appreciating in this world. One day, each of you will be required to do much more than what we're asking here. You'll be providing for a family, balancing mortgages and car loans alongside of insurance, electric bills, and all the while making sure you have enough to buy food and enjoy recreation. Some of you think all this happens naturally. It doesn't. It is a process, and it begins with reading a book, thinking about it, and writing down your thoughts."

"This has nothing to do with the real world," Bart spewed out.

"Wrong again," she corrected him. "It has nothing to do with *your* world. And unfortunately, for you, and for those whom you share your life with in the future, your world will never be the better world."

She stared at him, not backing down. He finally grew uncomfortable and broke the gaze.

"Okay, enough of Gatsby and Fitzgerald," she said, trying to lighten the mood. "Today, we start a book for pure pleasure."

Sighs of relief were released.

"This is Rebecca by Daphne DuMaurier," she explained as she brought out a box with the new books. "This is a classic mystery thriller."

"How classic?" Bart mumbled.

"Probably too classic for you," she smiled, "but I'm sure the rest of the class will enjoy it."

There were a few giggles at this, but Meg was really not amused. She had seen too many just like Bart come through her classes over the years. Big egos, just enough sports ability to make them popular in high school, but not enough to take them to college, much less beyond. He would probably marry some girl right out of high school, work a low paying factory job, have a kid or two right away, never make enough to keep his head above water, eventually divorce and move on to something even more mundane. She wished she could shake him into reality, but only he could find it for himself.

After reading for most of the period, Alissa raised her hand.

"Yes, Alissa."

"Can I ask you a personal question?"

The class stopped reading and looked at Meg with expectant faces. *Uh oh.* This appeared to be another one of those situations where everyone knew something except her.

"I suppose you can ask it," Meg told her. "I won't guarantee that I'll answer it, however."

"Fair enough," Alissa agreed. "We know that you went to Texas last weekend to see Mr. Private Eye."

Suppressed chuckles sounded.

"We couldn't help but notice that you showed up Tuesday with no ring, not to mention you were really cranky."

More giggles.

"Then today, you show up with a new ring on the same finger. You're not really cranky anymore. You're more in one of those *inspiring* moods you get into at times."

"*Inspiring?*"

"Yeah, you know—when you try to inspire us to change the world. I mean, Miss Mac, for heaven's sake, you even tried to inspire Bart to have a brain."

The class laughed. Meg smirked. Even Bart smiled.

"I suppose you deserve an explanation. You'll all know soon enough anyway." She stood and went to the center of the room. "I did go to Houston. The result of the trip was a break-up with my fiancé."

The girls moaned.

"No, Miss Mac," said one girl. "He was really cute! I'm so sorry!"

"It's okay," Meg assured her. "There was a good reason. It's not a real heartbreak situation. I was, well am, see … it's like this …" She was struggling to explain it. The class, however, was listening intently.

"Perhaps you should put it in essay form for us," Bart muttered.

"Perhaps," she agreed. "Gee, this is harder than I'd anticipated."

"Just spit it out, Miss Mac," Alissa encouraged.

"Thank-you, Alissa. I'll keep that in mind."

She was amused that the class was so interested in this particular subject. She was uneasy, however, because what she was about to tell them seemed so unorthodox. They would know within a week, though, that she would be marrying Phillip. Not only that, she would go from being *Miss MacAllister* to *Mrs. Anderson* over a weekend. She sucked in a deep breath and went on.

"Mr. Morris and I broke our engagement because I had feelings for another man."

The class *ooed* and *ahhed*. Every eye was on her now, intently waiting for the deeper explanation.

"When I came back, I knew I needed to tell this other man about my feelings. So, I did. He apparently felt the same, and so we're getting married ... now ... soon."

Eyeballs were wide in surprise, but no comments were made until Alissa whispered, "Wo, Miss Mac."

"It's not as weird as it seems," Meg tried to explain.

"Yes it is," said a guy in the front row.

"Okay," she agreed. "I suppose it is."

"Will you get engaged to me next week?" asked a boy from the back with a smile.

"It's not like that," she tried to defend. "I've known him for a long time. We've even dated in the past. He's been ..."

Suddenly she was interrupted by a squeal from Alissa. "It's Mr. Anderson, isn't it?" She fanned her face frantically.

"As a matter of fact, yes."

The class erupted, especially the girls.

"He's so cute!" yelled one girl.

"And those eyes!" said another.

Alissa came out of her seat and ran to get a closer look at the ring. "It's beautiful," she oozed. "Look! It looks like a little heart!"

"Let me see!" said several girls. Meg had lost control ... again.

"I can buy a better ring," insisted a boy.

"Dream on," someone laughed.

"The P.I. was nice, but Mr. Anderson is such a doll," said another girl coming to see the ring.

"I knew you loved him," Alissa insisted. "I'm glad you finally realized it. Boy, you almost blew it, Miss Mac."

"So ... does Mr. Morris need someone to pick up the pieces of his broken heart," mourned another. "I'm available for that job."

Meg was stunned. She just let the conversations continue. Rebecca would have to wait until Monday.

Bart came up behind her and whispered in her ear, "So, this is the *real* world?"

She smiled and nodded. "The real world is always full of little surprises," she told him.

"You call this little?"

She had to deal with questions for the rest of the day. By 6th period, the entire school knew the story of her breakup and her new engagement. Someone had even put a sign made from notebook paper on her door that said *Engagements Happening Weekly: Tune in Daily for More Details*. By the time she pulled into her driveway, she was ready to escape for the weekend. No papers to grade—thank goodness. She could go shopping tomorrow for a dress, and make all the necessary plans for the upcoming wedding. First, though, she had to call her mother.

"Mom, it's Meg."

"How are you, honey?" came the reply. "I've been so worried."

"I'm doing surprisingly well. I need to talk to you about something, though."

"Okay, I'm all ears."

"Do you think you and the family could make a quick trip down next week?"

"I suppose. Are you needing family?"

"Sort of," she said, trying to decide how to break the news. "It would be nice to have everyone here for my wedding."

Silence.

"Excuse me?" her mother finally asked.

"Mother, Phillip and I are getting married on Friday … next Friday."

More silence.

"Mother? Are you there?"

"Run that whole thing by me again, will you?"

"Phillip and I are getting married next Friday."

Silence again.

"Meg," her mother said slowly, "you wouldn't play on my emotions would you? You are telling me the truth."

"Totally truthful. That's the reason Kevin and I broke off the engagement. He knew I was still in love with Phillip."

Still silence.

"I knew it was true—I had to tell Phillip how I felt. He was tickled pink and now we're getting married."

"Meg," her mother said, still speaking slowly, "give me a few minutes alone, and then I'll call you back. And yes, we'll all be there—guaranteed."

"Are you all right mother?"

"I think I'm about to pass out, honey. I'll call you back in a little while. I'm not kidding."

"About the passing out, or the calling back?"

"Both," Meri said and hung up.

🌴🌴🌴

"Are you sure you want to get married on the beach?" Janet asked as they wrote down a few plans for the wedding.

"Absolutely," Meg assured her. "I wouldn't have it any other way."

"What if it rains?"

"How wonderful! It would just be that much more memorable."

"You're mother would die!"

"She almost did, you know, when I told her Phillip and I were marrying."

"I'm still thinking all this is a dream," Janet said teary-eyed. "You and Phillip ... getting married!"

"Tell me about it! On Friday!"

"Oh, no!" Janet burst out. "What about the honeymoon? What are you guys going to do about that? Neither one of you can get off work right now!"

"Who cares? We'll be at home ... together. We can honeymoon later in the summer."

"Home? Where are you guys going to live? Here or there?"

"Who cares, Janet? I assume there, at his place. We just got engaged. We'll work out the details as we go along."

"As you go along?" She was in full blown panic now. "You've only got one week!"

"Thank goodness," Meg mumbled. "I couldn't take much more of you in a state like this."

🌴 🌴 🌴

"Hello, bride-to-be," said Phillip as Meg answered the door later that evening.

"Hello, blue eyes," she said back.

"It's been killing me that I couldn't see you until now," he said as he came inside. He quickly pulled her to him and kissed her. She held him tightly still trying to believe all this was happening.

"It's okay," she assured him. "Soon, all our time will be our own."

"I can't wait. Friday isn't soon enough."

"And you wanted to wait until June," she chided him. "Have you had dinner?"

"Yuck," he said as he collapsed onto the couch. "Cold fried chicken from somewhere. I can't even remember where it came from. Ira brought it in while we discussed plans for the station."

"Ira, huh?" Meg said uneasily. "I suppose you told him about us?"

"Didn't have to—news travels fast in this community."

"What did he say?"

"Congratulations, and he hopes we have a great life."

"No snide remarks?"

"He doesn't hate you, Meg. Contrary to what you believe, he actually admires you. He thinks you have fortitude and insight."

"Funny way of showing that admiration."

"I really don't want to talk about Ira right now," he smiled. "We have more pressing matters at hand, you know?"

"Such as …"

"Where do we live, for starters?"

"Your place." Then she creased her brow. "If Ira approves."

"I was hoping you'd say that. No offense, but I don't care to live with Craig and Janet while we adjust to married life."

"I like your place …"

"Our place," he corrected her.

"Except for one thing …"

"Uh oh," he said cautiously. "What is it?"

"Your bed."

"My bed? That's pretty shaky territory there. What's wrong with my bed?"

"Don't you think it might be too small? I mean, you're thirty-two, I'll be thirty in a month, and we've slept alone all these years. A full-sized bed may be a little cramping. I've slept in that huge, king-sized bed for years now."

"I wasn't actually thinking we'd be fighting for our space," he winked. She blushed.

"We have to sleep, you know," she shot back.

"I suppose. I could go for some sleep right now."

"You're not taking me seriously," she said sitting up straight. "I want to buy a king-sized bed."

"Okay, we'll go tomorrow and pick one out," he agreed.

"Not tomorrow. I have to get a dress tomorrow and book the caterer and order the flowers …"

"Okay, we'll drop by a furniture store in the middle of doing all that."

"You can't go with me!" she insisted.

"Why not? It's my wedding too."

"You can't see the dress before the wedding day!"

"Why not? Will it vaporize into thin air?

"Maybe … no one knows … and we won't be the first to find out. Janet will go with me tomorrow."

"I want to see you tomorrow too!" he protested.

"You will," she said leaning over to kiss him. "And the day after that, and the day after that, and so on and so on."

He calmed down and held her quietly for awhile.

"I could get used to this, you know?" she said to him.

"I hope so. My family is thrilled about all of this."

"You called them?" She sat up again.

"Oh yeah … first thing this morning. Mother cried. Mary Ann and Julie screamed and allegedly danced with glee. Thomas was astonished. All in all I'd say it was a pretty good reaction."

"Can they come?"

"Mom, Thomas, and the girls can. Matthew and Terri don't want to travel with the baby again."

"I can understand that," she nodded. Easter had been a big disruption for little Nathan.

"James has some major papers due and probably won't make it."

"That's fine. I like your sisters the best anyway."

"They adore you. This is so wild. I'm actually talking about *my* family."

"Honeymoon," Meg interjected.

"What?"

"Are we going to do a honeymoon thing, or just wait until the summer?"

"Ah," he smiled as he mulled a thought. "I know exactly what to do."

"You do? What's kicking around in that brain of yours?"

He pressed his finger to his lips and shook his head. "It's a surprise," he grinned.

"A surprise? You're giving me a surprise honeymoon?"

"We don't have much time, just a weekend, so I can't do much. But it'll be ... well ... different."

"I've always liked different."

"I'm sort of banking on that," he laughed.

"Oh my, Phillip Anderson. What have you got up your sleeve?"

He pressed his fingers to his lips again and shook his head. "You'll see soon enough."

She leaned back on his chest and closed her eyes. He gently ran his hand down her hair, and she marveled at how natural this all seemed. She thought being with Phillip again would be awkward at first, then eventually it would begin to settle. Instead, it was as if this was how it was always supposed to be. She sighed and softly whispered out the word *paradise*.

"Not yet," he sighed back, "but we're awfully close to it."

Chapter Twenty-Eight

"We can have it hemmed up about an inch by Wednesday afternoon," said the saleslady as she measured the bottom of the dress Meg had chosen. "You can try it on again then, and if any last minute notions must be ..."

"I don't want it hemmed," Meg told her.

"Unless you're planning to wear exceptionally high heels, you will need it hemmed," the lady insisted.

"I don't plan on wearing any shoes," Meg smiled at her. Janet rolled her eyes. The woman was disgusted.

"You're going barefoot?" she asked.

"Yes, Ma'am," Meg confirmed.

"Are you sure?" she asked again.

"She's sure," Janet told her, not thrilled with the idea herself.

Meg removed the dress, and the lady took it to the back to ready it for purchasing. They tried to suppress their laughter when she left the dressing room.

"This," Janet said, trying to gain control, "will be your worst stunt ever. Your mother is going to die."

"My mother doesn't need to know."

"Your mother knows everything. She'll find out. At least Spiro's not in the wedding."

Meg grinned.

"No!" Janet insisted. "He is not going to be in the wedding?"

She burst with laughter at Janet's expression. "No, but I did consider letting him run free during the whole thing."

"Meg!"

"Just considered it," she reassured. "He will be safely locked in the house upstairs ... not even chained to the deck."

She purchased the dress, put it into the van, and marked it off of her list. She and Janet then visited several more stores before stopping for lunch. Janet was so excited that she had talked non-stop for the entire morning. Meg was hoping that some food would shut her up for a brief while. No such luck.

"Okay, I suppose we need to start getting your stuff moved into Phillip's," she continued. "We can just take van-loads over at a time."

"Phillip and I will do that. It'll only take a couple of trips. I'm mainly taking clothes and books and music."

Janet, teary-eyed again, just stopped to stare at her for a moment.

"What?" Meg asked her, feeling uncomfortable with the stare.

"I can't believe you two are actually getting married ... and this Friday at that!" Then she went into full blown panic mode again. "There's so much to be done! We'll never get it all together by Friday! I just know we won't!"

Meri and Susan flew in on Sunday afternoon. They were a welcomed change from Janet's manic mode which had caused her to break out in tears every couple of hours or so. These two were level-headed and calm. They jumped right in with the planning and took a lot of responsibility off both Janet and Meg. Sunday evening after church, Meg managed to sneak away to Phillip's for a little time alone.

"Talk about your whirlwind romances," he said as they sat out on his deck listening to the waves lick the beach.

"Whirlwind?" she said skeptically. "There's nothing whirlwind about us! It's taken ten years to get here!"

"Eleven," he corrected her. He stared at her adoringly, making her wonder why she ever broke it off in the first place. "Why did we wait so long? I should have made you marry me years ago. I should have never taken *no* for an answer."

"You're right," she smiled. "You should have just ... well ... made me see ..." She stopped.

"What is it, Meg? I should have what?"

She looked out at the moon over the beach. Should she come clean with him about all her fears? She needed the freedom to be with him in total honesty with no barriers between them. She had learned that from Kevin. Small things can become big if they're not dealt with right away.

"I need to talk to you about something," she reluctantly decided.

"Anything ... you can always talk to me about anything ... for better or for worse, right?"

"Right," she nodded as she swallowed the dread invading her throat. "I have some fears about marrying you ... well ... at least in the past I did. Right now they're more of embarrassments than fears."

"What are they? Have I hurt you in some way?"

"No," she assured him. "Never. It's nothing like that. It's more like I've hurt you, so to speak." She was quiet as she tried to collect her thoughts. Why had it become so hard to express herself of late? Perhaps it was because everything had become so complicated.

"Meg," he said reaching for her hand. "You haven't hurt me. I told you—all the past is in the past. It's over. We move on from here."

"No, it's not," she said in frustration as she stood up and walked to the rail on the deck.

"Then what is it?"

"I feel like damaged goods," she finally owned up to the truth about all her issues where he was concerned.

"You shouldn't," he laughed. "What's damaged about you? You're perfect!"

"No," she sulked, "I'm not. I always felt like you should have someone worthy of your calling."

"What are you talking about? What calling?"

"I knew you would be in youth ministry. I somehow couldn't bring myself to be your wife because I knew I wasn't … a virgin." She said it. It was out. Catharsis was supposed to be good, wasn't it?

"I'm not a minister anymore," he countered.

"But you will be," she said to him as he came and stood in front of her, brushing the hair from her face. She looked into his blue eyes, full of tenderness and love for her. "God's not through with you yet. I know that, and many others know that. You may not yet, and that's fine. But it will happen. What do I tell those teenage girls when they look to me as an example?"

He pulled her to him. "The truth, Meg. I won't pretend that I don't want to beat the whatever out of Alan every time I see his face. I won't pretend that it doesn't bother me that I won't be your first. But for heaven's sake, I'm in love with you! I have been for years! I would have married you long ago if you would have let me! Was this the hold-up?"

"I think so, but I still worry about it. I'm humiliated, Phillip. I want to belong only to you, but I feel like I gave a part of myself away long ago. In one way, it all seems like a dream, like it never happened, like Alan never really existed and that part of my life was just something fabricated. Then I see him, and it all comes back. It's this pitiful reminder of how weak I can really be."

"Not just you, Meg," he assured her, "but many others like you. Don't you see? You alone are qualified to help others deal with the same thing. Think of the girls at the home. Think of girls like Carmen. Your story can give them hope."

"Yeah, but it can give others an excuse—*Meg did it! Why not me?*"

"Please, Meg. Anybody looking for an excuse to justify anything will use whatever reason they can come up with. If it isn't you, it'll be something else. I've heard some of the most preposterous justifications with Scripture for things that God has called abominations! You can't help those who don't want to be helped. You can't convince those that don't want to be convinced. You can't move those who don't want to be moved. You work with those you can. You give them your all, and then you help them to grow into all God made them to be."

She looked up at him with her mouth wide open. "Great words," she said slowly. "You should take them to heart yourself."

"I know," he said with sadness and hurt. "I know. I've just come to that realization, though. It's hard when you're in the midst of the battle to forget your wounds and keep on fighting."

She took his hands and looked up into his face. "This time, soldier, you won't be alone—I'll be there to help with the healing, and to carry the flag in the midst of the battle when you're too weak to hold it up for a while."

"And I, you," he said back. "See, Meg? See how foolish we've been? All these years we've wasted."

"They haven't been totally wasted." She smiled and looked out at the moon over the Gulf. "At least we won't waste the next ten years."

"Eleven," he reminded her, "and besides ... I mean ... has there been anyone else since Alan ... you know ... he was it, wasn't he?"

"No!" she jerked her head back. "I mean yes! What I mean is he was it ... no there wasn't another man I was ... well ... you know."

"I know," he said quickly. "That's what I'm saying. That in itself is quite a testimony. Think about it—for all these years you've committed yourself to purity. There aren't many who can say that. Most people sort of give up once they've messed up. I know. I've counseled with endless numbers of teenagers and college kids who just couldn't see the point in stopping once they started. You can be an inspiration for the many like that."

"I suppose," she slowly agreed. "It's just such a touchy area with me. I've been so perfect in every other way. And even if I messed up, it was never permanent ... it could be fixed or altered or started over. But not this."

He looked at her and smiled with all gentleness and understanding.

"What?" she asked. "There isn't anything humorous about all of this."

"Actually, there is. Think about it. We've sat and begrudged ourselves over the fact that we didn't marry nine years ago, or seven years, or sometime before now, but do you realize what has happened?"

"I'm not following you at all."

"Maybe you needed eleven years to prove that you weren't as bad as you thought you were."

"I'm still not following you."

"Meg, you just spilled out to me that one of your biggest guilt complexes in life has to do with the fact that you lost your virginity during your senior year in high school. It possibly even affected your decision about staying or not staying with me long ago. Now, all these years later, you haven't compromised. You've proved to yourself, and to anyone else who may question you, even to me, that your purity is an issue to be reckoned with and not taken lightly. I have no problem with that. Those who know you now have no problem with that."

She gazed back to the Gulf. That seemed to make a lot of sense. She looked up toward heaven and thought a quiet prayer—*Is that what You've been doing all these years?* She felt a peace. All this time she had worked to compensate for the biggest mistake in her life, yet it wasn't the penitence that brought the healing. It was simply living without making the mistake again, something she didn't even have to work at.

She turned back to him, amazed by his wisdom and comforted by his acceptance. She really believed she could marry him with a pure heart.

"It honestly seems like it never happened," she told him again. "It was so long ago. I've just never been able to forgive myself and let it go. I've kept dragging this guilt around with me year after year. I guess it is time to move on."

"I should say so," he agreed. "And not just move on, but move on with me. Meg, has it sunk in with you that we're actually going to be married?"

"It's so weird, Phillip, because a part of me can't believe it's happening, but another is feeling like it was always inevitable."

"Yes! Exactly! Like this is totally right and we aren't throwing it together in a week's time."

"Well, I can't agree there. I'm definitely feeling the one week's planning," she told him wearily. "But it would be more miserable to wait any longer. I am ready to be yours … now … soon."

"Friday," he smiled.

"Yes." she smiled back. "Friday."

As Meg pulled into her driveway, she was still feeling peace and release from her conversation with Phillip. She walked in the door and was greeted by a frantic Janet.

"Where have you been? It's so late! I was worried about you! You're always in bed by 10:00, especially on school nights."

"I was at Phillip's, Janet. For heaven's sake, would you calm down?" Meg pleaded. "You've been so out of control since this whole wedding thing started. What are you going to do when I move out? Call to make sure I'm in bed?"

"I certainly hope not!" Susan declared, sitting calmly on the couch with Meri. "That could be bad for newlyweds."

"Of course not!" Janet exclaimed. "But I won't have to worry about her then. Phillip can!"

"Janet," Meri said with restraint, "Meg has lived alone, and done so very responsibly I might add, for many years. I think she'll be fine without the need to be checked upon."

"It is late, however," Meg agreed, "and I need to get in bed. I'll talk to you all in the morning."

She turned to Janet and said, "Relax, and sleep well. You need it."

Meg went to her room, but instead of showering, she immediately knelt beside a recliner that overlooked the water beside the sliding glass door. She began to cry as she released, really for the first time, her guilt and pain over her past.

I am so sorry, Lord, for ever doubting that I could be worth anything to You. I know Your Word, and I know Your love, and I've known Your forgiveness for almost everything, but this one thing I could never let go of. Perhaps Phillip's right. Maybe all these years of waiting have simply been a way of You bringing about my own forgiveness … for myself.

She was silent for a moment and let the sense of release continue to flood over her.

If it was Your plan for me to be with Phillip all these years, but I lost this time because of my own stubbornness, I'm sorry. I asked You to make Phillip happy. I never dreamed that answer would include me. But I think You for that privilege. Now, I ask You to help me be the wife he needs me to be. I believe You want Him back in the ministry. I don't know when or where, but I believe that. I also know that if it happens, for the first time in my life I'll have to take a backseat to someone else. Dear God! Can I do that? Can I give up being in control for the man I love most in this world? Only with Your help. And … can I be a help to him rather than a hindrance? Can I keep my mouth shut when I'm supposed to? Can I say things to others with tact rather than frankness?

She stood and slid open the door. The breeze from the Gulf immediately bathed her face. She looked over the place that had become her home, her haven, and her healing.

And can I leave all of this to follow him to who knows where?

She leaned on the railing and turned her face toward heaven.

I know I love him … with all my heart, but I'm not stupid enough to think that will ever be enough. Please, Father, teach me to lean on You and rely on You always for this marriage. Let me be strong where he is weak. Let me teach him how to love a family.

She smiled as she thought of his face and his wit and his unending over-analyzing of every situation.

And please give me patience with him. I've never had to be with him for 24 hours!

🛬 🛬 🛬

"We have a wedding gift for you, Miss Mac," said Alissa from the back of the class.

"Really? And what would that be?"

"You don't have to grade any papers on *Rebecca!*" the vibrant girl exclaimed.

"My, but I was so looking forward to that. I was planning on taking them with me on my honeymoon."

The class moaned.

"You can't do that, Miss Mac!" Alissa protested. "Mr. Anderson will leave you then and there. He deserves your whole attention for the weekend, you know. It's your honeymoon! Do I need to explain the facts of life to you?"

The class laughed this time.

"Actually," Bart said, "he needs your whole attention for the first few months. I think you should just call off all papers for the rest of the year."

"And the final exam," agreed another guy.

"I'm pleased that you're all so concerned with my upcoming nuptials, but Mr. Anderson and myself both have careers to worry with at the present. We will continue work as usual, and then have a real honeymoon this summer."

More moans.

"I'm not an expert on marriage," Bart continued, "but I understand that too many irons in the fire can make for a bad one. We really don't mind you sacrificing us for the sake of your marriage, Miss Mac."

"Actually, Bart, I am impressed with how you are thinking. Perhaps you will do more than pump gas one of these days."

The class ooed at this, then Meg told them to open their *Rebecca* books and read the next three chapters. Moans.

"I'll get it," said Meg as she left the glass porch where all the ladies were assembling bird seed bags for the wedding.

"Phillip!" she said in surprise as she opened the door. "What are you doing here? It's only five thirty."

He came in, gave her a small kiss, and walked to the porch to greet the rest of the ladies.

"New hours," he said as he grabbed a cookie from the tray. "I'm working nine to five now. Gonna be a married man soon. My hours need to coincide with my lovely wife's."

"How thoughtful you are," Meri said smiling. "You should have married him long ago, Meg. He could have taught you some congeniality."

Janet laughed, obviously in a manic *happy* at the moment, as opposed to manic *stressed*.

"Right," Meg said sarcastically. "And I'll teach him how not to be overextended."

Everyone laughed at that.

"I do hope you'll begin to slow down on some things once you're married," Meri stated.

"I'll tell you what, Mother, I'll give you a list of all my activities, and you tell me which ones I need to let go of."

"You do that," her mother agreed, although Meg was actually teasing. "I learned long ago that there are many important things one can do, but you can't do them all. Others need the privilege of working too."

"Don't you know, Mother, that ten percent of the people do ninety percent of the work?"

"Only because the ten percent won't get their hands off of the work," her mother retorted.

With that, there was total silence from everyone. Phillip looked to Meg and raised an eyebrow. He then looked back at Meri.

"Wow," he said. "I hope Meg grows up to be just like you."

"Fat chance," Meg chided. "I'm not marrying a millionaire heir."

"But I am," he smiled.

Monday evening was wonderful. They went over the last of the details with Craig who would be performing the ceremony. The plans were drawn for the chairs on the beach and the placement of the tables for the reception. The MacAllisters would entertain the Andersons on Saturday until Meg and Phillip returned from the mysterious honeymoon. Janet cried a few more times as she watched everything come together. Meg had never seen her so emotional and was beginning to hope that the wedding would get here quickly just so she would settle down.

Tuesday was not so pleasant. She struggled to keep her mind on her classes as it wandered to all that still needed to be done. Rain was a possibility, but she refused to move the wedding indoors. Janet had cried twice before Meg left for school worrying about whether the flowers would be ready on time. And where on earth was Phillip taking her for the honeymoon? All he said was that she should pack light and extremely casual. After school, she would begin packing the van with the first load to be taken over to Phillip's. He would come by after work, have supper, and then they would begin the moving process.

When she finally managed to get away from the classroom at the end of the day, she was startled to see a man leaning against the back of her Porsche. As she came closer, she tried to make him out. She could see he was a repairman of some sort, dressed in a work uniform with a cap.

"Excuse me," she said as she approached the car. "May I help you?"

When he turned around, she dropped her satchel. It was Kevin Morris.

"Hey, Meg," he said as he turned to greet her. "How are you?"

"What are you doing here?" she asked, reeling over the sight of him by her car.

"I've just bought another house," he explained. "It's on the same street as the Deweys' house."

"I see," she said feeling extremely awkward. She didn't quite know what to do or say. She picked up her satchel and unlocked the car.

"I'm fixing it up right now," he went on. "It needs a lot of work. I think it'll be perfect for a young couple just starting out, so I don't want to sink too much into it. It needs to remain affordable."

"That's very thoughtful of you," she managed to get out. She couldn't think of anything to say, and she couldn't kill the weirdness she was feeling.

"I understand congratulations are in order," he finally revealed.

"So, you know," she sighed, slightly in relief.

"Yep. Good news travels fast … apparently happens fast too."

"Did you expect me to sit around and lick my wounds?" she spouted off without thinking.

"A little," he confessed. "A week would have been nice."

"I didn't plan it, you know? It just happened. I was merely telling him how I felt, and why we broke up, and the next thing I knew, we were getting married."

"Look, it doesn't matter," he said sincerely. "That's the reason I broke it off. I hoped the two of you would make it work, and you did. I'm really here to do what I just did—congratulate you."

"You're being too good of a sport. You're supposed to make me feel guilty and rotten about it."

"All I ever wanted was to make you happy."

"Puh-leeze," she whined. "I hope you imagined some happiness for yourself in our engagement."

"Give me the privilege of at least being the martyr here. It makes the whole thing easier to swallow."

"Thank you," she said as a lump formed in her throat.

"For making you feel guilty?" he laughed.

"For dumping me. I would have married you, you know? But you were right. My heart belongs to Phillip … always has and always will."

He removed his cap and ran his fingers through his damp, stringy hair. He smiled over at her and then kissed her gently on the cheek.

"See you around … Margaret," he smiled.

"You too, Mr. Morris."

She watched him walk off, get into a rental truck and leave. There was still a part of her that loved him too, but she knew it wasn't the same that she felt for Phillip. Kevin was a spring of fresh water that had burst into her life for a short time, but Phillip was a waterfall, never ending and always flowing. Phillip was a part of her, and she had no doubts that she belonged with him ... forever.

Chapter Twenty-Nine

Meg and Phillip spent the afternoon moving her belongings to the condo. Much to her surprise, Ira had told Phillip to take the afternoon off in order to get it done. No matter how nice Ira had been, she still wouldn't accept that he agreed with all of this. Meri made a light dinner for them, and then they worked on into the evening. As it neared nine thirty, Phillip suggested they stop and pick it back up on Thursday. She was beat and agreed.

She walked out onto the balcony from the room that would soon be her bedroom and smiled as she breathed in the sea air. How wonderful it would be to have all of this planning and packing and moving over with so she could just settle down and actually live with Phillip.

"A penny for your thoughts," he said, coming up from behind and putting his arms around her. She stuck out her palm.

"What?" he asked.

"Give me my penny," she teased.

He reached into his pocket, pulled out a coin and placed it into her hand. "How about a quarter—that's all I've got."

"Inflation," she smiled as she turned around to face him. She pulled away from his embrace and took his hand as she led him to stand on the edge of the railing with her.

"I was thinking again about how close I thought I was to paradise. Look at this place—the beach, the waves, the breeze, and a small town where I can move mountains if I want to. I was thinking I had it made. Then you came back in and upset the whole apple cart."

"Sorry," he said puzzled, "I think."

She laughed. "Yeah, you've got a lot to be sorry for," she teased. "You've changed my whole perspective on paradise. Up to now, I thought life was perfect, yet I'm scared to death that Friday won't ever get here. I'm so afraid that if I lost you again, I couldn't go on."

He smiled.

"It's a good thing God works in mysterious ways," she continued. "Only He would make me get engaged to another man in order to realize that I loved you all the time. Had all of this not happened I would be sitting at home, grading papers, mumbling to Spiro, and thinking that you needed a good woman in your life to straighten you out."

"Oh, really?"

"Really," she said sternly. "You were a wreck, you know? And I knew you needed someone. Only I was too pig-headed to realize it was me. Now, here I am, realizing that I needed you just as much. Had God not done it this way, I would have taken credit for the whole thing and put it all down on paper so we could make sure we did it right."

Thank-You, God, he whispered to heaven. "I couldn't have handled perfection."

"The truth is—neither could I. I'm ready for a change. I'm ready for adventure. I'm ready to be challenged instead of calculated." She paused then added, "I'm ready for marriage." She thought on the idea. "I'm ready for life with you."

"Are you expecting difficulty?" he asked cautiously.

"Yep."

He laughed. It had always been difficult between the two of them, yet they couldn't deny they loved each other desperately. She also needed to open a can of worms and tell him that she had seen Kevin that afternoon. Now was as perfect a time as any, seeing they had agreed that life would always be full of little surprises and tension between them.

"Guess who I saw today?" she asked.

"The tooth fairy?"

"Close," she remarked. "Kevin Morris."

Just as she expected, he spun around and glared at her.

"He was waiting at my car after school."

"And he wanted ... what?" Phillip asked soberly.

"Would you believe to congratulate me?"

"He's a better man than I am then."

"No, he's not," she said as she took his hands and pulled him to her. "You did the same thing."

"I didn't mean it, though—pure pretense on my part."

"Perhaps it is with him, too."

"No—he gave you up." He paused. "I never did."

"I'm so glad," she said as she pulled him into a warm kiss.

Wednesday seemed to bring even more feelings of anxiety. Before leaving for school, Janet read a list of all the things that still had to be accomplished before the wedding. She cried a few times before Meri reprimanded her for being so negative.

"If you don't stop," Meri had told her, "this wedding is going to be halted out of sheer emotional exhaustion."

Meg wanted to applaud. She and Phillip should have just run off somewhere for the weekend, done the deed, and come back happy. Janet was grating on her nerves, and she hated feeling that way. Her sister-in-law had always been a breath of fresh air, but right now she was like a mosquito buzzing around everyone's ears. One wanted to swat her, but knew it would do no good.

School was worse. She couldn't concentrate on a thing with her classes. She had actually decided secretly to cancel all assignments for the week and just let the students *enjoy* their reading rather than analyze it. She wouldn't tell them until Thursday, however.

After school, she packed the van with a few more things, then went out to the deck to breathe. She couldn't have been there more than forty-five seconds when Janet appeared beside her, frantic. Meg held up her hand to stop any conversation.

"Whatever it is," Meg said rudely, "I don't want to know."

"The florist burned down!" Janet yelled.

She felt her face turning pale, then she smiled. "I don't care," she said calmly. "I don't need flowers."

"Of course you need flowers!" Janet blubbered. "You can't have a wedding without flowers! We've got to call another florist and make a new order and ..."

She put her hand over Janet's mouth. "Janet, please!" she found herself yelling. "Craig and Phillip and myself are the only ones in the wedding! All we need are three simple roses! That's it!"

"But your mom, and Phillip's family, and ..."

"Three ... simple ... roses," Meg re-emphasized. "That's ... it. And I don't even care if they're from a florist. Just pick some from a neighbor's yard if you must." Janet stared at her with red, swollen eyes. "You've got to get a grip, Janet. You're driving me up the wall, not to mention everyone else in the house right now."

The whimpering red-head collapsed to the seat, put her face in her hands and shook her head. "I think something's wrong with me," she finally admitted. "It's like I've totally lost control of my emotions. I'm scared, Meg."

She sat beside her and put her hand on her shoulder. "You're just an emotional person," she assured her.

"No—not like *this*. I hate this feeling. I think there's something wrong with me physically."

"Like you're sick or something?" she asked. Janet nodded. "How so?"

"I've felt horrible since last week. I'm tired and nauseous, and I've pegged it on just the excitement of the wedding."

"Maybe that's all it is."

"No! This emotional thing is crazy! I literally can't control it. Maybe my mind understands something that I don't. I'm scared."

"There you go!" Meg said with discovery. "You've worked yourself into believing that something serious is wrong with you. Maybe it's PMS?"

Janet began crying this time. "Not for a whole month! Things just don't feel right. I think I have cancer or something!"

Now she understood. Janet really was scared.

"Sometimes stress can play nasty tricks on our bodies," she reassured her. "I could be the poster child for that this past year with all that's been going on. Living with me hasn't been a bed of roses, you know?"

"Awwww, don't say roses," Janet whined again.

"Forget the roses," she said quickly. "Look, let me call the doctor, and we'll get you in immediately."

"I tried. I couldn't get an appointment until next week. I could be dead by then!"

"I said to let *me* call the doctor. I'll get you in tomorrow."

She shook her head. "No, I want to wait until after the wedding. I don't want to know anything right now."

"It would give you peace of mind."

"Or just the opposite," she mumbled.

They sat quietly on the deck for a few moments, letting the salt air and the gulf-breeze still their thoughts.

"Did the florist really burn down?"

"Meg! Do you think I would make up something so bizarre as that two days before your wedding?"

"I would," was all she could say with a smile.

"It's true ... the florist did burn down ... and you would be horrible enough to make it up."

With that, Janet was finally able to laugh.

🌴 🌴 🌴

Meg was a favorite teacher again as she announced to each class they would not be required to turn in a writing assignment this Friday. Cheers and yells reverberated down the hallway, and kids encouraged her to get married every weekend. Several mentioned that it was a very real possibility seeing how often she changed fiancés. She just smiled and ignored the snide remarks. Close to two o'clock, the secretary knocked on the door and called her out of the room.

"Please don't tell me this is bad news," Meg groaned as the lady handed her a note.

"I can't tell you," she smiled. "I'm not sure what kind of news it is. It's a number that Carmen Delancey left for you. She says it's somewhat urgent that you call her tonight after six."

She took the number and looked up at the secretary.

"She didn't say at all what she wanted?"

"No, sorry. She didn't sound very desperate, but then, Carmen was good at masking her feelings."

"No kidding," she sighed. "Okay, I'll give her a call tonight."

"I know this probably isn't something you want to deal with on the eve of your wedding, but I didn't have the heart to tell her that. You did so much for her. I didn't think she would be calling if it weren't really important."

"Oh, no problem," she assured. "You did the right thing. The world doesn't stop for my wedding."

"It ought to!" the lady laughed. "Who would have thought this could have happened so fast?"

"I've got your roses," Meri told Meg as she came through the door that afternoon.

"Really? Where'd you find another florist? Tampa?"

"Nope, the pastor."

"I forgot all about his green thumb! He's always had the most beautiful rose garden I've ever seen ... even prettier than yours. And you pay all that money to keep it up."

"I know," her mother grimaced. "Perhaps when he retires, he can move in with us and keep our garden."

"Fat chance," she sighed as she dropped her satchel on the floor and plopped onto the couch.

"He has plenty of yellow roses for everyone," her mother continued. "Janet thinks it's *just quaint*.'"

"Did she cry about it?"

"Yes," came the controlled reply with a stern expression.

"Mother, what's her problem?"

"Beats me," she said glancing down the to-do list.

"I'm worried about her. What's she doing now?"

"Sleeping."

"Well, that's better than crying ... I suppose."

"Hello?" came Carmen's voice on the phone.

"Carmen! It's Miss MacAllister. What's up?"

"Oh, Miss Mac, I forgot all about talking to you. Thank-you for calling."
She was surprisingly cheerful.

"No problem. What can I do for you?"

"Well, a lot, perhaps. Carole is getting married."

"Really?"

"Yeah—I guess it's good. She seems to be really happy. It's some guy
who she sort of worked for, if you can use those terms. He began to pay
her boss a lot of money to save her just for him. Anyway, he apparently
wants to marry her."

"Wow, that's ... well ... unusual, I guess."

"Yeah, whatever," she chuckled. "I don't get the whole escort thing
myself. Why a lady would do that, who knows? Why a man would marry
her? Go figure."

"So, where does that leave you?"

"Where ever I want it to," she explained. "He doesn't really want me to
move in with them because they'll be traveling a lot. He offered to hire a
nanny, or get me my own place, or whatever I want."

"And what does Carole say?"

"She says I can do whatever I want."

"And what do you want?" Meg quizzed.

"I want to come back to Treasure Cove," Carmen told her. "That's
where I belong. I've done well here. I work, go to church, and keep up with
my schoolwork. But I'm lonely. I miss the home. I miss my friends. I miss
your class. I don't want to stay here if I don't have to."

"I understand. Do you want me to talk to Mr. Roberts?"

"I already did," she said slowly, sounding down for the first time in the
conversation.

"And ..."

"I can't come back without financial backing. Because it isn't mandatory
for me to be there, because the courts haven't had to step in, the money
they get can't be used to support me. It has to go to kids who need to be
there because there's nowhere else to go. I understand that, Miss Mac, and I
don't feel bad about it."

"What if somebody backs you?"

She was silent. Meg now understood the reason for the call. She knew
this had to be hard for Carmen who was so independent.

"He says I could come back. Miss Mac, if you don't want to do this ..."

"Say no more!" she said quickly. "You know I want to do this!"

"I hate asking," she began to apologize.

"I'm honored that you would do it, Carmen. You've come so far from
when I first met you."

"I could have never done it without your gentle shoving."

Meg thought about that phrase—gentle shoving. How funny. She supposed that was the best description she'd ever heard of her tendency to make things happen.

"Well," Meg laughed, "let me *shove* you one more time. When I get back from my honeymoon, I'll talk to Mr. Roberts and we'll get this thing moving."

Total silence became loud.

"Well," Carmen said, obviously disappointed, "okay then. I've got a lot I can do until the summer. Thanks, okay?"

"Not this summer—I can have you here by next week easily. Do you want to wait until the summer?

"You're getting married this summer, right? In June?"

Meg laughed hard, and then felt horrible because the girl was clueless. "No, honey," she explained, "I'm getting married tomorrow!"

There was silence again, then she let out a slow, low, "Wo—you guys moved it up quite a bit."

"Oh boy, how do I explain this? See, Kevin and I aren't getting married. I'm marrying Phillip Anderson tomorrow."

"Wo," Carmen said a little louder. "I don't even want to know how that happened, but I will say that I think it's a good thing."

"I'm glad you approve. I should have called and told you, but everything happened so fast. I assumed someone probably texted or called you about it."

"My phone died several weeks ago. Carole didn't want to spring for another one."

"I'll take care of that when you get back to Treasure Cove."

"It's not a big deal. Just being home will be enough." Meg could tell by her voice that she was smiling. "And, by the way, congratulations. You guys belong together."

"Thank-you."

"Where are we going?" Meg asked again as she and Phillip drove toward Tampa Bay. "Janet is probably having a cow right now because I'm not there with her putting the finishing touches on my wedding plans."

"Let her have a million cows," he smiled. "There are other important things, you know, than just the wedding."

"Tell Janet that!"

"Your mother will. She knows we're here and why."

"Wish I did," she mumbled.

"You will," he said as he pulled into a huge warehouse. "Soon enough."

They got out of the Porsche and made their way to the building. When he opened the door, he led her into the office.

"Phillip," said a man from behind the monitor of a computer. "I was beginning to give up on you." He got up and greeted them.

"You must be Meg," he said as he extended his hand. She shook it and nodded, vaguely recognizing the face, but not placing it.

"That I am," she replied. "But I'm at a loss as to who you are."

"This is Gary Jasper," Phillip told her. Meg knew the name.

"You're the furniture guy!" she exclaimed, now recognizing him from his commercials.

"Bingo!" he yelled. "Give the girl a recliner!"

"Actually," Phillip reminded him, "it's a bedroom suit we need."

She looked up at Phillip and smiled. She had forgotten all about the bed situation.

"Right this way," Gary said as he led them through a door into the huge warehouse. They walked to the section where the bedroom furniture was displayed. She was overwhelmed by the choices. His commercials had promised the widest selection in southwest Florida, and she believed it now.

"I don't even know where to start," she said in exasperation. "If you would have told me I could have thought through it and had something in mind."

"I didn't want you to think through it," Phillip explained. "I wanted you to see it, like it, and then let me buy it for you."

She smiled and shook her head. "You will cure me of predictability yet."

She turned to Gary Jasper and asked, "How did we manage to get here after hours?"

"Very persuasive fellow you're marrying," he replied.

"I knew we could never make it down during store hours," Phillip told her. "I guaranteed him we'd buy one tonight … from him … if he'd let us in."

She looked at all the furniture again. There were so many choices, but she needed to make a decision … tonight.

"Okay," she sighed, "let's narrow it down at least. King-sized sets for starters."

"Gotcha," he said in understanding as he led them to a particular section.

It took two hours just for Meg to narrow it down to three sets, then another hour to get it down to two. After that, it was a mere twenty minutes until she and Phillip had agreed on a bedroom suit. It was an off-white poster bed with a dresser, chest of drawers, and two nightstands. They would deal with linens at another time.

It was after midnight when they returned to Treasure Cove. He parked the Porsche in the garage and walked her to the door.

"I don't suppose I'll be jogging with you in the morning," he asked.

"No," she said quickly. "I'll go down the beach, and you go up the beach. We shouldn't chance a meeting by doing that."

"Shoot, I'm not going to run if you're not with me," he told her. "I hate it! I just run to be with you."

She smiled and said, "How sweet. Will you keep running with me after we're married?"

"Depends on how much of a nag you become."

She punched his arm. "I'm gonna have to work on you really hard. Janet says it takes a good year to break a husband in."

"I look forward to it," he grinned. "Tell me again why I can't see you tomorrow."

"I have no idea," she said with a yawn. "Something about luck or such. It's like the wedding dress. You can't see it or me on the wedding day. I don't know what the deal is, but I don't want to be the one to find out if any of that mumbo-jumbo is true."

"You've never been one to be superstitious."

"I've never been one to get married before either. Life is full of little surprises."

🌴 🌴 🌴

When Meg got to her room, Spiro was fast asleep at the foot of her bed. She walked over and sat next to him. He roused and looked sleepily up at her.

"Poor, baby," she soothed. "You've been rather neglected this past week, haven't you? It'll all be over soon. Although, I don't think I've ever mentioned to Phillip that you sleep on my bed. Hmmm. That may be a slight problem."

She got up to change when Janet walked in. Immediately she began to panic inside, thinking she was about to be reprimand for being so late.

"Don't get hasty," Janet told her. "I just couldn't sleep, so I thought I'd get some warm milk. I heard you come in ... thought I'd say goodnight."

Meg smiled with relief. Janet was probably half lying. She assumed the sleeplessness was most probably due to her coming in so late, but at least Janet was being level-headed for a change.

"How do you feel today?" Meg asked her.

"The same," she replied as she sat next to Spiro with her milk. "Did you find the perfect furniture?"

"Oh yeah. It's beautiful."

Janet stared around the room pensively, then held back a tear.

"What is it?" Meg asked, though in honesty she didn't really want to know at this hour of the night.

"I'm going to miss you," she smiled.

"I'll just be down the beach."

"I know, but it will be very different from having you right here," she pouted now. "I've never had a sister. And then losing my mother when I was sixteen was hard, not to mention my brother too. It's been like having a family again."

"Well, look at it this way," Meg joined her on the bed, "you're not losing a sister, you're gaining a brother, and we'll both be right down the beach from you."

"I know, but I'll still miss you. I'm so happy for you two, you know? It's still like a dream to me."

"Tell me about it."

"I've always admired you, Meg. I've always wanted to see you have everything your heart desired. I feel the same about Phillip. Even though he wasn't a Christian yet, he was wonderful to me after Mom and Ben's death. He and Amy were the only two kids my age that really let me talk with them. It was almost like he knew how I felt and he could understand my questions."

"He did know how you felt. He'd been through so much by the time he came here."

"I know. I love him as a brother. This will make it official," she said cheerily.

"Well, I can't identify with you there," Meg grinned. "Never loved him like a brother."

"I should hope not!" she giggled. "You'd better get to bed. You do realize you're getting married tomorrow?"

"Is that tomorrow?" she asked.

Janet looked at her wide-eyed. "You are kidding, aren't you?"

"Yeah, but did you hear? The florist burnt down."

Janet shook her head. "You and Phillip deserve each other," she said as she got up and waved goodnight.

"That's a scary thought."

"You're telling me!" she whispered loudly.

Chapter Thirty

Meg awoke to Spiro licking her face as the breeze blew through the screen of the balcony doors. She pulled him to her and cuddled a while as she realized this was her last morning to awaken in this bed, in this room, in this situation. She gave a long stretch and glanced at the clock.

"Nine seventeen! When was the last time I slept this late, Spiro? I'm guessing years."

A knock sounded on the door, and she said to enter. It was Susan, smiling big and carrying a wrapped package.

"You're finally up, I see," her sister-in-law said as she came over to the bed and sat down beside her.

"Finally indeed. For the record, I never sleep this late."

"I imagine you never get home as late as you did last night."

Last night. It had been wonderful. She and Phillip had picked out their furniture together. They had talked and dreamed again like years before. He had teased her, and she had needled him back. They had laughed and enjoyed the prospect of their future together. Could all this really be happening? Could this actually be the day she married Phillip Anderson?

"Hello?" Susan sang. "Are you somewhere else?"

"Most definitely," she grinned.

"Lovely gown," she scowled as she pointed to the Miami Dolphin's jersey.

"I like it," she defended.

"Well, we aren't out to just please Meg anymore, now are we?"

"Are you saying I have to give up my jersey when I get married?"

"I'm just saying there are more appropriate things for sleeping." She handed Meg the package.

"Okay …" She cautiously took the gift. "I open it now?"

"Please. It's sort of a private present."

"Oh no," she groaned. "Kind of like panties and a slip for your tenth birthday party?"

"Kind of," she admitted with a playful smile.

She carefully unwrapped the package. Once she opened the box, she

240

discovered two beautiful, lacy, revealing pieces of lingerie, one white and one blue.

"Wow," Meg whispered holding up the white one. "What's the point of wearing it? There's nothing to it to begin with."

"That's the idea," she beamed. Meg blushed.

"I can't wear these! I'd have to turn the lights out before I left the bathroom!"

"Look at the blue one," Susan redirected.

She gently took it out and held it up to the light of the glass door and shook her head. "I can't believe you think I would wear something like this to sleep in," she chided as she swayed the nighty back and forth. "I can't sleep in this."

"It's not for you to sleep in," Susan explained causing the blush all over again. "Besides, why don't you show them to Phillip tonight? Lay them out beside your over-sized football jersey there, and then ask, *Honey, what would you like me to wear tonight?* See what he says."

She folded the lingerie and placed them neatly back into the box then shook her head as she got up and placed the box next to the gym bag she would be packing for the honeymoon.

"I'd like to talk to you about something else also," Susan said seriously.

"Not more lingerie, I hope."

"No—just about marriage."

Meg sat in the recliner next to the balcony door and gave Susan her full attention.

"I know you probably think I'm the worst source to be giving you marital advice," she began, "but I know what makes a good marriage, and I know what ruins one. It all revolves around communication. When Herbie and I married, I couldn't imagine that we would one day live together as strangers. We were so happy ... so in love. We dreamed our dreams and shared our feelings. No one ever explained to me that a day would come where we'd have to fight for the time, energy, and even interest to do that. After awhile, he would come home and tell me about his day, and I would listen just long enough for him to take a breath so I could start in about the kids and the house and the problems I was experiencing. Before long, he stopped talking, I stopped talking, and we never listened or dreamed again. The kids added to a lot of that, but the kids are wonderful. I know God gives us children as blessings, but sometimes those blessings come at a price. What I'm saying is this—don't ever lose what you've got right now. It'll start to happen, and you'll have to fight for it. As your marriage ages, make yourself listen to him. Make him feel as important to you then as he is now. Make him believe that he's the greatest thing that ever happened to you even if he hasn't taken the garbage out, or been able to take the kids off your hands long enough for you to shower, or even if he forgets your birthday or anniversary."

Meg looked at her with deep sympathy and regret. She was so beautiful, so vibrant, and so loving. She was a wonderful mother and a wonderful person. How could Herbie ignore her like he did?

"Don't pity me, Meg," she said sharply. "I'm my own worst enemy at times. Herbie didn't walk away from me on his own. I pushed him away quite a bit. I was maybe too secure in things you shouldn't put security in."

"How can you stay with him?"

"I love him. I always will," she explained. "I don't want anyone else. He's the father of my children. He's the love of my youth. I don't know how to bring him back, but I somehow believe that I still can. Perhaps, one day, he'll get right with God, and then God can bring the changes. I wish I had known the Lord back then as I do now. I would have been so different."

"I hate him," Meg told her frankly.

"Don't," she insisted. "He's trying hard to be his own man, not your father's or your grandfather's shadows. They're hard men to live up to."

"He doesn't deserve you."

"Oh, I think we pretty much deserve each other," she smiled sadly.

🏝️ 🏝️ 🏝️

After breakfast, Meg went out to the beach to check on how the setting up was going. Craig was helping the men place chairs in the sand, and Janet was frantically helping others set up tables in the grass on the side lawn. Meri was merely watching, not saying anything except to assure Janet that everything was going fine. She walked up and put her arm around her mother.

"I'm getting married today, Mother," she said, startling the lady.

"I know," she smiled. "Pinch me."

Meg did.

"Ouch," she winced. "I believe it—you're getting married for real."

"You're not mad that I'm doing it here, on the beach, instead of in the church, are you?"

She smiled. "Meg, I've never expected you to do the conventional. This is perfect. You and Phillip deserve the most unique wedding in the world. I can't imagine a better place."

"Me either. I did want Spiro to be the ring bearer, you know? Janet wouldn't hear of it."

Her mother glared at her for a moment. "I wouldn't put it past you."

Janet came gliding up grinning from ear to ear. "It's beautiful, isn't it, Meg?"

"It really is," she agreed with a hug. "Thanks for all this."

"I so wish we had more flowers," Janet complained. "Pastor Hill brought these few over this morning—he said it was everything he had. I bought some ribbon yesterday to make you a bouquet and Phillip and Craig boutonnieres."

"You've gone above and beyond the call of duty."

"Not at all! You deserve the biggest, prettiest, most special wedding in the world! I'm going to see to that!"

"Thanks." Meg hugged her again. "I really do appreciate all you've done. I would have never gotten this elaborate."

Janet started to cry again. Meg rolled her eyes at her mother who just smiled back and shrugged her shoulders.

The rest of Meg's family came in from the airport around twelve thirty. They greeted each other and joked with Meg about whether she was sure this was the right guy, or if she wanted to change her mind one more time. She ignored most as she watched Herbie and Susan greet each other. He gave her a gentle hug and spoke few words. Her kids, however, adorned her with kisses and smiles. Mitch, obviously intoxicated from the flight, said very little. Michael hadn't come with him, a disappointment for Meg, but probably best for Michael. He would have been ignored in the business of the weekend.

Meg also knew Phillip's family was coming in from South Dakota about now too. She couldn't wait to see them and was glad she and Phillip had decided on just one night for the honeymoon so they could come back and visit with the Andersons. The honeymoon. Surely Susan didn't expect her to wear one of those ridiculous pieces of lace on the first night. She felt her face flush again. When was she going to stop doing that?

The doorbell rang and she rushed to it, hoping to get rid of the blush before anyone noticed. She opened the door to find, much to her shock, Ira Epstein.

"Ira," she said in surprise. "Hello? What are you doing here?"

"I have something for you."

"Really? For me?"

"Stop looking so shocked," he said bluntly. "Yes, for you. Now come out to this truck with me."

She followed, wondering what on earth he would have for her on her wedding day. He motioned for the driver to open the back.

"I understand you had a few complications concerning certain arrangements," he began. "Despite what you may think, I actually like the idea of you marrying Phillip."

"You do?"

"Yes, I do. Phillip needs you. I don't need you, mind that fact, but Phillip does."

"You think so?" she asked, still recovering from her shock at his being here.

"I know so. Why do you think I so eagerly offered him a high position at my station with his not having worked in broadcasting for years?"

"So he could marry me?"

"Some of that," he admitted. "You almost blew it, engaging yourself to that Texan. All I could do was pray. God is not the least bit impressed with my money, you know?"

She smiled and nodded as the back door to the truck swung open. Her jaw dropped. It was filled with dozens of arrangements of yellow and white roses.

"Ira," she breathed out, "where did you get these?"

"Ft. Myers," he said matter-of-factly. "Phillip told me yesterday about the flower situation. He was so proud that you just took it in stride and accepted the pastor's few roses. It can be a good thing, having money, you know?"

"Yesterday? How did you get this many arrangements overnight?"

"Like I said," he told her, "money can be a good thing at times. The florist and his employees worked all night for me. I suggest you get someone to start strategically placing these things. You're getting married in about three hours."

"Ira," she said slowly as she turned to him, "I would hug you if I was a huggy person ... or you were a huggy person. But since we're not, may I just shake your hand and say thank-you?"

He reached out his hand. "I like you, Meg. And thank-you for not hugging me—I don't like you that much yet."

They laughed together, a first, and then she went in and brought out Janet, Susan and Meri. When Janet saw the truck, all fountains turned on until she realized someone had to put the flowers somewhere. She then panicked and began frantically calling the men out to unload them to the lawn and the beach. She hugged Ira desperately. He looked at Meg and she just shrugged her shoulders.

It was two o'clock—only two hours until the wedding. Meg's heart pounded with excitement. Flowers were everywhere—the beach and yard had been transformed into a paradise. Silver punch bowls were tested as yellow liquid cascaded into the bottoms. Crystal plates and pastel napkins were placed in various locations around the tables. Men and ladies dressed in white and black outfits began placing empty trays on the tables as they discussed the best positions for each dish to be served. Spiro bothered everyone, growling at some who seemed stranger than others, and following some who had shown him affection on and off.

"Are you nervous?" came Herbie's voice from behind her. He hadn't actually spoken directly to her in over four years. She turned and stared at his dark eyes.

"Should I be?" she asked.

"I doubt it. You guys will probably do okay."

"Why do you think that?" she asked curiously, a bit surprised that he had considered her marriage at all.

"You're going about it the right way," he said flatly.

"How's that?" She couldn't believe he was even having a discussion with her.

"You're mature. You've both faced reality long before now. You're beyond *happily ever after* and all that. You've got your feet on the ground instead of your heads in the clouds. That'll help."

"What about your marriage?" she found herself asking before she stopped to think ... again ... for the millionth time in her life.

He laughed. "My marriage ... I don't know about my marriage anymore. I suppose I love her still—I just don't know her anymore."

"Start over."

"With or without her," he half-asked.

"With her, of course! She's wonderful, Herbie. Can you not see that?"

"I see it," he said, still flat with no emotion. "Believe me, I see it. It's not as simple as that, though. There's a lot of hurt thrown in there now. A lot of horrible things have been said, and a lot of horrible things have been done. You don't just erase that."

"You could try," she urged. "You know she still loves you, don't you?"

He winced. He apparently knew. He glanced out at the beach then looked over to the lawn. "This will be a nice wedding," was how he ended it as he headed down the steps of the deck.

"Phillip just called," Susan came in to tell Meg as she dried her hair. "He wanted to know if it was okay for them to come on over. I told him it was. Is that all right? Are you ready to lock yourself in this room?"

She glanced at the time—three o'clock. "It's fine. Consider me locked away."

Her sister-in-law smiled. "You're going to be a beautiful bride. How are you going to do your hair?"

"I have thought long and hard about that," she confessed, "and I have no idea. Phillip likes it long and straight, my mother likes it piled up on my head, and Janet likes it rolled and full of curls."

"Well," Susan said as she came on in and gently touched a long strand of Meg's hair, "you are marrying Phillip. Let's concentrate on what would be most incredible to him when you walk down that beach today."

She nodded. They began to try different things. Some were funny, some were unique, but they decided on leaving it long while braiding two long strands on either side to pull to the back.

"Perfect," Susan smiled. "This is Phillip's Meg."

Meg stared into the mirror. It was perfect, and for the first time she thought she might actually cry. She was going to be Phillip's bride today, in just a matter of minutes now. A knock sounded on her door.

"I'll see who it is," Susan said, going to the door.

In came Julie, Mary Ann and Clara Anderson. When Meg saw them, she thought for sure the dam would break. Mary Ann ran to her and hugged her hard.

"I can't believe you're going to be my sister-in-law!" she exclaimed. "Oh, my gosh! You look absolutely beautiful!" She pulled away and looked her over.

"Wait until you see the dress," Susan told them as she left the room.

Julie came over to hug her also. "I'm really glad you guys are getting married. Can I hold Spiro during the wedding?" She reached down to pick him up.

"You sure can," Meg smiled as she pictured Janet panicking to see him out of the room and on the beach with Julie. "That would be wonderful."

Clara came over next and looked up at her, smiling with those blue eyes just like Phillip's. Turquoise pools began to form as she reached up to caress her face. "I knew you were the one—I knew it."

Meg smiled, but the tears finally came to the surface. She felt them begin to roll down either cheek. Reaching down she hugged the woman that would become her mother-in-law within the next hour. She felt such a connection with her already, although she had only seen her twice in her life. No words could express the depth of emotion she felt at this moment. She was now crying.

Clara pulled her away and shook her head. "O, goodness, don't start that. You'll have red, puffy eyes for the pictures. Quickly, think of something that'll make you smile instead."

"I can't," she cried. "Everything is so incredible right now that all I can do is cry."

"Mary Ann," Clara ordered, "make her laugh. Do something."

No good. Mary Ann was crying too.

"Julie!" Clara tried the younger sister. "Help us."

Julie, ever calm and collected, reached into her purse and produced some folded up sheets of notebook paper. "This is what I found out about dogs with heart disease," she began as she unfolded the papers for Meg. "It was pretty interesting."

Clara gasped. "Telling her information about her sick puppy is your idea of cheering up?"

That was all it took—Meg loved irony so the laughter came. She took the papers and immediately began to have Julie explain about each section. She glanced over to Clara who was trying to dry her eyes without smearing mascara, while encouraging Mary Ann to do the same. Then, as if on cue, Janet walked in. She observed the scene, the tears, Meg's eyes, and then she burst into sobs herself.

Chapter Thirty-One

"It's three fifty-five!" Susan yelled through the hallway. "Craig, you better find Phillip and head down to the beach!"

"Three fifty-five!" Meri exclaimed as she bustled toward the bedroom door. "Oh my! I had no idea! Meg, get your shoes on and let's all head to the porch!" She clapped her hands to get everyone moving. "Quickly now!"

"I'm not wearing shoes, Mother."

"I know!" The mother of the bride was starting to panic a bit. "Get them on! Hurry!"

"No, you don't understand—I'm not wearing any shoes."

Her mother smiled at her, still not grasping the idea. "I know, honey," she said patronizingly. "Please, get them on. Now would be a good time."

Janet came up and put her hand on Meri's shoulder. "Mother," she said slowly. "Meg isn't wearing shoes in the wedding—she's going barefooted."

Meri turned sharply to her daughter and stared in amazement. "You wouldn't." Meg just smiled and nodded. Holding up her hands in surrender, she acquiesced. "It's your wedding. Whatever." She came over and kissed the bride on the cheek and looked over the placement of the floral wreath around her head. With a tearful smile she told her, "You are a beautiful bride, regardless of what is or is not on your feet." Then she promptly left for the beach.

Craig came over and hugged her. "I need to get down there with the groom. I love you sis," he said as he looked in her eyes. "I'll see you at the sandy altar. Janet, come with me, why don't you."

Janet hugged her also and then began to look around the room. There was slight panic in her eyes when she asked, "Where is Spiro?"

"With Julie."

"Not on the beach?" she pleaded.

"On the beach."

"Whatever," the red-head managed through a weary smile. "I'll see you when you are Mrs. Phillip Anderson." She started to leave the room, but turned quickly for one last word. "If that dog gets loose ..."

Meg interrupted her, "It'll be cute and funny and wonderful and memorable."

Craig pulled his wife through the door as the panic in her eyes began to grow.

"Well," Susan mumbled as she brushed past the couple on their way out, "do you think anyone should tell her the mascara has dripped way past her eyelashes?"

Meg and her father shook their heads emphatically.

"Point taken." She turned to Meg. "I suppose we need to move you and your bare feet to the back porch."

"Your mother took that very well," Herbert chuckled. "You're uniqueness has grown on her the past few years."

"It never seemed to bother you. Why not?" Meg asked him.

"I learned long ago that the world is full of those trying to be carbon copies of others. The ones who stand out are those who dance to their own fiddle."

"Or march to the beat of a different drummer?" she teased.

"Or, as in your case, never try to fill anyone else's shoes."

They laughed as Meg, her father, and Susan left the room for the back porch.

Once on the glassed in porch, Meg's stomach felt as though it was flipping somersaults. *Could this actually be happening?* Susan opened the outer door so they could hear the music. Immediately the gulf breeze flew into the room. Meg felt her hair blow slightly as the skirt of her dress swayed in the salty sea air. She smiled—this was what she wanted her senses to capture when she married the man of her dreams. As the processional started, "The Great Gate of Kiev" by Modest Mussorgsky, her heart raced. Looking through the glass she saw Phillip and Craig walking side by side down the beach to the front of the group. She couldn't see her groom clearly, but his white linen shirt and slacks flapping in the gusts captured the essence of his free spirit. All she wanted at that moment was to take his hand and walk the beach—their beach. As the men stood in place, she saw him wave to his family and give them a thumbs up sign.

"I believe it's our turn," her father said as he put out his arm.

"Oh, Daddy," she confessed, feeling weak, "I don't know if I can even make it down the stairs. I can't believe how nervous I've suddenly become."

"That's what dads are for," he winked. "Didn't you know?"

Susan hugged her one last time and straightened her hair. "When we get down the stairs, stop for just a moment and let me adjust your dress. Then off you go."

"Okay," Meg nodded as she took a deep breath. "Let's go."

Susan opened the door and Herbert MacAllister stepped out onto the deck. He guided his daughter to the stairs where she stopped for a moment to take in the view. Everyone came to their feet. There were the girls from the children's home smiling with Alissa waving beside Mr. Roberts and Ira. There was the church staff all sitting together. There were teachers from school. There were people from church, her Sunday school class, the choir members, and many others. There was Phillip's family, smiling and crying at the same time, with Julie holding Spiro tightly in her arms. Then there was her family. Her mother was beaming with pride as she saw Meg, while Janet blew her nose from sobbing. Herbie was actually smiling. Mitch's mind was lost somewhere, but Andrew was beside him, teary-eyed she noticed as he reached up to wipe his eyes. Then she saw Phillip. He was smiling bigger than ever before. Suddenly everyone else disappeared and he alone was left on the beach. She barely noticed that she was walking down the steps until her feet touched the sand. It was warm and comforting and familiar as it sifted between her toes. She stopped so Susan could adjust her dress, then she and her father began walking between the two sections of chairs. The music played on, making her feel like a queen as she stepped next to a beaming Phillip. When it stopped, she felt sure that everyone else must hear her heart pounding.

"Friends and family," Craig began, "we welcome you to this joyous event—the joining of two souls into one."

She tried to pay attention to all that was being said, but her heart was flying and her mind was drifting. The only thing that could bring her back to earth was the constant squishing of sand between her toes. Craig went on and on, saying words she assumed were important, but she wasn't hearing them. She hoped the video turned out so she could actually remember the ceremony one day. She vaguely heard her father say, "Her mother and I," but felt a warm tingle rush through her body as Herbert placed her hand into Phillip's. Craig said more words, and the next thing she knew, Phillip was repeating vows to her. Then it was her turn. Craig spoke, she followed. He spoke again, she followed along, pledging her life and love to the most beautiful pair of eyes she had ever seen that stared down on her now with such adoration. Soon, Phillip was placing a ring on her finger. As she looked up, the breeze blew, making her hair fly behind her and causing Phillip's to tousle about. It reminded her of the first time they had met, his long blond locks blowing in the wind, standing there appearing like a god before her eyes. He now seemed bigger than life again as he repeated more vows. She placed the ring on his finger and spoke the words they had written days before. She was glad she knew they were meaningful, because at this moment she wasn't hearing them. She knew the pronouncement of husband and wife was next, but there was a pause instead. Thomas, Phillip's father, came up to the couple and handed Phillip his guitar.

"Meg," Phillip spoke, "I wrote this for you—for this day."

He began to play a beautiful progression of chords and then started to sing, his voice rising above the growing breeze, melting into the afternoon. She was so lost in the whole moment that she barely heard the words, but the melody moved her to tears. She watched as he sang to her, eye to eye. She was a princess, and this was her coronation. As he finished, the crowd applauded and he handed his guitar back to his father. She barely heard Craig pronounce them husband and wife, but when he did, she could swear her heart exploded. And as Phillip bent down to kiss her, she truly felt like a new woman. No longer alone in this life, she was now a part of someone else—the two had become one.

A bark, followed by a high-pitched squeal brought her back to reality for the first time. Spiro came running from beneath the chairs and jumped straight into her arms. She held him close and found herself laughing as Phillip reached down to pet him, then took him into his own arms.

Craig announced, "Ladies and gentlemen, I proudly present to you for the very first time, Mr. and Mrs. Phillip James Anderson." He paused for a moment, then added, "and Spiro, their oldest child." With that, there was much applause and laughter, and people began to leave their chairs to greet the bride and groom.

🌴 🌴 🌴

For an hour Meg and Phillip mingled with their guests, having little time to speak together. They glanced at each other occasionally, but that was as close as they could get. Pictures were made, the cake was cut, and the celebration began. She continued to respond to all her visitors but was growing weary of all the conversation. She wanted to be with Phillip, alone, and now. However, every time she thought she was through with one group of people and tried to find him, someone else would demand her attention.

"Miss Mac," Alissa cooed, "you look awesome!"

"It's not *Miss Mac* anymore, you know," she corrected her.

"Oh, my gosh!" the girl squealed. "You're right! How do I stop calling you that? You've always been *Miss Mac*."

"Think of the tall blond she's living with now," Lana suggested. "*Mrs. Anderson* will come out easily then."

"I can't believe it," Alissa went on, "that you get to wake up to that every morning."

"Me either," Meg confessed as she waved goodbye, making yet another attempt to find Phillip.

"Well, well, well," came a voice from behind her with a hand on her shoulder—Ira Epstein. "You did it. Now, I am anxious to see many happy returns from this investment."

"There will be no returns at all if I never find my groom in this crowd," she complained. "I'm beginning to wonder if there was ever a wedding … just this crazy reception."

"Oh, trust me," he smiled. "There was a wedding. I witnessed it. You were beaming, young lady. I must admit that you have made quite a beautiful bride."

She stared in amazement. "Thank-you, Ira. You are full of surprises today."

"I'm always full of surprises," he winked. "Now, go find your groom."

She searched for Phillip everywhere and continued being stopped by people to chat about meaningless this and that. Perhaps he had gone to the restroom—she decided to head to the house and see if he was there. As she approached the deck, suddenly someone grabbed her from behind and pulled her into the basement door. It was dark in there and she was beginning to wonder if she should panic. The light came on, and there stood Phillip before her.

"I'm sorry, Meg," he apologized, "but I didn't think I could wait another minute to tell you how absolutely radiant you look today."

She smiled and leaned up to kiss him. "Thank-you," she said wearily. "I've tried to find you all afternoon, but could never wade through everyone."

"I just want you to know how totally in love I am with you … and … and … how incredible you look today. I can't stress that enough. Meg, when you walked out onto that deck, I thought my heart would stop. You looked like a picture from a movie. Your hair, that dress, your flowers … and that smile. Oh, Meg," he whispered, "I couldn't breathe."

She kissed him again, longer and more passionately. "Let's leave now," she pleaded. "I want to go away with you *now*."

"I wish," he smiled. "Just a little longer. They're all here for us. We owe them a little time."

"I want to be with *you*," she whispered. "I don't want to wait around here forever."

"Just a little longer," he said again as he took her in his arms and kissed her more. "You looked so free and light today—it was as though you had winged feet and were floating across the sand."

She giggled. "I was," she grinned as she pulled up her dress to reveal her bare feet.

"You didn't!" She nodded. "You were barefoot during the wedding?"

"I haven't put a shoe on either foot all day long."

"No fair," he said as he pulled her to him again. "I had to dress respectably."

"I'll give you a foot massage tonight," she promised. "That is, if you ever get me out of here."

"As soon as I possibly can," he breathed as he kissed her one more time before insisting they leave the basement.

As they came out, Janet immediately bounced toward them. "None of that, you two," she scolded.

"We're married now," Phillip protested.

"Everyone's been asking for you," she continued. "I've been hunting you down like crazy!"

"We weren't in there that long," Meg defended.

"Exactly what were you doing in there?"

"None of your business," she said emphatically. "We're husband and wife now. Anything's legal."

"Oh my," Janet blushed. "We'd better get you two off on the honeymoon soon."

"My sentiments exactly," Meg agreed with a tiresome groan.

They patiently stayed around another two hours, and then Phillip began to say they needed to get on the road so they wouldn't arrive too late that night at their destination.

Meg made sure Susan had put her overnight bag into the Porsche.

"Complete with everything," Susan assured her, "even the nighties."

Meg didn't blush this time, but thanked her.

The guests undid their mesh bags of birdseed and lined up for the bride and groom. When everyone was ready, the couple marched between the lines of friends as handfuls of seeds barraged them. They waved goodbye as Phillip opened her door for her, helped her in, dress and all, and then ran to his side. He started the Porsche and sped away, cans dragging like chimes behind them announcing to the world that Meg and Phillip had finally tied the knot.

"So, when do I find out where we're going?" she quizzed him as she took his hand and kissed the back of it.

"Not yet—you'll know soon enough."

"If I pout really badly, will you tell me?"

He laughed. "You know me better than that. I have the stubbornness of a mule. I waited all these years for *you*, didn't I?"

"Yeah, but it's your wedding day," she sighed. "I thought maybe I could get away with it."

"It's not far from here," he said as he pulled off the interstate.

"Good," she moaned. "I was about to start pouting anyway ... just to see if it might work."

He drove a few miles down a familiar road, and then turned into the state park where they had been the day she told him she had found his mother. She realized this must be the destination, but couldn't imagine where they'd be staying. The park had some rustic cabins, but she hoped he hadn't planned for them to spend their first night together in a bug-infested, un-air-conditioned firetrap.

"Exactly where are we staying?" she attempted again.

"You sure are an impatient little thing, aren't you?"

"On the contrary, I think I've been fairly patient," she defended. "I know nothing. Well, I know that we are here, in this park, in the middle of nowhere."

He stopped the Porsche and pointed.

"There you go," he said. "Right between those two big oaks."

She looked and realized there was a huge fifth-wheel camper parked right at the spot where she had given him the plane tickets for South Dakota. He remained parked as he grinned at his accomplishment. She understood how significant the whole place was, and then turned back to him.

"You are beyond incredible," she laughed. "How did you ever come up with this?"

"It was too easy actually," he confessed. "It was here that I realized I was still in love with you."

She remembered. He had kissed her, only to be confronted with the fact that she was seeing another man. This night, however, she would belong to him alone, totally and unconditionally. He couldn't have picked a more perfect place for their first night together.

"Where did you get that massive camper?" she asked as he finally pulled up beside it.

"It's Ira's."

"No way!" she said with unbelief. "He's ended up doing more for this wedding than anybody."

"I told you he liked you, but you refused to believe me."

"I believe, I believe," she finally admitted.

He got their bags from the trunk of the car and then unlocked the door to the camper. He motioned her to walk on in, and she managed to finally get the dress through the small doorway.

"Nice," she said looking around. "Very nice. I've camped in tents too many years now."

"What ever happened to that driving camper your parents owned?"

"They sold it years ago," she told him as she plopped down on a couch in a side pull out. "They never camped in it anyway. We'd just ride from place to place in it."

"How did you get into camping?" he asked as he turned on the air-conditioning. "I just assumed it was a family tradition."

"Hee hee," she mocked. "I'd hate to see our family camping."

"Your family's not that bad."

"We're all spoiled. Why camp when you can stay in not just a hotel room, but a suite? Why cook on a fire or camp stove when you can eat out?"

"So, how'd you start?"

"I don't know really," she thought. "It seems like in college I camped a couple of times and thought it was so cool. When I graduated and started working with the kids at the children's home, I thought it would be a neat experience for them to go camping now and then. I bought a tent, a stove, and several sleeping bags. Spiro and I fared it alone the first few times, then I started taking a few girls with me."

"You and Spiro by yourselves?"

"Yes."

"That's dangerous," he noted grimly.

"That's why I married you," she grinned as she pulled him beside her on the couch. "Now I can camp anytime I want. This, however, does not count as our first camping trip."

"Why not?"

"This is not camping—this is a glorified house."

"You're not too offended are you?"

She laughed. "You're the only man in the world who would take a millionaire's daughter on her honeymoon in a camper!"

"You don't have it quite right. You're the only millionaire's daughter who would think it was wonderful to go on her honeymoon in a camper."

She nodded. He was right. She thought this was completely perfect, and couldn't imagine Paris or Venice being any more fitting.

"I've got to get out of this dress," she grumbled, "and then get something to eat. Susan told me she loaded us a bunch of plates from the reception."

"I didn't eat a thing," he complained. "I'm glad you only have to get married once."

After changing, they rummaged through the plates of food.

"This is so good," She said with a mouthful of spinach dip.

"You've got a piece of green stuff stuck right here," he motioned.

"Oops, sorry," she said as she found it and ate it. "Hand me the chicken wings, please."

"Here you go." He placed the container in front of her. "They're really good. Do you know how to make those? It's like they have honey on them or something."

"Let me see." She took a hefty bite. "Mmmm! Delicious! I can make these! What's in that plate?"

He opened the container and looked in. "Something chocolate."

"Pass it," she commanded. "Must have chocolate."

"What if we eat so much that we get sick," he suddenly thought.

She stopped chewing for a moment. "That'd be bad. Should we stop, or take a break ... or something?"

"Probably. Why don't we go sit out by the river bank?"

"Good idea," she said as she began closing Styrofoam containers. "By the way, are we going to get into trouble for camping here? This isn't a designated spot, you know, and they're very particular about that."

"Nope," he said as he took the containers from her and placed them in the refrigerator. "I pre-arranged the whole thing. There's a notice on the front of the camper."

"So we won't be disturbed tonight by some frantic park ranger stumbling upon us?"

"Shouldn't be," he said as he pulled out two folding chairs from a closet.

"This is nice," Meg said as they watched the moon over the river and listened to the water rushing over rocks and between cypress trees. "Let's leave the beach, buy a camper, and move next to the river."

"How about a trailer?" he asked.

"Nope ... you mean a mobile home."

"Oh yeah."

"I could do that," she told him.

They sat quietly for a while enjoying the cool of the evening, the singing of crickets and the moving river. It felt wonderful to not be rushed or panicked or checking things off a list. They sat and relaxed, saying a few words occasionally, but always going back to silence. Then thunder began to rumble in the distance.

"Hmmm," Meg spoke. "How far away do you think that is?"

"I don't know, but it definitely seems to be coming this way. Did you notice how the breeze suddenly got cooler?"

"Yes," she said dreamily. "I love rain storms. They're so violent, yet refreshing at the same time."

"That's a scary analogy," he said turning to her. "Violent? Refreshing?"

"Well, don't knock it," she told him sternly. "We became engaged during a violent rainstorm. Was that not refreshing?"

"You've got me there."

The thunder became louder, the lightening closer, and soon small drops began to fall sparsely around them.

"I don't know what you're thinking, Meg," he finally said, "but apparently we're going to have to go inside sooner or later. If you're as nervous as I am right now, you're probably wondering how long we can out last this rain."

She smiled and chuckled. "I suppose you're right. It's like the anticipation of those piano contests I used to compete in. I couldn't wait for them to come. I'd practice and prepare and pick out clothes and make plans, but when it actually came time to play, I'd be as nervous as a cat."

"We could eat some more," he suggested.

Suddenly, a huge bolt of lightning struck nearby. They jumped, grabbed their chairs and rushed inside. Phillip went to the fridge and began taking some containers of food out when she stopped him and placed them back into the fridge. She then put her arms around him and kissed him. He held her tightly and returned the kiss. When she finally pulled away, she made him follow her to the bedroom where she had laid out two lace nighties and a football jersey.

"Susan said I should let you pick which one I should wear tonight."

He stared with wide eyes as he ran his hand across the white one, then the blue one. "What's with the jersey?"

"My gown of choice for eight years," she told him. "Susan thought you might enjoy something different."

"Yea for Susan," he whispered. "I like her more and more each time I'm around her."

"Just not more than me, I hope," she said as she began to kiss him again. Heaven on earth. *We may not need any of these pajamas tonight.*

🏝️ 🏝️ 🏝️

Meg barely slept that night as the storm raged relentlessly. When she awoke the next morning, she immediately looked out the window next to the bed to see if they had been carried away into the river. Phillip sleepily questioned what she was looking at. She told him she wondered if her Porsche had been washed downstream in the rain. He smiled, then wanted to know himself if it was still there.

"It's still there," she confirmed. "It's a lot cleaner than it was last night."

"You are a restless sleeper," he moaned as he closed his eyes. "I'm glad you suggested that king-sized bed. I don't know if I could do this every night ... flip-flop, flip-flop."

She threw a pillow at him and lay back beside him. "I'm not a restless sleeper. In fact I sleep very soundly. It's just we're here in this metal box beneath really tall oak trees with millions of bolts of electricity crashing all around us. Didn't it bother you a little bit?"

"Not a bit," he mumbled. "You're flip-flopping, however ..."

Another flash of lightening struck followed by a thundering boom. She jumped—or flip-flopped—yet again.

"That's it!" she exclaimed, jumping up from the bed and putting on her jeans beneath her jersey. "I'm getting something to eat, then I'm leaving. You're welcome to join me if you like."

He sat up in the bed and gave her a puzzled look. "You're walking out on me during our honeymoon?"

"Don't take it personally. I'd walk out on anyone during a storm like this." She made her way to the kitchen area and began rummaging through cabinets. "Are you with me or not?"

"I guess with you," he said with a yawn as he got out of bed.

"Did you get anything for us to have for breakfast?"

He smiled, embarrassed, as he shook his head.

"You didn't get any food?"

"I confess," he said as he came up to her and wrapped his arms around her waist, "I wasn't thinking of food at all when I planned this trip."

"Well, your heart was in the right place," she said as she gently kissed his cheek. "But don't expect me to always be so forgiving."

"Whew," he whispered, "I wasn't expecting such mercy now."

"It is our honeymoon," she said, breaking his embrace and opening the refrigerator. "We must thank Susan for this food at least."

"I need coffee," he mumbled as he leaned against a cabinet.

"Tough luck," she replied. "Men what's wants coffee, must needs bring it along."

"Men what's wants coffee," he corrected, "marry women what's can remember to bring it."

"Well, at least we've got a microwave. You want some chicken wings?"

"I want coffee," he moaned again.

She looked over at him as he dropped onto the seat at the table and then shook her head with a smile. "Let's change, pack, and go eat somewhere."

"With coffee?" he asked hopefully.

"Yes," she smiled as she pulled him up, "and a buffet or something. I'm starved!"

"Probably from the flip-flopping."

"I'm gonna leave you here," she warned.

He held up his hands in surrender. "Just curious, how did we end up with the football jersey last night?"

"My gown of choice," she reminded him.

"I hate to say this," he grinned, "but I really like it. I'll never look at a football uniform quite the same again."

Chapter Thirty-Two

Meg and Phillip packed their few items, locked up the camper, and managed to get soaking wet from the few steps to the car. They went to the first restaurant they happened upon, a small diner, and stuffed themselves with lots of fatty foods and coffee. She had to admit the food was quite good and promised she wouldn't judge a restaurant by the amount of grease left on the tables, chairs, or floors anymore. They decided to go to the MacAllister house first assuming everyone would be there. After visiting a couple of hours, it was determined they would go to the Crab Shack for lunch. After eating, the Andersons went back with the couple to the condo for the afternoon.

"Phillip, look!" Meg exclaimed as she walked into the bedroom to find new curtains with pastel shells matching the new bedspread. "Did you do this?"

"Are you kidding? I don't have tastes this good."

"Guilty," came the confession from Clara as she joined them. "I wanted to do something for you, but didn't know what. I saw the new furniture in here and looked all over for the linens, thinking I would make it up for you. I found nothing. I talked Thomas and the girls into going shopping with me last night. We picked it out—sort of a wedding present."

"Oh, Clara," Meg said, "you're being here was enough present for us."

"No, I wanted something tangible for you to remember us by. I figured you could think of us us every night as you turn in."

"Or every morning when I have to make it ..."

"There you go," the older woman said with her gentle laugh and smiling blue eyes. "Morning and evening."

"Thanks ... Mom," Phillip said as he kissed her cheek. "It means more than you know."

"Yes," Meg agreed with a hug, "more than you could know."

"Okay, stop it, you two!" Clara demanded. "I'll be blubbering as bad as

Janet if you don't."

🌴🌴🌴

That night, Phillip and Meg said goodnight to his family, and went to their own room. He collapsed as he neared the bed, sinking into the deep comforter. "Ahh … I'm so tired. It's been all I could do to not take a nap today."

"You should have said something," Meg told him as she lay down next to him. "I would have gladly entertained your family."

"I can't believe you're not beat too," he mumbled.

"Maybe I am, but women can handle lack of sleep better than men. That's why God let us have the babies."

"I believe it. I can barely keep my eyes open."

"Hmmm," she said softly.

"Hmmm? What does *hmmm* mean?"

"Well, I just thought I'd wear something a little different tonight."

"You mean," he shot up from the bed, "you don't have a football jersey beneath that robe?"

She smiled as she stood up and began to untie her robe. "Well, if you're too tired…"

"Tired?"

🌴🌴🌴

The first two weeks of married life were truly bliss. Meg struggled to keep her mind on school, but managed to get through each day having accomplished all that was necessary. Phillip worked at his job with new inspiration, vowing to make the station better than ever before. The only one struggling with the arrangement was Spiro. From day one he had refused to sleep on the new bed. He had been so chastised over the years for jumping on any beds other than Meg's, both at the beach house and in Houston that he simply stayed off all strange beds. Even when she would place him on the bed, he would slouch down as though he were in trouble. Only if she or Phillip held him would he be comfortable. She bought him a small doggie bed that lay on the floor beside her, and he appeared to be comfortable with that.

Meg's thirtieth birthday rolled around quickly. She had been dreading this birthday the entire year, but when it finally hit, she rather enjoyed it. She had thought her life had been far from what any thirty year old's should be … until two weeks ago. Being married to the man of her dreams had somehow eased the blow of aging a bit. As she awoke that morning, she found herself smiling at the prospect of the future, although what the future held was unclear. She had already written a resignation letter for the school when she thought she would be marrying Kevin and moving back to Houston. She had been looking forward to not teaching. She didn't know why—perhaps it was just a need for change or a sabbatical. Whatever the reason, she had not torn up the letter. In fact, its presence began to loom in her mind even more.

"Happy birthday to you! Happy birthday to you! Happy birthday, dear Meggy! Happy birthday to you!" sang Phillip as he entered the bedroom with a bed tray loaded with breakfast.

"Meggy?"

"The song lends itself to two syllables there. I improvised, and that's what came out." He placed the tray down in front of her and kissed her good morning.

"You cooked this?" she asked in disbelief.

"Actually, no. I went down to Mazie's Diner and got us some hot plates. I did make the coffee, though."

"You make wonderful coffee," she smiled. "How did you manage to leave the house without me knowing?"

"Well, contrary to our first night together, I have discovered that what you said was true—you indeed are a sound sleeper. I get up two or three times a night, but you're always out like a log."

"Told you," she said as she took a big bite of eggs. "I didn't realize you got up every night."

"Every night," he told her as he took a bite himself. "Nature calls, you know?"

"Nope, I don't know," she said with a mouthful. "I don't think I've ever had to get up in the night to go to the bathroom."

"Never?"

"Well, a couple of times a year, maybe … like when I've had a lot to drink before I've gone to bed."

"Jeesh," he moaned. "I can't imagine sleeping through the night like that."

They ate a little more of their breakfast when Phillip produced a small box.

"What's this?" she asked.

"Oh, gee," he sing-songed, "perhaps a birthday gift?"

"Well, now, let's see what we've got here." She carefully opened the small package. Once the paper was removed, she carefully opened the blue velvet box to discover a beautiful diamond necklace that perfectly matched her engagement ring. It had two diamonds cut and placed together to give the appearance of a heart.

"Phillip, it's beautiful." She was awed. "Did you have this one made too?"

"Sure did," he smiled as he took it from the box and placed it around her neck. She kissed him several times as he tried to hook the clasp. "You're making this difficult."

"Life's never easy," she teased.

Each class at school managed to have a "party" for her, making it impossible to get any work done. She decided since she didn't turn thirty every day, she should just go along with the celebrations. When her last period rolled around, she was sitting at her desk making adjustments in lesson plans for the next day. She was so caught up in her project that she didn't notice the girl standing at her desk. Finally she spoke, jarring Meg from her work.

"Miss Mac, I'm back," came a familiar voice.

"Carmen!" Meg cheered as she jumped up to hug her. She had changed so much. Her hair had been trimmed, her clothes were colorful and attractive, and she was even wearing a small amount of make-up. "I can't believe you're actually here! What took so long? I was beginning to think maybe you had changed your mind."

"Carole wanted me to stay for the wedding, so I did. It was really gaudy, Miss Mac. I would have been embarrassed for her had she not thought it was the grandest thing in the world."

"I hope she'll be happy."

"Who knows?" Carmen shrugged. "Maybe she'll be happy for at least a little while. Or maybe it'll last. He's got a lot to offer her. No rugged good looks or anything, but a whole lot of dough."

"Maybe that's what she needs. Some women crave security and to be taken care of. Perhaps your mother is one of them."

"Perhaps," she nodded thoughtfully. "What about you? Is that why you got married?"

"That's doubtful," Meg laughed slightly. "Mainly it's because I'm head over heels in love with him."

"What about Kevin Morris?"

"Well, I suppose I'm caught there." She fidgeted with her pen as she tried to think how to explain her muddled love life to a teenager who had never known what normal was. "A possible life with him was very appealing. I did love him, you know?"

"I guess. I suppose love is different for different people."

Meg nodded with a smile—that about summed it up. "Thank you for understanding."

"Thank you for ... well ... for everything," she said, eye to eye, something that rarely happened.

"My pleasure, Carmen."

🏝 🏝 🏝

That evening, Janet and Craig hosted a birthday party with way too many people for Meg's tastes. Apparently, though, her sister-in-law's mood swings had begun to fade—she was literally glowing with excitement. Even though Meg wasn't thrilled about the party, she was thankful something had been able to help all the gloom and doom for a little while.

"Did you see the doctor?" Meg asked her when they got some time alone after everyone had left.

"Yes," she beamed. "I'm just fine."

"Thank goodness." She breathed with relief more to herself than for anyone to actually hear. "I was getting worried."

"Well, he says it's a condition that should remedy itself eventually."

It must not be very serious if she was taking it all so easily. "So, what exactly is the problem?"

"Hormones," the redhead beamed again. "It'll clear up on its own in a little while."

"Well, I guess just knowing that makes you feel better." It was still hard to believe how well she was taking it.

"Yes it does, and you can't imagine how much."

Craig came into the kitchen with some dirty plates and kissed Janet on the cheek. "How's my lovely bride?" he asked winsomely.

"Doing wonderful," she crooned back.

"Yuck," Meg groaned. "Even Phillip and I aren't that bad and we're newlyweds—it's disgusting on ya'll."

"Well," Craig winked at Janet, "perhaps we're feeling like newlyweds again, having you out of the house and all."

"Whatever. I can do without the lovey-dovey though, thank-you."

"Then you'd better leave soon," Craig teased, "because we're just getting cranked up. The night is young."

"Janet," Meg said sternly, "make him stop, or I'm leaving all of this for you to clean up alone."

"That's okay," she said dreamily. "Craig and I can do it."

"I think I'm gonna be sick," Meg mumbled as she left the kitchen to find Phillip and Spiro.

"Apparently, Janet's problem is on the way out," she told Phillip as they sat on the couch in their own home to unwind after the party. "She says the doctor said it was something hormonal and should be over in a bit."

"Thank goodness. She was beginning to grate on my nerves."

"Promise me," Meg said as she curled up next to him, "that if I ever get wacky like that, you'll let me know."

"I can't imagine you ever being emotionally out of control," he laughed.

"Oh, imagine it. I came really close several times this past year." She looked at him seriously. "And I mean it too—let me know if I start to lose it."

"I will—I promise." He pulled her into an embrace and held her.

They sat quietly for a while with the back doors open so the breeze could blow in from the gulf and the waves could sing to them. She felt content, complete. She never imagined she could feel completely freed from the past or so excited about the future. Healing had taken place in her life, and she knew now that she truly lived in Paradise.

"Penny for your thoughts," he whispered as he stroked her long hair.

"You've become rather nosey about my thoughts of late."

"Not become, but always have been. I've just recently developed the nerve to ask."

"I see. Well, I was just thinking about how God has healed me of all the past through you. I never thought I could feel like this—free, pure, right. The hope of ever having those things seemed gone."

"I'm glad." He pulled her around to face him. "Meg, I can't tell you how much I love you, or how wonderful it is to be your husband. Words can't describe it. Also, I can't tell you how much it means to know that yes, you messed up long ago, but you never did again. It's almost like a gift. On our wedding night, wow, what can I say? I had no regrets ... none at all."

"And I believe that. In fact, when we were pronounced husband and wife, I thought I would explode! It was like, BOOM, we're one now!"

"I saw it on your face," he smiled. "You glowed that day. You were the most beautiful woman I'd ever seen."

"And in my eyes, you were the only man I'd ever loved."

"What about Kevin?"

"I know it sounds strange," she tried to explain, "but what I feel for you and what I felt for him were so totally different. He was ... oh, I don't know ... an easy escape maybe? My only chance for change, perhaps? I wasn't desperately in love with him ... comfortably in love, perhaps, but not desperately."

"What's the difference?"

"Comfortably, I could live without—desperately, I couldn't."

"Then I must be desperate too."

🌴 🌴 🌴

During school later that week, Mr. Roberts had left a message for Meg to come by the children's home after classes. She went, and was presented with quite an option. How many changes could one woman make in a year's time? She would have to think and pray long and hard before deciding. She went home and did just that. After awhile, she pulled up her resignation letter on the computer and read over it. Is this really the step she wanted to take? She continued to pray and think until Phillip came home and found her on the back deck.

"What's that?" he asked as he kissed her hello and sat next to her.

"The resignation letter I wrote when I thought I would be moving to Houston."

"Really? Are you still thinking of leaving teaching?"

"Yep. I was made quite an offer this afternoon."

"Tell me about it," he said as he picked Spiro up to cuddle him.

"Well, I got into teaching because I wanted to change not necessarily the world, but rather the *worlds* of kids. I grew up incredibly privileged. I actually resented it in a way. No one expected me to do great things. No one expected my brothers to do great things. Our lives were set. Whatever we wanted in life, we could have or do simply because my dad had an unending supply of money."

She shifted in her seat and reached over to pet Spiro.

"That wasn't good enough for me. In my eyes, my brothers were losers who were wasting their lives. I wanted to be great simply because I had the ability, not because I had a rich daddy. So, I decided to excel in everything I did. I made sure I had the highest grades. Thus, I became valedictorian. I worked like a dog playing tennis, thus I played number one on the team. I practiced more than ever required or expected on piano, thus making me an incredible, award-winning pianist. I just wanted to inspire other teenagers to do the same."

She stood as her speech became more emphatic.

"I had every reason to just float along, but I knew I was better than that! And I proved it!" She faced him. "Phillip, that's why I teach—to get kids to believe that they're better than whatever life has dictated to them. I've succeeded with many and lost many more. But it's been a good journey."

"A journey that I'm presuming you're about to end from the way you're talking," he said seriously.

"Mr. Roberts offered me the position of Dean of Girls at the home."

"Really?" he said in unbelief. "They're creating a position for you?"

"He said these girls need guidance and planning and mentoring, which is what I've done to some degree all these years. He and the rest of the board decided it should be done full time."

"The rest of the board?" He raised his eyebrows in shock. "Aren't you on the board? Did you get asked or was this a total surprise?"

"Total surprise," she confirmed. "He talked to them all privately to tell them what he was thinking. It was unanimous."

Phillip smiled, let Spiro down, and stood up to touch her cheek. "I know I don't get a vote on the board, but I can't think of a better position for you ... or a better mentor for those girls."

"Not being haughty," she said soberly, "but I agree with you. It's like this is what I was created to do, Phillip, at least right now. I don't know what the future holds, but for as long as I can, I can move the worlds of these girls in a new direction."

"Move on!" he shouted. Spiro began barking after the yell. "Let's go for a walk. Spiro needs to run some."

"Great idea. Let me put this letter on the counter. I need to turn it in tomorrow, I suppose."

"Don't suppose, Meg—know."

"Thank you," she said smiling. "Have I told you lately that I really like having you in my life?"

🏝️🏝️🏝️

Friday after school, Meg turned in her resignation much to the dismay of the superintendent and the principal. She explained her new plans, and they both agreed it would be wonderful for the home but a great loss for the students of Treasure Cove. She thanked them for their form of flattery, but insisted that God was in control and would provide an ample replacement. At this, the principle winced, as he and Meg had butted heads over and over concerning religious matters. He told her for once he hoped she was right because she would be a hard teacher to replace.

She felt a need to celebrate. Immediately crab legs came to mind. She didn't want to go out, however, so she dropped by the market to buy several pounds. As she checked out, the lady working the register stared with wide eyes as she scanned all the crab legs.

"We're having company," she defended, feeling the need to justify the large amount. Then, after thinking for a while, realized she should have explained instead that it takes a lot of crab legs to equal enough meat for a meal. She laughed at herself as she loaded the groceries into the car, realizing she always had this need to appear perfect. Would it ever end?

She began the crab boil when she got home, and patiently awaited Phillip's arrival. She and Spiro sat on the deck while she began a new novel. She couldn't concentrate on the book though. She could only think about all the ideas coming to her mind for the children's home. Finally, she put the book down, got a pad of paper and pencil, and began putting all her thoughts onto paper.

"Wow," Phillip said as he surprised her on the deck, "you're mighty busy for someone who just resigned."

"I don't look at it as resigning—it's like I've moved on."

"I bet the school board is in disagreement with you," he smiled as he sat next to her and cuddled Spiro. "Do the students know yet?"

"Nope," she shook her head. "Next week is the last week of school. I figured I'd tell them on Tuesday since exams start Wednesday."

"I don't envision a happy group of kids."

"We'll see," she said.

"So what's on the stove?" he asked. "Shrimp?"

"Crab legs."

"Yes!" He followed with a celebrative jig.

Chapter Thirty-Three

When Meg awoke on Saturday morning, she began to get out of bed to go jog as was the norm.

"I'd like to appeal," Phillip moaned as he rolled over and pulled her back down.

"Okay, appeal then," she grinned.

"Do we have to jog on Saturdays? Can't we take a day off?"

"We take Sundays off," she insisted.

"I know, but that's not really a day off. We have to get up and go to church," he explained. "I would like to at least sleep in with you one day a week. You know, just lie around, maybe watch a little Saturday morning TV. Besides, since Spiro can't run long distances with us anymore, it's not fair for him. Every day we lock him up in here and then take off."

"Oh, my, you are pulling at the old heart strings, aren't you? Using Spiro to make me stay?"

"I'm desperate," he pleaded. "Don't you ever want to just stay in bed and sleep in?"

"Every morning," she confessed. "I just discipline myself to get up and run. I have to with the way I eat. Think of those crab legs last night."

"You could stand a little meat on your bones. Let Saturday be the day your body just gels."

"I don't want my body to gel!" she protested.

"Now what is that scripture about your body not being your own anymore? It belongs to your husband, I believe."

"So, if my husband wants me to be fat, I should just be fat?"

"Exactly!"

Meg did not jog that Saturday.

🌴🌴🌴

On Monday morning, Meg woke up feeling horrible. Her head hurt and her stomach was miserably nauseous, not to mention she had been to the bathroom in the middle of the night—something that never happened.

Phillip rolled over to kiss her good morning.

"We'd better get jogging," he said to her.

"I feel miserable," she told him. "I don't think I can move, much less jog."

"What's wrong?"

"I have no idea," she moaned. "My head is throbbing and I feel like I'm gonna throw up if I move. It's not flu season, so I don't know what's going on."

"Can I get you something?"

"Maybe a cool rag."

"Coming right up," he said as he jumped out of bed and ran to the bathroom. He came back with a cloth and placed it on her forehead. "Can I get you some pain reliever for the headache?"

"Yeah," she said weakly. "You better make some coffee."

"Coffee with an upset stomach?" he questioned her.

"I've got to get some energy before I go to school."

"Maybe you shouldn't go."

"I've got to," she said as she began to sit up. "Exams for seniors are on Wednesday, and juniors have them on Thursday and Friday. I can't get a sub to come in today. I'm the only one who can review with them."

"Okay, one coffee and two Tylenols coming up," he said slightly panicked as he blustered out of the room.

She got up, still feeling terrible, but managed to get dressed and down some coffee.

By mid-morning, she was feeling better, but not a hundred percent. She assumed it was a mild little bug and was almost back to normal ... at least until lunchtime. She got her meal and sat with a group of senior girls in the cafeteria. After one bite of food, her stomach began to churn immediately.

"Are you alright, Miss Mac," asked Alissa. "You look really pale."

"I thought I was," Meg answered, "but I'm beginning to wonder. Is it me, or is it the food?"

"I've always told you this food is horrible," Lana interjected. "You kept insisting it was fine."

"Whew," Meg breathed as she sat back in her chair, "this isn't settling well at all."

"Tell me about it," Lana groaned with her.

Phillip came into the cafeteria and surprised Meg as she tried to drink some iced tea.

"What are you doing here?" she asked him.

"I was concerned about you," he said as he pulled up a chair beside her.

"Awwww," said the girls in unison.

"She felt bad this morning," he explained.

"She feels bad now," Alissa informed him.

"Really?" He felt her forehead. "You don't feel fevered."

"Awwww," the girls crooned again.

Meg rolled her eyes at the unwanted attention. "I'm fine, really. I'm just a little nauseous. I think I'd better hold off on lunch too. Perhaps I can have a good supper."

"Do you feel like steaks? I could pick some up on the way home and we could grill out tonight," he suggested.

"Awwww."

"Would ya'll stop," Meg complained. "Steaks sound really good. Yes, I think I could eat tonight."

"Okay," he said trying to smile as he glanced down at her full tray of food. "Are you going to eat your lunch?"

She shook her head and pushed it away.

"May I?" he asked as he pulled the tray towards him.

"Ooooo," said the girls with disgust this time.

"One day you girls will realize that this is some of the best food you will ever eat," he warned.

"I doubt that," said Lana.

When Meg got home, she lay on the couch and, to her surprise, fell asleep with Spiro lying next to her. She was out until Phillip came home and began grilling the steaks. She opened her eyes to see him on the deck turning the meat. Slowly she got up and went out to him.

"Hello," she said as she put her arms around him from behind.

"Hello yourself," he said, turning around to face her. "You look better this evening."

"I feel better … and I'm starved. I must have had a bug or something. I can't believe how tired I was. I had to go to the bathroom last night. It must have messed up my whole schedule."

"Glad you're feeling better," he said with a kiss. "I hated seeing you so sick."

"I think I'm on the mend. When did you get in?"

"About forty-five minutes ago. I put the potatoes on to bake and then marinated the steaks. I wasn't sure how long you'd been napping, but thought I should go ahead and start grilling them."

"Forty-five minutes!" she exclaimed. "I slept through all that?"

"Yeah. I wasn't even trying to be quiet. You must've been really tired."

"I guess I was. Perhaps I'll sleep better tonight," she said as she lifted the lid on the grill to smell the steaks. "Mmmm. I'm starved. How much longer?"

"About five minutes."

"I'll go get ice in the glasses," she turned toward the kitchen then pointed in the opposite direction. "Gotta go to the bathroom first."

🌴 🌴 🌴

Tuesday morning was worse. Meg knew she needed to jog. It had been since Friday morning that she had exercised, and she felt terribly lazy about not doing it. The nausea, however, was intense. Having heard her voice moan, Spiro stood up on his hind legs, placing his paws on the bed beside her.

"Come on up, baby," she coached him, but he still wouldn't join her on the bed.

"Good morning," Phillip said as he entered from the bathroom.

"Not," she replied.

"What's wrong?"

"I feel sick again. No headache today, but the nausea is about to win."

"Oh, no. You want another damp cloth?"

"No," she groaned. "I think I'll just take a shower. Maybe that will refresh me."

"Okay," he said as he helped pull her to her feet. "I'll put on some coffee."

"Good idea."

Meg was fine the rest of the day, except for telling the students she wouldn't be teaching next year. Her junior classes were mortified. They couldn't believe it. They begged her for another year. She explained her new position and how good it would be for the children's home. Some thought it was great, some resented the home. Either way, she assured them all a wonderful teacher would replace her and they would enjoy being forced to work under someone else as much as they had her. Moans always followed.

That evening, Meg decided to go to bed earlier than usual. She and Phillip lied down and turned on the television. Spiro, for the first time, jumped up in bed with Meg.

"Phillip!" she yelled. "Spiro's in bed with us!"

"Hey, buddy," he said as he pet him. "Have you decided I'm not that bad after all?"

The pup nuzzled himself next to his mistress, and before long, both of them had fallen fast asleep.

🏝️ 🏝️ 🏝️

Meg woke up Wednesday morning feeling completely worn out. She blamed it on her two trips to the bathroom that night. Spiro was still next to her, lying very still.

"Hey, sweetie," she said as she pet him gently.

"Sweetie?" Phillip questioned her sleepily. "Did you call me sweetie?"

"No, silly, I was talking to Spiro."

"He's still up here?" he asked as he got up on one elbow. "He hasn't moved all night."

"Poor thing. He probably was afraid he'd be kicked off."

She quickly hopped out of bed and headed toward the bathroom.

"Feeling better this morning?" Phillip asked as he watched the sprint.

"Actually, no, I've just gotta go really bad ... again."

"Again? How many times did you get up last night?"

"Twice!" she yelled from the bathroom. "This is getting ridiculous!"

"Are you going to jog?"

"I don't think so," she yelled back. "I'm afraid I'll throw up if I do."

"You want me to put on some coffee?"

"Please," she called back. "I'd better shower again. I am so tired and so sick."

"I guess that means you're sick and tired, huh?"

"I'm not laughing, Phillip."

Meg showered and then began to dry off. When she came back into the room, Spiro was still lying on the bed in the same position she had left him. She put on her robe and went over to him.

"Poor thing," she said as she sat next to him. "You're more tired than I am."

She tried to rouse him so she could pick him up and put him out for a walk, but he wouldn't move.

"What's wrong, baby?" she asked as she tried to pick him up. He still didn't move. Fear shot through her mind, and then her body tingled.

"Phillip!" she yelled. "Come here quickly!"

He immediately ran up the stairs to the bedroom.

"What's wrong?" he asked out of breath. "Are you okay?"

"Something's wrong with Spiro!" she screamed. "Phillip, what's wrong with him?"

He came over and gently picked him up in his arms. He felt for a heartbeat and then put his face next to the dog's nose. He looked at Meg strangely and shook his head.

"No," she said softly. "No. Phillip, no." She began to cry as she took her pup, his limp body lying in her arms. "Phillip, no," she was sobbing now. "Spiro! Please! Don't do this!"

She lied down with him on the bed and cried for a long time. Phillip left to make her a cup of coffee. When he came back, she was in the bathroom throwing up.

"Meg, I'm so sorry," he said helplessly as he handed her a damp cloth. "What can I do? Do you want me to call in a sub?"

"No," she said wearily as she shook her head. "Today are finals for seniors. I need to be there."

"What can I do?"

"I hate to say this," she began, "but go down to that sorry vet here in Treasure Cove, and pick out a little casket for Spiro."

"You need to do that, Meg."

"No!" she cut him off quickly. "I can't face that jerk, Phillip. Pick out anything. You know me, and you knew Spiro well. You can get something appropriate."

"I'll do it," he said as he took her in his arms. She began crying again.

"I can't handle this, Phillip," she sobbed. "I can't handle this today. I'm so sick, and then this happens."

"Don't go in, Meg," he told her again. "Let me sub for you. Tell me what I need to do, and I'll follow your orders precisely."

She shook her head. "Thank you," she whispered. "That's more than sweet of you, but I'm obligated to do this. I owe those kids to be there today."

"Are you sure?"

She nodded and went back in to where Spiro was. She sat down next to him on the bed and gently rubbed his small body. She cried again.

"Do you want me to pick you out something to wear?" Phillip asked as he handed her a cup of coffee.

"Thank you, please," she said taking the cup and swallowing a small sip. "We'll give him a proper burial at the beach house this afternoon."

"Let me call the music minister at the church and tell him we won't be there tonight," Phillip suggested. "At least give yourself a break somewhere."

"Okay," she finally agreed. "I don't think I could make it anyway."

She looked up at him as he stood anxiously beside her at the bed and said, "I feel so sick, Phillip. Normally when I throw up I feel better. I don't right now."

He kneeled down next to her. "This isn't a normal situation. If you don't feel better tomorrow, let's call the doctor."

"No problem," she agreed weakly.

🌴 🌴 🌴

Meg struggled through school that day. She had a difficult time controlling her crying, but the nausea did leave by mid-morning. She explained to her classes about Spiro, which usually brought several girls to tears, which in turn started her up all over again. Everyone was sympathetic with her, which made the day a little easier. She managed to eat some lunch, but barely kept it down.

After school, she went straight home and was surprised to find Phillip waiting for her.

"What are you doing here?" she asked as he met her at the door.

"I didn't want you to be alone," he explained.

She reached up to kiss him and then walked into the living room. There she saw a beautiful little blue casket with an arrangement of yellow roses on top.

"Oh, Phillip," she whispered as the tears began to flow again, "you're so wonderful."

He held her tightly until she could stop crying. She walked over to the little casket and slowly lifted the lid. Phillip had laid him inside sweetly and placed his rubber ball next to him.

"I feel foolish being so upset about an animal, but I can't help it," she explained. "I guess I loved him too much."

"That's a silly statement," Phillip told her. "You can't love any living thing too much. You are only at fault for not loving enough. And you, Meg, are not guilty of that."

"Thank you," she replied tearfully. "I'm so grateful to have you with me right now. I appreciate you being here when I got home."

"Don't mention it," he smiled at her.

"I think I'm gonna throw up again," she said wearily as she headed for the downstairs bathroom. She did.

They took Spiro to Craig and Janet's and gave a fitting memorial service. It wasn't too much as Meg didn't want to be ridiculous over an animal, but she felt a need to experience closure as she would with anyone she had loved. Janet and Meg both cried way too much, but neither seemed able to control it. The guys placed the small casket into a hole beneath a beautiful blooming hydrangea bush. As they began to cover the casket, Meg had to leave to throw up again. When she finished, she came back down to say a final goodbye.

"You need to see a doctor," Janet insisted. "Three days of this sounds serious."

"I know," Meg agreed. "Perhaps it will be as simple as something like what you have."

Janet smiled so big that Meg almost got angry. She felt horribly sick, yet Janet was smiling at the prospects. Instead, she grabbed Phillip's arm and insisted they go.

Thursday and Friday were so hard for Meg that she began to wonder if something were seriously wrong with her. She had lost pets before, even grandparents, but she couldn't get over the overwhelming loss. She cried at least once during every class as she already missed the seniors that would be graduating on Friday night. She didn't throw up again, but fought the nausea off and on through both days. Phillip tried to get her not to go to the graduation ceremonies, which merely elicited more emotional display on her part. That night, she and Phillip attended the graduation, which she sobbed through. They sat next to some children from the children's home who had wanted to come. Carmen asked Meg several times if she would be all right, to which Meg nodded as she continued to cry.

Saturday morning, Meg awakened determined to go jogging. She ran to the bathroom first, even though she had used it twice again during the night. She didn't throw up, but felt as though she could.

"Are you feeling better today?" Phillip asked when he realized she was going to jog.

"Not really, but I've got to get out of this rut. I'm starting to feel like Janet. I've got to get back on track."

"You're not feeling better, though?"

"No," she admitted. "I could throw up again if I thought about it."

"Don't jog, please," he pleaded. "I'm really concerned about you. We can walk the beach if you want?"

She shook her head. "I need to move around."

"Well, let's walk then. Please?"

She looked over at him as he sat up in bed. His eyes were so full of concern that she found herself crying again. He quickly came to her and held her for a moment. He then picked her up and put her back in the bed. She lay down and went back to sleep for two more hours.

When she awoke, she could smell bacon frying. It took her back to summers as a child in Treasure Cove. Her mom would always make a big breakfast at the beach house, and the smell of bacon would always be so strong. Meg loved it. She knew that Phillip must be really concerned if he was actually cooking breakfast. She was hungry, something that had barely happened all week. She smiled as she got out of bed and made her way to the kitchen.

"You must be feeling better," he said when he saw her.

"Sort of," she told him as she walked to the stove to smell the bacon. "I'm most definitely hungry."

"That's good, but I would suggest you cook the eggs. I'm not very good at that at all."

"Okay, then, let me teach you how to cook eggs. Then you can cook them for me every morning now. See?"

"I'll try," he said hesitantly.

🌴🌴🌴

Sunday and Monday mornings were no better. Meg had yet to go jogging, and it was all she could do to make it out of bed. Phillip did make breakfast for her both days, but she could barely eat. Monday morning she decided to just go back to bed since school was over. She did miss Spiro, and wondered how she would ever make it through the summer without him. These thoughts, of course, brought her back to tears again, which made her more upset, and found her in the bathroom throwing up again. When Phillip came home for lunch, he insisted she call the doctor and make an appointment immediately.

"Meg," he told her gently, "you told me to tell you if you ever started acting like Janet. Well, you sort of are. Now, you have good reason, with Spiro and all, but the sickness and the emotional roller coaster you're on are getting worse."

"Am I that bad?" she asked. He nodded. "Yuck. Give me my phone, and I'll call Rosenstein."

"Thank you," he said as he handed her the phone.

As Meg sat on the cold bed in the office covered with sterile paper that crinkled every time she moved, she remembered why she hated doctors' offices—the smell. That faint smell of alcohol mixed with whatever else it was made her nauseated again. She also hated coming to Dr. Rosenstein. His thick German accent made it hard to understand most anything he said. She often had to make him repeat things two or three times in order to clearly grasp what he was saying. She could go somewhere else, but he was a faithful church member and a wonderful Christian. He was also a very good doctor. She couldn't understand him, but he always made her better. He was funny too, although she didn't always catch the humor the first time around.

"Vell, vell, vell," he said as he came in with a chart. "Vat is de problem vid Meg? Are ve not de picture of health today?"

"No, I didn't bring any pictures," she half said, not sure what she was responding to, seeing that she understood only a few words he ever said.

"Shoo are so funny, Meg," he laughed. "It is too bad zat shoo do not get ill more often. Vat is happening zat vould bring shoo here?"

"I've been horribly sick this past week."

"Vat kind of zick?"

"Nauseous, tired … almost all the time."

"I zee," he said as he jotted down some notes. "Haf shoo fomitted?"

"Thrown up?" she asked. He nodded. "Several times."

"After eating?"

"Sometimes, and sometimes after crying or after smelling something, or ... it's real inconsistent, yet quite persistent."

"I zee," he said, writing a bit more. "Are zere any more zeemptones?"

"Zeemptones?" she asked.

"Any sing else wrong?" he clarified.

"Oh, yeah ... well, I'm having to go to the bathroom all night long. I've never done that before. I think that's why I'm so tired. Could that be it?"

"Hmmm," he said, scribbling down more notes. "Are shoo defecating or yoorenating at night?"

"Excuse me?"

"Number von or number two when shoo go potty at night?"

"Oh," Meg blushed. "Number one ... just urinating."

"Okay," he said with resolve. "Did shoo take a yoorin zample ven shoo came in?"

"What?" she asked.

"Did shoo go pee pee in ze cup?"

"Oh yeah," Meg nodded. "I did that."

"Vedy goot," he smiled. "I haf an idea I might know chust vat ze problem is."

"Really?" Meg asked with hope.

"Ve vill see," he said calmly as he patted her shoulder. "Sit tight, and I vill be back in a vew moments."

She breathed a sigh of relief. He didn't seem to be concerned. Perhaps something like this was going around and she had caught a good case of it. Of course, it was totally possible that he could have told her she had a fatal disease and she had missed it all together. She laughed at the statement about going pee pee in the cup. She wished Phillip could have been here to laugh with her. Poor Phillip. They had been married barely over a month, and she was already messing up on him. He had been good to her, though, and she vowed to make it up to him when she got over this problem.

After what seemed like hours, Dr. Rosenstein came back in with a smile.

"Vell, vell, vell," he said in greeting again, "shoo haf most definitely gotten shooself in quite a sichoohation."

"Am I gonna be okay?" she asked. "Will this thing work its way out of my system?"

"Most definitely," he nodded. "It tis not veally an illness, but more of a condition."

"A condition?" she wondered. "But it's not permanent?"

I shood zay not!" he laughed. "Shoo are pregnant, Meg!"

"I'm what?" she asked again, thinking he had said pregnant, but sure he must have meant something else.

He got right down into her face and said slowly and deliberately, "Shoo are going to be a mommy. Do shoo understand?"

"I'm pregnant?" she asked in unbelief.

"Dat's vat I said de furst time, but shoo didn't hear. Shoo are pregnant."

Meg could feel the blood leave her face and knew she was about to pass out. Dr. Rosenstein immediately helped her lay back. He called for a nurse to come in and help.

"I take it dis is a big sooprise," he said as he elevated her feet.

"Big sooprise," she said slowly.

"Glad to see shoo didn't loose shoor sense of humor," he smiled. "Are shoo using birth control?"

"Sort of," she mumbled out, feeling herself coming back to total consciousness.

"Zort of?" he laughed. "Dere iz no zort of. Either shoo do or shoo don't."

"What about the sickness?" Meg wanted to know. "How long will it last?

"Depends," he explained. "Shoo coult be ofer it next veek, next month, or be von of de unlocky vons dat has it for de whole nine months."

"Nine months!" she exclaimed. "How do you know?"

"Shoo don't," he smiled at her. "But shoo get a cute itty bitty baby at ze end of it all."

Chapter Thirty-Four

Meg stumbled out of the office in a daze. She didn't know whether to laugh or cry—she was having a baby. This possibility had not even popped into her head. She assumed they would be married a couple of years and then start *thinking* about having children. But now? She drove carefully to the station to tell Phillip. She wasn't quite sure what to say or how he would take it, but she kept replaying the picture of him holding his little blue-eyed nephew during Easter. Tears came to the edge of her eyes again. Could she handle nine months of this emotional wreckage?

She pulled into the parking lot at WJBA and was stunned for the second time that day. The whole place had been beautifully landscaped. Had Phillip done this too? The outside of the building had been redone with white vinyl siding, and there was even a new sign to replace the one that had been there for probably fifteen years. She walked to the receptionist's desk and asked if Phillip was available.

"Yes, Mrs. Anderson," she replied. "You go on back and I'll buzz him that you're here."

"No," Meg said quickly. "I want to surprise him."

Meg smiled at the sound of *Mrs. Anderson*. The kids at school couldn't get out of the habit of calling her *Miss Mac*, but she never complained. The year would soon be up and she wouldn't be returning, especially now—there was a baby on the way.

She approached his door warily, trying to choose her words. How did she tell him he was going to be a father? Until a few months ago he was a nobody. Now he was a son, a brother, an uncle and a soon-to be father. She knocked gently and cracked the door open.

"Meg? Is that you?" he asked as she barely peeked through.

"Just me," she said as she walked on in.

"I've been so worried. What did Rosenstein say?"

"He said I needed to see another type of doctor—an OBGYN."

"What?" he asked as his face went pale. "What kind of doctor is that—a specialist of some sort? Did he not know what was wrong?"

"Yes, Phillip, he knew," she said, realizing he was clueless. Okay, she would try a different angle. "He said I'm not really sick—I just have a condition that should be remedied in a little over seven months by this point."

"Seven months!" he exclaimed. "No way! Meg, I'm so sorry. Maybe this new doctor can help."

"Not really," she sighed. "All he can do is monitor my condition in the meantime."

"Well, we'll find another doctor," he insisted. "Someone who can get you through this better."

"Phillip, sit down and relax," she said calmly. "This doctor will do fine. He handles cases like mine all the time. It's a very common condition."

"What's it called? Maybe we can find someone who …"

"It's called pregnancy," she interrupted. "I'm six weeks pregnant."

His jaw dropped as he flopped down into his chair. He stared at her, first into her eyes, then down at her stomach.

"Are you sure?" he asked.

"Positive," she smiled. "At least I think that's what Rosenstein said. He's so hard to make out some times."

He stood and began to pace in front of the windows. "You're really gonna have a baby?" he finally asked.

"No," she corrected him, "*we're* going to have a baby—me and you together."

He sat back down and then stood back up. "Are you okay with this?" he asked her.

"Having your baby?" she smiled. "I'm more than okay with it. I'm thrilled."

"Oh, Meg," he breathed out a huge sigh, "I don't know what to say. I wasn't even expecting this. Did you know … or … well … did you think that maybe …"

"No, I had no idea."

He finally jumped up and gave a loud yell. It startled Meg as well as several others in the office. People began to appear at his door to see if all was fine.

"You'll never believe this," he began, but Meg stopped him.

"We've had some good news," she interrupted quickly. "Nothing to worry about. You can go back to whatever it was before Phillip scared you."

They left and then Phillip quizzed her as to why.

"Janet," was all she had to say.

"Oh, yeah," he mumbled softly as he took her in his arms and held her tightly. "This will be hard for her, won't it?"

"I'm sure it will. She's wanted children for so many years … and here we are, barely married … and have a baby on the way."

"I can't believe we're having a baby." He shook his head in amazement. "Is this real? I mean, just last month I married you and thought that nothing could ever top that … but being a father … Meg …"

"I know," she smiled again. "It'll take some time to get used to the idea. At least I know why I've felt so strange this past week. No matter how long I might be sick, I can handle it knowing that there's a very good reason."

"Meg," he whispered again, "we're going to have a baby."

"Yes, we are," she said as she laid her head on his chest. "I suppose I can't accept the position as dean now."

"Why not?" he asked as he pulled her away.

"I'm staying home with my baby, Phillip. I can't be one of those career women and moms at the same time. My mother was always so busy. I swore to myself that if I ever had children, I'd be home with them. No nannies or modern day style—no daycare."

"Really?" he asked. "I never pegged you for being a stay at home mom."

"Does that bother you?"

"Are you kidding?" he laughed. "I can't imagine anything better for a kid. I would have given everything to have been cooped up with a lady who thought I hung the moon during my childhood. I just always thought you were so driven … so business oriented … that …"

"I've changed, Phillip—I'm a wife, and soon to be mom. I'm ready to do just that for a while."

"Then I couldn't be happier," he grinned. "But when do we tell everyone?"

"Heavens, I don't know," she blew out a long breath of release. "We've got to break this gently to Janet first. Once she and Craig know we can announce it to others."

"Can I tell my family?" he asked excitedly. "They're way up in South Dakota. They'll never tell Janet."

"Yeah," she nodded. "Let's tell them tonight."

"All right!" he yelled again. "I'm gonna be a daddy! I'm gonna be a daddy!"

"I think I need to go," she said softly. "I'm going to lay down for awhile."

"Absolutely! I'll try to get home early so we can celebrate. Anything I can pick up for dinner?"

"Be creative," she said as she kissed him goodbye. "But don't forget some dill pickles and ice cream."

"What?" he asked puzzled.

"Never mind. See you later." She turned back and blew him a kiss. "I love you."

"Me too." His eyes and smile had never been brighter.

As June passed, Meg found the nausea lessening, but the overwhelming tiredness still prevailed. If she had to choose one, she would choose to stay tired but not sick. She found herself really missing Spiro however, as the summers had always been a wonderful time for them. If she wasn't careful, she would find herself crying over him often. Phillip offered to get a new puppy, but she refused. Spiro couldn't be replaced.

Another thing plaguing her was that she had not yet told Mr. Roberts she wouldn't be taking the new position at the home. She would have to tell him about the pregnancy, which brought up the number one problem on her list—Janet. She still wasn't ready to face her with the wonderful news, especially with how fragile she had been.

"You've got to tell Mr. Roberts, Meg," Phillip urged her, "and soon."

"Ugh … I know," she moaned as she roused from a lazy nap. "I dread it. They created this position for me, and I all but promised them I'd do it."

"Things change, you know?"

"Yes, believe me, I know," she said as she stretched and sat up. "I don't know which I dread more—telling Mr. Roberts or telling Janet."

"Janet seems really happy of late. Perhaps she's come to grips with this whole children thing."

"Perhaps, but she's also gaining weight again. Have you noticed?"

"Hmmm, yeah," he said slowly. "I was hoping it was just me."

"See what I mean? With this illness she's got and the emotional instability, now topped off with gaining weight, how do I tell her? She's kept that weight off for more than ten years! How could she be gaining it all again?"

"She's not fat, Meg," Phillip insisted.

"No," she agreed, "not yet, at least."

"Look," he tried to give some positive direction, "which do you dread the most?"

"Oh gee," she said sarcastically, "would I rather have my hair pulled out or my fingernails pulled off?"

"It's not that bad."

"It seems like it," she moaned again.

"Just think, which seems worse?"

"I suppose telling Mr. Roberts," she finally decided. "He's been so sweet and supportive of my work there these past years. To tell him I can't take the job would be horrible."

"Then tell him first," Phillip said brightly as though the whole thing had been solved.

"Just like that? Just pop up off this couch and run down there and spill the whole thing?"

"Just like that," he affirmed. "Then, when you get back, we pop over to Craig and Janet's and spill the whole thing out to them."

"Boy, you sure are optimistic," she groaned.

"Meg," he said as he sat beside her and flashed those adoring blue eyes, "I'm going to be a daddy. I want the world to know. The woman of my heart and my dreams is carrying my child, and I'm just about to burst. The sooner we get over the difficulties surrounding all this, the sooner we can get on to the joy. See? And think about this—my family and your family will be down here in one week for summer vacations. Do you want to keep all this secretive then?"

She laid her head on his shoulder and took his hand. He was wonderful, and this baby was the most precious thing that could have ever happened to him. He was right. If she couldn't do it because of her own fears, at least she could do it for his happiness. She reached up and kissed him, then jumped up from the couch. "I'm outta here," she smiled.

"Wow," he said, standing with her. "That was quick."

"You're very convincing," she said as she went to get her shoes.

"Run that by me again," Mr. Roberts said with a slight twinge of anger as Meg informed him she would not be taking the position.

"I can't take the job," she said again, softly.

He ran his fingers through his curling hair and closed his eyes for a moment. "I can't believe you're telling me this," he said with a controlled calm she knew he wasn't feeling.

"It was a hard decision, Mr. Roberts," she tried to explain. "I've wanted to tell you for awhile, but just couldn't get the nerve."

"You've resigned your teaching position," he began going over her actions. "You told the girls you were coming. I don't understand."

"Something has developed that I didn't expect."

"How long have you known about this?" he asked, still on the verge of losing his temper.

"Almost a month."

"A month!" He lost it this time. "You've known for a month that you wouldn't be coming and you never let me know? We've been making plans! We've been raising the money for your salary! Did you think we would just roll over and smile when you refused us?"

"You don't understand," she tried to explain.

"I don't care, Meg!" he continued. "It was rude and reckless of you to string us along like this! This isn't like you! You're responsible and quick to act! What were you thinking?"

"Mr. Roberts," Meg said with some authority this time, "there are other circumstances in my life now ... some other people ... that had to be considered in this decision. My life is more than just coming here, you know?"

"Excuse me?" he said angrily. "Now you're justifying your actions?"

"I am pregnant!" she finally admitted. "I didn't want to spread this information out too soon!"

Mr. Roberts was speechless. He sat down immediately and just stared at her, his demeanor suddenly changing.

"I've known about three weeks," she continued. "I've been really sick, and really tired. I wasn't ready to let the cat out of the bag. You see, Janet and Craig have tried for years ..."

"Meg," he interrupted her, "you don't have to say anything more." He smiled at her, got up from his chair and came over to hug her. "You as a mommy, huh?" he laughed. "Congratulations!"

She was stunned. He had just been so angry, now he was gentle. She was struggling to change emotional gears as quickly.

"I need to explain," she tried to say.

"Explain what?" he laughed again. "I've got five kids of my own ... saw my wife through all five pregnancies. On the contrary, you're doing quite well."

"Thank you," she said as she tried to continue, "but we haven't told anyone yet because ..."

"I'll say you haven't!" he smiled. "Trying to keep this a little secret, huh?"

"Not deliberately. Well, sort of ... see ... it's about Janet and Craig."

He nodded knowingly. "I understand. When Janet came up here to help with tutoring, she talked some about her frustrations. She doesn't know about this yet, I take it."

Meg shook her head.

"You need to tell her," he said with all anger gone. "For your sake, you need to tell her. How is Phillip? I bet he's bursting at the seams! And my goodness, this is quick! I suppose, however, you guys are a little bit older than the average newlyweds ... getting a faster start, huh?"

"Not intentionally," she blushed.

He laughed heartily this time. "Oh, my goodness! Surprise! Surprise! You know what, Meg? Those are the best ones. They just sneak up on you and steal your hearts! God works in the most unusual ways!"

"You can say that again," she mumbled.

"Meg, tell Janet," he pleaded. "You've got nine months of wonderful anticipation coming. Don't squelch it. She's going to have to know sooner or later. Let her get over the shock, and then she'll be right beside you, enjoying this pregnancy and expectancy of a new little life."

Oh no. Meg found herself on the verge of tears once more. Mr. Roberts noticed and laughed yet again. He put his arm around her and led her out of his office to the front door.

"Meg," he said as he looked her in the eyes, "mum's the word here until you give me the go-ahead. But please, don't wait too long. We need to start taking in resumes, and we need to tell the children. I don't want to do either until I can say, *Guess what? Meg's not coming because she gets to take care of her own kid for a change!* Okay?"

She nodded, wiping a tear, then hugged him and left for the radio station to talk with Phillip about dealing with Janet once and for all.

The plan was to go and look at the progress being made on Craig and Janet's house. Then they would sit and discuss the new baby. If everyone was holding up emotionally, they would go out to celebrate at the Crab Shack. If not, Janet would pout at her house, and Meg would pout at hers.

"Here's the great room," Janet said breathlessly as she pointed out the features. "See how these doors open onto the deck? And I insisted on a fireplace."

"Well, you'll sure use that a lot," Phillip said sarcastically.

"I don't care, Phillip," she defended. "I loved our fireplace in Texas, and I want one here. We do have enough cold days in the winter to be able to enjoy it some. Besides, what's Christmas without a fireplace?"

Meg nodded, having always loved a fire in the hearth with stockings dangling down.

"It's called Christmas in Florida," Phillip reminded her.

"Bah humbug," the redhead retorted.

She led them through several more rooms. The house was beautiful. It was being painted at the time, so the finishing touches would soon be on the way. Meg found herself wishing to build a house too, something she never imagined before. As Janet led them into one of the bedrooms, Meg was stunned—Noah's ark paintings and border covered the walls.

"This will be a nursery someday," Janet explained. "Don't you just love Noah's ark?"

Meg felt a thud at the bottom of her stomach, and she actually began to feel faint. Phillip, taking in the whole scene, quickly came next to her.

"Are you all right, Meg?" Janet asked her. "You look pale."

"No," she said quickly. "No, Janet. I am not all right ... not at all, in fact."

"What's wrong?" Craig asked. "Do we need to go back to the house?"

"Yes," Meg insisted. "We all need to talk."

They walked back up to the house and sat down. Craig and Janet had concerned faces, and Phillip just held her hand knowing that the news would be even more difficult now. They had assumed that Janet had come to grips with not having children, but the nursery proved she was as optimistic as ever.

"We have some news," Meg began. "I haven't known how to tell you. I've been through this in my mind so many times, but I just don't know how to go about it."

"Oh no!" Janet blurted out. "What's wrong? Are you really bad sick?"

"No, Janet, that's not it. Jeesh! This is so dog-gone hard! If I didn't love you guys so much I would just blurt it out! I don't want to hurt you."

"Meg," Craig insisted, "please get on with it. Whatever it is, we can take it."

"I'm not so sure. It's a very touchy area with you two … well, especially with Janet."

"Meg," Janet said, "I'm trying not to be offended right now. You know you can tell me anything. I'm a bit hurt that you're holding out."

"Well, it's just that you two have wanted children for so long," Meg tried to explain. "I know your frustrations with all of that."

"You know?" Janet said with a smile.

"Well, yeah," Meg said confused. "You told me."

"I told you?" Janet asked as confused as Meg. "When did I tell you?"

"At Christmas," Meg reminded her.

"Christmas? We didn't know at Christmas!"

"What do you mean? You told me all about it at Christmas. You were struggling with being childless. It was the biggest hurt of your heart. You were trying so hard to come to grips with that."

Janet laughed, "Oh, that! It's okay. No problem."

"Well, maybe not," Meg tried to get out. "See, it appears that … well … we found out a few weeks ago. Oh rats! I can't do this, Phillip!"

"Meg!" Janet blurted again. "Would you say whatever it is that has gotten you so upset!"

"We're going to have a baby!" she finally yelled out.

Janet looked at her confused. "Who is?"

"For heaven's sake, Janet! Do I have to spell it out for you? Phillip and I are going to have a baby. I'm pregnant. It'll soon be two months."

Janet's eyes grew wide with excitement and a smile grew across her face. She jumped up and grabbed Meg from the couch and hugged her. Craig grabbed Phillip's hand and congratulated him, then insisted Janet let him hug his sister.

"This is so wonderful," Janet said with tears. "You guys won't believe this. We haven't told anyone because we were so afraid that … well … that there might be complications."

"You knew I was pregnant?" Meg asked, still confused by the whole scene.

"No!" Janet squealed. "I am too!"

Meg felt herself getting dizzy again. Phillip sat her back down on the couch and Janet sat beside her.

"All that craziness I was experiencing around your wedding was due to the pregnancy," Janet explained to her.

"You knew then?" Meg asked.

"No, silly! Remember, I told you I thought I was sick? Well, when I went to the doctor … boom! It was all spelled out."

"Why didn't you tell us?" Meg said a bit hurt.

"You're one to talk," Janet shot back. "I had a good excuse! What's yours?"

"What's yours?" Meg insisted.

"Because of all the complications in the past of getting pregnant, the doctor said it could be possible that things may not go well … that we might lose the baby. He suggested we give it four months before we started telling anyone. Its four months now."

"So, when were you going to tell me?" Meg asked her.

"Your parents are coming down in a week. We thought we'd say something to everybody at the same time … you know, a big announcement."

Meg smiled and even began to laugh. She had been so afraid to tell Janet, yet Janet had been carrying her own child the whole time.

"One of us needs to put this in Reader's Digest," Meg suggested.

Janet hugged her again as tears began to flow. Meg, though she hated to admit it, was doing the same.

"Can we put up with this for another five months?" Craig asked Phillip.

"Five?" Phillip replied. "I've got seven more to go."

The celebration at the Crab Shack was bigger than anyone had anticipated. Janet, who had held the news of a baby longer than Meg, began to spill everything she had kept inside. For the first time, Meg and Phillip were able to really share the excitement of what was about to happen, as well as Janet and Craig. It was an evening of joy and anticipation, one that would never be forgotten.

Chapter Thirty-Five

"Wow," Phillip said in awe as he gazed around the condo. "This place looks incredible. It doesn't even look like the same house."

"A woman's touch," Meg mumbled as she arranged a few pillows on the couch. "I told you so, you know?"

"You did indeed," he smiled. "No argument from me on this one."

"What?" she said in mock surprise. "No snide remarks? No sarcastic innuendos?"

"I'd be a fool to," he laughed as he came over and picked her up and spun her around.

"Phillip! Put me down before I throw up all over you."

He gently placed her feet back on the floor but continued to smile. "I don't care if you do throw up me. This is wonderful. My family will be here this afternoon for two whole weeks, and you're going to have a baby … and my house now looks like Martha Stewart made a visit. Throw up away, baby!"

"Sometimes, I worry about you," she said with a grin.

"Let's go get the recliner," he said as he grabbed the keys.

Phillip's grandmother, affectionately known as Grandma Corrie to his brothers and sisters, had moved in with Clara and Alex just a month ago. She had come to the point where she could not care for herself alone anymore. She had lived in Wyoming for over twenty years and as a widow for fifteen. Phillip couldn't believe he was going to meet a grandparent. She was unable to lie down, so they were to get Meg's blue recliner and bring it over for her to sleep on and pretty much live in during the visit.

Phillip and Craig loaded the recliner into the back of Craig's small pickup and brought it over to the condo. Meg made sure they placed it where she could have a good view of the beach anytime she wanted. Grandma Corrie had never seen the beach and was excited about the visit.

"This will be perfect," Meg breathed as she sat in the recliner and swiveled around to see the gulf. "Your grandmother should enjoy her visit."

"My grandmother," Phillip repeated softly. "Meg, how much more can I take—all these new additions to my life?"

"God knows how much, and He is the giver of all good things."

They waited impatiently at the airport as the plane was slightly delayed. Phillip paced while Meg attempted to read a book. She didn't want to tell him, but she was struggling with thinking about Spiro because she often flew with him. She could remember how he hated to get into the cage before boarding the planes, and then how excited he would be when they reached their destinations and she would let him out. If she had to make a trade off somewhere, she supposed a new baby for a loving, faithful companion was acceptable, but it was still so hard.

"There it is!" Phillip yelled as the plane taxied into the unloading position. "Where's the wheelchair?"

"Over there," Meg said pointing to a corner where he had parked it. He immediately ran over and wheeled it toward the area where they would wait for the family.

It took several minutes before passengers began to appear, and then it seemed to go on and on with no Andersons showing. Phillip grew more impatient with each person who was not a member of his family.

"Phillip," she reminded him, "your grandmother is with them. They'll probably be the last ones off. If she needs this wheel chair, she probably walks very slowly."

"Yeah, right," he agreed. "I'm just so excited!"

Passengers continued walking through, and finally, right at the end of the line, came Phillip's family. Mary Ann was out first, running over to hug Meg, then Phillip. Julie followed her, also greeting Meg first. Clara then appeared, carrying a big purse, followed by Thomas who was walking with Grandma Corrie holding onto his arm. Clara found Phillip and hugged him tightly—then she greeted Meg.

"Hello, little mother," Clara whispered to her. "How are you doing?"

"Better than I ever thought possible," she replied with a smile.

Grandma Corrie was ushered to the wheelchair, but she refused to sit down until she had greeted her grandson. She was even shorter than Clara, and stockier. Meg knew Grandma Corrie's hair must be every bit as long as her own because it was pulled up and rolled into a full bun on her head. She had the sweetest face she had ever seen, with smiling eyes and unusually smooth skin for a woman of ninety-one. Grandma Corrie reached up for Phillip's face. He leaned down and she pulled him directly in front of her. She smiled graciously and looked deeply into his eyes.

"You are a child of promise," she smiled and spoke with a slight foreign accent. "Did you know that?"

He shook his head.

"God has preserved your life, just like Moses," she continued. "He has great plans for you. I am thankful to see you face to face. This is such an answer to so many prayers."

Everyone stood quietly as Phillip helped the elderly lady into the chair. Then Grandma Corrie motioned for Meg to come to her. She walked over, almost in awe. The woman had such a commanding presence to be so small.

"And you," Grandma Corrie said as she took Meg's hand into her own, "hold the promise of God within your hands."

Meg didn't understand what she meant, but literally felt a warmth flood her entire body as though God himself had just spoken words of prophesy to her. Then she noticed, which nearly took her breath away, the same blue eyes shining back at her that she had seen in Phillip and Clara.

"Welcome to Florida," Meg said to her. "We have so looked forward to meeting you."

"You have no idea," Grandma Corrie replied. "You have no idea."

🌴 🌴 🌴

The evening with the Andersons and Grandma Corrie was wonderful. Phillip grilled steaks for all, and Meg baked some potatoes and made a salad. Most of the conversation centered around the new baby, except for the few times Mary Ann reminded them all that she absolutely must go shopping for a swimsuit the next day. She would be in Florida for two weeks and must have the latest fashion in order to truly make the most of her experience. Grandma Corrie said few words, but she smiled, almost glowing, the entire time. Meg still wished she could pick out the accent, but it was too vague to place.

"Where is your grandmother from?" Meg asked Phillip as they crawled exhausted into bed that night.

"I'm not totally sure. I think Mom said something about meeting Grandfather in England … or maybe it was France. But I don't think that's where she's from."

"You're no help."

He chuckled, "I'm sorry. It was one of those brief history lessons I received during Christmas. I was in such a fog that I don't remember a lot of what happened. I was trying to concentrate on my family, but your face kept creeping up to the front of my mind. I kept picturing you snuggling next to a warm fire with Mr. Wonderful while enjoying the chilly Christmas in Texas."

She turned to look at him. "You never told me that! You were thinking about me?"

"Obsessed," he confessed raising one hand as the other held her tighter.

"I thought I had lost you … just when I realized that I really, really wanted you. It was hard."

"And I'm so sorry," she said kissing the back of his hand. "If I had known how you felt, I would never have gotten involved with Kevin Morris from the start."

"Meg, remember, no more apologies. Perhaps if it had not been for Kevin Morris, we wouldn't be here, together, in our bed, expecting our first child."

"First?" she asked. "Are you planning on more?"

"At least ten or twelve."

"Can you afford that many kids?"

"Your daddy's a millionaire. We can have twenty kids if we want. We can adopt twenty kids if we want."

She smiled, gave a small laugh, and then whispered "He's not the only millionaire."

He leaned up on an elbow and looked at her strangely. "What do you mean?"

"Let's just say that I've made some really wise investments over the years with a lovely chunk of inheritance I received when I was twenty-one."

"What kind of chunk, and what kind of investments?"

"My chunk was Five million."

He gasped, "You have five million dollars?"

She shook her head and corrected him, "Oh, no … I invested most of it. I have considerably more now."

Phillip let go of her and stared at the wall in a daze.

"Are you okay?" she asked him.

"I don't know," he said softly. "I always assumed you'd have access to your dad's money, and I was determined to never, ever use it for any reason. I was going to provide for you, but … wow … you yourself have several million dollars … on your own … free and clear."

"Is that a problem?"

"No!" he said quickly. "It's just … well … for lack of a better word … unexpected."

"But it's not a problem?" she asked again.

He shook his head. "No. I just didn't know."

"Good," she smiled as she made him lay back down, "because it's considerably more now."

He sighed. "Are there any other surprises you haven't told me about?"

"Definitely," she giggled. "I wouldn't dream of letting our marriage get bored."

"I don't imagine that's a problem we'll ever face," he quickly added.

The next morning after breakfast, it was decided that Phillip would take his family shopping so that Mary Ann and Julie could buy swimsuits, although Julie really didn't seem to care. Meg wanted to stay with Grandma Corrie so she could relax and be refreshed for the rest of the day. Being on her feet seemed to wear her out.

"You have no idea what tired is yet," Clara told her. "Wait until the eighth and ninth months."

"I can hardly wait," Meg moaned.

"You sure you don't want to go," Phillip asked her. "I could wheel you around in Grandma Corrie's wheelchair."

At that, Grandma Corrie chuckled.

"No thanks," she waved him off. "I'll just stay and rest."

The truth was that she wanted to talk with Grandma Corrie. The woman fascinated her to no end. She wanted to find out who it was behind that third pair of blue eyes. Shortly after everyone had left, she pulled up a chair next to the recliner and began to talk.

"Where are you from, Grandma Corrie," she asked her.

"Oh, here, there and everywhere," the lady teased as her eyes danced with joy, speaking in her slow and deliberate manner with that unusual accent.

"That accent of yours," Meg went on, "is from where?"

"Good question," she replied. "You just can't place it, can you?"

Meg shook her head.

"It is a strange one, birthed from a strange story."

"Please tell me," Meg pleaded. "I am way too curious for my own good, I'm afraid."

The aged woman laughed a hearty laugh for someone so fragile looking. "You are a treasure. There is no such thing as too curious. We are all curious. It seems that you just have the nerve to pursue your curiosity. That is good. It means you don't live in the darkness too often."

Meg laughed and nodded her head as she said, "It also means I tend to overstep my boundaries, put my nose in places it doesn't belong, and find out way too much information that I probably shouldn't know!"

"Ah, but it helps you change the world, does it not?"

"I suppose it does," Meg agreed, wondering how much the woman knew about her.

"My father was a pastor in Germany," she began, speaking slowly. "Years before the Hitler regime took over, God told my father he must leave Germany because of impending danger. He did not want to go, but God told him He had a plan for my father which did not include Germany. So, we moved to France. I was a young child. I hated France. It was beautiful and charming, but I did not know the language, and I was lost there. Other girls made fun of me because of my language, and still others at how I dressed. My mother began to teach us English. She was so intelligent.

"Two years later, the war broke out and Father said we must move to England. It was a hard transition also. He had no skills but pastoring and teaching the Word, but no one in England would hire him to teach because his accent was so thick and Germans were not a favored nationality at the time. Father began working odd jobs wherever he could. It was humiliating for such an educated man to gut fish, clean toilets, and scrub floors, but he believed God wanted him there, so he pushed on.

"As Jewish refugees began to come from Germany, many were hopeless and confused. Why was God allowing this? Why was there such hate for them? Many had lost family, parents, children, brothers and sisters. They felt guilty for leaving and despair at losing everything.

"My father, being from Germany, could talk to them, as well as interpret for them. He began to minister to them in our home. Many began to come to Christ, and within two more years my father was able to begin a legitimate church."

"How wonderful," Meg whispered. "That's an incredible story."

"Yes, child," Corrie went on. "God is always incredible. When we listen, trust and obey Him, His power overwhelms us. My father taught us that. Many in the family thought he had made a stupid mistake, throwing his life away because he claimed God spoke to him. But as he ministered to these hopeless, lost people, we saw lives transformed.

"When Captain James learned about our church, he would come there for services on Sundays, and would attend weekly Bible studies when he could make it. His mother's parents had been German immigrants in America, and he took great pleasure in listening to my father preach in their language. He had a choppy grasp of it, and loved the chance to speak it with our congregation. I was twenty-one now, and he was twenty-five. He was so tall and handsome, and such a man of God. He would bring soldiers with him who would bring gifts for the children in the church whose parents could afford nothing. One Christmas, and of course these converted Jews had never celebrated Christmas before, Marcus James dressed up as Santa Claus, had collected many gifts and came bursting into the church during a Christmas feast. He proceeded to call out the names of the children, one by one, and deliver them the most wonderful little treasures. He then explained the legend of Saint Nicolas and the love of Christ. I fell in love with him immediately after that.

"He began to visit with my father in our home. These visits often ended with him and me sitting on the outside steps talking about the incredible power and wisdom of God. After several months, he showed up one night almost looking devastated. As we sat together that evening, he told me his term of service was up and that he would be leaving within the month. My heart was breaking. I could not imagine living without him. I was secretly in love with this incredible man. Then he surprised me. He asked if I would return to America with him as his wife."

"How exciting!" Meg said.

"Oh yes!" she agreed. "My father was not too pleased at the prospect of me living over the waters, but he knew there would never be a more Godly man to give his daughter away to. So, as they say in America, the rest is history."

"What a story," Meg told her. "You should write a book."

"I do not want to talk about me any longer," Grandma Corrie said seriously.

"Okay," Meg agreed, thinking the woman was tired, "but thank-you for sharing that story."

"I must talk about you and my grandson."

Meg looked at her startled. "Me and Phillip?"

"Yes," she affirmed. "There is much I must tell you, and I fear this may be the only chance I have."

"What is it, Grandma Corrie? Is there a problem?"

"I hope not," she laughed again. "But God has much for you two to know. I must tell you all this in private. God has directed me to do such. Do you understand?"

"I'm not sure." Meg was confused. "What is it that I need to know?"

"First," she began, "I have always known that Phillip was alive."

"What?" Now she was shocked. "Who told you?"

"God," she said flatly. "When Clara told me of her baby's death, I mourned and prayed. But God strengthened me and told me the child was like Moses, and that he was alive and protected for a great purpose."

Meg felt that wave of awe again that had overwhelmed her when Grandma Corrie had first spoken to her.

"That devil senator had tried to kill him, and he had lied to my daughter, even about the child being a boy."

"Why didn't you tell Clara?"

"First, she would have thought I was crazy. She did not share my faith at that time. Second, when Clara did come to Christ, to tell her the child was alive would have made her search for him. God told me that must not happen. Her life would have been in danger also."

"What did you do?"

"I prayed and prayed and prayed," she continued. "Sometimes I would pray all night if God would lead. I prayed for Phillip's safety, for God's hand in his life, for God's purpose to be accomplished. Then, fifteen years ago, I began to pray for you."

"For me?" Meg asked astonished. "God showed me to you?"

"The power of God is incredible! When you finally came into his life, I prayed and prayed and prayed. Did not Satan try to destroy you also?"

"Yes," she answered stunned. "Yes, he did. I thought my life was ruined at one point."

"Ah," she replied knowingly, "but the power of God can heal all wounds."

"Yes, but not until now—this year."

"I know," the sweet woman gave a gentle smile, Phillip's smile, Clara's smile. "I prayed during your wedding that God would overwhelm you with His love and that you would finally know His healing touch."

"And I did," Meg nodded, still amazed at all she was hearing.

"Yes," she acknowledged. "God's power can overcome all things. It is so important that you never forget that. There is much ahead for you and Phillip."

"In what way?"

"God has laid His hand on that man. He chose him from the beginning for a mighty purpose. He chose you to be there with him."

"What purpose, and what am I supposed to do?" Meg wanted to know.

"That, I can't tell. I just don't know," she said. "But God is going to use him, and you are the strength that will see him through it."

Meg stood up and began to pace. This was all so overwhelming. Either this lady was old, senile and crazy, or God was speaking directly through her about things to come.

"I am not crazy, Meg," Corrie said sternly, her accent almost sounding thicker. Meg turned to face her quickly.

"Has God always spoken to you like this?" Meg asked her.

"No," she said shaking her head. "He has only spoken to me about Phillip and you. I have interceded for you both all these years. Now it is your turn to begin seeking God and interceding. It is time for you to become what God has intended all these years. My time on earth is short now."

"No, Grandma Corrie," Meg began to plead. "I'm not ready for this … this … responsibility you keep talking about. I have felt your prayers! I need those prayers still."

"No," she said soberly. "You need the power of God in your own life. It is time for you to stop seeing God as merely your friend. You must see Him as your very life and breath. You must seek His face and His power. You must become the vessel of strength for Phillip. God has much for him to do."

"But what?" Meg asked again. "What's he supposed to do? He's been so hurt by the ministry, I don't see him going back to a church for years."

"God does," she said with authority. "And you must be the one to convince him that he is to go."

"When?"

"Before this year is up," Corrie said.

"This year?" Meg exclaimed. "He'll never go! It's too soon!"

"God has chosen you, Meg, to move him there."

"I don't have that kind of power!" she insisted, knowing that Phillip's pain and rejection still ran deep.

"But God does!" Grandma Corrie said loudly as she stood to her feet. "I have seen the power of God at work, Meg. He is so much greater than your simple faith can understand at this moment! Do not deny what God is wanting to do in your lives! Satan has tried to destroy Phillip. Think of it! He tried to kill him from the beginning! But, God was able to preserve his life. He tried to keep you from him also. But look! You are his wife, his helpmate, you carry his child, and you alone have the key to open the doors that God has laid out for him. You alone will help Phillip fulfill the will of God! I am passing the mantle to you ... right now ... this very moment."

"Grandma Corrie ..." Meg's voice trailed off as she felt utterly helpless ... and speechless.

"I may die in peace now."

"No!" Meg insisted. "I can't do this without you. I don't have that strength."

"No, you don't, but God in you does. It is your turn to become the woman God created you to be. Seek His face, dear girl. Obey His call. Take on the yoke He offers to you."

Meg felt herself tremble as Grandma Corrie spoke. Somehow she believed what this lady was telling her. Somehow she knew that she was more than just Phillip's wife, but the catalyst for change.

"This year?" Meg whispered. "He won't be ready this year."

"Do you question the timing of God?"

Meg looked out onto the gulf and felt such fear at all that was happening. "I don't question the timing of God," she admitted. "I question my own weakness and my own lack of knowing God the way you do."

"Then seek His face. God is not that far away. He is powerful, He is awesome, and He is here. Meg, I must pass this mantle to you. It is your turn. Do not reject what God has ordained."

Meg sat back down in the chair and stared out the glass doors. She would never believe that she could have the faith and integrity and wisdom of God that this woman had, yet here she was, realizing that she must. Grandma Corrie, in another feat Meg imagined impossible, fell to her knees and began to pray. She immediately joined her and began to weep. They prayed for an hour and a half. Meg couldn't understand how this woman could stay down there so long. Then she realized this must be a habit she'd had for years.

Dear God, Meg prayed silently in her mind, *can you make me like her? Can I ever have that kind of strength?*

And as she prayed that very prayer, Grandma Corrie prayed out loud, "Dear God, clothe Meg with Your strength and wisdom. Make her a woman of prayer and obedience. Show her Your power."

When they finished, Meg was amazed that the elderly lady could get up from her knees so easily. Then she remembered what she had said—the power of God was incredible.

"You must not tell this to Phillip," she told Meg.

"Why? I can't imagine not telling him."

"You are to be his strength, not his prophet," Corrie instructed. "You are to seek God on his behalf."

"He's so gifted—I know God can use him greatly."

Grandma Corrie laughed again then said, "God does not use giftedness. Gifted people cannot do anything without God. God uses broken and contrite hearts. Always remember that, Meg. Broken and contrite hearts He will not despise. He can change the world with a broken man, but a man of pride and great ability can change nothing. Never think the vessel is more important than the Treasure."

"Yes, ma'am," she said softly. "I feel as though I still need to pray. How can that be possible?"

"Go to your closet, Meg," Corrie said gently. "God will call you to prayer often now. Go to your closet and obey Him."

She nodded as she left the lady alone in the room and literally went to her closet, closed the door, and knelt again.

"Dear God," she said slowly, "help my unbelief."

Chapter Thirty-Six

July Fourth was a wonderful holiday. Everyone spent the day at the MacAllister beach house eating, swimming, playing badminton and volleyball, and talking. As the day neared the close, they sat in the living room sharing just a bit longer. Grandma Corrie was very quiet. In fact, Meg had never seen her talk or act as animated publicly as when they had been alone that one afternoon. If she hadn't known better, she would have believed, as the rest of the family, that she was senile, forgetful, and barely aware of anything. Yet anytime Meg was alone with her, the woman smiled and laughed and talked of the power of God.

"I got a really disturbing letter from Amy yesterday," Janet began as the silence started to grow. Janet somehow always felt it her duty to disperse moments of quietness. "She said Nikos had to demand the resignation of their youth/music minister."

Immediately Phillip blurted out, "Oh, great! I suppose he's turned into one of those bashing, controlling pastors too now!"

"Phillip!" Janet yelled back at him. "No, he's not! He had a very good reason!"

Suddenly the silence became overwhelming as everyone stared at Phillip.

"I'm sorry," he said defensively. "I've just had some bad experiences, okay?"

"But Nikos," Janet went on, "was your college roommate for two years. You could have a little more respect for him than that."

"I said, I'm sorry," he retorted, but obviously still agitated.

"The guy had an affair with one of his youth. Now she's pregnant, and he wants to leave his wife and two kids to marry this seventeen year old."

"Unbelievable!" Craig exclaimed this time. "That's terrible!"

"How do we know?" Phillip interjected, still upset.

"How do we know?" Janet shot back. "Are you suggesting Nikos and Amy have made something this horrible up just to make a man leave a church?"

"It can happen," was all Phillip would say.

Before Meg knew what she was saying, she found herself uttering out loud, "Nikos is a man of God."

All eyes now turned to her.

"What did you say?" Phillip asked her.

"I said, *Nikos is a man of God.*"

"You don't know that," Phillip insisted. "You don't even know him that well!"

"True," Meg agreed, "but I did spend some time with him that one summer after high school. He was a good man, a Godly man. But I know his reputation more. Sometimes a man's reputation says more about the man than knowing him personally."

"Well said," jumped in Grandma Corrie to everyone's surprise. They all stared at her for a moment, as she went back to smiling sweetly and being still and quiet.

"Reputation?" Phillip asked her. "What do you know of his reputation?"

"We've prayed for him at church all these years that he's been in the ministry," Meg explained. "I've heard of the churches he's pastored and the ministries he's started and the people he's helped. Great changes have happened to others under his ministry. I can't say what he's like as a person, because frankly I had a hard time understanding his accent, but God's used him mightily—Nikos is a man of God."

Phillip sat quietly for a moment. His family stared in shock at his outburst. Janet was near tears as she adored Nikos and Amy, and Craig was getting rather hot about the whole conversation. The rest of the MacAllisters didn't seem to mind because hot discussions and controversy were common at their family gatherings.

"I'm sorry," Phillip finally managed. "It's just that it's so hard to get over the egotistical, maniacal morons I've had to work under who call themselves *men anointed by God.* The only anointing they had ... had been in their own minds!"

"That doesn't mean all are like that, Phillip," Craig said. "We've been through this before. You had some horribly bad luck."

"No such thing as luck," Grandma Corrie muttered again, eliciting stares as she sat back and smiled.

"That's right, Phillip," Meg agreed. "There is no such thing as luck. God has his hand on you, and has had for all these years. Those men weren't accidents or bad luck."

"Amen," said Grandma Corrie. All stared again.

"So, then God gave me all these wounds? He's responsible for all the garbage I had to go through?" Phillip said with frustration.

"No," Meg quickly disagreed. "You are responsible for your wounds. You responded to a bad situation, to many bad situations, in a way that made you vulnerable."

"Thank-you, Dr. Freud," he said sarcastically.

Suddenly, Grandma Corrie stood up from her chair.

"Mother, sit down," Clara demanded.

Corrie did not. She walked over to Phillip and put her hand over his hand. She looked deeply into his eyes, her own filled with tears, and said, "Is it not time, my son, to let God heal *all* of those open wounds?"

"Mother," Clara said loudly, "sit down!"

"His power is incredible, even to the changing of souls," Corrie went on. "Is he not the Great Physician?"

"Mother!" Clara yelled.

"It's okay," Phillip said to his mother as he took his grandmother's hand. "She's right. I've let this fester in me for so many years that I can't even think about the goodness or healing of God. It *is* time for me to let go of this."

He stood up and led his grandmother back to her chair. He then reached his hand out to Meg. "Come with me," he said as she took his hand. He then looked to his family and said, "You guys can drive back alone. Meg and I will walk back by the beach. I have some things I need to get off my chest."

As they went down the back steps of the deck onto the beach, he held her hand tightly. They walked briskly for a moment until they were out of sight of the house. He then stopped, fell to his knees, and began to weep loudly. Meg quickly knelt beside him and held his head in her arms. She began to pray silently that God would erase the pain and heal the wounds that still hurt him so deeply. The more she prayed, the harder he seemed to cry. She'd never seen a man so broken in her life. Then Grandma Corrie's words came back to her, *God uses broken and contrite hearts. He can change the world with a broken man, but a man of pride and great ability can change nothing.*

After several minutes of weeping, Phillip began to settle down and wipe his eyes. Meg reached over to dry them also.

"I felt the power of God shoot through her hand and into my whole body," Phillip said slowly.

"What?" Meg asked.

"When my grandmother touched me, I felt something literally shake me," he tried to explain. "It was as if ... as if ... I can't explain it, Meg. I just knew that I had to let go of all this baggage I've been carrying around. Meg, what if God still wants to use me and I'm sitting here living in my condo on the beach— just enjoying the high life? What if I'm taking the wide path that leads to destruction while totally ignoring the straight and narrow? It's not just about me anymore. I have you, and I have our baby. I can't ignore God's call anymore."

She reached over to caress his cheek as she smiled softly. His expression melted as she gently moved a strand of hair on his forehead.

"I have felt the power of God too," she told him. "I've been so shallow and so flippant with Him. I've done great things thinking they were under His direction, but I've never really known what the direction of God was."

"God has done great things through you," he insisted.

"No," she said emphatically. "I've done great things in my own power. I am smart. I am forceful. I am manipulative. And to top it all off, I am rich. I can do anything I want to do Phillip, and that's exactly what I've done. I've done good things, but that doesn't mean I've done God's things. I want to know His power and His life in me. I want Him to be the reason that I live and breathe."

"Me too," he confessed. "What is so sad Meg is that I've been there. I've known God and His power and His wisdom, but I let these ... these ... these self-centered men, not God centered, ruin my life and my love for God."

"The one thing I am sure of is that God's hand has been in my meeting and marrying you," she told him.

"Me too. Together, Meg, you and I, committed to Him, we can do anything God wants us to do. You just need to know that I'm weak. I've been destroyed inside—no confidence left in me. I can trust God again, but I still hurt. And I'm afraid that I won't be able to stand up under another man who sets out to control me ... or destroy me."

"I'll be your strength now," she assured him. "I'll be your haven. When you can't go on, I'll intercede to the Father on your behalf so you'll know that power and life lies in Him. You'll know that you can go on. I'm going to be your biggest ally on earth and your quickest link to heaven."

He stood and then helped her carefully to her feet. He held her hand as they silently started back down the beach toward their house. "I really hope you mean that," he finally said. "You don't know how brutal people can be when the devil's convinced them they're doing God's bidding while all along he's whispering his evil plans in their itching ears. I think I can do this again if you really mean what you just said."

She stopped him and gazed up into those turquoise eyes. "With all my heart I mean it. I belong to you now. I am not my own any longer."

"Are you sure, Meg? You've always been so independent and in control. Can you take this role of just following me wherever the wind blows?"

"Not the wind, Phillip," she corrected him. "I'll follow you wherever God leads."

He put his arms around her and held her tightly as the breeze began to pick up and thunder slowly rumbled in the distance. "I'm so thankful for you," he managed to get out. "God really is good, Meg. He really is."

🌴 🌴 🌴

As the Andersons prepared to board the plane back for South Dakota,

Meg and Phillip promised to come up for a visit when his vacation time came around the first of August. They began saying their good-byes in order to leave, when Grandma Corrie stood up from her wheelchair. Phillip immediately went over to help her. Meg followed. She looked at both of them and smiled a knowing smile.

"God is good," she said with strength. "He is a powerful and mighty God. You are to never forget that."

"We won't," Meg told her.

"I am thankful I got to see you both," Corrie continued. "My heart has peace, and I know that God is now in control. I will say goodbye forever now."

"We'll be up in August, Grandma Corrie," Phillip reminded her. "We'll spend some time together again then."

"No," she said gently. "This has been our time together. I have fought the good fight. I have run the race. I am now ready to see my Redeemer's face."

"Grandma …" Meg began, but was interrupted by Corrie.

"Don't spite me this," she said. "I am ready to see the salvation of my God … for my faith to at last be my sight. This world is not my home. I have accomplished His purpose, and I am ready to go."

They both hugged and kissed her, and then watched her leave through the hallway on Thomas' arm.

"Don't take too much of what she says seriously," Clara said as she told them goodbye. "She's very old. She's not quite all there. She's been that way for several years."

"She's a loony," Mary Ann spouted out.

"No, she's not," Meg told them both. "She's just been living in a world that's not easily understood on earth. Her citizenship is somewhere else."

"Sounds like science fiction to me," Julie mumbled.

"Perhaps," Meg smiled as they hugged goodbye. "But I bet it's been a nice world."

As they watched the plane taxi down the runway, Meg looked to Phillip and asked, "Do you think we'll ever see her again?"

He shook his head and said gently, "Not in this life."

Two days before Meg and Phillip left for South Dakota, Corrine Hedwig James left her temporary home for the one she so longed to see. Phillip was able to perform the ceremony as well as sing, and Meg played for the service. Meg felt that Grandma Corrie deserved so much more than she had received in this life, especially in her later years, but she knew that now she was receiving the only reward she had ever sought—to see her Redeemer's face. She longed to tell Phillip all that she and his grandmother had discussed but would keep her word and not say anything. If Grandma Corrie thought it was something that should not be spoken of, Meg respected her and trusted her enough to keep it between the two of them.

The rest of the visit to South Dakota was wonderful. Meg fell in love with the log cabin she had seen once before, not quite a year ago. She began secretly planning to have one of her own some day. She and Phillip doted on little Nathan who was now crawling and responding to everyone. Although Meg wasn't even four months pregnant yet, the desire for her baby became stronger. She found herself praying for her unborn child often during the day and asking God to mold her into a mother that could raise her children in the wisdom and power of God.

She also had the chance to spend much time with Mary Ann and Julie. They adored her and hung on her every suggestion. Julie had even let her hair grow out, hoping that it would soon be as long as Meg's. They all visited Mt. Rushmore, the Badlands and spent an afternoon in Wall, South Dakota. Meg had never traveled much. There hadn't been much time growing up. Because Meri's parents had lived in Treasure Cove, that became the destination for all vacations. Meg began to envision her and Phillip and their children traveling across the United States, camping and visiting and traveling and seeing everything they possibly could.

The plans for Christmas were made so that conflict would not occur between the two families. The Andersons agreed to have Christmas the day after the 25th so that Phillip and Meg could be at the MacAllisters, and Terri and Matthew could be at her family's house. Mary Ann was slightly disappointed claiming that she didn't know if it was physically possible for her to avoid opening presents on Christmas morning, but agreed to try. Julie, ever patient, thought it would be wonderful because the whole family would be together for the first time. When they questioned her about this, claiming they had always been together at Christmas, she responded by saying, "Not with Meg."

The rest of August passed quickly. Meg had to admit she was a little depressed as school began and she wasn't a part of it. It was the first time in her life that she hadn't been at school that she could remember. It also made her long for Spiro again. She found herself spending a lot of time at the children's home *filling in* until they selected a dean for the girls. She still spent much time in prayer. She couldn't help but remember what Grandma Corrie had told her—she and Phillip would be leaving Treasure Cove before the year was up. She decided to go ahead and begin Christmas shopping so that if they did leave, she wouldn't have to worry about it at the last minute. She laughed at herself as she shopped in September because she was famous for frantically searching out the perfect picked over gifts on Christmas Eve. When Phillip went with her, he asked why on earth they were shopping so early. She simply said that their families had doubled and they had better start sooner this year.

*   *   *

The first weekend of October, Meg had Alissa, Lana and Carmen over for the first time since she had married. Alissa and Lana were now freshmen at Gulf Coast Christian College, and Carmen was spending her last year, and a full year at that, at the children's home. Had anyone seen pictures of Carmen this time last year and now, it would be impossible to believe this could be the same person. As the three girls laughed and giggled over everything, Meg found herself praying that God would do great things in Carmen's life. She had done much for Carmen, but she also knew that God could do even more.

"Just like old times, huh girls?" Meg asked as she rolled the Monopoly dice.

"Bite your tongue!" Carmen blurted out. Everyone looked at her in surprise.

"Well, come on," she defended. "You guys are in college, Miss Mac, excuse me, *Mrs. Anderson*, is now married, getting fatter by the day, and doesn't even teach anymore. Then there's me! Jeesh! I have a life! Now, somebody tell me how things are still the same."

They sat quietly for a moment then Alissa said, "Okay, you win. Everything's different."

"Except that I am NOT fat," Meg insisted.

"Puh-leeze," Lana moaned. "You've already started wearing those little moo-moo type shirts."

"It's a maternity shirt!" Meg defended. "Regular little shirts are a bit too confining now."

"Getting fat," Carmen whispered.

"Growing a baby," Meg said sternly.

"Whatever," Alissa said. "But the fact still remains, you are getting bigger. But in my opinion, I just want to say, *finally*! I mean, you've been pregnant forever. I was wondering if you had made the whole thing up! Where was this little baby?"

"It takes nine months to grow, you know?" Meg teased her. "Did you not pay attention in human physiology?"

"Not if I didn't have to!" Alissa laughed. "I hate science!"

"But there's another difference too," Carmen said seriously. Everyone looked at her. "Spiro."

They all nodded, and Meg felt that twinge of loss again. He and Carmen had been close during the months she had lived with Meg.

"I still miss him, too," Meg confessed.

"I don't think he was really a dog," Carmen mused. "He was a little human packaged up in one cute bundle. Do you think dogs go to heaven, Miss Mac?"

Meg thought for a moment then said, "People have always told me no, but I've never found it in the Bible. I mean, God used that donkey to talk to Balaam. Perhaps animals know God in a way that we can't understand … a simple way. This isn't theologically correct, but I'd like to think that Spiro is running around up there chasing a yellow ball."

"Me too," said Carmen.

"Me three," said Alissa.

"Whatever," Lana moaned. "Sometimes you guys can be downright icky with sentimentality."

The next Monday afternoon, Meg had been reading in the blue recliner that had managed to stay at her house even after Grandma Corrie left. She had read, prayed, cleaned up a little here and there, but had finally drifted off to sleep. As she slept, she dreamt of Grandma Corrie falling on her knees next to the chair praying for her. Then Grandma Corrie, in her dream, looked up at her and said, "It won't be long now." As Meg tried to question her, she was roused by a very pale-looking Phillip.

"Are you okay?" she asked as his expression caused her concern .

"I'm not sure," he said in a whisper. "Something has just happened, and I need to talk to you about it."

She immediately sat up in the recliner and gave him her full attention. "What's going on, Phillip?" she asked in fear. "What's wrong?"

"No, no," he quickly reassured her, "it's nothing like that. I got a strange and unexpected kind of phone call today."

"From whom?" she wondered as her curiosity peaked.

"Nikos Andropolos," he said flatly.

"Okay. What did he want with you?"

"Take a wild guess," he said as he undid his tie.

"I'm clueless," she told him impatiently, "and in no mindset to play twenty questions."

"His church has been looking for a youth/music guy for three months. Every resume that's come to the committee they've rejected. He says they don't feel God has shown them the man yet. They haven't pursued a single one."

"How sad. I hate that their youth are suffering through all of this because of the infidelities of the last guy."

"Well," he went on, "Nikos said that the day the guy read his resignation, God put a specific name on his heart, but he continued to ignore it because he didn't think this guy would even consider the position."

The thud hit her stomach like a rock. She looked up at him and mouthed the word, "You?" He nodded. "Heavens, Phillip, you?"

"He said Janet has told Amy about all my problems and disgruntledness. When God put my name on his heart, he thought it was just his own desires. We had talked often about serving together when we were roommates. We used to plan the ideal church."

Meg stood up and began to pace.

"Don't pace," he pleaded. "You make me nervous when you pace."

"This is it, Phillip," she said as she sat beside him on the couch.

"I don't know, Meg," he said weakly. "What if I can't even work with Nikos? What if I'm beyond repair?" His eyes grew wide with fear as he turned and said, "What if it's some sick trick the devil's playing to mislead me away from the station and back into hell?"

"No, Phillip," she said gently. "God doesn't operate like that. You need to give Him as much credit to lead as you give Satan credit to mislead. What if this was what God had planned all along—you and Nikos working together, sharing a common vision? What if this was what Satan knew too, or had an inkling of? Maybe this is why he tried to destroy you?"

He stared at her with an astonished look. "Wow," he breathed. "How do you come up with this stuff?"

"God is awesome," she found herself saying. "He has plans for us that are for good and not defeat."

"Nikos said the committee finally asked last night what on earth was going on," he continued. "They couldn't figure out why God was so silent when their church was in such need. Apparently, to top off the whole shebang, three of their teenagers, two guys and one girl, committed group suicide last week."

"Oh, no!" Meg cried out. "Phillip, no!"

He nodded sadly. "And Nikos feels responsible because he hasn't called me. Anyway, he told the group that God had laid a man on his heart, and that he would contact me on Monday. It's Monday."

"What do you think?" she asked him.

"I think it's time for me to get back on the straight and narrow, obey God, and honor his call in my life."

Overwhelmed, she put her arms around him and kissed the top of his head. "God is powerful, Phillip," she reiterated. "He will provide what you need to do this."

"He already has," he said as he sat up and looked into her eyes. "I'm a new man because of you, Meg. I can do anything with you by my side."

"No, Phillip," she corrected him, "we can do anything with God on our side."

"You want to help me make a resume?" he asked. "Nikos said to make it very simple, nothing fancy and no padding of information. He said to include what God is leading me to think about the ministry there."

"What is God leading you to think?"

He thought for a moment, rubbed his stubble and shook his head. "The only thing that comes to mind is that God is awesome and powerful, and that if He wants me there, He can do anything He wants through me to accomplish His purpose."

"Let's get to the computer and write that down before we forget it," Meg insisted.

After finishing the resume, they printed it out, prayed over it, and then put it in the mail that evening. The rest of the week they said little to each other about it. They understood that the process of a committee choosing one out of many often took several days or even weeks. They were prepared to wait a long time, and were totally caught off guard by a phone call on Friday night.

"Hello?" Meg said as she picked up the receiver.

A thick accent answered her back, "Hello! Is this the Meg MacAllister Anderson?"

"Yes, it is," she replied.

"This would be the one and only Nikos Andropolos."

Meg was stunned. She couldn't speak.

"How does the prospect of moving to northwest Alabama appeal to you?" he asked.

"Uh … well … I suppose that if God wants us there, then the prospect sounds great," she finally said.

"It is good to hear you say that, because you do realize now that when God calls Phillip to a church, He is also calling you."

"I hadn't quite thought of it that way, but I suppose you're right."

"I know I'm right. I have been married a long time now, or so it would seem," he laughed. "Many children and a wife will change your life and your priorities drastically."

"How many kids do you guys have now anyway?"

"Five, with another on the way," he laughed again.

"You make me tired just talking about it!" she groaned.

"When is yours expected to make its arrival?"

"Sometime in February."

"Perhaps it will be an Alabama baby?" he suggested.

"Perhaps," she said quietly. This was the first time she realized that the baby might not be born in Treasure Cove. She had just assumed, with each doctor visit, that they would still be here for the birth. Her heart sunk for a moment. No Janet or Craig with her, a church full of strangers, a new doctor, and a new house all were very insecure possibilities for her first child. As she gave the phone to Phillip, she sank into the recliner and prayed that God would give her everything she needed to make this move. She had only thought about Phillip these past few months, and not herself. Now she was feeling fearful.

When Phillip hung up, he gave her the news.

"They voted unanimously to consider us this evening. They want us to fly up next weekend in view of a call."

"Next weekend?" she asked shakily.

"What's wrong? Are you having second thoughts?"

"No," she said gently. "I just hadn't thought about having the baby up there."

"Me either," he confessed. "It all seems to be happening so quick. I could tell him we need more time if you want."

She shook her head. "It's not about what we want, Phillip. It's about what God has planned for us. Perhaps we've been here too long already. If God wants us there, he'll meet all our needs … even our emotional ones."

"Are you sure?" he asked again.

"I'm not sure about anything in my own strength," she said with a hesitant laugh, "but God is awesome and powerful. I'm confident in Him."

"Whew," he smiled. "I'm so glad you're on my side."

"Why's that?"

"That confidence will come in handy if we take another church."

"Perhaps this church is different," she suggested.

"I doubt it," he said. "Just because the pastor's a great guy, well, that doesn't say much about the deacons."

"Phillip!" she exclaimed. "You have got to stop all this."

"I know, I know, I know," he said quickly. "Meg, I'm scared."

"Well, stop it right now," she insisted. "God is leading us there, not shoving us."

"Yes," he admitted. "Yes, He is." He then looked up and said, "God, please help my unbelief."

Chapter Thirty-Seven

As they boarded the plane, Meg tried to squelch her anxiety. She wanted to be excited about this new possibility, she wanted to be strong and confident for Phillip, but she was scared. Added to that was the thought of being around Amy for an extended time … perhaps even living near her. They had never gotten along—Amy was serious and stern and Meg had always been a bit silly and carefree in her younger years. Amy had been responsible and calculating where Meg had been adventurous, always pushing the limit. What kind of mother was she? What kind of wife was she for that fact? Would she try to change Meg? Would she offer pushy advice? Would she stare disapprovingly at her and her life?

"What in heaven's name are you thinking about?" Phillip asked her as they lifted into the air. "I certainly hope it's not me with that look on your face!"

"It's not," she forced a laugh, imagining how horrid she must appear. "Amy and I never got along very well."

"I know. Hard to forget."

"Maybe I've changed enough that she won't bother me anymore."

"Or maybe she's changed," he suggested. "Motherhood can do that to a lady."

"Perhaps," she mumbled doubtfully.

🏝️ 🏝️ 🏝️

Coming out of the unloading area, Meg immediately spotted Nikos. His dark, wavy hair had actually grayed a small bit, and following right behind him was Amy—she was beaming. Her long, blond hair was the same as ever, French-braided down her back reaching to her waist.

"My friend and brother," Nikos said as he embraced Phillip.

"Meg," Amy smiled as she reached out to hug her also. "Do you think anyone our age still wears their hair like this except us?"

Amy making a joke? Meg caught her breath. "I doubt it," she replied with a guarded chuckle. "I've been wondering if I'll want to mess with it anymore after the baby comes."

"Trust me," the tall blond said as she took Meg's arm, "this is the easiest do possible. You just wash it, let it dry straight, and then throw it into a braid or pony-tail or bun—well, that's to impress the deacons' wives." She gave a hearty laugh catching Meg by surprise again.

"Meg," Nikos said coming over to her with his thick accent, "you look exactly the same!"

"I was thinking the same about Amy," she said as they embraced.

"But not me?" he mocked.

"What's with the hair, man?" Phillip asked him.

"You don't like my highlights?" he laughed. "It's called a wife and children! Yours is coming, my friend!"

The drive to Clayton was peaceful and nice. The men sat in the front of the Andropolos van, and the ladies sat in the middle seats. Meg couldn't believe how easy Amy was to talk to, or even yet, that Amy was actually talking. Her eyes glowed as she talked of her children, her homeschooling, and her anticipation of the next child. Meg was almost overwhelmed. She'd been trying to figure out how she was going to manage one, much less six! Nikos told Phillip of the events from the past few months at the church. She managed to hear only bits and pieces, but from what she could put together, things had been stressful. One man, a deacon, had decided to pretty much run the church because he didn't think Nikos was moving fast enough. Most were behind Nikos, but only a few voiced actual support because this man donated much to the money bags of the church. This particular deacon wasn't even sure the church needed another *reckless young man up here leading their teenagers astray.* Perhaps Phillip was right—just because the pastor was wonderful didn't mean the rest of the church would be.

They went to Amy and Nikos' house and greeted the five children plus a babysitter. Hannah was eight, Katie was six, Jason was four, Caleb was three, and baby Brianna was almost one. Meg breathed deeply as each child greeted her politely and went back to whatever they were doing before their arrival. Amy had hugged each of them and introduced them by name, age, and favorite food. Each child seemed to adore her, and Meg was about to admit that she may adore this new Amy a bit too.

Amy prepared a scrumptious meal, and the entire family, plus Phillip and Meg, sat around a huge picnic table in the dining room of the pastorium. Shortly after dinner, members from the committee that had chosen Phillip began to arrive at the house. Meg sat with her mouth open as Amy insisted that Meg relax as the three older children carefully and orderly cleared the table while Amy loaded the dishwasher. Before any child left, they would ask Amy if there was anything else to do. When she assured them they were through, they left with a hug for their mother and skipped out of the room. While Amy finished, she suggested Meg go into the great room and meet the members. Amy referred to them as the *cream of the crop* in the church, and said these very people would one day become her dearest and most treasured friends in Clayton.

As she sat down in the great room, meeting several of the five-member committee, she kept wondering where the children were. She could vaguely hear them in the distance, but couldn't figure out exactly where the small noises and squeals were coming from. Soon she forgot all about the children as Rhonda Evans and Becky Lewis began talking with her. Amy had been right. After ten minutes, she felt right at home with the two ladies. Soon Amy joined them, and Meg felt as if she had known them her whole life. They talked of the wonderful doctor that would most probably deliver her baby. He was a church member and an excellent obstetrician. Clayton considered themselves blessed to even have an OB/GYN in the town. That was two down, Amy being actually nice and then a good doctor in town, and who knew how many left to go. At least Meg could go to sleep that night with some of her fears alleviated.

"The committee thinks you're wonderful," said Nikos. "They like you too, Meg," he winked.

"These are wonderful people here," Amy injected. "They really are. This is a wonderful church. The people have been so supportive and cooperative with Nikos' ideas."

"Except for that one deacon, huh?" Phillip asked with apprehension.

Amy giggled. "You mean Harold Hastings?"

"That's the one," Nikos agreed. "I told him about Harold on the way home today. I thought he should at least be forewarned before meeting with the deacons tomorrow night."

"He's a jerk," Amy mumbled, again shocking Meg to no end. She had never heard Amy say anything about anybody before, except for maybe Meg, but at least it was always to her face.

Noticing her expression, Amy quickly explained, "You'll see what I mean soon enough. There are some people in churches, Meg, that are not there for spiritual reasons. Harold is a power freak. He runs a business ..."

"... with an iron fist," Nikos interjected.

"... and thinks he should be able to run anything his money's been put into," Amy continued. "In his mind, that includes the church."

"Does the church just go along with him?" Meg asked.

"To his face, sort of," Amy went on. "But whenever we have private voting, he loses by a landslide."

"He always wants a hand count," Nikos said grinning, "but fortunately for us and the church, it is in the constitution that if anyone calls for a secret ballot, it has to be done."

"Is this guy going to give me a hard time tomorrow?" Phillip practically stuttered.

"Probably," said Nikos and Amy in unison. They then laughed together.

"Is this really funny?" Phillip asked nervously.

"Sorry, Phillip," Nikos said as he tried to control his smile. "Every church has some Harolds. Thank God we only have him! He has been a breeze to deal with because the church likes me. They believe that God has placed me here, and they believe in what God is doing here. He has been on every committee that has ever chosen a pastor ... except mine!" Nikos and Amy began laughing again.

"It doesn't bother you that this guy is set against you?" Phillip asked him.

"Why should it? God brought me here, not Harold Hastings. When God is ready for a change, He will let me know. Until then, I am secure in the power of God."

"I wish I could have that security," Phillip confessed.

"You will. I am your ally here. The people trust me. The committee tonight loved you. Harold Hastings will answer to me if he has any problems with you. Understand?"

Phillip nodded, not fully convinced he was ready to face Harold Hastings tomorrow night. The rest of the evening, however, was delightful. Amy led Meg down to the basement which had been converted into a huge playroom. The children were playing blissfully as the two ladies entered.

"Do you have school down here?" Meg asked.

"No," Amy said quickly. "We have school upstairs in the great room. This is their escape room. They know that when they come down here they are free to run and play and have a blast. Upstairs we behave and act properly."

"I see. They are very well-behaved."

Amy laughed. "Don't judge them too quickly!"

"But they're perfect," she insisted.

"Of course they are! They've been told this weekend is extremely important and that they are to display their best manners. If they do, we will go camping on Monday and Tuesday. This will probably be the last week we can tolerate the weather for camping."

"You camp?" she asked, again surprised at the enormous change in this woman.

"Oh, yes," Amy said as she took baby Brianna in her arms. "With a large family and a modest one-income salary, we learned that our investments needed to be wise and enjoyable to all. Camping sounded like the perfect answer ... and it was."

"Cool," was all Meg could say as baby Brianna reached out to her.

🌴 🌴 🌴

"It's so chilly and fall-ish up here, isn't it?" Meg asked Phillip as she cuddled next to him in bed that night. "The leaves are already starting to change."

"I've never seen leaves change like that before," he said as he held her close.

"Whose bed is this anyway?"

"The oldest girls—I can't remember their names.

"Uh … Hannah and Katie, I think," she mumbled pulling the covers up to her chin.

"Cute kids."

"Cute family."

They lay quietly for a few minutes, so long, in fact, that Meg had almost drifted to sleep.

"What are you feeling about all of this?" he finally asked her.

"Hmmm …" was all she could manage to say.

"I'm serious—what are you thinking?"

She turned toward him and touched his cheek gently. "My fears are quickly losing ground. How about yours?"

All he said were two words—*Harold Hastings*.

🌴 🌴 🌴

The next day was spent sightseeing with the entire family. They borrowed the church van and went all over the area. Meg was dizzy from so much riding. They picnicked at a park and then talked for a while more as the children played. She knew Phillip was dreading the meeting with the deacons, although he was trying hard not to show it. She reassured him several times, reminding him that both she and Nikos would be there.

The evening came too quickly. They went with Nikos to the church where a nice supper had been prepared. Meg knew immediately who Harold Hastings was by his demeanor when he walked into the building. She found herself eyeing him off and on all evening trying to size him up. He definitely had an intimidation about him that began to wear on her as the time for questioning Phillip approached. They all sat their chairs in a semi-circle around her, Phillip and Nikos, at Harold's insistence. Several others suggested they just go to the sanctuary, but Harold won out. It looked more like a setup for an inquisition than a time of gentle banter.

"This seating vote was not by secret ballot," Nikos whispered with a grin as they took their places in front of what appeared to Meg as an interrogation panel. One man led in prayer, a very moving prayer for guidance and wisdom, and then the questioning began. At first it was tame. The questions were basically about their backgrounds. Nikos managed to keep things light, and the deacons and their wives were very charmed by Phillip's winsome personality. After about fifteen minutes, however, Mr. Harold Hastings raised his first question.

"All this has been nice and pleasant," he began, "but the truth is, we are supposed to entrust our precious teenagers into your leadership. What promise do we have that you're up to the job? You've managed to quit most of your ministries in about two years, from the looks of this here resume."

Harold Hastings sat back, his grayed hair greased down to his head, his belly lopping over his belt. He folded his arms as though he had sent the final blow. Meg watched Phillip carefully. She knew he had to be nervous, but he appeared calm and collected on the outside.

"I have no promise for you, sir," Phillip finally said, and then he said nothing else.

"Is that it, boy?" the man asked incredulously. "That's all you've got to say?"

"In response to that question … yes sir," Phillip replied. "Anything else?"

"You bet!" Harold said immediately. "Why don't you have any plans or promises for this church? You think we're just going to pay you a salary so you can loaf around and do whatever comes to mind?"

"No, sir, of course I don't, but I have yet to meet any of your teenagers. All I know is that one girl is pregnant from the former youth pastor, and three others took their lives recently. That sounds pretty serious. I'm assuming that I'm going to be responsible for a lot of emotional healing around here for a while. As God leads me, I'll obey Him. But I won't even begin to presume what needs to be done at this moment, and I will absolutely *not* make any promises about anything."

Harold Hastings sat back, obviously not pleased with the response. Meg watched as the other deacons and wives began to roll their eyes and sit uneasily. She realized this was a battle. Her only thought was to begin to pray for Phillip, and she did.

"What I want to know," Harold went on, "is what you plan to do about all this mess? We're, in a sense, hiring you to clean it up, I suppose."

"Then you've got the wrong man," Phillip said quickly. "I don't clean up messes I don't make, sir. I will help to bring healing, but this church is responsible for the clean-up. I didn't hire the former youth pastor, nor did I ever counsel those three kids."

"You only think those are your biggest problems coming here," said a man on the edge of the row who was obviously disgusted with Harold's line of questioning.

"You stay out of this, Davis," Harold said sharply. "I gave you all your time of sweetness and small talk. I'm ready to get serious with this young man right now. And what I want to know," he said as he turned toward Phillip again, "is what you plan to do. Are you going to be bringing in pool tables and other gambling devices into the church in the name of ministry? Hmm? And what about these so-called rock concerts? I suppose you're planning on dragging them around to those things too. I don't care how many times they mention Jesus, they're still of the devil."

"God has revealed that to you personally, sir?" Phillip asked. "Because if He has, we may be in conflict here."

"Aha!" Harold yelled as he stood to his feet. "He's no different than that other fellow!"

"Oh … yes … he … is," Meg found herself saying slowly and deliberately as she glared into the intimidating face of Harold Hastings.

"Excuse me?" he said in shock that she had spoken. "I don't recall you being addressed in any of my questions."

"You have just accused my husband of something horrific, and you don't even know him," she began. "Not only that, but he is a man with a heart for God. If you start accusing him of things that are wrong, you have God to answer to … *sir.*"

"Well, well, well," Harold said as he stood from his seat and thrust his hands into his pockets. He began to walk around them, as though he actually were interrogating them.

"Please sit down, Mr. Hastings," Nikos asked.

"I will not!" he exclaimed. "I believe I have just been insulted."

"No, sir," Meg remarked. "You have merely been corrected. And if you don't mind, would you please sit down. You're being extremely rude. If you want to question us, it would be proper for you to sit and look at us eye to eye rather than pace behind us as though you were a Nazi general trying to scare something out of us by interrogation. If you want to know anything, we'll answer you in a diplomatic way, but we will not cower to your intimidating, and frankly, ungodly tactics."

She tried to ignore the looks everyone in the room was giving her. She knew they were all in shock, and she was afraid she had just blown Phillip's call to this church. But there was no way she was going to just sit back and let this man play his games while lives were hanging in the balance. She also knew that if they bowed to his devices at this moment, it would define their relationship with him if they did manage to come. They would be his puppets. She may not know much about church work, but she sure knew a lot about running a multi-billion dollar oil business, and she had seen many Harold Hastings come through the doors of MacAllister Oil.

Deacon Hastings carefully walked back to his seat and sat down. "I do not believe I have ever been so insulted," he said. "I was called a Nazi. I'll have you know that I fought against the Nazis in World War II, and I do not appreciate the comparison."

"Then," she managed to smile, "you know exactly how we feel. And for the record, I didn't call you a Nazi personally, sir. I merely stated that your behavior was Nazi-like. Thank you for respecting us enough to behave honorably toward us during the rest of this interview. Now, may I ask you a few questions, Mr. Hastings?"

Once again, looks came from everywhere. Nikos was suppressing a grin, and Phillip was biting his fingernails.

"By all means," Harold said as he crossed his arms and leaned back in his seat.

"What do you do for a living, Mr. Hastings?" she asked.

"I run a business," he said. "Not that it's any of your business."

"Did you want that to be a secret," she shot back.

"I didn't say it was a secret," he said sternly. "I said it wasn't any of your business."

"Well," she continued, "I assumed you were a professional man, the way you conducted your questioning … straight to the point … sort of cut to the chase approach."

"Thank-you— I think."

"What positions of leadership do you hold in this church?" she asked him.

"I don't see as to how this is relevant. We are to be questioning you, not you us."

"On the contrary," Nikos broke in, "this is a time of questioning for both parties. We are as much on trial here as they are, Mr. Hastings."

"May I continue?" Meg asked Harold. He nodded reluctantly. "Would you answer my question? What positions of leadership do you hold here in church?"

"I teach Sunday school," he began reluctantly. "I am chairman of the deacons. I am in charge of the ushers."

"Is that it?"

"Is that not enough for you?" he asked her rudely.

"No, that's plenty," she told him. "I assumed you were very involved. You're a leader, Mr. Hastings. That's obvious. But how do you handle your leadership? Do you have class members call you on Saturday night to find out what you're going to teach Sunday morning to know whether they should show up or not?"

"Of course not," he said slowly. "But they have their own books. They know what I'll be teaching."

"Has anyone ever told you to stop teaching those particular lessons? Have they ever said they didn't agree with your teaching style? Have they ever called you old-fashioned or out of touch?"

Several chuckled at this question because he obviously was old-fashioned.

"No," he said.

"What about your business?" she continued. "Do your employees ever ask what on earth you think you're doing? Do people ever tell you that the ushers are a mess and that perhaps you don't know what you're doing there? Or what about your position as a deacon? Has anyone told you lately that you're way out of line in how you handle things in this church?"

"Of course not!" he exclaimed.

"And why not, sir?" she asked.

"Because it would be rude and it would be wrong!" he insisted.

"Then why should my husband, with no information whatsoever concerning your teenagers other than that some of them are slightly messed-up, be demanded to give you a detailed account of what he plans to do, how he plans to do it, and with what methods he plans to do it? You're a businessman. Use your business sense for something other than mild intimidation."

Harold Hastings stood to his feet and began pacing behind Meg, Phillip and Nikos again. Meg rolled her eyes, knowing that the entire council of deacons was watching her.

"I think it's clear what we have here," Harold said. "We have a woman who isn't submissive. We have a lady who is in control. We have a man who will be ruled by anything other than the Word of God. I vote right now that we dismiss the consideration of calling this man to our church."

"I vote that we recommend Phillip Anderson, and his rather intelligent, level-headed wife, to the church tomorrow morning for the position of youth/music minister," said the man on the end, who had spoken up previously. Harold shot him a hard look.

"I think you should reconsider, Mr. Davis," Harold said sternly.

Mr. Davis smiled and said, "I personally like Meg. I really like Phillip. I also like the fact that you don't seem to like them. You didn't like Nikos, and he's done wonders for this church. I'm guessing, not on that fact alone, that Phillip and Meg are just what this church needs too."

"You're on shaky ground, Davis," Harold said as he walked over to him. "I will pull my money out of this church so fast it'll make your head spin, son. Where will you and your little preacher boys be then?"

"Perhaps in the middle of God's will," Meg said from behind him. He spun around quickly and stuck his finger in her face.

"Unless you are prepared to supplement this church with a large amount of money, young lady, I'd suggest you and your husband leave this room right now."

Meg just smiled. Phillip didn't move, and Nikos stood up.

"I suppose that makes it about as clear as it can be," Nikos said. "Mr.

Hastings has made sure you understand tonight that it is his will and not God's will that he wants to see carried out in this church. Are you men ready to vote on Phillip?"

"Wait just a minute there," Harold demanded. "You are not in charge of the deacons! I am!"

"May I say one more thing?" Meg asked as she stood to her feet too.

"I don't think so," Harold said harshly.

"If you pull your money out of this church, I will gladly supplement this church's budget until it can make up for your loss," she said.

Harold Hastings laughed out loud at this remark. "That's funny, lady! Do you know how much money I pour into this church on a yearly basis?"

"I don't have a clue," she smiled as she shook her head slowly, "but you apparently don't know how much I'm worth either."

"Oh, really?" he said, still laughing. "Why don't you tell me how much you're worth?"

"You know that MacAllister gas station right on the edge of town?" she asked. He nodded. "My father is Herbert MacAllister, president of MacAllister Oil."

For the first time, Harold Hastings was speechless. He looked around the room at all the faces staring at him. He wanted to say something, but it was obvious there was nothing he really could say. He finally reached over for his coat hanging on the back of his chair. "I suppose you all think this is a victory," he said bitterly. "It's not! I will not be pushed out like this, especially by a woman!"

He glared at Meg and then left the room. Once the door to the outside slammed, men begin jumping up from their seats cheering with glee. Women were hugging each other and talking excitedly. Nikos was praising the Lord and Phillip was just sitting there, looking as pale and faint as the evening he had been at the dinner with his father, the senator. Meg reached over and took his hand.

"I'm sorry," she whispered into his ear as tears began to well up in her eyes. "I have a long way to go in this ministry business. I won't mess up the next one, I promise."

He turned to her and smiled with wonder. "Do you realize what you just did here?"

"Made you a station manager for another year?"

"You just kicked the devil out of this church!" he laughed.

"Meg!" said Mr. Davis as he came over to her extending his hand. "Let me shake your hand and welcome you to First Baptist Church of Clayton, Alabama! My name is Ricky Davis, and this is my wife, Kimberly."

Kimberly and Ricky shook her hand.

"I think we're going to get along just fine," Kimberly grinned. "You just single-handedly dealt with the biggest problem this church has ever had."

"Meg," Nikos said gently as he realized she was struggling. "What you did was of God. His power and wisdom were all over you. And as for your money, God will always provide. Mr. Hastings never could understand that we are fine without him. Your little offer, however, will be very reassuring to those in the church who have been duped by his threats."

"I didn't mean to do that," she found herself saying. "It just happened. I wasn't so irate that he was attacking my husband as much as the fact that he was questioning a man of God without reason or regard to his calling."

Nikos laughed again, "I'm sorry for laughing, but every church needs a Meg MacAllister Anderson! Perhaps God will now be free to work here abundantly with all the rubble cleared away."

Chapter Thirty-Eight

"She didn't!" Amy exclaimed as Nikos and Phillip gave her the details of the meeting.

"I didn't mean to," Meg defended.

"Meg," Amy continued, "this church has been so responsive to God. Everything Nikos has initiated they have embraced. God has changed lives and moved unbelievably, but every step has been uphill because of Harold Hastings. He didn't want Nikos here, and he refused to support any program he started, but the church followed. He would have done the same to Phillip. I know it sounds strange, but I believe God used you here to break the evil hold he had on this church. I just feel it! We're free!"

"That we are," Nikos agreed. "Phillip, are you ready to take us on?"

"Shoot," Phillip yelled, "I'm ready to take on the world! I just found out I married General Patton!"

"A general in God's army," Nikos laughed.

"Who would have thought it?" Amy said stunned. "You were so far from this the last time I saw you ... rebellious and causing trouble everywhere. This is wonderful! I have the feeling we're going to be the best of friends. Can you imagine that? Me and you?"

"Yesterday? No," Meg confessed. "Today? I'll believe just about anything."

🌴 🌴 🌴

Meg excused herself early and went to the bedroom to pray.

God, was I right? I feel like I was wrong. Did I say wrong things? Everyone keeps telling me that I did the right thing. I don't even feel like I was in control. I feel like I embarrassed Phillip and usurped my right place. God, give me some kind of peace, please?

As she stayed on her knees, she heard the voice of Grandma Corrie in her mind. *God is going to use him, and you are the strength that will see him through it.*

Phillip finally joined her in bed that night, carefully climbing in beside her.

320

"I'm awake," she told him softly, still struggling with her tears. "I didn't enjoy that tonight at all."

"I did," he said as he pulled her close. "Meg, I wish someone would have said that to every pastor and several deacons at every other church I've been at."

"I feel so drained," she groaned. "I'm tired, I'm weary, both emotionally and physically, and I know this can't be good for the baby."

He reached down to touch her tummy and gently rubbed his hand back and forth. "Our baby," he said softly, "will be fine. She will have a strong mommy to take care of her."

"She? You know the sex now?"

"It's a girl," he said with confidence. "At least, I feel like it's a girl."

"We can find out, you know?"

"No," he said quickly. "We agreed to let it be a surprise."

"Yeah, but you're lying here making predictions," she complained. "We're not supposed to do that."

"Sorry," he said gently as he kissed the top of her head. "I won't talk about our little girl again, at least until she's born."

Phillip was called unanimously the next morning. This was the first vote in the history of the church to be completely unanimous. Nikos didn't even preach. Phillip sang a song accompanied by Meg. It brought the church first to their feet, and then to their knees. The rest of the service was spent in prayer, praise, and anticipation of their arrival. Phillip told Nikos he would really like to finish out the year at the radio station. He knew that was highly irregular, but felt like starting the new church during the new year would be appropriate. Nikos agreed, and then they immediately began to search for a house. Meg was again moved by the goodness of God as they found a lovely log cabin with three bedrooms overlooking a river. It had never been lived in because the people who had built it had moved on before it was completed. They made arrangements and contracts to have the cabin finished before the first of the year. On the way back from South Dakota after Christmas, they would stop by and make any other necessary arrangements.

"I look forward to serving with you both," Nikos said as they prepared to board the plane. "This will be a moment in history for the work of God."

"And Meg," Amy told her, "don't worry about things for the baby. As soon as you're settled in, the ladies want to give you a baby shower. It will have to be quick, though, if that baby's coming in February. They can sometimes be early, you know?"

"Not with my luck," Meg smiled wearily.

"You might be surprised! The only thing predictable about children is that they are so unpredictable."

"You certainly ought to know," Phillip muttered.

🏝️ 🏝️ 🏝️

"So, how do you feel about everything?" Phillip asked her once the plane was in the air.

"Confident. At peace. Secure. Excited," she replied.

"That bad, huh?" he teased. "Do you think January is too late?"

"I need that much time to say goodbye to Treasure Cove," she said somewhat sadly. "I'm excited about the future, but that has been my home for eleven years. I got my life together there. It'll be hard to let go of it."

"I know the feeling—that's why I came back."

"However, it's time we both moved on, and I'm ready, but it'll still be hard."

He said nothing, but nodded in agreement. She knew it was overwhelming for him too. But she had the confidence that God had led them to Clayton, and in that confidence she would rest.

As the exhaustion and reality of the last several days overtook her, she drifted off into a deep sleep where she dreamed of her and Grandma Corrie sitting in rocking chairs looking over the river on the deck of the log cabin in Clayton. The elder woman said nothing, but smiled knowingly. Meg felt peace about everything as the baby began to kick from inside, only she did not realize it was the baby at first because she had never felt it kick before. She awoke and immediately grabbed Phillip's hand.

"What is it?" he asked panicked.

"Feel that?" she said. "She's kicking! Can you feel her?"

"My gosh, Meg!" he exclaimed. "Maybe it's not a girl. She's strong if she is."

"Takes after her mother, I suppose," she smiled sheepishly.

"That she does," he agreed. "Most definitely."

🏝️ 🏝️ 🏝️

The holidays were approaching way too quickly for Meg's liking. Even though she wasn't working, her life was stressfully full with packing and planning and then helping Craig and Janet move into their new home. She felt she had lost the entire month of November. She and Phillip along with Janet and Craig were boarding the plane for Houston before she knew it to spend Thanksgiving at the MacAllister home. Janet, who was now eight months pregnant, had been warned to take the flight easily, perhaps even not at all, but she couldn't miss Texas at Thanksgiving. She promised the doctor she would not sit too much, walk too much, eat too much or do anything else too much if she could go.

Meg, barely six months now, was showing too. She felt the life inside her move often and found herself smiling at each jab. She especially got tickled whenever she would play the piano. This always seemed to stir the baby. She had been asked often what was so funny during the offertories.

"You look absolutely radiant," Phillip whispered to her as the plane took off.

"Well, thank-you," she said back to him as she took his hand.

"I really meant it," he said, his eyes dancing in the sunlight pouring through the window. "I've always thought you were the most beautiful woman I'd ever laid eyes on."

"You're embarrassing me."

"You don't understand," he continued. "These past few months you've just glowed."

"They say pregnancy does that to a lady." She could feel her cheeks blush.

"No," he insisted, "it's more than that. It's as though you've just ... well ... settled into life differently or something. I hate to say this, I mean ... you know I'm a progressive thinking type of guy, but coming home and finding you there ..."

"... usually asleep on the couch ..." she grinned.

"Yeah, but it's just a warm feeling. I appreciate the fact that you're going to stay home and raise our child."

"I couldn't do it any other way ... at least not for me. Whenever I do something, I do it wholeheartedly. I'm almost afraid that I couldn't balance a baby with anything else."

"Do you think you can balance a baby with me?" he asked looking a little pitiful.

"Maybe not at first," she admitted, "but we'll work hard at it."

"That's good enough," he said with a tiny kiss.

As they entered the MacAllister house, the family finally appeared. Meri and Andrew were there to greet the couples, and Marguerite appeared from the kitchen to see the two pregnant girls.

"Oh, my goodness," she exclaimed in her thick accent, "I cannot believe the two of you are bringing me babies next year! It's about time is all I can say!"

"Meg," Andrew said with shock, "I've never seen you so ... so ... big."

"And I've never seen you so pale," she said back. "This is normal for pregnancy, little brother."

"Yeah, I know, it's just that, well ..." he struggled to explain.

"Yeah, yeah, yeah," she smiled, hugging him anyway. "It gets worse, however. Look at Janet."

"Yeah, but I've seen her fat before," he explained.

"Bite your tongue, Andrew!" Janet exclaimed.

Meg showed Phillip up to her room, everything in place as it always had been. He said nothing, but just stared.

"This is overwhelming for you, isn't it?" she finally asked him.

"Very."

"I'm sorry," she said as she came over to him. "I just assumed you understood how rich we were."

"I did too," he said with a swallow, "but nothing could prepare me for this. The limo—the house. Meg, you have a grand piano in your bedroom! In fact, this bedroom is bigger than some church sanctuaries, not to mention some people's houses!"

"I know that," she said gently. "It doesn't seem right or fair. Can you see why I'm so free with giving my money away now?"

He simply nodded.

"You know what?" she smiled mischievously as she snuggled up next to him. He shook his head. "I've never slept with a guy in here before. You have that honor."

He smiled now as he took her in his arms. "I'm not sure I'm up to the job," he said cautiously.

"Too bad. You've already applied, and a bit obviously I might add," she touched her tummy. "Let's go downstairs and see the rest of the family."

"Hmmm," was all he said as she led him to the door. He then stopped, turned back to view the room again, and said, "You have a grand piano in your room."

"Come on," she said dragging him, "you'll get over it. Besides, it's only a baby grand."

He didn't get over it as soon as Meg would have liked. He seemed to mope and stare in awe for the rest of the afternoon and on into the evening. As the family ate dinner, he ate very little, reminding her of when he first returned to Treasure Cove. She tried to joke him out of his mood, but nothing seemed to move him. As everyone else made their way to bed, he and Meg stayed huddled on the couch in front of the fire in the family room.

"I don't even know how to make a fire," he confessed as she cuddled next to him.

"I'll show you," she said dreamily. "It's not too hard."

"You know, I've never felt so inadequate in my whole life," he finally confessed.

"Phillip, please don't say that."

"Do you understand how totally intimidating all of this is?"

"Actually, I can understand. I know how all this looks to you."

"I mean I knew how wealthy you all were, but throwing out a few financial figures can't compare with all that I've seen today. For crying out loud, Meg, I've never ridden in a limo my whole life. I remember you now telling me that's how you went to school."

"It was an embarrassment for me," she confessed.

"I recall, but it's still a fact that you did. Your house in Treasure Cove is so modest compared to this. I just pictured a nice two story place where you all lived comfortably, but for heaven's sake, you have a ballroom in your house!"

"You need to understand that all this is just home to me. I know how awesome it looks to you, but this is where I grew up. It's, well, normal ... in my eyes."

"Gee, that's really comforting," he said sarcastically."

"Snap out of it!" she suddenly demanded. "Phillip, if this were the kind of life I had wanted, I wouldn't have married you."

"That's a big comfort there too," he said, still drowning in his self-pity.

"It should be. I don't care for all of this. In fact, there've been times in my life when I resented it. I can remember wishing that I had a normal family and lived in a normal house. I remember hearing other kids talk about going camping or playing board games or cards with their families. I suggested it once to my mother—she said, *That's nice, dear. Perhaps the help could play with you sometime.* I told myself at that moment that I wanted to grow up and be poor. And the help did play with me, by the way. Then I grew up and realized that they had to play with me. What a letdown. Do you know what it's like to wonder if anyone ever really cared for you?"

"You knew your parents loved you," he said. "You guys had great summers on the beach."

"The beach was not Houston. It was three months of bliss. I sometimes think it was those summers that held this family together. Home was not like the beach."

"This is all so hard to swallow. It's like you guys pretended to be normal while in Florida, but in reality ..."

"No, Phillip," she corrected him, "we didn't pretend. I didn't pretend. I hated this life. All I could ever want is what I've got now. I have a wonderful husband, a man who genuinely loves me, and not for my money. We're happy, we're simple, and we're expecting a child whom I want to raise in a simple loving environment. I don't want this and I never have."

He put his arm around her tighter, and held her close. He sighed deeply and said, "I hope you always feel that way, Meg, because a minister's salary will never, ever come close to this."

"Thank God," she said with a comforting smile. "Now, how 'bout we take a walk upstairs and, well, you know, break in my old bed."

"I just have one question," he said. "When you have trouble sleeping at night, you don't get up and play the piano, do you?"

"Haven't yet," she told him, "but then, I've never had trouble sleeping."

"I believe that," he smiled. "Unless you're in a metal camper beneath a tall tree with an electrical storm raging all around."

🏝 🏝 🏝

The next morning, Thanksgiving, Meg was awakened by Phillip's plucking out *Heart and Soul* on the piano. She rolled over and groaned as she put the pillow over her head to block the sound.

"Are you complaining about my playing," he asked loudly.

She jerked off the pillow. "*Heart and Soul*? the ill-fated song that everyone and his brother can play, and usually horribly I might add."

"And good morning to you too, Sleeping Beauty," he smiled back as he continued playing.

She moaned as she crawled out of bed and trudged toward the piano. "Move over, Liberace."

"You're not gonna hit me, are you?" he asked warily. "You look vicious."

"Have you ever heard me play *Heart and Soul*?"

"Of course not. You would never play *Heart and Soul*—you play Beethoven."

"Oh, trust me, I can play *Heart and Soul*."

"Nope."

She took a deep breath and then began to play difficult arpeggios with her left hand. Her right hand finally joined in, playing a complicated version of the well-known melody. After the first verse, she transposed the entire song into a minor key and began playing the arpeggios with her right hand while pounding out the melody in deep, dark tones with the left. When that verse was finished, she transposed yet again, and ended up making the whole thing sound like a music box.

"Must you always impress me?" he asked.

"Now," she said triumphantly, "please don't ever play that song again."

🏝 🏝 🏝

The rest of the family began to arrive as dinnertime approached. Mitch came with Michael and immediately retired to the family room to watch football. Meg knew Phillip wanted to watch whatever game might be on, but he stayed close by her side, as this was their first Thanksgiving together.

326

Phillip and Michael became good friends right away, and Phillip ended up with the boy on his shoulders for most of the morning.

When Herbie, Susan and the four children arrived, Meg noticed a marked difference in their attitudes toward each other. Herbie actually opened the door for her. He gently held her elbow as they walked into the kitchen to look over the preparations. He asked to be excused as he left to go watch the game also. Susan seemed to be glowing again, just as when she was a schoolgirl. Meg desperately wanted to get her alone and find out what was happening, but that wasn't to happen anytime soon. Preparations were in full swing, and everyone began to give Marguerite a hand.

"Why don't you go join the guys with the game," Meg suggested to Phillip. "I'm going to be pretty busy in the kitchen for a while."

"You don't need me to bake a cake or something," he asked bending down to kiss her cheek.

"Please, no," she said sternly.

"Gee, you don't like my piano playing and you don't like my cooking. Why did you marry me?"

"Because you drive a Durango," she said flatly.

"Oh, great," he said as he left the room with Michael on his shoulders. "Miss Porsche," he mumbled just loud enough for her to hear.

Chapter Thirty-Nine

Meg, Janet, Susan and Meri stayed busy, and perhaps a bit too silly, until dinner time as they worked with Marguerite. There was much teasing and laughter, and Meg thought to herself that this was what a holiday was meant to be like. She felt the baby kick often, especially when Susan would burst out in laughter, or Janet with one of her high-pitched squeals. She would then think of Phillip. This was his first Thanksgiving ever with a family of his own. She finally snuck away from the kitchen to find him and wish him a proper happy Thanksgiving.

"We haven't seen him in about an hour," Herbie told her as she asked the men where Phillip was.

"He didn't come to watch the game?" she asked.

"He did," Mitch told her, "but then said he was only interested in the SEC and left."

"I think I saw him with Jose'," Andrew said.

"Jose'?" she asked.

"You haven't been married a year yet, and you're already losing your husband," Herbie smiled. Meg looked at him in shock, amazed that he was actually interacting with her.

"I'm just kidding, you know," he said soberly.

"I know. Since when?"

"Go find your husband," he shot back, "or I may try to tease you again. I don't want to risk being beheaded over it."

Andrew laughed. "It must be those pregnancy hormones."

"Pregnancy hormones? What about testosterone …why did God think that was such a good idea?" she mumbled as she left the room to continue the search.

She didn't find him until the dinner bell rang. Sure enough, he came walking in with Jose' as well as a big smile. Apparently he had lost Michael somewhere in the process as the little fellow came in holding Mitch's hand.

"Where have you been?" she asked him to the side as she took his hand and led him to their section of the huge dining table.

"Learning stuff," was all he would say.

"What kind of stuff?"

"You're just a little too nosey," he complained as Herbert MacAllister called everyone to silence for the prayer.

Once again, Meg noticed how Herbie pulled out Susan's seat for her, and then made sure she was comfortably positioned before he sat down himself. Several times during the passing of food they actually spoke and smiled at each other. If she didn't get Susan alone soon, she would make one of her famous *Meg faux pas* and openly ask what on earth was happening.

The meal was festive and wonderful. She reminded Phillip several times as he kept filling up his plate that Marguerite would have some wonderful desserts. He assured her he could handle one or all of them. He did. Then everyone retired to the family room with a roaring fire, a big screen TV playing two channels at once, both broadcasting football, of course, and some relaxing conversation.

"Susan and I have an announcement," Herbie blurted out suddenly in the middle of several different things going on. Immediately everyone gave him their full attention.

Meg's heart sank, however. Her worse fears suddenly surfaced in her mind. The whole congeniality thing had probably been the result of them finally deciding to divorce. She had seen it happen before. A couple barely communicating for years finally makes a decision of finality and the tensions drop. She braced herself.

"Man, this is sort of hard to say," Herbie choked out.

The lump grew in her throat.

"You all know things have been less than perfect for us for years," Susan started in.

"Let me tell them, Susan," he insisted. "You can tell your family tonight."

She nodded obediently as he went on. Meg took Phillip's hand and squeezed it hard. She couldn't imagine family life without Susan.

"We've done a lot of thinking this year," Herbie continued, "and finally come to some conclusions about our marriage." Meg looked to Susan for some indication of the announcement, but she just sat stone-faced as Herbie explained what was happening. "You all have been very patient with us, putting up with us during our ups and downs ..." he continued.

"Would you get on with it," Susan suddenly insisted. "Stop dallying around."

"Okay, okay, it's just going to be shock for everyone. I thought I should build up to it."

"I hate build-ups," Craig mumbled out. "Just say what you've got to say."

"Agreed," Andrew chimed in. Apparently everyone was on the same wavelength as Meg here, and all were anticipating the dreaded, but inevitable news.

"Okay," Herbie said as he took a deep breath, "Susan and I are going to have another baby."

"What?" yelled Mitch as Janet let out one of her high pitched squeals. Meg's baby jumped, and the lump in her throat now turned into tears.

"A fifth kid?" Andrew asked.

"We are getting to be a prolific family, aren't we?" Meri said with a sweet smile as she stood up to hug her son.

"I suppose you'll be wanting a raise again," Herbert teased.

"No, Dad," Herbie said, "but I have decided to stop the weekend business trips for awhile."

"Those are your schedulings, not mine," Herbert said.

"I know." Herbie gave a regretful wince.

Suddenly, another loud squeal erupted from Janet, but this time it sounded slightly serious. "You guys are not going to believe this," she said in a panic, "but I think my water just broke!"

"No way," Craig said calmly, "you're not due for another three weeks."

"Babies can come early," Meri reminded him sternly.

"Not for Janet," he laughed. "She's late for everything. It's more likely that she would be three weeks late than three weeks early!"

Everyone laughed, except Janet. "Look! Either my water just broke, or I just wet all over myself."

"Have you been having contractions?" Susan asked as she walked over and began to assess the situation.

"For weeks," Janet said, still panicking. "And I must confess they've been a bit stronger today, but never painful."

"Don't worry," Susan smiled, "the pain will be here soon."

"Somebody contact Bert," Herbert said as he began to take charge. "I think we're having a baby today."

"No!" Janet insisted. "I can't have this baby here! My doctor is in Florida!"

"We have good doctors up here too," Meri said calmly. "You'll love them. In fact, I'll make a call now." She left.

Craig helped Janet up from couch, and yes, something had broken for sure. Susan took her to change clothes while Meg packed a suitcase for her. Within fifteen minutes, Craig, Janet and Meri were on their way to the hospital, followed by a caravan of other cars.

"This is the craziest thing I've ever seen," Susan laughed as they followed the limousine.

"This is the craziest day I've ever seen," Meg said as she tried to catch her breath from all the running around. "And what's with you guys being pregnant again?"

"Isn't that hilarious?" Susan said as they sat alone in the car. "Can you believe it?"

"No! Could you please explain this to me?"

"It's really your fault, you know? After your wedding, Herbie said that we used to be in love like that and he wanted to know what happened. I told him I still loved him, but that our lives had changed so much that we somehow lost touch of each other in the process of growing. He said he didn't want to keep on going like we were—living like strangers in the same house. He either wanted us to somehow reconcile or separate."

"What a jerk ..."

"No, Meg, he's not a jerk at all. He took the initiative to put us back together. That took a lot of guts."

"But what about all of his little affairs?" Meg asked her. "Why couldn't he have taken some initiative before being unfaithful?"

"Oh, Meg, he never was unfaithful."

"Yes, he was, and everyone knew it!" Meg couldn't believe Susan would deny this known fact.

"No, he wasn't," she assured her. "He said he knew the rumors were going around, and somehow he didn't even mind them, but he couldn't bring himself to ever cheat on me. He thought about it, even planned it occasionally, but he never came through with it. He hoped the rumors would draw me out and make me combative so we could talk. But you know me, ever patient, somehow thinking he would come back to his senses and scared to death to push a point."

"He never cheated on you? You really believe that?"

"Yes. I told you I still loved him, and that he wasn't this horrible person you pegged him out to be. He's just not good at putting on masks and pretending things are great when they aren't."

"No kidding," she breathed sarcastically as she tried to rethink her brother's behavior. "So, you guys are totally back together?"

"Totally," she confirmed. "He's been spending much more time at home and has tried to reschedule as many of his business trips during the week so he can be home on the weekends and go to church with us."

"Unbelievable." She was dumbfounded.

"He even wants us to buy a camper for Christmas."

Ah, a camper. Meg's weak spot, her dream for the ideal family. Had Herbie changed that much?

"The kids are thrilled. I'm thrilled."

"And you're having another baby ..."

"Yes, and apparently Janet is having one today," she said as she pulled into the hospital parking lot.

Janet had the baby indeed shortly after they arrived. Within three hours,

Amanda MacAllister was born, weighing in at six pounds and eight ounces. She was beautiful with a head full of red hair like her mother and light blue eyes like her father. As the entire MacAllister family gathered together in her room, much to the chagrin of the nurses on duty, Craig gave another Thanksgiving prayer. He thanked God for the promise and possibility of new life, for families being healed, and for the love and warmth in the room. Meg cried, yet again. If she didn't have this baby soon, she was going to become emotional Jell-o.

Meg and Phillip flew back to Treasure Cove that Sunday alone. Janet and Craig would stay another week in Houston until they felt comfortable flying with the baby. Meg packed boxes and crates that next week until she was sick of seeing them. She had Phillip to put them in the spare bedroom so she wouldn't have to look at them again until they were to be unpacked in their log cabin in Clayton, Alabama. All arrangements were made concerning the move. The week after Christmas, the moving van would pack up their belongings and then Phillip and Meg would leave Treasure Cove.

"What do you think of Alan Parsons?" Mr. Roberts asked Meg on one of her visits to the home before Christmas.

"I try not to."

"I need to know," he told her. "He's been recommended by the college dean to serve as a dorm parent for this next year."

Her jaw dropped. Alan molding young minds?

"That bad?" he asked her.

"I'm the wrong person to ask," she said truthfully. "I don't know him now. I knew him years ago, and the man I knew years ago I wouldn't even recommend to clean toilets at a truck stop."

"He's done some volunteer work here with us this past semester, and the kids have loved him. He's been gentle and caring with them—a wonderful role model as a man. We don't get many male volunteers. He put down two references—you and John Mason. Mason gave him glowing reviews."

She let out a deep breath. True, Alan was a different person, but she couldn't bring herself to trust him implicitly, especially with young, impressionable boys. He had hurt her badly. How could she take the chance of letting him hurt children?

"You're struggling with this, aren't you?" There was concern in his eyes.

"More than you know," she confessed. "He was the guy who, well, years ago in Houston, that I…rats! I hate even talking about it!"

"You compromised yourself with?" he asked. She nodded. "Do you think you can't be objective about him?"

"I can't be objective about him at all. I'll admit that he's changed. He seems to have made a complete turnaround, but I can't get over what happened to me."

He nodded in understanding, but then he looked her in the eye and said, "Perhaps it's time you do get over it."

"Excuse me?" she said a bit hurt by his remark.

"Meg, you have carried that baggage around with you for years. I've listened to you whine and complain about it a long time. What have you actually? Nothing as I see it. God's blessed you with a wonderful husband and a baby on the way. He's even so forgiven you that He's allowing you to accompany Phillip back into the ministry. I don't know who it is exactly that you need to forgive—Alan or yourself. But you need to do it."

She nodded as the words stung. She still wanted to punish Alan for her years of guilt. God had forgiven her, and God had forgiven him. Why did she still struggle with this so much? Why couldn't she just let go of all of it and move on?

"I don't know how," she finally confessed. "I guess I've nursed this grudge for so long that I can't seem to let it go."

"Find a way," he said seriously. "Don't do it for Alan, but let go of it for your own sake."

🏝 🏝 🏝

As Meg and Phillip made the final packing list, a thought occurred to her. "We have three vehicles, Phillip."

"Yep," he agreed, "and I've been trying to figure out how to get them up there."

"We only need two."

"Okay … which one do you suggest we ditch?"

"I want to keep the Porsche," she said immediately. He grinned and nodded in agreement. "I'd like to keep the Durango," she went on. "It'll make the perfect family vehicle in a couple of months. I don't want to even imagine dragging baby stuff around in that Porsche. I get cramped just thinking about it."

"So, are you saying you want to get rid of the ugly, brown van?"

"Yes," she slapped him playfully. "That ugly brown van has done some wonderful things I'll have you know."

"Then let it keep doing wonderful things, but with somebody else. Give it to the children's home."

She looked at him with a smile.

"What?" he asked. "What did I say?"

"You said to *give* it away. I was thinking the same thing. I sort of assumed you'd want to sell it."

"It's not mine to sell—it's your ugly van."

"No—it's God's. It was bought for a single purpose—to haul kids around from the home. It's done that well, regardless of its color."

"Why brown?"

"Phillip!" she yelled. "Lay off of my van!"

"It's ugly, Meg," he teased her. "Why not blue or lime green?"

Suddenly a thought occurred to her. She stood up from the couch and walked out onto the deck.

"What is it?" he asked as he followed her. "You look like you've seen a ghost."

"That's exactly it," she told him as she looked up into his eyes with a serious face.

"What? What's going on?"

"I know exactly who that van should go to."

"Who?"

"Alan."

"Alan Parsons?" His eyes grew wide.

"Yes, we need to give that van to Alan Parsons."

She waited for him to explode. He usually did when Alan's name came up. She hadn't mentioned him for months hoping they could both forget him. She wasn't prepared for his response.

"Alan Parsons," he said gently. "You know he's going to be working at the home next year?"

"I didn't know for sure."

"Meg," he touched her cheek, "I couldn't think of a better person to have that ugly old van."

"You mean it?" she asked in unbelief. "You don't mind?"

"I mean it," he smiled. "He's a good guy. I'm sure glad people aren't holding my past over my head like I've done with him this year. How miserable."

"I can do this in good faith," she finally admitted. "Maybe this will bring me the release that I've needed."

"And me," he nodded. "Shall we go make a delivery?"

"Let's draw up some papers first," she said as she pulled out her phone to call her lawyer.

🌴 🌴 🌴

Meg and Phillip knocked on the dormitory door. The look on Alan's face said it all when he opened it and saw them there.

"Wow," he breathed, almost as if in awe. "You guys … come in, please."

They walked into the small room and he offered them a seat on his bed.

"Can I get you something?" he asked, obviously anxious to please them.

"No, thanks," Meg said. "You probably know that we're leaving Treasure Cove in a couple of weeks."

"Sure do," he smiled gently. "I think it's great that you guys are going back into the ministry. That church is blessed to get you."

"Phillip, maybe," she chuckled, "but I've already run one deacon off."

Alan laughed softly. "No, they're blessed. I wish God's best for you both. And Meg, I've wanted to say this for a long time, but, well … I didn't think it would be proper … so … I … well, just never said anything."

"What is it?" she asked.

"You glow with that baby inside," he blushed. "God has really blessed you guys. I'm very happy for you."

"Thanks, Alan," Phillip said. "And now we want to bless you."

"Look, you guys," Alan paced slightly, "just the fact that you've let me stay here, go to your college and go to your church has been more than enough. Please don't make me anymore indebted to you."

"Oh, we can't help it," she teased. "We want you to think about us often after we're gone."

"I'll pray for you guys every day," he told them.

"Here," Meg said as she pulled the keys from her pocket and tossed them to him.

"What's this?" he asked confused.

"Keys," Phillip grinned. "Haven't they taught you anything at this college?"

Alan smiled shyly. "Keys to what?"

She got up from the bed and aimed his shoulders toward the door. Phillip opened it and pointed to the van outside.

"I don't understand," he said as he turned around to face them both.

Phillip produced the title to the van and handed it to him. "That ugly thing is now officially yours."

Punching Phillip's arm Meg argued, "It's not ugly! It's practical."

Alan was just staring at the paper, the keys, the couple, and then the van. He was trying to put it all together. "I don't get it. What exactly is all this?"

"We're giving you the van," she explained. "We don't need it, and you do."

"Giving it?" he asked.

"It's no sports car," Phillip grinned, "but you can't haul many kids around in one anyway."

"You're giving me that big van?" Alan asked them again.

She took him by the hand and led him outside. She opened the van's door and made him get inside. She put the key in the ignition and said slowly, "This … is … your …van. Can't make it much clearer than that?"

Alan took out the key and looked at them both. "Why?"

"Because it's ugly," Phillip teased again.

"Phillip, stop it!" Meg insisted. Then she turned back to Alan. "Because it's your turn to be blessed. We believe God wants you to have it."

He got out of the van and stared at the keys. "I don't believe it," he said shaking his head. "I don't deserve this, especially from you guys. I can't accept it."

"You don't have a choice," she told him. "It's in your name and you own the title now. Do with it what you want. I suggest you retire the bicycle for recreational purposes only and begin using this thing for your major traveling."

"You're serious," he said as he looked at the title again. "Why me?"

"We needed healing as much as you did, Alan," she tried to explain. "This puts us all on level ground now. I've forgiven you—you've forgiven me. See?"

"What about you?" Alan asked Phillip. "Have you forgiven me too?"

"Totally," Phillip told him. "Just as God has forgiven me."

Alan began to smile again. Tears welled up in his eyes and much to Meg's dismay, in hers also.

"I don't know what to say," he told them. "Words aren't adequate."

"Let's just say *goodbye*," she suggested.

She hugged him tightly and realized that she was totally released from the bitterness, the guilt and the pain. She smiled as tears rolled down her cheeks when Phillip embraced him also. As they waved goodbye to Alan, she now understood why forgiveness was important. True healing could only happen when full forgiveness was finally given.

Chapter Forty

"She's so beautiful," Meg said to Janet about baby Amanda as they flew to Houston for Christmas. "I can't wait for mine to get here."

"Meg," Janet told her, "it's the most incredible thing that's ever happened to me. I sometimes get up in the middle of the night to just stare at her. I can't believe I have a baby!"

"You're a wonderful mother. There's a part of me that wished our children could grow up together. I pictured that when I found out we both were pregnant."

"I know," Janet said sadly, "but God knows best, doesn't He?"

She nodded.

"It's ironic," Janet went on, "that your children will grow up with Amy's instead of mine."

"Very," Meg laughed. "What's even more ironic is that Amy will probably end up being my best friend!"

"Marriage and motherhood have mellowed her well. "I've always said that the two of you were more alike than you realized."

"Who would have thought it? I just hope I don't run off any more deacons. They may fire Phillip before he has a chance to even warm the soil up there!"

🎂🎂🎂

Christmastime at the MacAllisters was quite an adjustment for Phillip. He was, once again, overwhelmed by the house as the decorations were beyond description.

"Do you guys charge for people to visit during Christmas?" he asked Meg as they prepared to greet guests at the annual MacAllister family Christmas gathering.

"Please, no," she moaned. "Having the family over is enough. No strangers, please. Although you are about to meet some of the strangest people in your life tonight."

Phillip was exhausted after the party and confessed that perhaps a small

337

family was beginning to look more appealing.

"Oh, my," she teased him as they snuggled under the blankets in her room. "We're not going to have six kids like Amy and Nikos?"

"Let's just settle for five like Susan and Herbie. How do you remember all those people's names? I couldn't tell you one person I met tonight."

"Name tags," she mumbled as she snuggled closer to him. "One thing I won't miss about Florida is the warm weather almost all the time."

"Hmmm," he barely moaned out as he had already begun to drift.

"Good night," she whispered as the baby began to kick again. "I don't imagine I'll be drifting off as easily tonight," she smiled and rubbed her tummy.

🌴 🌴 🌴

After several days at the MacAllisters, Meg and Phillip flew to South Dakota. Mary Ann and Clara were waving excitedly as soon as the couple appeared from their flight.

"Now this is a proper greeting," Phillip mumbled to Meg as he spotted his mother and sister.

"Tell me about it," she replied. Money couldn't buy everything, and she had admitted that she would have traded the wealth anytime for a normal, happy, close family.

"Oh, my gosh!" Mary Ann yelled at as she came over to Meg. "Look at you! You're so cute! Mama, look at her tummy!"

"How precious," Clara said as she touched Meg's abdomen. "How much longer?"

"Two months," Meg smiled.

"I'm here too," Phillip complained. "I'm the daddy. I had part in this."

"Stop whining," Mary Ann teased. "She's cuter than you. Face it!"

The next few days at the Andersons were full blown with festivities. They had so many traditions built around Christmas that Meg actually began to take notes so she could be ready for them all next year. Phillip had shared some of them with her last year, but she wasn't prepared for all they did. Being extremely pregnant did manage to omit her from a few activities, beginning with football and ending with a jump in the icy creek. Clara and the girls seemed to cook constantly. There were cookies and cakes and pies always coming out of the oven, and the house smelled downright delicious. Meg had hoped for snow, and she wasn't disappointed. The day after Christmas a good snow fell, eliciting even more activities—snowmen, snow angels, snowball fights, and sledding. Meg, of course, sat them all out, but planned next year to make up for her plight.

"Are you ready for the move?" Clara asked her as they sat beside the fire one evening when everyone else had gone to a movie.

"I think so. Everything's packed that needs to be packed."

"You'll only have one day home when you get back from here, then you're off?" Clara asked. She nodded.

"You should have given yourself some more time. You're going to be exhausted after leaving here and then turning right around to move."

"I don't care," Meg smiled at her. "I wouldn't trade anything for my time spent here with y'all. This has been the most wonderful Christmas ever."

"You only say that because you didn't have to jump into the creek."

"You just wait," Meg laughed, "I'll be right in there with the rest of them next year."

"Fine, and I'll stay in here and watch the baby."

"You should see Janet's baby—she's so beautiful and perfect."

"Every baby is," Clara smiled.

"I suppose," she yawned dreamily, beginning to feel weary from being so busy. "Do you miss Grandma Corrie?"

"Not really. She had had one foot in the grave for so long that when she did finally die, it was a blessing."

"I really liked her," Meg confessed.

"She was a unique lady."

"She was a wonderful lady," Meg countered.

"In some ways," Clara agreed, "but it was hard having her for a mother. She was always so staunchly religious. She was uncomfortable with our American culture, so she didn't socialize at all. I never had friends over or had a party. She spent so much time with her nose in the Bible and on her knees."

"Is that bad?" Meg asked.

"It is when you're five years old and you crave someone's attention. She was a good woman, but she wasn't connected here. I suppose that's one reason why I rebelled so much during my teen and college years. I wanted to punish her, and even God I guess, for all I thought I missed during my childhood."

"She seemed to really walk with God."

"She did," Clara agreed, "but at a big price. She was always telling me what God had said to her, and she was always right. I remember being jealous of God. I wanted her to love me like that."

"You don't think she did?"

"As a child, no, I couldn't understand it. As I grew older, I realized that God was her only security. He and my father were the only ones she felt comfortable with. Father was gone a lot, so that left the Lord. When I married and had children, I promised myself I would be involved in every area of their lives. These silly traditions and things we do are just fun things that seem to add up year after year. The creek thing started about ten years ago. It had been so warm and we were all complaining that it didn't even seem like Christmas. James said he might as well go swimming. He was dared to do it, so needless to say, he went into the creek. Mind you, it was still extremely cold. Before long, we all ended up in the water, and the rest is history."

"How do you balance God with children then?" Meg wondered. "It doesn't sound right. It sounds like a contradiction."

"Children are gifts of God," Clara began to explain. "He gives them to us to enjoy. Some people don't recognize that. They see children as burdens, as responsibilities that are mandates rather than privileges. They're only children for a few precious years, you know?"

She smiled and nodded as she rubbed her tummy. "Clara, I want to be everything God wants me to be, but everything my children need me to be too. How do I know I haven't lost the balance?"

Clara laughed. "You *will* lose the balance ... and often. You'll find yourself so busy changing diapers and washing clothes and keeping up the house that you'll realize you haven't prayed in days. Then other times you will be so caught up in the Father that you'll realize no one has clean clothes and there's nothing in the cupboard for dinner!"

"What do you do?"

"You say, *Amen*, and then put on a load of clothes and go to the store for some food!" she exclaimed. "Everything in life isn't overly spiritual, Meg. Sometimes being really spiritual means carrying out the mundane duties that God has ordained for you to do. Changing diapers is as much a part of the will of God for a mother as leading a Bible study or carrying food to the elderly."

"Yeah, but how do you *know*?"

"If you don't care for your children and family, no one else will take up the slack. When their needs are met, then you know you can move on in another direction. As they grow, so does your freedom to move out. But don't ever think God would have you leave your family for His work. His work is your family ... at least while your family is with you."

"Someone should teach a class on this."

"Remember that," Clara smiled. "Perhaps you'll do just that one day."

"My mother didn't balance very well either," Meg confessed. "In fact, we had very little family life. We had our summers and that sort of made up for everything else, but the rest of the year was the pits. I don't want that."

"Then you won't have it," Clara told her. "You are a good wife. Phillip is so happy. I'm imagining that you'll settle into motherhood just fine and learn the balance quickly."

Phillip and Meg returned to Treasure Cove on Tuesday, said goodbye to all of their belongings on Wednesday, and spent Wednesday night at Craig and Janet's. They talked about what the future had to hold for both of the families and also struggled with getting teary over leaving each other again after such a short time of being together. Later that night, when Meg heard Janet get up with the baby, she sneaked into the living room.

"Do you mind all the getting up at night?" she asked.

"Sometimes I do wish she would just give me one good night's sleep," Janet confessed, "but usually I just find myself thanking God that I have the privilege of holding her and feeding her in the middle of the night."

"Do you wish you didn't nurse her?"

"Never," she whispered. "I wouldn't change this for anything."

"But then you have to get up with her all the time," Meg complained a little. "Don't you think Craig should do it sometime too?"

"Not at all," Janet said as she smiled at Amanda. "Before long, she'll be independent and on her own. I won't ever regret that there was a time in her life that she was totally dependent on me. Meg, this is what I've always wanted. I won't short-change this time for anything. It's very possible that this will be the only baby I ever have. I want to absorb every ounce of it I possibly can."

Meg nodded. She could understand. She longed even more to meet the little being that was growing bigger and stronger inside of her each week.

On Thursday morning Phillip and Meg said their final goodbyes to Treasure Cove. They left early for northwest Alabama, promising the doctor they would stop every couple of hours for Meg to walk around. They drove the Durango and towed the Porsche. Nikos had asked them to call when they reached Birmingham so they would know when they would arrive. The plan was to spend the night at Nikos and Amy's and then unload the moving van the next morning.

When they finally arrived at Nikos', the yard was so full of vehicles that Phillip had to pull over across the street. As he helped Meg out, people began to pour out of the pastorium. Meg couldn't count them all, but there had to be close to fifty people. They greeted the weary couple with much excitement and anticipation. A covered dish dinner was awaiting them inside, and everyone fellowshipped for close to two hours. Meg became reacquainted with several ladies she had met on their first visit, and met several more who were excited about her arrival.

The next morning, the same fifty or so were at the cabin when the moving van arrived. They ordered Meg and Phillip to just stay still and tell them where everything was to go. Within one hour, the entire cabin was set up with furniture, and ladies had helped Meg totally unpack boxes to set up the kitchen.

That evening, Phillip made a perfect fire as they sat cozily in their great room admiring their new home.

"I thought you couldn't build a fire," Meg said as she snuggled close to him.

"Jose' taught me," he smiled.

"When?"

"At Thanksgiving."

"I see," she said.

"I think I'm gonna like it here," Phillip said contentedly.

"I'm worried," Meg had to confess.

"Worried? You? I thought you had the world by the tail!"

"I've already run off one deacon," she reminded him. "What if I ruin your whole ministry? What if I'm not cut out to be a minister's wife? I've always had my way, Phillip. In some ways, I suppose I'm a spoiled brat. Do you think I can really be what you need here, or will I blow it for you?"

He laughed heartily as he pulled her close and said, "You'll be the perfect minister's wife! As I see it, no one here will be the least bit concerned about what I do as long as you're around."

"That's not very comforting," she said with a punch.

"It is to me," he teased. "Besides, you like conflict and challenge. Welcome to the next boxing ring."

"I don't want to be the center of conflict and challenge," she pouted. "I just want to be a sweet, gentle wife and mother."

"Good luck," he chuckled.

🏝️ 🏝️ 🏝️

Meg woke up exhausted as the nurse took her blood pressure yet again. In the corner of the room was a bouquet of two-dozen yellow roses.

"How many times do you have to check my blood pressure?" she complained.

"Every two hours, Mrs. Anderson."

"Where did the roses come from?" she wondered.

"It is Valentine's Day," the nurse smiled as she put the thermometer in Meg's mouth. "I'm assuming your husband."

She smiled. Of course—yellow roses on Valentine's Day. She would have to ask him about last year's yellow roses. She had never confronted him with that.

"Where is that husband of mine?" she asked the nurse.

"On his way here," the nurse smiled. "He's hijacking your beautiful daughter from the nurses in the nursery. They're rather upset about it too. She's such a sweet baby."

"I want to see her again so bad," she said, literally aching to hold her baby. "I've only held her once since the birth. They gave her to me and then whisked her away."

"Your husband hasn't left the baby's side."

A knock on the door called the attention of the two ladies.

"Come in," Meg said, still very exhausted.

"It's me, Mommy," came Phillip's soft voice as he opened the door. He walked in carrying a tiny bundle in his arms. He came over to Meg and sat next to her on the bed.

"I'll see you in a couple of hours," the nurse said headed for the door. Meg didn't hear. All she wanted was to see her baby.

"Let me hold her, please," she said to Phillip.

"Okay," he said hesitantly, "but only for a little while. You need to rest."

"I can hold her and rest at the same time."

Phillip gently handed the little girl to her mother. Meg peeked into the small bundle and gasped with delight.

"Oh, my! Phillip," she whispered, "she has your eyes ... and your mother's ... and your grandmother's!"

"I know," he beamed. "But look at that nose ... just like yours."

"She's more beautiful than I ever imagined."

"Happy Valentine's Day," he whispered as he kissed her forehead. "I personally arranged this, you know, her being born on Valentine's Day."

"Yeah, right," she mumbled. "A few hours earlier would have been just fine. How long was I in labor?"

"Fourteen hours after we actually got to the hospital."

"I could have handled three like Janet," she said wearily.

"Well, it's over, and you did great. And look what we've got—a Valentine's baby."

"That reminds me, are those from you?" she asked pointing to the roses.

"Of course—I always send you yellow roses for Valentine's Day."

"Last year too?"

His sheepish smile said everything.

"That was naughty of you," she said sternly. "My class was extremely confused. Kevin sent roses too, you know?"

"I didn't care," he confessed. "I was so in love with you that it hurt."

The baby yawned, causing her parents to melt.

"How precious," Meg sighed. "We have to choose a name now, you know?"

"What are you thinking? We picked several."

"In my opinion, there's only one that can fit those blue eyes," she said as she looked up at him.

"You want to name her Phillip?"

"No, silly," she said as she looked back at the baby. "Corrie ... how could we call her anything else?"

"Corrie," he said tenderly. "Perfect. How about Corrie Meredith ... after you and your mother?"

"Corrie Meredith Anderson," she tried out. "I think it fits perfectly. What do you think, little Corrie?"

Corrie yawned again and then shut her tiny turquoise eyes in contentment. Meg looked up at Phillip and smiled. He gently placed the little blanket up around the baby's ear.

"We did good, Meg," he said. "God blessed us with a precious gift."

"That makes two this year for me. I have a Phillip, and I have a Corrie. What more could I possibly want? This has got to be paradise, Phillip."

"Nope," he disagreed. "Paradise is still to come. This is just a taste of paradise."

"It has to be close," she confessed. "How can anything be better than this?"

"I'll agree. We're so close to paradise at this moment, I can almost feel it," he whispered.

"I *can* feel it," she insisted gently. "I really can."

He bent down and brushed a soft kiss on her cheek, then another on the baby. Meg saw the pools in his eyes again. Suddenly it occurred to her that everything she had ever done in her life for anybody could never compare to what she had given him at this moment. She also realized that anything she had ever sought to fulfill her own life was now meaningless compared to this. Healing had happened, and it had sneaked up on her when she least expected it. She looked up at Phillip, then back down at Corrie. He was wrong—this indeed was paradise.

Coming soon by Daphne C. Murrell

THE THIRD KING

Third in line to the throne, young Andrew Braisogn has no aspirations to follow his father as monarch. He is talented, sensitive, and desires nothing more than a normal life away from the microscope focused at the royal family. But as fate works its way through the lives of his brothers, he may be forced to step into a role that will destroy all his dreams.

Evangeline Dorvain has fought the battle between royal and common her entire life because of her mixed blood mother. Her father, however, a full-blooded royal, is one of the country's most respected military lawyers. No one is quite sure what to do with the beautiful, strong-minded young lady who seems to ignore bloodlines and boundaries. As she rises quickly in the world tennis circuit, suddenly the tiny nation of Braisognia is in the global spotlight and the country is forced to honor her.

As Andrew and Evangeline cross paths, a forbidden friendship develops in which they both find great comfort and acceptance. But the ongoing hate and struggle between the classes threatens any happiness they might ever find alone ... or together.

For more books or recordings, check out Daphne's website at www.daphnemurrell.com or amazon.com.